Consequences

C R Saxon

HCS
HATTON CROSS STEAMPUNK
PUBLISHING

First Edition
Copyright © 2023 C R Saxon
www.hcspublishing.com
All rights reserved.
ISBN: 978-1-955644-06-8

Acknowledgements

To my amazing, supportive, and totally awesome husband and alpha reader: Thank you! Thank you for helping me make this book a reality. I love you oodles!

Thank you to my totally awesome beta reader, Minlu – loved your suggestions and thoughts! And thank you to everyone who helped get this book published.

To everyone reading this, thanks for giving my story a try. I hope you enjoy it!

Unseen Scars:

Cost of Victory

Mirrors and Dreams

Pain of Darkness

Consequences

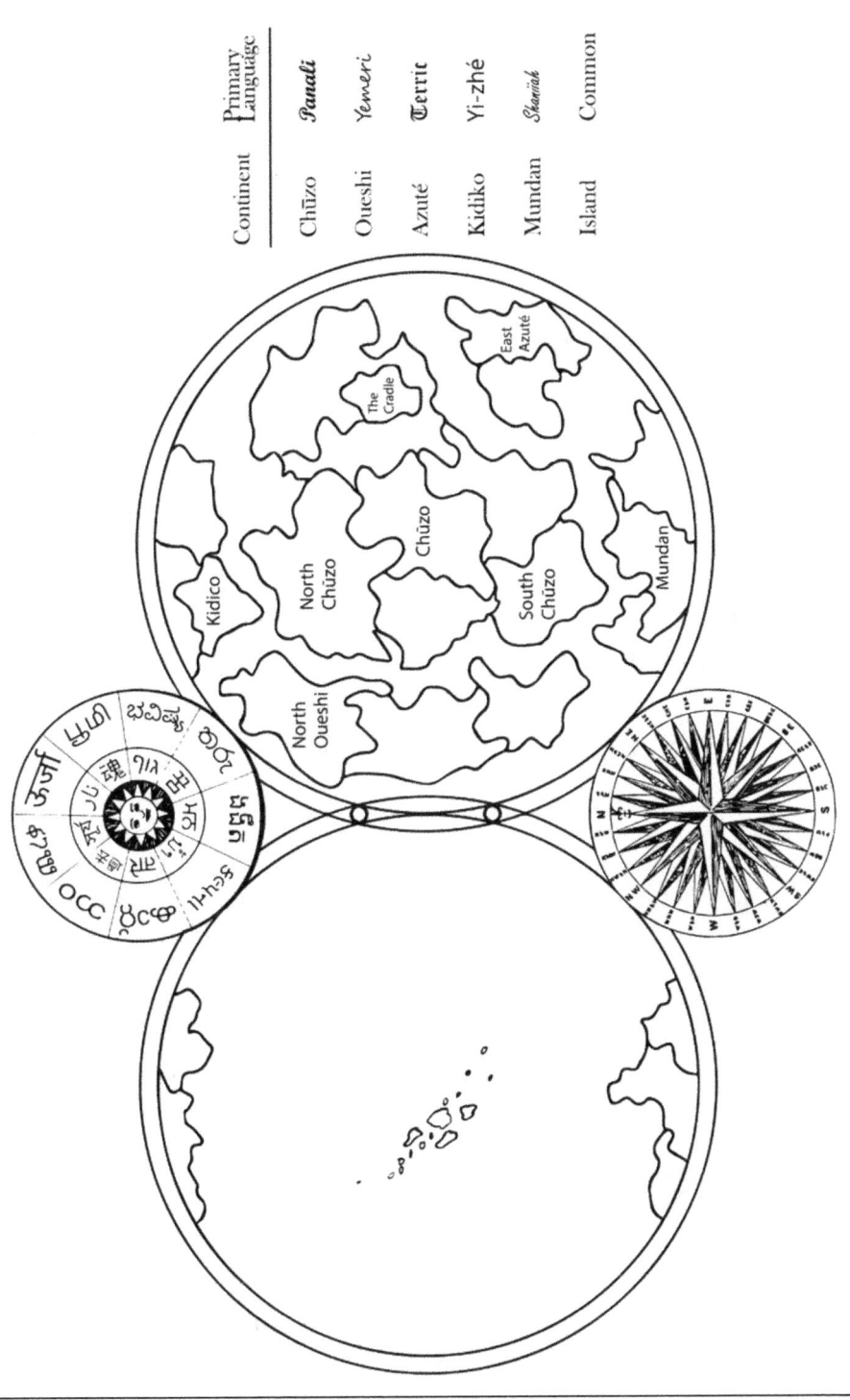

Continent	Primary Language
Chūzo	*Panali*
Oueshi	Yemeri
Azuté	𝕿errit
Kidiko	Yi-zhé
Mundan	*Shaviak*
Island	Common

THE CHARGES

 Humawit
Earth

 Zavun
Sun

 Û-ya'ïn
Water

 Iinamï
Heart

 Saikun
Fire

 Śarī-a
Body

 Shēnó
Life

 Dyzlar
Stars

 Ogani
Dreams

 Wézi
Moon

 Dashū
Souls

 Pigosa
Darkness

 Erviv
Wind

 U-Ech
Mind

 Kámua
Past

 Umbacano
Imagination

 Ajulagrá
Future

 Táqua
Energy

ABILITIES

 Athletes run faster and farther than Olympic humans. They're stronger and more agile with superhuman stamina. Athletes are often trained as Fighters to fulfill future political duties. Athletes and Fighters both are small and lean.

Fighters have less stamina than Athletes but greater fine motor control, process and react faster, and are ambidextrous. They're unable to digest animal proteins.

 Healers control the energy inside of living things. They expertly manipulate cells and encourage them to die or grow. Reading living energy allows them to "see" what's going on inside organisms and what has happened to the body.

Energists control and manipulate the naturally existing energy around them. Though they can access living energy, they risk killing the creature they pull the energy from. They're born without hair pigment.

 Artists stimulate and maipulate brains through visual stimulation using images, movement, and sculpture they create. Their art carries their intended messages to the viewer regardless of how abstract the idea or differences between viewers.

Weavers stimulate and manipulate brains through auditory stimulation. By telling stories and creating music, they seemingly alter reality for the hearer. A Weaver's voice triggers this stimulation unless they consciously choose not to. They're born with vitiligo.

 Thinkers' minds constantly work to understand the world around them to the deepest detail. Though Thinkers try to focus on one specific interest or two, they'll study and contemplate anything that grabbs their attention. Nothing bothers them more than not being able to understand.

Tinkerers are driven to use their knowledge to create. Their minds have an uncanny ability to easily figure out and understand what's needed to bring their ideas to life, but they have difficultly processing the world outside their head. They're born with unusual eyes.

 Telepaths constantly experience the minds of those nearby, making their brains. more resilient against illness. They process mental stimuli at superhuman levels while engaged in everyday activities. With effort, they can access deeper parts of a person's mind and can even force simple commands.

Mind Talkers choose to access another's mind and can reach forgotten and hiddend parts. They can easily manipulate and control a mind they've accessed. They're born with hypotrichosis.

Languages:

Common – Generally used by the majority of the world

Oŭndo (Ō-o͞on-dô) – Considered an extinct language; origin unknown

Yuehio (Yo͞o-chi-ō) – The Grassland's traditional language

Elemental voice – regardless of the language spoken the hearer can always understand.

Titles:

Dinta (Din-tä) – North Oueshi "lesser prince"

Nuwa (No͞o-wä) – East Azuté "queen"

Nu (No͞o) – East Azuté "king"

Zi (Zē) – East Azuté "prince"

Inoa (E-nō-ä) – West Kidico "general's daughter"

Mwä-tonô (Mwä-tō-nō) – Unknown origin "heir of Tonō"

Tonō (Tō-nō) – Unknown origin – a name from legend

Kōjomä̀ (Kō-jō-mä) – Unknown origin – means nothing nice

Jinku (Jin-Ko͞o) – Oŭndo for trainee or heir

Kalj (Kal-j) – Heir to the Emperor of Kidico

Rä-yŭmon (Rä-yo͞o-män) – A title Oya refuses to claim

Chapter 1

I'm failing again...

Failing...

Like always...

How do I face the Duchess with all my failure?

Dry coughs shook the half-drunk cup of milk tea in Ferdinan's hands. He hadn't wanted it. Wasn't hungry. But Jon forced it on him and he regretted every sip.

Uncontrollable shivering intensified the nausea. Coughing...

Pale red dotted trembling, blue fingers when he uncovered his mouth. His stomach lurched, making him groan. Pulling the blanket tighter, the skeleton stood – easing past Oya and Jon in the swaying world of black spots. There was sound – a voice. But everything oozed and glopped together.

Stick legs staggered. Black dots multiplied, swarming. Everything blurred. And minty milk charged up his throat. Warmth enveloped bony, blue fingers and something cold hit his shoulder...then his knees.

Move. Get out of the way... Get out... Black spots drifted lazily around each other. He was tired. *What can a defect do? I'm failing... Failing her like I did grandmother, like I did everyone...*

Stick legs ignored demands to stand – pleas to move.

All that existed were swaying black dots and an uncomfortable warmth cooling in his bony hand... Until something blunt impaled his shoulder and stinging needles wrapped around him.

***

Where are you Śań-a? It hadn't answered her call or commands since escaping the cavern. Oya needed it to heal her leg and her dear friend. Neither would Ferdinan last much longer without its help. Delicate fingers tugged at the steel locket around her neck. *Giving up those connections gave me enough energy...*

Wild green eyes drifted to her dying friend as the growing giant lifted him to his feet. Uncertain looks and intense glares followed the two boys out of the cart. At first, she thought it was their unusual appearances, but the harshest glares were directed at Jon.

Ferdinan was too sick to notice, but neither she nor the growing giant missed them. *Just get them to Samuel...* The glowing orbs in her peripheral were unusually still – as if holding their breath. *Will that be enough?* Would Ferdinan live that long? *Śañ-a! I need your help!*

Sighing with the falling snow beyond the window, Oya closed her eyes – opening them again on her twilight beach. Golden brown hands smoothed over blood red hair, turning it black, speckled with sunshine and shadows and stretching it down past her hips, then brushed over her eyes, returning them to the gold speckled black she loved. "Tanan!"

No response. Again. No matter how many times she called. No matter how much she searched she couldn't find Tanan. *I just placed Śañ-a with her, she's young and... It wasn't that long ago.* Oya paced.

Can Śañ-a be truly lost? It wouldn't be the first one, but... Losing Śañ-a... The loss of U-Ech was devastating. But Śañ-a? Could humanity come back from that? *Where do I start? Where do I look for it?* If Kámua hadn't been broken...

Looking out over the endless purple sand Oya considered her options...bare feet carrying her aimlessly.

Ajulagrá can tell me if Śañ-a has a future. That was something...

Moonlight glinted off the sand – calling out. Making her sigh. *I already have too much.* But it was her duty. And Dashū completed its mourning with her. If only Śañ-a was so easily found.

Delicate fingers slipped into the sand and lifted the chunk of broken mirror. She squeezed it tight, but it didn't hurt her. Nothing could hurt her here. Not physically.

Are you sure?

𝒴ℯ𝒶.

He's not worthy and he has no right to you.

𝒥 𝓈ℯℯ 𝒽𝒾𝓈 𝓌ℴ𝓇𝓉𝒽 𝒶𝓃𝒹 𝒥 𝒹ℯ𝓉ℯ𝓇𝓂𝒾𝓃ℯ 𝒽𝒾𝓈 𝓇𝒾𝑔𝒽𝓉.

I know... My dear friend would be a better choice.

𝒴ℴ𝓊𝓇 𝓌𝓇ℴ𝓃𝑔. 𝒥 𝓌𝒶𝓃𝓉 𝒽𝒾𝓂. 𝒽ℯ'𝓈 𝓅ℯ𝓇𝒻ℯ𝒸𝓉.

It wasn't Oya's place to laugh at a charge's choice, but that boy was far from perfect. Normally a charge knowing the guardian they wanted made her job easier. But the amount of work for this one...

She waved the broken mirrors into existence and reassembled the shattered pieces. Mostly. Dashū always tested its choice first.

There're things I need to do. Will you give me time?

Yes. Thank you.

"Ozar!"

Three breaths and the giant stood before her. It took another moment for him to bow. "Rã-yŭmôn."

Oya approached the empty spot beside the giant. "Ajulagrá, I have a task."

Please be quick — you pulled my keeper at an inconvenient time.

"Piloting a vehicle?"

Addressing Oueshi's Laual.

Ozar stood quietly – pretending he was comfortable being ignored.

"The Five are of no concern to me." *Neither could a continent's leader compare to the importance of the charges.* Gold-flecked black eyes bore into Ajulagrá. "I can't find Śarī-a or Tanan."

She has no more futures.

"And Śarī-a?"

There're many.

Oya breathed out slowly. "Ajulagrá. Guide your keeper to the one who'll secure Śarī-a's safest future and quickest return. Its abilities are sorely needed."

"Why not call the leader here?" Ozar looked down, apologizing.

Oya's gaze didn't waver. "I only met Tanan."

We'll leave as soon as we can.

"Is there anything more, Rã-yŭmôn?" Ozar asked timidly.

"Go."

The two vanished.

Holding a person to their ancestor's sins wasn't fair. But considering how Ozar's line had benefited – was still benefiting... No. It was simpler than that. She'd uphold the earlier Rā-yŭ's decree until their sin was rectified. Unfortunate. Ozar was a good man.

Regardless, she couldn't do much until Śarī-a was found or Samuel healed her leg. Not physically, anyway. *Time to test the Jinku's limits.*

Running golden-brown fingers through gold speckled black hair turned it white and when she rubbed her face, aged skin replaced her youthful smooth. Becoming Muulam for Yuyu worked well. Reaching out, Oya called the younger Tinkerer. *If she doesn't accept a second charge, I'll have to find someone else.*

***

Am I being paranoid? Since getting Ferdinan and Oya on the train, the other passengers glared at him. *Why?* Jon quietly tended to them as best he could. So why? What was he doing wrong? At least his ally was finally sleeping. So was Oya, which was unnerving for some reason. As terrible as this train ride was, it kept Ferdinan from exercising. *How has he not died yet?* Ferdinan's disturbingly sunken face looked hollower as he slept. *How can anyone do this to themselves?*

I'm so tired. But he only had to get Ferdinan and Oya to Samuel. His big brother would heal them both. If only he could convince his ally to not go home, but Ferdinan wouldn't listen to healer Yahmo or him.

For hours he watched over them until wicked green eyes popped open, startling him. And that crazed smile... "Our stop is soon."

Jon felt bad waking the gent. Exhaustion clouded colorless crystals as his ally jerked away. Cracked lips offered a weak smile and blue tinged the skeleton's skin.

Oya rambled. Commenting on how she hadn't seen anything since crossing the North Chūzo boarder and asking how much colder and snowier it'd get. Every word was in Oŭndo. *Is this the kind of stuff they usually talk about?* Jon didn't get all of it, but he understood most.

"*Oya...*" Burning red Ferdinan looked at his blue fingers. "*Your cuffs. How many sets did you...?...?*"

"*Two. But I only brought one with me.*"

4

Ferdinan held out a bony hand – overgrown hair hiding his face. *"May I see them?"*

Grinning, she handed over a little sack latched at her hip. Taking it, Ferdinan opened a small tool kit.

I need mom. Why won't he let me call her?

"I'm sorry, you can't use these for a while."

Inhuman green eyes dimmed when Ferdinan opened them and disconnected the power sources before doing the same to his set.

At least I won't have to deal with those death cuffs... *"Thank you. That'll safe keep us many in ways."*

Blank blue crystals stared at him – unblinking and surprised. Surprise morphed into mourning. *"You learned Oŭndo."*

I stole something precious from him... It wasn't Jon's intention; he was simply tired of them ignoring him with Oŭndo. *"You speak always it around me. And I immersed camp was at the – me grandmothers taught every day. Program and your..."*

Oya giggled. *"They did have fun teaching him."*

Ferdinan apologized. *"Learning was the respectful choice..."*

Giggles filled the awkward silence. *"For being the most populated country, I haven't seen any buildings or people."*

"North Chūzo been you've never to?" Jon wasn't sure why that was both difficult and easy to believe.

"I haven't made it that far."

"We've passed two...?...and a number of larger towns." Boney fingers sealed the access port on the cuffs. *"Look for the...?...."*

"The...?...."

The exhausted skeleton jerked awake when blue crystals drifted close. *"The places that look like sitting gardens."*

"Those were...?...? For what?"

"Train stations."

Disbelief scrunched Oya's delicate lips to the side.

"Disrupting the ecosystem's wrong." Shaking boney fingers returned the cuffs - interrupting Oya's response.

She waved the lifeless bangles. *"Afraid I'll fly away?"*

"Using them on the islands is fine and there in Azuté..." Ferdinan huddled deeper inside his blanket - paling. *"But the world isn't ready. Especially at the conference... Keep them stored 'til we reach Jon's estate."*

"What kind of conference is it to worry about such a simple thing?"

"These aren't simple. And... There'll be military leaders. If the world isn't ready, militaries certainly aren't. I don't want them misused." Boney fingers clutched at his stomach. Closing his eyes, he breathed out.

"We can skip the conference and go straight to Jon's estate. Evelyn would love these."

Horror twisted Jon's face - and Ferdinan's. *I won't allow those anywhere near Evelyn.*

"You and Jon should travel to the Artimus's. But please don't show them to Evelyn. I don't want her getting hurt."

Jon listened silently. Hoping. But each of Oya's attempts to get Ferdinan to not go home, subtle or direct, ended the same until the gent drifted off - shivering uncontrollably.

Jon placed another blanket on his ally. He didn't think it'd help much, but couldn't stand seeing a sick child shiver like that.

"How bad do you think it'll be?" Wild green eyes shot back at the glares assaulting them.

"His family hurts think I him."

"I'm trusting him to you 'til I have mobility again." Nothing about Oya expressed surprise. *"Can you do that much?"*

Jon wanted to cry. He was done a year ago but wasn't allowed to stop yet. When would it finally be over? *"Yes."*

Chapter 2

The skeletal support'll work...but how do I attach them to her hands...? The point was for her to live normally, to give Yuyu back some of what he stole...she lost. And...Elbie couldn't stand seeing her in pain. She never complained, but whenever she rubbed her hands or had to force her exhausted fingers to keep moving just so she could talk... *I'll always feel at fault, won't I?* Even if he didn't, he wanted his sister to be able to work again. To create without being dependent on anyone.

Elbie's study of the human hand was fascinating. *Attaching them for unimpeded wear... And getting them to respond with the fingers instead of after... Her hands are still growing.* Master Ferdinan's titanium bones and adjustment electrode were perfect for the supports. But the material would need to be replaced often... Bulkiness and bunching would be a problem... *If the second skin didn't turn to goop when removed...*

"Choice paralysis?"

Startled, Elbie jumped. A smile bloomed when he saw Haoyu. The plethora of food and spices reminded him of his task, tinging his cheeks pink. "What do I make when I can make anything?"

Perfectly straight white hair swayed with Haoyu's giggles. "Anything you've been craving?"

"Not really." *What'd make her happiest?* "Yuyu loves pepitos..."

Dark eyes glowed as white hair swayed. "Those're tasty, but so much work. Would you like help?"

"Nilo promised already." *You need to pack for your fieldtrip.*

Haoyu smiled. "I'll help with dinner. Joy's cooking with loved ones."

Guilt flared. *Yuyu loved cooking with her family...* "Sounds fun."

"For the fieldtrip..." Haoyu turned to the shelves. "I'm sorry."

Elbie studied the vegetables. "Breakfast's a surprise."

"Oh?" Haoyu's cute smile made his dark eyes glow. "What?"

"A surprise!" Mischievousness laced Elbie's lips. "Mirotti pal is-"

"When did you learn to make those!?"

"I...I'm not sure. Master Ferdinan taught me..." *Where is he? Is he ok?* "Yuyu loves them. I didn't know you'd had them."

"Last break when the North Chūzite ambassador came." Haoyu floated higher to grab cinnamon and clove from a shelf Elbie couldn't reach. "You'll need these. He doesn't seem like he'd enjoy baking."

"Baking, sewing, cleaning...life skills are vital for everyone." *Fruit. Vegetables. Seasonings. Pepitos take three cups of cornmeal. A cup of flour for the mirotti pal... Also butter and... What meats arrived?* "He taught us recipes we could cook with or without a kitchen..." *Was that part of our training....? What purpose did it have if so?*

Haoyu chose a citrus the size of their heads. "How's this one?"

"Perfect!" Elbie giggled, taking it. *A little too big, but it looks ripe.*

Haoyu returned to the high shelves. "How's your printer?"

"The carbon arrived today," Elbie beamed. "I should know soon."

"I can't wait to celebrate your accomplishment!"

I hope we're celebrating, not commiserating. Regardless, he needed to finish here and meet Nilo to make the food for his picnic with Yuyu. And prepare for breakfast tomorrow. Excitement welled up. *She's going to show me the design for the pet robot.* Whatever Yuyu came up with, it was going to be cute – and fun to build. *What animal did she choose?*
***

Golden fingers jabbed at his fresh wound while Zephyr studied the Duchess's reports. *Treatments work but the infection's spreading fast and we don't have the resources to make enough...* Decimated farms and wild food preserves... *How long 'til the ecosystem collapses; is this what happened to the Cradle of the World?* Stopping it would be impossible if it crossed their boarders... *How many'll die without those resources?*

Then came the unrest. Animosity toward the Duchess rose despite her being the only reason there was food. Her storage program provided precious time to figure out the disease, but his people were hungry and scared. To them, she failed like the corrupt nobles she was purging.

The tightness took control again, so he jabbed his wound mercilessly until he could breathe. *Focus.* After days of struggling, the Prince found one viable idea to get the materials without causing a panic. He hated it. The Duchess would too. But they needed those resources. Even if it was terrible. With no better options and the infection spreading, Zephyr composed a message. Sending it was painful. But he did. And then he ran. Only to be bombarded by more painful things. School, country, the elf's impossible task. And her words.

"The guilt, shame, and regret o' past years will fill us 'til we drown. We hope and swim 'til we reach the shore, and there we come to groun'."

Guilt. Shame. Regret. Zephyr was drowning.

When his dearest friend and rival appeared by his side, he slowed to not outpace her. She deserved a better friend than him, but she'd worry if he ran away and... Remembering her blade pin his lung – the pain he caused her. *I owe her this. Whenever she wants to run or fight I will.*

Color and sunshine filled the flowered meadow. Using his friend for this was shameful. Greedy. Terrible. But he needed it as much as she needed to fight. Stance low, he waited for her attack. Denila turned her run into a sidestep. *Attack!* He wanted to yell. His chest was so tight. He needed the pain. *Please!* Onyx eyes closed, teeth grit against the goo. She leapt. Unable to dodge, he guarded – her kick vibrating through him, easing the goo. But there was too much. It was too tight.

How many times can I let her hit me before she worries? Recalling Captain Rutoric, he grabbed her leg and shifted – forcing her back to him. A hard kick landed against his hip, breaking his grip and letting her summersault away. Grinning at the pain-soaked relief, he charged as she rolled to her feet. And when she turned, her grin met him. One reminiscent of that elf and the conversation he tried forgetting.

"Reliving it taught you nothing?"

I don't understand. What truths? The elf gave him one – the two parts of him hid what he is. *How has no one seen I'm a monster?*

Denila's fist materialized, knocking his head sideways. *What am I doing? Focus or she'll stop!* She took advantage of him regaining his footing, not with another strike, but by sweeping his legs from under him. A fist flew toward his gut – but not as quickly as it should have.

She's hesitating... Fire flared. Zephyr rolled and pushed himself to his feet. *Watch! I'm fine!* Feigning a forward dash, he swerved and somersaulted behind her – popping up to his feet while she was still turning. Grabbing her arm, he used her own momentum to pull her across his shoulders and throw her to the ground.

9

A ridiculous win because she was worried about a monster. Her face twisted – desperate to unfreeze her lungs, but she got to her feet and readied her next move. *I'm a monster.*

Denila sprung forward and he barely swerved. *The elf wouldn't have spent so many dreams tormenting me if she didn't see the monster I am.* A reddish-brown fist approached – a feint. Blocking low, he spun away. *I'm a monster.* The ease with which a natural Fighter shifted between left and right gave them the advantage and Zephyr an excuse to let the next strike land. To soak in every ounce of pain. *Please see it.*

Uppercut to his kidney. *Kill it.* Sweeping kick to the side of his knee. *Kill the monster.* Roundhouse to his jaw. *I don't want to be a monster anymore!* A thrust came and he barely caught it, twisting her fist and stepping behind her. Denila threw her head back.

The sky loomed and her face hung upside down. *Didn't see that...* At least his nose wasn't broken. *I need to be careful...* If she hurt him enough to need a Healer... His throbbing face pushed back the goo one heartbeat at a time. Her worried voice blobbed in his ears. And he grinned. "You win."

A fist rammed into his upper arm jarring his face and sending blessed pain through his body. "That's not what I said!"

Cringing, he braved a glimpse. "I apologize. Thinking was difficult for a moment."

She offered her hand and pulled him to his feet. "I'll take the win. Time for my exit interview."

***

Blankets, pillows, and dining ware for two filled the tiny garden maze Elbie showed her a while ago. *Guess I'm early.* It was more likely her little brother was late because he was too ambitious for a picnic lunch, but Yuyu didn't mind waiting. It gave her time to study the torn piece of paper that was in her hand when she woke up this morning. Like U-ya'in, it was alive and talked to her. But unlike the mischievous water that loved to tease and play, this was wonderous.

Looking at the bit of yellow paper, possibility sat in Yuyu's hand. A Tinkerer's paradise. Every thought she could imagine. How to build it. Everything she dreamed of making... *Umbaccano's amazing.* Pink eyes shifted to the gloves hiding her hands' gruesomeness. If only she could give it her full potential. But there was one who could. He'd love it.

Yuyu told it all about him. His amazingness. Gentleness. Genius. Every incredible idea. Her years with him. How proud she was of him. All she wished for him. Until she was in tears. Not because she was sad or happy. Warmth and pain filled her. *Is this what love feels like?* Soft? Comfortable? Full of hopes, joys, and sorrows of the one she cared for?

Umbaccano listened – filling her with a different kind of warmth. One more amazing than she imagined a hug felt, if they didn't hurt. *You'd love Elbie's talent and perseverance and mind! You'd love him.*

I want to meet him.

***

Regal clothes, exotic face paint, and elaborate hair adorned the man who sired him. The man Herrard would replace once he chose a spouse. "Negating the worst and minimizing animosity, well done."

"Thank you, sir." The Kalj's smile hid his anxiety. He did his best to account for every issue the treaties Xhou and the Duchess negotiated would cause, but Herrard wouldn't know how insufficient his solutions were until his world tour of meetings started. *If only this was all...*

The man's expertly painted face and perfectly silent bells added to Herrard's stress. *I need to practice the face paint again...* And revisit his stillness training. A Kal's presence should never be heard, only felt, until they spoke. *I hate bell training.* At least the various hair styles were fun even if protocols dictated which he was to wear in each circumstance.

A thick brow rose high. "How'll you convince the world leaders?"

"There'll be turmoil regardless." *I hope my plan works.* Herrard's fingers combed through his long hair. His would be done in elaborate styles soon too. "I'm sending ambassadors to each country to minimize fallout. If Oueshi's Laual and the Kyos assist, this should go smoothly."

"How quickly can you contact everyone?"

Sitting up tall, Kalj Herrard bowed to the Kal. "Everything'll be arranged by the time I graduate."

"Good. This'll prove your merit for Kal splendidly." The plain man smiled – tired and excited to see retirement nearing. "Send me your plans and I'll start preparing the ambassadors."

"Thank you. I'll contact the rest of the Five." *Better practice hair and painting my face...* Appearing in an official capacity was a pain...

***

"I'm sorry!" *I took too long!* Yuyu was sitting on a pillow reading when Elbie returned with the food. *That's a strange face she's making.* He hurried and laid out everything. "What's wrong?"

Yuyu put her screen down. "Human bodies are disgusting."

Ah... Maturation lessons. "That's part of being alive though."

"Yeah..." Pink eyes turned to the ocean. "I'd rather know what to expect than be surprised."

"Knowing what's normal is nice too..." Elbie blushed.

"Would you like to know?" Pink tinged her cheeks. "It's going to get weird soon. They split the lesson into male and female bodies this time."

Strange... But that wasn't his hope for today. "Maybe later. Here."

Yuyu leaned in. "Pepitos! My favorite!"

Giggling, Elbie handed her a plate. "I made cinnamon milk also."

"You're amazing!"

~

Lunch was wonderful. Spending time with his sister eating delicious food Nilo helped Elbie make...more accurately, Elbie helped Nilo. But Yuyu smiled and enjoyed every bite nonetheless.

"You're looking...intense. Sessions with Norger still no good?" Sunlight shone off pink eyes as Yuyu put down the toy Norger gave her and rubbed her hands.

Elbie gave a strained smile. This wasn't what he wanted to spend his last afternoon with her talking about. "He's...good with programing..."

"And?"

I hate it. Master Ferdinan would have him build what he wanted after studying similar programs. Not give him a program and a list of modifications then do it for him. *Why does he think I'm inept?*

Mismatched eyes stared at his trembling hands. Master Ferdinan made him feel capable of anything - acknowledged his efforts and helped him find the right directions. Mistakes. Doing things wrong. It felt like the normal creation process, not failure. But Norger...

Every time Elbie shared his work, Norger was surprised he exceeded expectations – as if expectations were the limits of ability. *I'm not as incompetent as he thinks, am I?* Burning cold tapped his hand. "Elbie?"

"Sorry. I got distracted." Elbie offered her more cinnamon milk, which she turned down.

Yuyu picked up the little toy and spun it. "Norger's pretty stubborn."

It was probably rude, but Elbie didn't want to think about the new Lead. "Have you been able to remember your first year of training?"

The abrupt change in topic startled Yuyu, but she smiled. "No."

"Master Ferdinan made sure we were comfortable and our yearmates were sympathetic." Elbie forced his own smile.

"Remember how? Other than the greeting?"

Elbie thought hard. "He supervised meetings with my suitemates."

"I forgot about that." Yuyu spun the toy, lip twitching. "I remember regular lectures about no one having the right to touch me and he'd step in if anyone didn't respect that."

"Same." Elbie smiled. "Didn't your dad work with Master Ferdinan before you started...or do I remember wrong?"

Yuyu paused. "I remember playing in my empty dorm and dad being there in the lab..."

"Should we invite one of her parents to stay over break?"

Pink eyes narrowed as she thought. "Good idea. When do you think they'll tell us her name?"

A mischievous little grin took over Elbie's face. "Maybe we don't have to wait."

~

Yuyu was going to ask what he meant, but Umbacano interrupted.

Introduce us.

A smile bloomed and quickly faded as Yuyu remembered when she tried showing Elbie U-ya'in's shell. *I thought that wasn't my place...*

It's my place to choose who I wish to meet.

13

Golden light surrounded Elbie and confusion coated his face, but he shook it away with a sheepish smile. "It's working."

"Your printer? I want to see!" *You will too, Umbaccano. Then I'll introduce you. I promise.*

Ok.

Jumping up, Elbie escorted her to Ferdinan's lab.

"Growing a diamond..." *He's amazing!* Pink eyes followed the little machine as it ran back and forth. It was impossible to see change from layer to layer – but over many...

Introduce us.

Opening the glass pendant shot jolts of pain through her fingers, but the torn corner of paper came out easily. "What do you think of this?"

First, Elbie was confused. Then, mismatched eyes grew wide and his smile brighten. The golden glow from earlier surrounded him again. "You remembered! He's so cute! You did this advanced of a prototype on your own? You're absolutely amazing!"

Confused, Yuyu studied the paper. It folded itself into a paper bird and morphed into a real one. Bright yellow with soft feathers. It's crown and tail were as regal as the Five Masters. Black eyes glistened. Orange dots speckled its cheeks and the tips of its wings. It was beautiful and majestic. *A bit ostentatious?*

This is how he's chosen to see me.

He does love birds. Elbie and Umbacano studied each other, taking each other in. Simply experiencing the other. "Its name's Umbacano."

Elbie offered a finger. The bird hopped up; head cocked to the side. Joy radiated from them as they fell into a trance. Like when she first experienced the charges... *Watch over my little brother while I'm gone.*

Pure excitement consumed her. And the room and the world! Excitement and unfettered joy of finally finding a home. Finding a family... Elbie's smile was beyond description.

Chapter 3

Found you. Finally. Ash covered winter clothing and masks, making them shadows in the snowy woods beyond the courtyard. They were ready, but the child noble came prepared. He carried a girl with a braced leg and, walking ahead, a sick boy scanned the area. *Pathetic.*

Nobles who wouldn't face their citizens weren't competent to lead. But forcing infirm children to act as shields? Disgusting. Dishonorable. Unconscionable. The boy especially... *Is he a Ragnian Camp survivor?*

Using someone who'd survived that as a shield...! *We waited too long to remind them of their place.* But they were rectifying their mistake now. Nobles weren't allowed to fail anymore, to place themselves over citizens. *We're done. They'll pay as warning to their successors.*

Drifting snow softened the world, but not the rock in his hand. Hands that'd grown thin. Not like the adults surrounding him...but still unhealthy. Because nobles shirked their duty to go without so their citizens had enough. *Don't hit the girl, only the child noble.*

Drawing his arm back, he flung it with all his anger and hunger! And it flew. *Fulfill your purpose, rock.* Dark eyes grew wide. Time crawled. Shaggy hair appeared and the rock sliced the camp survivor's cheek as he herded Ferdinan and the girl into the corner of a covered sitting area.

Rocks flew. That tall, bony body shielded the girl as stick arms protected Ferdinan's head. More rocks drew blood and tore through the survivor's clothes. He wanted to scream for everyone to stop! There was only one target. Only one deserved punishment. But he froze, horrified at the blood oozing down the boy's cheek. *I hurt an innocent person...*

Rocks stopped and Trac, their speaker, stepped forward. He lifted a rod high above his head and tried pulling the survivor away, but the child spun and grabbed the hand holding the weapon. The crowd screamed out the nobles' injustices, failures. Trac struggled to break free from a child who looked barely able to stand.

"Halt!" The survivor called out. That word wasn't panicked or desperate. It was firm and held the strength and force of absolute authority – shocking the crowd to silence.

"Stand aside. Our business is with Lord Ferdinan."

"I'm Lord Ferdinan. I'll submit, but I can't allow you to hurt the innocent."

Fury radiated through Trac's mask at the lie. "This is our duty!"

The sick boy studied the mob. Ferdinan said something, but the survivor kept searching... "Our eyes! It's impossible to fake my eyes!"

Uncertainty washed over the courtyard. Trac looked closely at the survivor, then turned to the one they assumed was Ferdinan.

The skeletal boy stepped forward and presented them to the crowd. Only two people had eyes like that. The Duke and his son. Faking dark eyes was easy, but ones that pale... *That can't be him.*

The healthier boy moved between Ferdinan and the crowd – injured girl holding tight to his neck. "Stop! Please! He's sick."

That skeletal face hardened. "This isn't your people, land, culture. Elsewhere I bend to your beliefs. But here you'll respect our customs."

Horrified, the boy turned. "No!"

"Citizens keep nobles in their place so evil can't take root and cause the country's downfall. I accept my people's will. While on our land, you will too. Stand down, Oueshian. Stay with Oya."

Oueshian....? Why use the girl's name but not his? He pushed the oddity away. There was only one they stood against today.

Two boys forced the Oueshian to the closest bench while Trac dragged Ferdinan to the center of the snowy courtyard. Years of anger and frustration at watching those he loved do with less and less...! But the red oozing down that skeletal cheek... *No. Our duty. We're starving. If we don't, our families will die.* But...those quivering bones...

The child noble shook, but wasn't afraid. Unbelievably pale skin was ashen where it wasn't blue. Boney fingers clutched at his chest. Every time Trac pushed him, pain twisted his face. Rocks flew once Trac took the noble's coat. But not his. *The crowd's too big, I'll hit an innocent...*

More blood soaked fabric with each hit, showing the boy was thinner than they. Much thinner. *To look like that he must be doing his job. Does he deserve punishment....?* The crowd advanced. Fury grabbed the noble, anger spewing more vapidly with each shirt they cut off...

The Oueshian stood but didn't move – held by invisible hands. The girl with the braced leg pushed herself to her good foot. She didn't shout.

Didn't raise her voice. But the authority she spoke with compelled the air to deliver her alien words to everyone present.

He didn't understand them and the mob didn't react. But there were two – a man on the far edge of the courtyard and a woman halfway between him and the girl. They listened intently. And when she fell silent, they turned and watched the crowd. Something green glinted off the edge of their ears and their faces held no emotion.

Why are they just watching? Why am I? No, it's my duty to hold nobles to the highest accountability! For our country! Our people! My family! His gaze fell on the mob. Torn fabric flew. Screams! *Joining now, I'll get hurt. Beaten or crushed....* Fury intensified. Snow turned to mud.

The Oueshian was frozen yet fighting to move. Alien eyes soaked in everything. The two with green on their ears watched, disappointed.

And rage, rightly held, deepened again. *How's there so much hate in us? Or is this fear...?* He couldn't see Ferdinan. Couldn't hear the noble anymore. But no one that sick could survive... Cold sweat broke across his skin as reality set in. *I don't want to be a person who beats a child to death. Even if it's expected. Even if it's my duty.*

He shook – terrified.

He shook – why was he the only one?

The two with the green on their ears cried silently. The tall boy fought to scream! The girl stood regal. Emotionless. And his ears rang. His heart twisted and thrashed against his ribs. He didn't want to see anyone die. He didn't want to be part of that death.

Rage and frustration, fear and helplessness beat down on a child already near death. *Why won't they stop? Even if he was healthy, this is too much!* He didn't know he stepped up or opened his mouth. But his weak, trembling voice drifted above the hate and despair. "Enough."

A few stopped. A few... A few listened, but not enough.

He wasn't in charge. He wasn't anybody, but... Clenching his fists, he dove into the fray, knocking Trac off balance to stand protectively over the child noble. His heart pounded. *Will they beat me too?* "Look at him! He's gone through worse than us already. Look!"

He expected violent backlash, but it was like their mouths were held shut and their bodies bound as they looked on the naked jumble of bones shaking in the muddy snow and struggling to breathe.

Melted skin wrapped the left side of his torso and upper arm. Countless scars marred the rest of his body. He was so thin... Welts and cuts and blood... A couple bones didn't lay right under tortured skin.

Whatever held the Oueshian let go and he flew forward - knocking him aside and taking Ferdinan in his arms. "Monsters! He's a sick child! I hate this! I hate this country!"

A frail hand struggled to rise as Ferdinan choked on breath and words. Whatever the child noble was trying to say, it only made the tall boy more upset. "No! I hate everything about this country! It's wrong!"

"Mind your place, Oueshian," the injured girl warned as the man with green wrapped around his ear carried her over.

Wheezing and half formed sounds left Ferdinan. He couldn't understand the child noble, but the Oueshian looked horrified and the girl nodded. Inhuman eyes turned to the crowd, "We might not agree or understand, but he's not angry. He's grateful you upheld your duty."

Colorless eyes closed and wheezing turned painful.

"I'm not a Chuzite, but I respected your customs as my dear friend wished, as he respected my own." The crowd turned to her, trembling at her voice. "Now go and know there stand three witnesses to this day."

Ice ran down his spine and the collective mob shuttered. But everyone left. Except him, who watched as the tall boy cried, frantic to hold and check on Ferdinan at the same time. The woman removed a blanket from her bag and carefully wrapped the child noble. And the girl... She was no longer regal, but rigid like a statue in the man's arms. And when she returned to life, the wheezing eased.

"Seems he finally got the punishment he's been wanting."

Horror twisted the Oueshian's face and emotions beyond description glared at her. "What...!"

Inhuman eyes rolled at him. "I don't think it's enough for him yet."

Ferdinan struggled to breathe as the Oueshian wrapped himself around the unconscious child and sobbed.

What've I done?

Chapter 4

"Congratulations!" Tuel hovered over the ocean, smiling bright. "That completes your apprenticeship. I'm proud of you!"

Panting and covered in sweat, Haoyu floated eye-level with his mentor and smiled just as big. "Thank you, Master Tuel! I can't believe how heavy water gets!"

"It does. Twenty cubic feet's impressive at your age. Don't move more 'til your energy capacity's grown." Tuel looked away. "And..."

The first time Haoyu called him "Master" felt more real than the title he was given. All of Haoyu's year called their mentors that. The mentors got in trouble for letting them, but it was adorable. Now Dæya insisted it had to stop since apprenticeships were ending.

"And?"

"You can't call me 'Master' anymore. I haven't earned that title and since you've completed your mentorship..."

"But...isn't that what you call a teacher?"

"No. 'Master' is an earned title and I haven't earned it." Mussing his apprentice's matching snow white hair, Tuel's gaze drifted toward the main island. "Ready for your fieldtrip?"

Dark eyes brightened. Haoyu chittered excitedly as they floated back to shore before suddenly falling silent – face strained.

"What's wrong?"

"Um... Elbie's not allowed to go. He'll be here alone..."

"He's not being housed with older students?"

"He is..." Haoyu's dark eyes drifted to the approaching beach. "But... He's gotten better, but Elbie doesn't talk about himself much, doesn't speak up when he should... With all of us gone, I'm worried no one'll notice if he needs help. That no one'll notice him."

Haoyu's the sweetest. "I'll make sure he's not alone."

"Thank you."

"Gladly. Gongie and Marcus'll help too. Ilu might, but he's busy with some home stuff."

"Gongie...?"

"Yes?"

A grimace tightened Haoyu's lips. "Maybe not Gongie alone..."

Did Ferdinan pass on his fear of Psychs? "He helps with the younger students regularly. Even got hurt protecting Yuyu from that menacing disk."

Haoyu giggled – looking away guiltily. "He acts strange around Telepaths. Gongie, Ninn, Qestra... Like he's preoccupied when they're near. That's why the disk almost hit Yuyu. He didn't react when it was thrown to him, so it veered to the closest active person."

That's what happened? I thought it malfunctioned. "I'll keep that in mind. Tell me more about him."

***

Angry bodies and screaming vitriol faded, leaving Jon in the snowy courtyard with the unconscious Ferdinan. *Don't die.* He was taking the gent to Samuel to get better. Dying here... *Why couldn't I move? How could I do nothing while he was beaten?! He'll die 'cause I did nothing!* Even now all he could do was hold the gent.

Jon wanted to flag down the nearest car to take them to the ports, but a woman warned not to move the gent since they didn't know how badly Ferdinan was hurt. Still, he had to hold his ally up or the skeleton couldn't breathe... *Who're those two?* They had no rods or bands in their ears, but wore a green cuff like Oya had at the camp.

Everything became a blur. Soldiers arrived then Jon stood outside the Samultz estate. Instead of Ferdinan, Oya was in his arms and a servant was coaxing him away from the skeleton. *When...?*

Various languages slipped off their tongue, but Panali jarred Jon's brain back to reality. North Chūzo's native language. The crowd spat so many words in Panali, but Ferdinan responded in Common... *Why didn't he address his people in their tongue?*

"I promise he'll be properly cared for."

"I..." Jon watched soldiers carefully place Ferdinan on a litter. All he could think about was learning Panali because North Chūzo was an

20

important ally. Knowing their national language was respectful and would make befriending Ferdinan easier. But he'd never spoken it with the gent. There were so many opportunities and he practiced it with other students... It was stupid, but Jon focused on this because it was safe to think about. Everything else was painful. Dangerous.

A cold finger poked his cheek. "*I'm sorry, what was that?*"

The servant bowed and gave Jon a sympathetic smile. "*Dinta, would you prefer our sons to share your rooms while you're here?*"

Jon's heart raced as he squeezed Oya tighter. He didn't want to be alone. But sleeping with strangers... "I'll stay with Ferdinan."

"I'll see what can be done."

***

Those clouds. They didn't match her dear friend's, but they'd taken root. It wasn't unexpected after watching Ferdinan be beaten to death. *Thank you, Shēnó.*

I can help you too.

She turned to the drooping orbs in her peripheral. They'd given her half of themselves so she could call Shēnó. *It'd be better to help them.*

I'll help all of you.

A glow only she saw filled the passenger's compartment and energy filled her and the orbs. *Thank you for the infusion of life.*

I'll return to Charlie now.

Thank you. Tell him I'm sorry for stealing you so suddenly.

Pure giggles danced around her. Then the car stopped. *What's happening?* An hour's drive and they saw nothing but snowy landscapes and amazing silvery winter flowers. *How do they survive in such cold temperatures?* And now they sat at a forest's entrance. *If winter looks like this, how beautiful are spring's colors?* And...where were the people and buildings?

Jon fought the soldiers reaching for Ferdinan while Oya studied the nature surrounding them. A man appeared from nowhere offering the softest blanket she ever felt. "Please follow me, Dinta, Miss."

Calming Jon's heart, she grinned at the man. "Where're we going?"

"Inside." After some to do, the man got Jon moving. Just beyond the tree line was a gentle hill. They didn't go up it or around. They walked to a flat side of it. *A door? Fascinating...* Studying the surrounding area...

It looked like a hilly forest with unusually kept gardens, but here and there light glinted and steam existed where it shouldn't. *Amazing!*

***

If she'd put the well-being of her country over that creature. Why is she so incomprehensibly stubborn when it comes to that thing? Given the choice, the Duchess would've given the defect to North Oueshi before she was forced to carry it.

"Surprising, hearing you bartering for a child like you would a shipment of vegetables." Shock washed over the Queen Mother and was replaced with indignation, but the Duchess continued before the woman could speak. "The answer's always the same."

Calmly the Duchess gazed at North Oueshi's leader, their strongest ally. *That thing isn't mine, nor am I allowed to relinquish it.* But it didn't matter. North Chūzo needed materials for the soil treatments. Materials North Oueshi naturally had in abundance. Caring for her citizens was her duty and honor, but pride had no place with death looming over the world, so the Duchess followed Prince Zephyr's suggestion and sent a contract the Queen Mother couldn't refuse. As much as they hated it.

This was necessary, but the consequences... "In exchange for the materials, we'll open claims to North Oueshi. Trained teachers'll be sent to help them adjust as their new families are approved."

"Why now?" A million thoughts flashed across the Queen's face. A golden prize with only one caveat – Chūzite teachers.

"Consider carefully what you do with that information." This offer gave away much. Both about North Chūzo's state and her understanding of North Oueshi's. "And what I could do with mine."

The Queen Mother's lips tightened. "What're your limits?"

"Claims will remain open 'til our need for those materials ends."

"And those being processed when the need ends?"

The Duchess's smile was strained. "Disrupting processing is detrimental to children. Those granted process will be given the option to complete it, but new claims will be denied."

"We can place children faster than you," Mother pressed, "continue 'til there aren't any waiting claim options."

A hard glare twisted the Duchess's face. "Pressing for more of my citizens won't erase your ancestors' sins."

Beautiful, dark eyes dropped before returning the glare.

Perhaps "ancestors' sins" was dramatic. No one knew why North Oueshi's birthrates had steadily dropped for four generations. Claiming children worldwide maintained their population. Until the blight. North Oueshi's loss didn't compare to East Azuté. No country's did. But it was significant. And there were fewer children available to claim.

"Read over the treaty. Mark any-" A chime interrupted the Duchess - one she'd been waiting for. "Your son arrived. Jon's rooms are set up to speak with family and friends as long as he wishes."

"Thank you. Please care for my children 'til they return to me."

***

They're supposed to be doing drills today... Gongie searched every direction. This island was inconvenient to reach, with little beyond rocks and wild vegetation. Sometimes Fighters and Athletes had rowing competitions this far out and Energists would race here and back. But today should've been safe.

Muddled thoughts and emotions sharpened, forming into distress. *Where are they?* There was only one, but being spotted would make things awkward.

Searching water and sky... By the time Gongie spotted the kayak, he recognized that mind. It was too late. An Athlete would spot him if he moved. *Please continue past...*

They beached beyond view of his boat. He had a chance if...

The golden Prince dragged the craft up the sand. Thoughts Gongie shouldn't hear bombarded him. Zephyr's mind was scarier than Ferdinan's. And...it changed recently. For the worse.

Being close to a mind in that much pain hurt. And Zephyr's distress grew continuously over the last year - becoming a physical ailment. Thick tar filled his chest, paralyzing his lungs, mind, body... And it kept intensifying.

Walk past. Run to the other side...

Zephyr vanished into the heavy vegetation, but that mind got closer. *Where is he?*

Shining silver...then a sharp pain coursed through his leg – pushing the tar down. But it was already growing back. *I'm trapped...*

"It needs to die." A sludge of emotions emanated from the older boy. *"I need to kill it..."*

I can't hear this, can't know. But the Prince's mind was too loud to be contained by a veil and he didn't want to be stabbed again.

"Why do we want to die?"

In his mind, silver took the form of a comically short blade. The symbol of relief. Escape. Light glinted off the blade's edge. Then it stabbed deep. Gasping, pain dragged Gongie to the ground.

"Reliving it taught you nothing?"

He didn't hear me... Emotions and intentions welled up in Zephyr – terrifying Gongie. He couldn't... *Should I show myself? Or endure?*

Silver filled his mind again. *No!* Gongie's body moved.

Rocks dug into the Telepath's back and skull and something pressed his neck and wrist to the ground. Horror. And distress. Thoughts, beliefs he'd heard one too many times from Ferdinan. That face twisted and onyx eyes tripled.

Forced thoughts crashed in, but Zephyr got off him. Haunting thoughts welled up and vanished suddenly – replaced by fighting techniques, adrenaline, and a too ambitious class schedule.

"You don't have to do that." Gongie gasped – fighting back nausea from the mental assault. "I know. I've known for a long time."

He'd known about the abuse and did nothing because he wasn't supposed to know. He known about this thing haunting Zephyr – the thing the Prince couldn't name. He'd known. And did nothing.

Panic and fear intensified – making him dizzy. Making the world sweep and sway. Every instinct inside Zephyr screamed to attack. To destroy the threat before him.

I need to run... But Gongie couldn't move.

Golden hands screamed though his voice was steady. "What are you doing here?"

"Th...this is w-where I always c-come..."

Of course. What do I do? Sighing deeply, Zephyr rested his head in his hands before glaring at the Telepath. "Say anything and there'll be no place you can hide from me."

***

Elbie stood there telling Ferdinan it wasn't his fault. But it was. He knew it. He killed another person. A child... Then Oya replaced the boy and confirmed it. She confirmed it... And Elbie stood before him again...

Over.

And over.

And sometimes Grandmother added her own accusations. Relaying the words of the twenty million who joined her. All those eyes... They cried! Because of him!

Every cell tore away from each other... Disintegrating.

Hoarse screams shredded his raw throat. His heart thrashed, beating harder and harder, faster, faster. Light brown eyes glared at him and the disintegration spread. There was no air. Black spots filled the world.

And Elbie told him it wasn't his fault. But it was. Ferdinan knew it was. Oya knew. Grandmother knew. The twenty million knew. Looking down, nearly colorless eyes watched his chest turn to dust...

Raw and rough – the screams returned, his throat frayed and bleeding. And his cells dissolved into atoms. Those light brown eyes radiated hate and disappointment. He failed...

He needed to cough, but there was no energy, no air, nor time between screams to. Black spots blobbed and oozed around the dust that was once his useless body.

And Elbie stood there telling him it wasn't his fault.

***

"Ooo! The gold stuff!" Xhou plopped next to his island brother and nabbed the jeweled container of lip paint and a brush – causing a ruckus of bells to sound in protest. Soon his lips were as golden as Herrard's and he was grinning obnoxiously. "It's like liquid silk."

An unprincely snort left Herrard, cringing when the bells jingled. "You're welcome to take my place. I'm sure an Artist could come up with something to make your hair look long enough."

25

"We tried that before." They both laughed at the memory. Two seven-year-olds convinced a little face paint and matching clothes would make them impossible to tell apart, and an entire palace humoring them. They weren't children anymore, but... "Want to?"

"Can't. I'm helping with the youngest students in a few hours."

Blue-black eyes sparkled. "Me too. I think they'd love it."

"And the instructors would definitely appreciate it." Herrard rolled his eyes, purposely jingling the bells on his cuff, but chuckled. "Think you can squeeze those broad shoulders into one of my robes?"

"I'd be more worried about dragging the hem along the ground." The Scientist lined up the pigment, prepped the creams, and organized the brushes. "Give me your face!"

Despite more laughing than focus, Xhou did a good job painting both their faces. Herrard pulled out head wraps - twisting and braiding them in place of hair. Soon they were tying each other into the Kalj's old ceremonial robes. Once all the ribbons, bobbles, and bells were properly laced and secured, they crowed the mirror.

"I think we've improved." Xhou snorted at the two colorful faces staring back at them - tinkling bells sounding through the room.

"Definitely. They'll never know which one is which!"

It was dumb, but they laughed. "You know, if I warn Elbie, he'd make sure everyone humored us like the adults did back then."

"Master Kezia's going to hate us." Hazel eyes and a too amused smile lingered for a moment. "Message him. I'll grab extra bells."

"Ha! All the adults are going to hate us if we bring those."

"But the youngest'll love them." Herrard dashed to his room, but froze before entering. "The middle students will be jealous when they hear they missed this."

"Guess we'll have to do it again for their welcome back assembly."

Chapter 5

The tunic and slacks provided by the Samultz were fine. Not as soft and elegant as Leonel's creations, but of a princely quality. *Of course, I am a prince after all...* Not as high ranking as Zephyr or Ozar. But still a prince by Chūzite rankings. *How will they treat Oya?* One who proudly bore no title? *But at the camp...* Long fingers and a fluffy towel attacked his sopping wet hair. After the cave-in...

Air grew thin. Jon turned on every light, but the dark beyond the window loomed heavily. He breathed out slowly – pushing away the surety of death. *They called her Rā-yŭmôn. Doted on her. Did all she asked...* When she told strange stories, they hung on her every word...

One story after another filled their tomb until he fell asleep...

Jon's heart raced and he stopped his thoughts there. He didn't want to remember. *What's the Chūzite equivalent of her rank....?* Fatigue hit hard. He felt ill. *I'm trapped alone in a giant room. Ferdinan... Where did they take him? Oya told me to watch over him...but...where is he?*

A man entered and bowed. "Dinta, the kitchens are open to you. We'd be honored for you to make use of them as you please."

Ice consumed Jon. *Kitchens...* He loved cooking – loved feeding people... But the offer made him sick. Ferdinan turned this pleasure into a chore. The camp stole the joy of creating magnificent dishes. There was no one here to feed...save Oya, but she didn't take joy in eating. Not like his family and island brothers. "Thank you, but I'll be focused on Oya and Ferdinan while I'm here."

"Understandable. They'll remain open to you regardless." The man bowed. "Miss Oya's playing in the gardens with our children."

Jon wasn't sure if he should worry or be relieved, but he nodded.

"You have a call awaiting from your mom." The man motioned to the giant screen attached to the wall nearest the bed, then offered the screen he was holding. "These are secured for you to contact your friends at school. Please use them for as long as you wish."

Mom....? Tears filled his eyes. Could he really talk to his family? Hear their voices? See their faces? Joy and hope and trepidation danced in his stomach. "Thank you. You're dismissed."

"I'll return later with dinner." The man bowed and left the room.

Sitting in the middle of the bed gave him the best view of the giant screen. *They arranged it this way for my comfort.* Drying his eyes, he accepted the waiting call.

A strange twisted sight wrangled a scream from him as he fell back, almost scurrying off the bed – until two voices he knew called out, apologizing for scaring him. Panting, he sat studying the screen for a long time. His mom's and Evelyn's faces were grotesquely morphed to look like...ogres. *What is this....?*

"Look at what my big brother helped me do! Now I match my stuffed ogre!" Joy squealed out of Evelyn as she held up the stuffed toy she'd gotten last break. "I wonder if it'll make me a dragon too!"

Why would anyone do this....? But Evelyn wanting it was all the reason Ferdinan needed. Regardless of how ridiculous. "If you send it to me, I can easily adjust it to make you a dragon."

"Big brother can do that though!" Evelyn giggled and squeezed his mom's arm. "I want to show *you* the pie I learned to make!"

It took a minute to find a smile, but Jon placed it on his lips. "Too bad. I like programming. I'm excited to see your progress with baking, though I'd love to see your actual faces...if I could."

Mom reached forward and they became human, then turned blurry for a long time. He hadn't meant to cry – not with Evelyn sitting there. Because worrying her would trouble Ferdinan.

But he didn't have words. Just tears...
***

How much does he know? What'll he do? And I threatened him... How much worse would that make the Psych's retaliation?

Lunch wasn't sitting right. *I need to leave – I need to fix this.* But without a legitimate reason Denila would worry. And Zephyr didn't know what to do anyway... *If he's known for years...* Nausea doubled.

He needed something better than this inane conversation to focus on. Grabbing his screen, Zephyr started the next assignment. Literature. Though distracting, it didn't stop his churning stomach.

A red-brown fist rested on a slender hip as midnight eyes rolled at him. "Looks like socializing's over. Back to work."

Grabbing a screen, Denila sat. Silence filled the room – making Gongie's face loom heavier. The terror that blanketed the Psych... Zephyr's stomach twisted and unbearable warmth filled his gut. Gongie wanted to run. He paled. *He's known everything? For years?* That warmth increased, crawling up his throat. Why was it so hot?

The consequences Gongie would face...but his cousin would already be destroyed. What'll happen to me? Zephyr gulped down air. Lunch turned sour. *To my people with no heir?* Intensifying. *My country?* Urgency filled his brain and Zephyr bolted from the room.

A few rounds emptied his stomach, but his body kept going and his mind spiraled. Waves of dry retching held him prisoner. *What'll he do?* There wasn't time between heaving to gasp in air. *How many will I destroy?* Dizziness made the nausea worse and the retching more violent. Panic drove his heart. And he couldn't stop. Not the Telepath nor his body from trying to expel his organs.

I'm a monster. Nothing can stop it. That's why the goo only grows – why it keeps coming back! Zephyr couldn't breathe or think or move. There was no running from that truth. No forgiveness. He was trapped. Trapped spasming on his knees. Trapped at the mercy of someone he didn't know. Trapped by the truth of what he was.

Something cool and damp rested on his neck, easing the awful heat. *Why? Doesn't she see what I am?* A strong hand gently rubbed his back and a voice he didn't deserve spoke softly – providing a path out of his mind. The cool cloth. A strong hand. That beautiful voice.

Dizziness abated and exhaustion settled in. *I'm so tired...*

When the retching stopped, Denila wrapped him in her arms. Held him. Waited for Zephyr to catch his breath, to relax.

***

"Nothing from an animal. Including fish," Sora smiled.

Samuel nodded. Going over this wasn't necessary – she had a great memory, but he had to make sure. "How do you greet him?"

"Is it the same?"

Samuel returned her smile. *Good, she remembers.*

"Offer my hand. If he moves away, pull back, but keep offering. If he stares at my hand instead of me, stop. If he looks at me, wait for him to move back and offer again. If he hesitates, don't move. Pulling away will make him feel rejected, pushing forward will scare him." Worry laced her lips. "He's still as skittish as he was eight years ago?"

What'll three days with his sister do to him? "He...struggles after being at the Samultz Estate." Looking at her was hard. They were matched to assure successful childbearing, but Sora was married with her own life and families. She knew a little about his, but not enough to truly discuss Ferdinan. "He doesn't like being touched. But after time at the Duchess's estate, he can't tolerate it."

"Understood."

"To make sure you do..." Samuel let his voice turn hard. "If you ever use touch against him, I'll have our matching revoked. You'll be removed from the program and banned from claiming."

An entirely new level of seriousness blanketed her. "What've the Samultz done to him?"

"Nothing we can prove."

"I see..." Leaning back, Sora considered his words.

***

Why hold a child responsible for something beyond their control? Oya observed Chūzite customs but didn't understand them. And Ferdinan... He'd never let a child suffer like that, so why? Alien green eyes shifted to sapphire. *Jon's being pampered.* Starlight hair floated to her hips. *My dear friend's beyond my reach.* Grinning her most crazed grin, Oya called Zephyr – looming over him when he appeared.

Golden hands danced but onyx eyes couldn't look at her. "I don't have answers yet."

She smirked. "Why would your cousin choose to be stoned and beaten when he could've easily prevented it?"

Words and color left Zephyr and his hands fell to his sides.

Tenalia hasn't been told yet. "He tried stopping his companions from traveling with him. Searched for shelter for them when they got off the train. He knew. Yet chose to go to his dukedom. Why?"

Zephyr tapped his forehead and dropped his hand to face it. One gesture after another started only to stop until his hands found the right words. "Thank you for telling me."

"That doesn't answer my question."

"North Chūzo's the longest surviving civilization for a reason." A golden thumb ran down his upper arm before extending his hand. "Keeping those with power in their place is vital to prevent the downfall of our people. It's why a noble's life is less than a human's."

Nobility aren't considered people...? A starlight eyebrow rose.

"It's a citizens' duty to punish nobles who failed them. In exchange for losing their right to humanhood, they're given the best education and training to protect our people and our culture."

"The opposite of ancient humans..." The elf almost laughed at how far that belief was twisted.

"What?"

"Humans once believed nobles were gods or descendants of gods. They were greater than humans. Questioning them was a sin. If worshiped and pampered, they'd prosper the nation." The elf gazed at the starless sky. "Later civilizations twisted it so the rich and powerful were considered blessed by gods and treated similarly."

"That's horrendous..."

Stretching, the elf smirked. "They would've loved your golden skin. What better proof to godhood than skin that shines like gold?"

"I'm not a god."

"I know." Sapphire eyes twinkled.

"Civilizations fall when the powerful aren't held to the highest accountability. Every time." Zephyr's hands flailed. "Which is why he'd never shame our people like that."

"True." *How do I keep my friend from returning here?* "In case I fail, you should know he's dying."

"What...?" Zephyr swallowed hard.

"Even if I succeed, if he sees you like this... You found the wrong answer." Zephyr looked away when she pointed at his thigh. "Fix your mirrors. I can't store them here forever."

"...what...?" Golden hands flew. "You can't report Ferdinan's been beaten and move on to something else–"

Placing a delicate hand on his shoulder, she sighed. "What can you possibly do for your cousin if you can't fix a couple mirrors?"

Golden hands moved reluctantly. "What do I do?"

"Find the pieces. Learn your truths."

"How...?" Despairing, two golden fingers tapped his sternum.

The elf studied him for a long time. "What's bothering you?"

Zephyr looked down. "There's a Telepath..."

"Why worry about him?" A curious smirk turned on the Prince.

"He knows. Everything I touch breaks..." Zephyr hesitated for a while before his hands moved again. "Destroying Ferdinan hurt someone he loves. Possibly broke them. What do I do about him?"

Her wicked grin grew too amused. "Nothing."

"What?" His hands jerked.

"Let him decide."

"Too many'll be hurt if he decides to tell."

"True," the elf nodded. "But what if he decides to help?"

"Why would he help me?"

The twilight beach shook and cracked before she could answer. Dark tentacles rose – wrapping around her. *Who's waking me now?*

"What's this?!"

"Time to wake up." A push forced the golden boy from her beach.

Wild green eyes scanned the world around her. Snow fell harder. The woman assigned to her knelt, pale and hand pressed to her chest. Behind her was a man Oya didn't recognize.

"You'll get sick sleeping out here." The woman wrapped a blanket around her. "Lady Emelica and healer Kannani request your presence to prepare you for the conference."

Grinning, Oya let the woman lift her and the man carry her in.

Chapter 6

"You haven't earned death."

Ferdinan froze - trembling. Steeling himself, he turned, eyes searching every inch of the abyss.

The ghostly image of Emil marred the surrounding black. *When did I last take that chemical? At the camp? Before? After?*

But it didn't matter. Nothing mattered. "I'll never be able to."

Emil's expression was hard to describe. Disappointment and frustration warped with things Ferdinan didn't have words for.

But it didn't matter. Nothing mattered...

His atoms tore themselves apart. Screams filled the black abyss. Then Kannani's light brown eyes glared at him. His chest constricted and he couldn't breathe, but he screamed anyway at his older sister's touch. Even Fighter's had physical limits, how hadn't he reached his? Her face vanished and his body stopped disintegrating, but his heart still leapt erratically. He still couldn't breathe...

Stick arms fought to push him up. If he could've, he would've laughed. Testing, he laid back and was drowning again.

He was so tired... It was all too hard... *Thank you, Kannani, for finishing it...* Tears welled up. Even if he hadn't earned death his older sister would give it to him. She'd know he needed to be stopped.

A bowl of porridge was placed on the stand beside his bed - its light scent turning his stomach.

"Eat." Kannani crossed her arms, glaring at him as if he were a snail infesting her favorite plant. "You are required to attend the conference. Embarrassing North Chūzo is unacceptable. So eat."

Blue crystals stared at the bowl. How did-? It moved to his lap, her hand hovered menacingly, threatening to disintegrate him again.

Bony fingers trembled. All of him shook. But he got the spoon to his mouth - gagging, fighting the nausea. Swallowing was harder than being still. Harder than seeing the death tally climb. Harder than knowing what he did to Elbie and Yuyu and Xhou's precious sister...

But he did it. Once. Then twice. Then thrice.

Oats and acid rolled up and oozed out. Stern lips hardened and her hand disintegrated his cheek. His arm. Knee. Shoulder. Back. Kannani's hand never stayed in one place long. Just long enough.

Each time he screamed, his heart thrashed. Vomit choked him.

And Emil stood shaking his head. "I hate you. Beyond word. Beyond emotion. Beyond comprehension."

Looking down, Ferdinan nodded. But it didn't matter. Nothing mattered. "So do I."

***

Giving him hints is cheating.

He can't believe there's more than one truth. The Elf winked at the mirror shard. *You can't test him if he can't find the test.*

Placing the shard in the fire, she opened the silver roads. Gongie was easy to find. *For his care of Ajani, he's earned a little trust.*

Standing outside the Telepath's dreams, she searched his mind. There was so much guilt – for being unable to help Jon, for doing nothing, for letting another suffer when they didn't need to.

Maybe they can help each other. Opening the door to his dream, she stepped into an empty classroom. Gongie sat on a stuffed sac reading. "A strange paradise."

Startled, the boy studied her for a long time. "I can't hear you. Your thoughts. Feelings. Presence."

"Well, I'm a figment of dreams."

"People in my dreams reflect the thoughts of those nearby. Which means I'm still alone..."

"You've only dreamed of nearby active minds?"

"It's rare I get a break from them." Gongie put down the screen and approached the obnoxiously tall elf.

She smirked. "This is my dominion. Nothing reaches here if I don't wish it."

Dark eyes stared. Contemplating. "Thank you for the break."

"It's not free, but enjoy it while we speak."

"Your price?"

"Why tell Zephyr you know everything?"

"Who are you?"

"The elf who haunts Zephyr's dreams. As you already know."

Gongie smirked. "That's why I asked who you are."

"My question first," the elf grinned back.

Sighing, the Telepath nodded. "The guilt's unbearable. Saying nothing... Ferdinan's broken as is Zephyr and I've hurt Jon deeply. It's unforgivable. I could've prevented this – everything. All the pain and brokenness... If I spoke up. If I gave the help they couldn't ask for."

"How could a child go against adults and their rules?"

"Those are just shields, excuses. It was easy hiding behind them... Easy... 'Til I scanned Ferdinan's mind."

"Oh?"

Shivers cascaded through him. "It broke from reality."

"What do you mean?"

"I lied, saying it was a waking nightmare." Shame paled Gongie's face. "I didn't know what to do. Jon was trapped and Ferdinan was the only one who could reach him. Even if it was just his body..."

The elf leaned forward. "And?"

"I scanned him." Gongie looked away. "Parts of his mind were torn out. I've never heard of anything like that. They were disrupting everything – weakening the defenses he depended on. There was so much hidden away about to break through and shatter him."

"You put the pieces back."

"Yes," Gongie nodded. "And strengthened the walls holding in things he couldn't handle."

"Want to atone?"

Gongie's face twisted. "Yes. More than anything."

"Have a seat."

***

"What would you like to wear today, Dinta?"

Huh...? Blankets rolled back - exposing Jon's head. *Tired. Go away.* An unexpectedly large wardrobe hung near the dressing mirror, all of it suited to an Oueshian prince.

"Master Lochi'll arrive after breakfast. I know she's not your normal stylist, but she trained under Master Kiswala."

Of course they searched for a stylist connected to Kiswala. "Thank you. I'll forgo a bath 'til after."

Considering his hair would be tamed shortly, Jon selected a knee-length purple tunic and loose, matching slacks. Soft, ornately decorated slip-ons complemented the outfit. *Impressive they put together this much in my size so quickly.* And chose well - purple was his favorite color. The traditional outfit reminded Jon of home... Every courtesy they provided made him long for his family more...

Oya was in the dining hall when he arrived. And... *That's what they provided for her?* Slacks and a wrap top. Simple work clothing. In winter... He stood uncertain. *She has no title, but...* She was still a student on the islands, a guest, and Ferdinan's friend. And the Samultz were Chūzite nobles. *Why would she request clothing like that?*

Food was served. There was plenty for him and Oya, but not lavish amounts. Neither was it as fine as he expected - considering everything else. It didn't bother Oya. And Jon was happy he didn't have to worry about feeding anyone, so he ate what he could.

Wicked green eyes turned on him. "I wonder how my dear friend's doing?"

Urgency and desire to find his ally swelled. A desire he almost forgot after being wrapped in his mom's voice. If Ferdinan died... He didn't want to know, but he needed to. He didn't trust the Samultz to tell his family. Or to provide proper death rites for the gent...

Jon didn't know where he was going. Wasn't aware of which hall or wing he was meandering. It would've made sense to go to the medical wing. It would've made sense. But he wandered down an uncomfortably dim hall. There was a sound. Something inhuman...

Escalating pain filled that sound. Screaming - shrieks... But it wasn't in this hallway. *Move faster.* Running. Running... *Think about where you're going...* But he couldn't. Turning onto a connecting hallway he didn't know was there, the shrieks grew louder.

Until they stopped.

Jon's pace slowed at the dead end. There were three doors. And he stood listening – waiting. But there was no screaming. No sound.

The first door was to a closet. The second, to an empty room. And the third was locked. Knocking, Jon waited. And knocked again. Maybe it was his imagination... But the urgency he felt increased.

The door cracked open and Ferdinan's second sister looked up. Surprise was quickly replaced with a gentle smile. "Dinta. I apologize, I wasn't aware you were visiting today."

He was screaming, but... Kannani was small. Slight of frame and on the shorter side like the Duchess and her sisters – Jon towered over her. *Could someone so tiny make him scream like that?* "I need to see Ferdinan."

"I'm afraid he's sleeping, but you're welcome to sit with him." Her smile softened. "I'll have a more comfortable chair brought."

The hall closet was bigger... A bed Ferdinan outgrew, a bedside table, a small trunk, and a simple stool filled the room. Two pillows propped the skeletal body up – a body gasping desperately for air... Clear bags fed into a tube protruding from Ferdinan's shoulder.

And... It was too much. An empty mind was safer. To not think.

Sitting beside the bed, he glued his eyes on the gent. Each strangled, gasping breath killed Jon's heart a little more.

***

Trains took Ozar from the North Oueshian winter down the length of the continent in comfort. Watching snow and ice turn into summer was fun. Until he stepped into oppressive humidity.

Trudging thick jungles in mid-summer was exhausting. Seeing the village's entrance brought the Hei-O great relieve. Then he saw it...

Buildings burned to their foundations were being reclaimed by ambitious jungle vines. *What happened?* Ozar felt sick. *Ajulagrá?*

Ṣarī-a still has a future.

Who did this?

I don't know.

But they're in these jungles?

Yes.

Removing his sweat drenched shirt, Ozar searched.

***

Ferdinan's older sisters waited with a couple impressive trunks. Neutral smiles painted their faces while the manservant placed Oya on the couch. *They look nearly identical. But nothing like my dear friend.* Even their pale skin was different from his. Kannani went to work unbracing her leg and redressing her wounds while the elder pulled colorful bundles of fabric from the trunks and hung them.

"Miss Oya, you'll need sixteen day outfits, sixteen attendee suits, sixteen dinner robes, and five gowns for the conference."

That surprised a snort out of her. "Excessive for two weeks."

"I assure it's bare minimum." The eldest gestured to the racks. "Choose at least that many, though you're welcome to all you like."

Alien eyes rolled at the excessiveness. If she didn't need Jon to stay with Ferdinan... *Too bad. He would've loved doing this for me.*

***

Pink eyes appeared – bag slung over one shoulder and a plate of sweet buns in her free hand. Asking for her bag and gladly snatching a bun, Elbie led the way downstairs – Umbacano flying around them.

"You're happy."

Sheepishly, he smiled. "Xhou helped me find her name."

"What is it?" The toy spun.

"Li-Nouha."

"Ah! What a beautiful name! What's her title?"

"She'll be Kidico's Apitá when her mother retires."

"Apitá..." Pink eyes looked up as Yuyu thought. "That's the General of Generals?"

Closer than I was. He had to look it up. "The Kal's strategist. Like your mom, but for a continent instead of a country. You're perfect to help her learn the skills she'll need."

38

"Fun! You'll help though."

"Of course!" Umbacano landed on Elbie's shoulder – black eyes focused on Yuyu's hands. *Once I figure out the material...* A universe exploded before his eyes. All the possibilities... It was... *What is this?* It was magnificent and dizzying and...

"I'm sorry you'll be alone."

It took a few blinks for the universe of possibility to disappear. He didn't know what it was, but he wanted it back. No, right now he had his sister to worry about. "I'll prepare for Li-Nouha and contact her family. Everything'll be done before you get back!"

Giggles filled the air and the boat loomed ahead. "It's ok to feel sad or lonely. You don't have to hide it."

Haoyu said the same last night. "I'm ok. I promise."

"Then I'll come up with lessons to counter what Norger does."

It was mean, but Elbie laughed. They chatted until the warning chime sounded. "I guess it's time."

"Yah..." Mussing his hair, Yuyu smiled. "See you in a month."

"Have enough fun for me."

"I will." Waving, she turned to join her groupmates.

Elbie waved back until she was out of sight. That idea and all the ways to make it work...it was perfect. Except...

Smile fading, he set his jaw.

Finding Master Ludwick was difficult, but the man invited Elbie to his lab once he was done talking to one of the Artist's instructors.

"What do you need?"

"Master Ferdinan mentioned he developed nanobots. Do you have his research?"

"I remember those. They didn't do what he hoped..." Master Ludwick's expression turned curious as he studied the boy. "There's a few years before you'll learn what you need to understand them."

Elbie cringed. Every discouraging word and look Norger gave hit hard... *I'm not good enough yet.* Umbacano lightly pecked at his ear and nuzzled his cheek before flying to Master Ludwick's head. The man studied him again – seemingly unaware of the ostentatious bird.

"They aren't dangerous, so it's fine if you want to learn about them." Looking around, "Let me find a sample and the research packet."

"Are...are you sure it's ok...since I haven't learned yet?" Umbacano pecked the Scientist's hair then glided back to Elbie's shoulder.

"Here they are." Grabbing a screen and a metal cylinder, Ludwick offered them to Elbie. "Anything you can't figure out, ask. I'm curious how much further you'll take them."

"Really?" Mismatched eyes brightened and Elbie leaned his head gently against the yellow bird. "Thank you very much!"

"Good luck figuring those out." Master Ludwick dismissed him.

Excited feet stopped a few steps past the door. That was easier than normal. And... *Why has no one noticed you?*

Yellow feathers ruffled and Umbacano nuzzled his cheek.

What was I...? Master Ferdinan's lab! I'll study there.

Chapter 7

The desperate gasps of a drowning person startled Jon. Rushing forward only caused Ferdinan to cower away... Boney fingers grabbed at his chest and nearly colorless crystals darted around the room. If the Tinkerer moved back any farther, he'd fall off the bed.

Half-naked and trembling, coughing... Glued wounds and angry welts overwhelmed grotesquely scarred skin. And an IV port hung loosely from a desiccated shoulder.

What do I say? What do I do? Jon wasn't prepared for this...

"I...I'm...so-sorry..." Ferdinan looked away, voice trembling.

What can I say that won't make everything worse? Silence held them hostage. Silence so loud, he almost missed the stifled quiet of shaky tears. But what could he do?

The door opened and healer Kannani entered holding a neatly folded outfit. She smiled at Jon and placed the bundle on the bed before addressing Ferdinan. "You're to answer to the Duchess. Bathe and dress. I'll get you in an hour."

"He's ill." Jon stood between them. "The Duchess should come to her sick child."

"*Be re...spectful, Jon. The Duchess...has millions...to worry about.*" Boney feet slipped off the bed and Ferdinan rubbed his face dry. "*Millions...more important than me... I'll go instead of...wasting her time.*"

Keeping his voice level was difficult. "*Family comes first.*"

"*Don't presume to know...what's best for a world you...don't understand.*" Pausing, Ferdinan focused on sucking in air. "Thank you, healer Kannani. I'll be ready."

Giving Jon one last smile, she left.

Undressing was a struggle for his ally. The gent was so weak. *I thought he was a skeleton back in South Chūzo, but he looked healthy then compared to now...*

Last block impossible amounts of muscle bulged under damaged skin. Now it was all gone. *How can he move? What's in that cocktail?*

Where skin wasn't bruised or angry red, it was jaundiced. Blue ate at his fingers and toes, lips, eyes, and tipped his ears. Every spinal nob, every rib... The grotesque curve of unpadded hips... Jon nearly gagged.

Stick arms forced Ferdinan to his feet, but weakened legs didn't carry him far. Rushing over... That jumble of bones cried out - huddled in a ball and shaking uncontrollably.

"It's ok. I'm just helping..." Lifting his trembling ally, Jon got him to the bathroom. Unlike the one given to the Dinta, this was barely large enough for a standing shower. A chair was placed inside. And a simple soap. *How can they treat him like this? No, he probably requested this.*

"Please leave..." Stick arms propped Ferdinan with the sink while Jon started the water. "I'm perfectly capable of bathing."

"I'm cracking the door." Swallowing was hard. "Don't close it."

Instead of answering, Ferdinan stepped into the shower. Jon wasn't satisfied but he left because he didn't know what to do. Hanging the robe and slacks Kannani brought, Jon found a hairdryer and made the bed.

It was too small. And clumps of hair on the pillow made Jon gag, but he cleaned them up anyway. Because it was better than thinking.

The shower stretched on longer than Jon expected. *Is he ok?* Carefully he edged toward the door and peeked through the crack. Soap filled Ferdinan's hair and ran down his body, but the gent wasn't bathing. He was sitting there crying. And it made Jon cry too.

Not wanting to think about what would happen to Ferdinan if the gent wasn't ready, Jon dried his face and knocked on the door. "You don't have much time. I'm coming in."

There was no objection. No fighting him when he rinsed the soap from the skeleton or helped his ally dry off.

Red, swollen eyes looked at nothing as Jon got him dressed and dried his hair - making more fall out. "Do you want it tied back?"

The gent shook his head but told him it needed to be.

This isn't Ferdinan... It was like the shower washed away what little was left of the Tinkerer. Like Jon was dressing his ally for execution. He hated it. "You don't have to do this."

Ferdinan looked down, body shaking, but Jon couldn't tell if it was from weakness, pain, cold, or fear. "Please stop making this harder."

The intention was to walk with Ferdinan to the Duchess's office, but it was the first thing his hosts hadn't allowed him. So he looked for Oya. Looked. But couldn't find her. Neither could any of the employees recall where she was. Though Jon wasn't surprised, he wished she'd behave like a normal person until they reached the boat.

***

It was unusual. Instead of standing before her desk, the Duchess drew open the curtains of her full-length windows and stood there waiting for him to approach.

Dry coughs shook Ferdinan's body and Emil's animosity doubled. He didn't hear the voice like before. Not because it wasn't there, but because it hated him beyond words. It should be better this way. But all those terrible things it told him were better than the loathing directed at him from his own mind – loathing that only added to his self-hatred.

And the hate that glared at him from those light brown eyes... Evening's dim framed them both and muted winter flowers filled his peripheral. Ferdinan didn't get a chance to kneel before dull steel crashed against his cheek.

"Remove your shirt." The Duchess ran a hand through her unusually short hair before scowling.

Bony fingers undid the ties holding his wrap shirt closed and let the simple cloth slide off. Open wounds were glued together and angry welts looked worse than they felt. Or maybe they didn't... Ferdinan hadn't felt much beyond Emil's loathing since the train.

"We allow you here, provide for you, and you do this?" Her voice was soft and hard and unforgiving.

"I apologize, Duchess." *I'm sorry... I tried... But I failed... Again.*

"You put our strongest ally in peril." The force of her fury came down upon his cheek, knocking him back. "We need North Oueshi's resources to save this country and you knowingly put their beloved last born in danger."

Stick limbs staggered as he moved to kneel before the Duchess. "I apologize. I tried..."

"Intentions mean nothing." Again that dull steel came down hard. "You're not even competent enough to be a defect."

Instinct made Ferdinan flinch, but the next hit never came. Instead, she grabbed his hair and forced him to stand. He towered over her, but she still glared down at him. Emil didn't laugh - just hated him more.

"You're a curse. A blight. Everything was good before I was forced to have you. Good for our people and our family. You destroyed all that." She brought her hand back and twisted her body.

She'd never put such force - so much of herself - into a strike.

Steel rammed his face, knocking his body to the floor. He should get up. Should kneel... But he was tired... *Stay on the ground drowning...*

The Duchess walked to the door and paused with her hand on the knob. "If they want a defect like you, they can have you. I'm tired of keeping you from destroying their family too."

Total disgust and animosity left - slamming the door shut.

Everything was numb. And it didn't matter. He didn't matter. He was a defect. A bane. A useless child.

He couldn't do anything for his country, his family, anyone...what was the point of his life? Why did he exist when he ruined everything?

I bring so much pain. Destroy everything. I want to stop. But I keep making everything worse... Curling up in a ball, he laid there shivering, heart beating erratically, gasping for air. *Why am I alive? Why was I born? I don't understand...*

He should leave. This was the Duchess's office and she had millions to worry about. He should leave... But it was so hard to move...

***

Not knowing what else to do, Jon put on the coat and winter boots he was given and searched for Oya outside. It amazed him how many types of winter flowers had been cultivated in North Chūzo. But the country itself was a giant garden. Everything was built to not affect the landscape.

There was a garden maze on the north side of the Samultz estate. Jon hadn't been here often, but every time he saw it, it was magnificent. And this time was no different. But there was someone unexpected.

At first Jon thought it was one of the gardeners. But when he got closer, he noticed the recorder. Concern and uncertainty paled the woman's rich skin and dimmed her dark eyes.

"Are you okay?"

She jumped back – studying him, obviously disapproving of his princely attire. "I see why he didn't say your name."

"Excuse me?"

"I would've never guessed you weren't him..." She looked at the recorder she held – expression firm. "You should check on him."

"What do you mean?"

She shook her head and walked away. "Go."

***

It was frustrating, but Oya told herself she wasn't surprised. It wasn't like Jon could manipulate people's perceptions and memories like she could. Still, he could move freely, unlike her. Giving him the desire for fresh air, she stole their conversation from his mind and turned to the orbs in her peripheral. A wink and an infusion of energy flowed into her.

Energy she needed to take hold of the manservant and keep them both unnoticed as he carried her to the Duchess's office. Since Ferdinan could see her, she cracked the door and listened instead of going in.

What hate she felt toward the Duchess became fully justified. Words that never should be spoken to a child...and that hit – the woman put all her soul into it. All in front of a picturesque window... *Odd...*

Though fuming, the small woman stopped at the door to throw one more dagger at her dying friend.

Delicate fingers tugged at the locket she always wore. *What sort of punishment do you deserve?* It wasn't just this, it was a lifetime of hurting her dear friend, of training Zephyr to do the same.

Unnoticed, the servant followed behind the Duchess until they came to an impressive library. And empty library. *Perfect.* The fewer people, the easier. Unholy fire flared in crazed green eyes as a golden-brown hand reached for the Duchess. *Is there anything-*

The door opened, interrupting Oya's thoughts, and a well-dressed woman entered – pale and shaky. "I have the video."

The Duchess took the screen she offered and clicked the opened box. The recording through the window was perfectly crisp.

"As you commanded, there'll be no doubt from the General that you struck Ferdinan. No rumors or uncertainty."

"Thank you." The smile on the Duchess's lips was strained, but grateful. "Make sure it's disseminated throughout the Dukedom."

"Are you sure? The consequences to your family..."

"We exist to serve the people. It's best for them, for our country and General that there be no question on who damaged that thing."

"But you didn't hurt him...he wasn't here most of his life." The woman looked uncomfortable arguing, but the guilt was too much...

"I won't let my people be divided by this. I won't let my General sow doubt in the portion who love her more than they hate me. I'm the villain who mutilated that creature. No one else. There's no monster in the country who could, save me." The Duchess stood tall, frail shoulders back and chin high. "I accept the consequences. As a citizen, you've done your duty and I thank you with a full heart and deepest respect."

Consequences...? It didn't take Oya much thought to realize what those would be. Not in a country like this. The two women sat and the Duchess made clear her desires and gave detailed instructions for how to protect her two youngest daughters. Listening... *There's no point in my being here.* But...if she found Śarī-a in time, she'd have to deal with this later.

What can I do when he finds out...?
***

When mismatched eyes drifted to his printer, Umbacano redirected Elbie back to the nanobots. *Master Ludwick's right.* He didn't know enough to understand them. But he *would* give Yuyu her hands back.

Neither did he stop until his brain reached its limits... Resting his cheek on the desk, he watched the printer until a chime sounded.

Sitting up, he turned to the door. White hair flew in all directions beyond its window. *Tuel?* Jumping off the stool, he hurried to open it.

"Master Ferdinan isn't back," Elbie flinched. *He already knows that.*

Tuel smiled. "I'm not here for him."

Air caught in Elbie's throat. "Is Haoyu ok?"

46

"Haoyu's fine. It's harvest time before the rains start." Tuel sat in the air, but hovered at Elbie's eye level. "Want to help this year? You're young, but Master Ticci approved if you want to."

This is unexpected... But he wasn't sure what to expect from the older Energist. "What do you need me to do?"

"Kitchens always need extra hands." Tuel rolled his eyes at himself. "Greenhouses need to be disassembled so we can store them."

Elbie almost giggled. Taking things apart sounded fun. "I'd love to help. Thank you for thinking of me."

A giant grin took over Tuel's face. "Want to fly?"

***

Taking the woman's advice, Jon searched for Ferdinan. It took a while, but when he found the gent, it was like the skeleton's soul was removed. Like he was too broken to cry. No words. No arguments... Ferdinan couldn't even look up.

Getting his ally back to the room and in bed was easy, though the Tinkerer recoiled whenever he got too close. The IV cocktail was brought shortly after. This time Jon studied the bags. Most of the ingredients he didn't know, but he knew where to look them up and it made him angrier at the Samultz.

Stimulants to keep him moving. Nutrients to force his organs to keep working. And late-term pain medicine. The kind given to people who wouldn't be alive the next week. *They care more about getting him on that boat than his needs...than about him. But refuse to let my family claim him!*

The next morning healer Kannani arrived with a small trunk filled with the cocktail. She gave Ferdinan instructions on how and when to administer it to get through the next day.

And Jon sat quietly because he didn't know what to do. He wanted to yell at them. To punish them for hating a sick child – their own brother... but it wouldn't change anything. And risking them retaliating...keeping Ferdinan here until the end... Jon hated all of this. So when they were in the car – tree line shrinking – he was relieved.

The drive to the pier wasn't long. Oya scrutinized every inch of the view, searching for hidden buildings. Ferdinan slept propped against the window – wrapped in his coat and blankets. And Jon watched over them both, counting the seconds until he finally would be with Samuel.

The plank was lowering when they reached the pier. Samuel and Sora waved... Breaths came hard and tears stung. He was so tired... And now he finally was done.

No more...

Chapter 8

Silver ribbons stretched across an endless black. They went every direction – randomly crossing each other before shooting out into eternity. Following these paths to the elf was eerie the first time Zephyr was here. It still was. But its vastness made him feel tiny. Insignificant. And that brought relief. No matter what kind of monster he was. No matter how vile and dangerous... Here he was insignificant. Inconsequential. Nothing.

If only it was the same in real life.

Setting his jaw, Zephyr found her presence. Larger-than-life and just as happy to let him die as live depending on his choices. Golden feet made their way to the twilight beach and an old woman in the distance. Snow white, wavy hair fell down to her hips and dark skin was weathered with age, but her movements and the glint in her eyes were too youthful. Past her was a familiar child and a fire, but the old woman waved her away before Zephyr could place her.

A grin as wicked as the elf's turned on him. As the old woman approached, she grew taller, younger, less human until she was the elf.

"I'd ask if you're my broken mind or something else." Golden fingers weaved and danced before tapping the bridge of his nose and drawing down the side of his chest. "But you wouldn't give me a direct answer."

That smirk grew more amused. "I'm who I need to be for the people who need me."

Pointing at her, Zephyr pressed a finger against each cheek, held an open hand perpendicular to the ground and brushed the other under it. But his tongue didn't move.

"If your greatest threat became an ally, would you accept their help?"

"What?"

"Gongie wants to help. Do you accept?"

Onyx eyes stared. *What's this insanity?*

A delicate hand waved open the silver roads. Expecting him to follow, she led him to a crowded classroom where Gongie sat trying to read. Older boys crowded around - each doing their own things, having their own conversations. It was chaotic and a little nauseating... *This is what it's like being a Telepath?* It looked miserable.

"Ready?"

Gongie jumped. Surprise faded to relief and a gentle smile. "I can't hear you. You aren't in your dorm, are you?"

A golden ring finger tapped his ear before his hands circled each other and one pointed at the Psych. "Can you hear everyone in the building?"

"Constantly."

No wonder he knows...

"Good luck," the elf smirked.

"You're leaving...?" Gongie looked nervous.

"I have other tasks. Other people needing my attention."

Instead of walking away, she faded out of existence. It was disconcerting... *Now what?* Annoyed, Zephyr returned to the silver roads - ignoring Gongie. *Do I want to do this? What's the point? A monster can't change...*

"Wait!" Gongie stumbled out of his dream and nearly off the silver road.

Golden hands grabbed the Psych and shifted his fall to land on the path. "Careful! I don't know what'll happen if you fall."

"Th-thanks..."

"Go back to your dream." Shrugging off the Telepath, Zephyr started walking. He didn't know where he was going, but he didn't feel like dealing with an audience.

"I'm here to help."

"Don't involve yourself with me. You'll only end up hurt."

"And if I choose to take that risk?"

"Then you're an idiot. Go away. I don't want you here."

The Psych didn't leave.

Would he wake up if I pushed him off? Shaking his head, Zephyr closed his eyes. Maybe ignoring the boy would work. *What does a mirror shard feel like? But it's not just a broken mirror, it's* my *broken mirror. Part of me...*

But what did he feel like?

I feel vile, corrupt, evil... He felt like that goo always strangling him – choking out his life... He was an infection... But he couldn't find that feeling.

"Is something supposed to be happening?"

Startled, the Prince stepped back, foot rounding the edge of the path. Between his reflexes and Gongie grabbing him, he didn't fall, but his heart was racing.

"I'm so sorry!"

"Stop." Golden fingers spread wide before moving. "Why are you still here? Go away!"

"That's all I've done for a decade." Gongie looked down. "I won't anymore. If I did the right thing when I first realized–"

"Minding yourself and following the rules are the right things."

"There're no rules here. I want to help. I won't see anyone else hurt 'cause I didn't try. Now what're you doing?"

"Figuring out what a monster feels like." Golden hands thrashed. "Yeah, it's stupid."

"But you're searching for mirror pieces." Gongie blushed. "The elf told me..."

"The broken mirror is part of me..."

Understanding and an expression Zephyr couldn't label filled Gongie's face. It irritated him greatly.

The Psych closed his eyes and let out a long, slow breath. *Just go away! Why does he want to be here?*

Slowly Gongie turned and walked – concentrating harder than Zephyr thought necessary. Following...took forever. But a door eventually appeared.

"Where did this come from?" Gongie studied it. "Where does it go?"

"I don't know." Steeling himself, Zephyr entered – Gongie on his heels.

His most cherished memory surrounded them – frozen. Colorful. Beautiful. And his heart sank. A monster didn't deserve joyful memories.

"Wow...I..." Gongie turned, taking it all in. "I'm not used to seeing this much human presence in a North Chūzite city."

"It was built to not impact the environment." Zephyr's hands moved hesitantly. "General Tenalia said honoring my Grassland's heritage was important, even at a North Chūzite ascension ceremony."

"That's...a way to put it..." Dark eyes studied the scene. "Looks amazing."

"It was..." *Now what?* Golden fingers tapped and bounced. "I guess...find a broken mirror..."

The memory came to life.

***

"Stop." Norger rested his head in his hands. "That makes no sense. How am I expected to do this?"

It'd make sense if you listened. Irritation grew to anger as rain pounded violently against the windows. Even Umbacano's comfort wasn't helping. *Please come back, Master Ferdinan.*

Sitting back, the Thinker rubbed the bridge of his nose. "Show me where you're at with your final project."

Warmth and anticipation filled Elbie – his own and one too intense to belong to him. But that was okay. He was excited to show the Lead. Excited to explain how far he'd come. And prove how capable Tinkerers were. Even if stupid Thinker programs were useless for them.

An Energist walked them to Master Ferdinan's lab in an invisible dome. It was like walking through a glass tunnel, fun and wonderous – making Elbie feel better.

Smiling bright, he ran up to his carbon printer. Another two days and it'd be finished. *Next time, print smaller ones. But a giant... Or hollow! And store a treasure inside for Yuyu!* Umbaccano cheerfully nuzzled his cheek. *She'd like that.*

Turning to the new Lead... Elbie's smile died. Instead of awe, interest, or curiosity, the older boy frowned.

"How did this get approved?" Wind bashed rain into the windows.

"Master Ferdinan..." *...thought it was a good idea.*

Frustration wrinkled Norger's brow. "He approved this for a second-year? How irresponsible."

Elbie stood shocked. *What's he complaining about?* And disparaging the best teacher on the islands! Elbie felt like yelling. He should defend his mentor, but no words came.

"How much of this did Lord Ferdinan do?"

White hot fire burst in his chest and words filled his tongue. "It's my idea. My design. I built it. Programed it. And fixed every issue Master Ferdinan and Xhou found." *I made this printer. It's my creation.*

Lips pursed and brow raised he glared disapproving – disbelieving. "Putting you in danger. Using you to build things he wants. The special treatment of being so rare must be nice."

Elbie felt something break. Umbaccano landed on his shoulder and a strange warmth like the golden light of a summer sun washed over him. It overpowered the anger. But it couldn't give back what Norger lost any more than it could stop the rain.

***

Why was moving so hard? Ferdinan's body wanted to – his muscles screamed, demanding he move. But they didn't hurt as much as they should. And moving was so hard...

Unwrapping the blankets. Looking at Jon or Oya. Opening the door. They were all too hard.

Retching seized his body when Samuel came into view – hugging Jon and checking Oya. But the Healer didn't come closer.

Closing his eyes, Ferdinan rested his head against the cold glass.

Tapping startled him. Muscles constricted and his heart raced. Letting out a shaky breath, Ferdinan looked – hands searching for a weapon.

Hematite eyes and a loving smile waited patiently. *Who...? She looks familiar...*

"Can I open the door, Ferdinan?"

He wasn't sure if he nodded, but she opened it. Impossible cold rushed in and attacked, but she knelt on the ground and looked in – offering her hand.

His body recoiled despite his wishes.

"It's been a while. Remember me? Sora?"

Sora...

It took a bit for his brain to work. *Samuel's wife...* The one the man was assigned to through their genetic matching program. *She has a spouse...who was it?*

It was a standard practice in North Oueshi to assign a wife or husband based on their compatibility to successfully bear children. But they could choose whoever they wanted as a spouse – someone they were happy with. Someone they loved.

The practice seemed odd at first, but once he learned of the fertility issues plaguing the country, it made sense. Every citizen was tested – but only those capable of having children were matched with a partner. Samuel was just waiting for Sora to decide she was ready. The man's block would be removed until they managed a successful pregnancy... *I need to die before she decides. I don't want to ruin another generation of Artimuses...*

She spoke softly, but he hadn't heard what she said. And that was rude. He should be focused on her, not stupid thoughts that didn't matter.

"You don't have to go. I'm just as happy taking you to the Artimus estate as I am helping you aboard the conference." She smiled, not moving. "Whatever you want. That's what we'll do."

I want to die. Emil's animosity exploded inside him and his weak, erratic heart told him stepping into the water would kill him without drowning. But he didn't have a choice. He had to represent North Chūzo. He couldn't embarrass his country.

Bitter cold hit harder when he removed the blankets. He rotated and Sora moved out of the way.

Slipping behind him, she grabbed his bag from the seat. He'd forgotten about it... Which would've been bad... The screen with Oya's histories was in there. And his itinerary for East Azuté. *I should message grandpa Huey. Make arrangements for the supplies to be delivered...*

Muscles cried out – pleading for him to move faster, to run, fight. But his feet weighed three times more than the rest of him. Moving was a chore no matter how much his body needed it. It was so hard...

Lumbering steps inched him forward until something jarred his body and he found himself wrapped in softness. Like the blanket he just removed – but softer, more comforting. That softness lifted him and held him in place until he was steady on his feet.

"I'm sorry, I know you don't like being touched, but I couldn't let you fall." Sora's smile didn't waver though it was apologetic. "Think you can make it?"

Ferdinan couldn't stop looking at her. Blue lips trembled and shaky hands took hers. That softness returned. Just soft. Yuyu told him her father felt like clouds. He didn't think she was lying but he couldn't believe there were people who weren't painful. Until Maelel. If Yuyu's father felt like clouds and Maelel like a gentle breeze... And now Sora... How many people weren't painful or disconcerting?

Softness wrapped around him and he realized he was crying. Realized she was strong. Realized he'd destroy her like he had everyone else. No matter how nice her touch felt. He'd hurt her. *You need to stay away from me...* But he couldn't push her away.

She stepped back and her gloved fingers dried his face. "You don't have to do this. You don't have to do anything you don't want to do."

"I do." His voice cracked, making him blush. "I'm sorry."

He hated everything about this. About himself. But not as much as Emil who made his feelings perfectly clear without a word.

But he still wanted to hold her hand...

"You've nothing to apologize to me for." She held out the hand he kept staring at.

It hurt. Being offered comfort he didn't deserve but desperately wanted. Tears filled his eyes but they didn't fall. They just kept looking longingly at her hand until it took his and guided him up the plank and to his cabin – catching him when his knees were too weak to hold him.

***

There were so many places to look. And an obscene number of mirrors. *Do mirrors hold significance to the Grasslanders?* Though curious, Gongie searched for a broken one. *It's nice here.* Enjoying so much energy and excitement without countless minds assaulting him...

Though Zephyr was growing more frustrated with each intact mirror.

The door... If it worked for the door, would it work for the mirror?

Closing his eyes and pushing aside the joy and color and celebration, the Psych focused. Guilt. Fear. Desperation to be better – to be more... And a deep longing for love... That was the golden Prince.

It was faint. Like a lost child crying softly in a giant crowd. Holding onto that scared child, Gongie walked. Sometimes it faded and he had to turn around. But when it grew louder...

He ran. And when he stopped it wasn't before a broken mirror, but a cluster of little shards. Reaching down... Something grabbed his hand...

This isn't your place.

"Excuse me?" No one was near... *Did I imagine that?* "Zephyr!"

The golden Prince came running, but recoiled when he saw the shards. And the memory froze.

What's happening...?

Green tinged Zephyr's skin and onyx eyes fixed on the broken pieces – like prey watching a predator. Kneeling, the Prince reached for it, golden hand trembling.

Why's he scared to touch them? Gongie knelt beside the Athlete.

"I don't know what'll happen. With the elf, there's no guessing..."

"It's ok. I want to be here. I want to help."

Zephyr scowled at him, but carefully scooped up the broken pieces.

The celebration vanished. And Gongie saw when it all began. Thousands of beatings all started the same way...until something changed. First, they were driven by a passion to protect, to preserve life. But quickly morphed into something desperate and terrified.

Onyx eyes stayed closed. Unable to look. Terrible pain coated the Prince.

Rancid metal filled Gongie's gut. *I could've prevented most of this...* But he didn't. And now he stood as a voyeur to another's most agonizing moments.

Golden lips whispered, "I'm a monster."

***

"That looks interesting."

Attacking ants landed on Elbie's shoulder – making him jump and scaring Umbacano.

"Sorry. I didn't mean to startle you." Ilu bowed and sat next to him. "May I ask what it is?"

"Something to help Yuyu." *Why's he here?* This boy had no reason to talk to him. But Ilu was Jon's suitemate. And a Healer. *Is he here to tell me what happened?* "Can I help you?"

The bright smile was unexpected as was the screen the older boy offered. "Heard you were studying hands. This might help."

"Thank you." Elbie finished researching, but turning down a thoughtful gift was rude. Opening the first article... he smiled. *This is more technical and detailed.* ...and filled with jargon he didn't know...

"Sorry it's advanced. Figured you already knew the basics." Ilu grimaced. "Hands are delicate and so vital to Tinkerers, I wanted to make sure you had the best information. I'll go over it with you after classes if you want."

"Thank you. I appreciate it." Umbacano fluttered to perch on the edge of the screen. Like everyone else, Ilu didn't notice him. *Why...?* Elbie blinked. Confused.

"Is something wrong?"

What was I...? "Sorry, I'm sure it's wrong to ask..."

"It's ok, I'll answer if I can."

It took a moment to find a question. "The beam... Yuyu struggles to speak without her hands being busy. I was wondering if it'll heal."

"Brain injuries rarely heal completely. She's lucky there's a work around to exploit..." The older boy paled – turning to the rain beyond the window. "I'm sorry. That was terrible to say. But you're intelligent, I didn't want you wasting your time finding real answers."

"Thank you." Attacking ants consumed his shoulder again – making Elbie flinch. *If I was so intelligent, I'd figure out how to make touch not hurt...*

Umbacano stopped fluttering around and turned his attention to Elbie. The beautiful yellow bird hopped over and nuzzled the young Tinkerer's cheek.

Elbie's mind filled with a universe of possibility.

Chapter 9

Oya gave Jon her wildest grin while Samuel removed the brace immobilizing her leg. *I got them both to Samuel, but...* The clouds over the growing giant's mind had taken root. And her dear friend...

A warm hand rested on her knee only to pull away. Disbelief filled dark eyes, forcing her gaze from Jon. It was the same look the healers at the hospital gave her. The same warped fear and confusion Herrard held after he woke her that day. *What do they see when scanning me?* But she needed her leg healed.

Jon paced – nervous, jittery. Anxious hands wrung each other and the dark clouds grew.

Reaching inside Samuel, she dampened the thoughts and feelings painting his face and magnified his desire to heal her. "I know. It's ok."

Samuel's curls bounced when he shook his head – fighting against her manipulation. And... It wasn't working. Just like at the hospital. Jon scratched at his neck, looking around. Frightened. Frustration twisted Samuel's face and he tried harder.

When Jon paled, struggling to breathe, and looking like he'd puke, she let go. *Time's up.*

Long limbs attacked the door – not stopping until the Thinker clutched the railing. Even from inside the cabin, Oya saw him trembling.

"Care for your brother. There's someone I need to talk to before trying again." Oya laid back. She needed a working body. But if an island Healer couldn't help her... Śarī-a hadn't been able to help either... Could Shēnó? At least enough for Samuel to succeed? Considering what she was, Oya wouldn't be surprised. And Shēnó was already nearby infusing Ferdinan with life. *Shēnó...what do you think?*

I'll try.

That's all I ask. But while Jon was being cared for, there was something she needed to check on.

Alien green eyes closed only to look out over her twilight beach. *How much longer will this exist? How much longer will it be mine?* She loved Ogani, but it deserved a guardian.

Smoothing golden-brown hands over herself from head to toe, Oya changed her hair back to black speckled with sunshine and shadows that reach down to her hips. And gold flecked black eyes she missed dearly. Her favorite yellow wrap top and comfortable shorts replace the exquisite clothing she'd adjusted to during her time on the islands. With one command Ajulagrá and Ozar stood before her.

"Have you found them?" Oya spoke to the light standing to the right of Ozar.

Śarī-a's missing but not lost. The village was forced to flee.

Ajulagrá reported everything they learned. Rage seethed under the calm façade she held. If she hadn't made a promise... Still, she'd find a fitting punishment for the woman with silver-streaked hair.

I need its host to make the transfer that'll anchor Śarī-a... No. She'd have to do more than that. The unprepared couldn't handle mourning with a charge and she needed its help now. "Report back as soon as you find them."

***

This was the nerve wracking one. Kyo's were short of world heroes. Better than leaders in Herrard's opinion since they earned that title, unlike leaders who were born to their positions. The Kalj scrutinized every inch of his hair for any strand out of place and fixed his face paint a dozen times. Adjusting the robes, Herrard waited for Xhou to signal the extra security was in place. Giving a nod, the Thinker left the room.

Once all three Kyo's appeared, he stood and bowed to them. "Thank you for responding quickly."

"I was surprised, this wasn't an alliance we would've predicted." Kyo Jorani acknowledged Herrard's respect and gestured for him to sit.

Doing as instructed, Herrard offered intel the Five gave him. Ending with the most concerning piece. "The Duchess arranged a second treaty with North Oueshi – trading orphans for minerals."

Two sets of annoyed, questioning eyes shifted on the screen – probably to wherever Leoniel Kyo's image sat on their displays.

"It's not simple." Lavender hair swayed as he adjusted a shimmery blue collar. "But the information you've shared clarifies things."

"May I ask?"

"They don't have enough food and desperately need those minerals to fix their lands. While wild edibles can sustain each country for a short time, it's not a luxury North Chūzo has." Leoniel gave a sad smile. "We lost too many children to the blight and distributing their population's the only way to keep them from starving. Even if it goes against their beliefs and customs."

I thought so. "Thank you."

"Why didn't you inform us?" The oldest Kyo asked, giving Leoniel a stern look.

"It was part of my quarterly report, Lan. If not for the Kalj's message, I wouldn't have realized its significance."

"Fair." She turned to Herrard. "I'd be best utilized in Chūzo."

Kyo Jorani spoke next, "I'd do best with the Five world leaders."

"I'll be in East Azuté distributing resources to the first wave of volunteers revitalizing farming regions." Leoniel bowed his head in apology. "But the Queen Mother and her sons have strong ties in various countries."

"I'll contact her." Grabbing a screen, Herrard prepared for the hardest part. "What's the best forum for private meetings with the various world leaders? Considering the delicate situation... If something goes wrong, famine'll only be the first problem."

***

Jon's mouth was too dry to swallow and he couldn't catch his breath. His pounding, jerking heart only made the nausea worse. He knew he should focus on the endless expanse of open ocean. Open sky... But he couldn't stop shaking and his hands were going numb... *What is this?! How do I stop it?*

It was all too much! Being trapped underground... Surrounded by hate on the train... Watching Ferdinan slowly dying in a tiny dark room...

His heart jumped and twisted erratically. Was it somehow damaged? But a few weeks without food couldn't do that... He hadn't abused his body for a lifetime like Ferdinan...so why wouldn't it stop?!

Strong, warm arms wrapped around tight.

Samuel...he can heal me... "My heart! There's something wrong with my heart."

61

Samuel shook his head calmly. "I know it feels that way, but your heart's fine. Can you believe me?"

Samuel wouldn't lie, but it was pounding and leaping and twisting. It felt like it'd explode. He couldn't breathe beyond a gasp and the numbness spread up his arm. His vision blurred and he pleaded. "Help me! Make it stop!"

"Focus on me." Samuel knelt and squeezed Jon's hands. "Breathe with me. Slowly breathe in and hold it until I breathe out. Can you do that?"

Jon didn't think he could but he nodded anyway. It wasn't easy, but he followed Samuel's exaggerated cues – squeezing his brother's hands and not breaking eye contact.

Nausea subsided. Feeling returned to his arm. His heart slowed.

"There. Good job." Samuel hugged Jon again and didn't let go until his little brother stopped shaking. "How do you feel?"

Jon kept squeezing Samuel. "I feel unwell. I have for a while."

"It's okay. I'm here now."

Before Samuel could offer more, Jon pushed him back. "For how long? How long before Ferdinan takes you away and I'm left alone again? I don't want to be alone anymore! I can't take anymore..."

***

I'll give them the space they need. Tugging on the nearest passenger's mind, Oya "asked" them to take her to Ferdinan's cabin.

There she sat on the bed beside her dear friend. He wasn't asleep but was unresponsive... Judging by the black clouds smothering his mind, she doubted he could do more than lay there. Delicate fingers combed through his thinning hair – coming away with a disconcerting number of strands. "Sleep."

It was subtle, but Ferdinan's body relaxed. Oya closed her eyes and when she opened them, she was on her twilight beach. But Ferdinan wasn't there. *Interesting...* Morphing into the elf, she opened the door to the silver roads and made her way to him.

His dream was unexpected. Instead of the joy she provided for him a year ago, the skeleton stood in the center of a twisted dark abyss as two memories played. Two she'd torn away.

The elf watched Oya confirm Rura's death before Elbie appeared and did the same. Back-and-forth. Round and round. Over and over...

"It's your fault."

"You're back?" The elf looked at Ferdinan's healthy doppelgänger. "He hasn't been reacting to you."

"I'm done. I don't care about him anymore."

"You sound awfully bitter for someone who doesn't care."

"Why would I care about anyone who created me to throw me away? He's not going to change. Nothing's going to change. So why fight anymore? He's given up too." Emil didn't look at her or Ferdinan, but he pointed to a spot just beyond the dream. "We know there's only one outcome."

"Possibly. But I have to try. I don't care if everyone else gives up – I will try."

Nearly colorless blue crystals finally met her gaze. They were bitter and angry and indescribably tired. "I know. It's all you've done since the hospital."

That made the elf pause. "Seems I'm not as sneaky as I thought."

"It wasn't difficult. You're the only one who cared enough to do anything." Emil shrugged. "Not that he can see that."

Nodding, the elf patted Emil's shoulder and went to the spot he pointed at earlier. The scarred edges where she'd torn the memories out remained. They weren't healing. Untrained stitches forced them in place. But they weren't healing.

Neither the memories nor the mind wanted to accept each other. But those stitches were firm and deep. *If I can't get him to Śañ-a in time, these memories won't matter. But the damage if I tear those stitches...* She didn't know what it'd do. Neither did she feel like making Ferdinan's final breaths any harder.

But she could stop this dream. She could take him to the path of joy she built for him. Returning to her dear friend, the elf banished the darkness and opened Evelyn's door. It hadn't been used nearly enough.

"This isn't where you belong."

Ferdinan looked longingly at it. But he didn't move. Skin wrapped bones stayed huddled on his hands and knees.

"Shouldn't she get to see her big brother one last time?"

"Why do you always manipulate me?"

"'Cause I care too much to let your stubbornness hurt you at every turn." The elf knelt beside him and helped him stand. "And 'cause I don't want you suffering more guilt."

He didn't fight her. Didn't say anything more. He simply let her walk him to Evelyn's door. And when joy and light shone through, he stepped forward on his own.

"It's not fair. None of this is."

"Such is humanity." The elf waved open the door to the silver roads...and an annoyingly familiar face appeared. *I wasn't expecting you.*

Emil scowled and pulled her back. Zephyr stood stunned. And the elf sighed. *He's perfect for Ogani. Too bad Dashū claimed him first.*

Stun turned to relief. The golden Prince stepped forward and knelt before Emil. "I'm so glad..."

"You really need to stop playing in my world." The elf stepped forward despite Emil's objections. "Don't breathe yet."

"What do you mean?" A golden finger tapped his temple and pointed at the elf.

"Zephyr, meet Emil. He's just as much Ferdinan as your veiled and chained reflections."

A million expressions twisted Zephyr's face as those words sunk in. "He's my fault."

"Yes, you bear responsibility."

"To a degree." The elf pulled Zephyr to his feet. *An unexpected opportunity...* "It's impossible for a soul as damaged as Ferdinan's to not have created a part to protect them."

Guilt forced onyx eyes closed.

"Let's go." The elf motioned to the silver roads. "I have work, so I'll talk as we walk."

Emil tried objecting but the elf silenced him. If everything worked, this would help him to.

She guided Zephyr to her twilight beach, giving him an offer he'd refuse. But one that'd benefit many. "You have the ability to make souls like Ferdinan's whole."

Bitter laughter spilled out of Zephyr and his hands danced. "Easily destroying souls doesn't qualify me to fix them."

Pausing, she waved the broken mirrors into existence.

Zephyr's lips twisted. "How'll that help me fix anything?"

"Regardless of how, would you take it if it could?"

"Monsters don't fix things...!" Zephyr's hands and words trailed off.

"Was becoming a man worthy to be General, to be Ferdinan's cousin, a lie?"

Zephyr stood shaking his head. "I wasn't lying. I simply understand the reality of my sins now."

"But becoming General isn't a choice. Only the type of General you become. Will you be worthy? Will you protect, uplift, and heal? Or will you say pretty words and maintain the standard 'til you can step down?" The elf patted his shoulder. He wouldn't accept today, but implanting the idea... "Consider it. Now, why did you come?"

Zephyr's hands started and stopped many times before shaking his head. "How do I fix the mirror?"

"First you need all the pieces." Sapphire eyes glinted when exhaustion and despair blanketed the boy. "And take Gongie with you."

"I don't want him there."

"Trust me." Giving her usual smirk, she waved him back to his dreams and walked on. There was plenty for her to figure out as well.

"One potential guardian..." The elf laughed. *Dashū has more patience than I do.* Which was why she was frustrated with herself. She'd worked with the two young Tinkerers during that show. They were special to her dear friend. And talented. But she never considered Elbie for Umbacano while Yuyu didn't hesitate.

65

Then there was the general frustration of picking a new charge to send. How could she test Yuyu's ability to be Jinku if the girl found guardians faster than she could?

***

Once Jon fell asleep, Samuel tracked down Oya. Healing her was simple...but... Something didn't feel right about it. Samuel couldn't place what it was – like a memory he knew he should have but couldn't find. Regardless, she was running around the ship now, enjoying the freedom of mobility.

He returned to his sleeping brother. Sora was caring for Ferdinan. And Samuel was going over the Tinkerer's medical scans.

Ferdinan's heart was barely functioning and seriously damaged. His organs were shutting down and his bones were dangerously thin. Everything was out of balance. *How much to push him into cardiac arrest?*

The drugs Kannani forced on the boy were keeping Ferdinan moving, but causing nerve damage... Then there was a drug he'd never seen. It wasn't flooding the boy's body like the others, but it was there and slowly decreasing. *What was this chemical doing for him?* This wouldn't be the first time the boy self-medicated, but it was the first time with something Samuel couldn't find record of.

How do I tell mom about Jon and Ferdinan? How secure are the connections here? But she needed to know. They needed a plan to get Jon healthy without drawing attention. And Ferdinan... He didn't want to tell mom to prepare rites, but other than keeping the boy comfortable, Samuel didn't know what else he could do...

Picking up a screen, he made the hardest call of his life.

Chapter 10

Gongie stepped onto the silver roads. *Can I keep coming here when we've finished?* It'd be nice. Especially without the annoyance radiating at him across the abyss. "I wasn't sure you'd come."

"She trapped me here."

Gongie grimaced. *She does seem forceful.* "I'm sorry..."

"You already know everything, just go back." Zephyr's hands and face betrayed his humiliation.

"I know you don't want me here. I know it's rude intruding on deeply personal things, but I can't do nothing anymore."

"Why does it matter? I'll be leaving soon."

"People I love will keep hurting and the future leader of a fifth of the world's population will be useless. That'll hurt more." Gongie swallowed hard. "There isn't much time. Let's find the pieces."

"It'd be better if everyone knew I'm a monster. They could deal with me accordingly."

How do I respond to that? "Of everything I know, I know your remorse is real. That's all I need to help you. Regardless–"

"Help me? You should stay away from me! What remorse? Everything I've done... Why aren't you running away? I know you're scared of me, I see it in your eyes." Golden hands flew. "And I don't blame you...you should be scared people like me exist."

Gongie stood tall. "I avoided you for years 'cause I thought you were terrible. But you were just blind. Monsters don't see their reflection and cringe, they don't worry about the damage they've done or the people they'll hurt in the future. Monsters don't care that they're monsters. They enjoy it."

"I didn't care. I felt he deserved it. Felt I was right! Everything I did to him...others... How can you say I'm not a monster?"

"You aren't. Not when you accepted this pain and opened your eyes."

Frustration blanketed the Prince. "Monsters can't change."

"Prince Zephyr." *This isn't my place. I have no right to say or do anything. And I don't know how to help someone who hurts themselves so they can breathe.* But he was tired of ignoring this. Tired of seeing their lives torn and twisted. If he said something, anything, Zephyr and Ferdinan wouldn't have become so broken. And Jon would've never lost the innocence they protected for years. "What makes a person human?"

"Excuse me?"

"I met someone who lost their humanity and wanted nothing more than to have it back."

"Did they regain it?" Zephyr's breath caught in his throat.

That was a hard question. The camp residents believed Gongie returned her humanity, but nothing about her changed – only the residents' view of her capabilities. Ultimately, that didn't matter. His answer needed to help the boy in front of him. "They did."

"How?" Disbelief made Zephyr's hands sloppy.

"We had to figure out what makes a person human."

"And?"

"The journey to finding your humanity is the only way to reclaim it." *Jon's decision...will this help him be a brother to Ferdinan? Will helping Zephyr fix things enough Ferdinan could accept us? Or is it too late? I helped Ajani find her humanity and it made everyone happy. If I help him, will it do the same? Or will I make it worse?* Gongie closed his eyes and concentrated until he found Zephyr's presence. "This way."

Beyond the door were forests. Quiet. Calm. Beautiful. A perfect contrast to the celebration. They searched. And like last time, Gongie found them. Shattered bits scattered along the bank of a small pond.

And when Zephyr touched them...

The chaos of a thousand voices took shape. "Serve and protect. This is your duty." "You need to master this to fulfill your duty – to serve and protect those under your care." "As his older cousin, it's your duty to protect him." They all said similar things. To a toddler who didn't know what those words meant, countless times as Zephyr grew into the Prince kneeling next to him, trying not to cry.

The pressure was unbearable and they were only memories. *How much worse was hearing this so many times?*

Something dark flitted through the trees - making Gongie's heart race. "What's that?"

Onyx eyes looked down, despairing. "I don't want to know."

But the Prince stood, lips twitching as he acknowledged each memory telling him his duty. And when he broke past them, the shadows took form. Zephyr looked away, but Gongie's gaze stayed fixed.

General Tenalia smiled at the tiny Zephyr. "Become the best protector. Serve our people well. That's all you have to worry about."

That's all? What a horrifying thing to say to a young child.

The shadow brightened. Tiny Zephyr thanked her before being sent to play. Little feet ran to a garden maze planted in a nearby meadow.

Short brown hair and nearly colorless eyes came into view. Turning from the flowers, Ferdinan knelt - head down.

Tiny golden hands danced. "Let's play!"

Obeying, Ferdinan stood, healthy and nearly as tall as the golden Prince. Every command Zephyr gave, his younger cousin obeyed. Until an older girl - nearly a young woman - appeared. She gave the Prince a hug and told him Tenalia was waiting. Smiling, he ran out of the maze.

Screams broke the beauty - tripping Zephyr. Inhuman screams... Pushing himself to his feet, the tiny Prince bolted for his cousins. But when he reached them... There was no monster, no fallen tree or fire. Nothing to cause distress. The young woman looked annoyed, and Ferdinan huddled in a ball, crying.

She smiled at Zephyr. "My Prince, why aren't you inside?"

"What happened?!" Golden hands flew as he rushed over.

"He thought a stick was a snake."

Looking at Ferdinan, little hands moved, but the Prince didn't speak and the young Tinkerer looked away.

"The General's waiting, my Prince." The girl lifted Zephyr to his feet and turned him toward the palace. "I'll get it inside in time to eat."

It...? Did she...?

Uncertain, but encouraged by her sweet smile, the tiny Prince did as he was told. The scene faded.

"What was that?"

"Kannani..." Zephyr's hands shook as they moved. "I've been failing for this long..."

"You were too young–"

"It's my duty!"

Another memory played – ending in the same lesson. And like the first, a shadow took form after. Showing a similar event. Over and over. One after another. The lesson – serve and protect. But the reality...

He was stopped from protecting every time...

As he grew, Zephyr anguished – not knowing what to do – being rebuked or ignored when he asked... Until he completely veiled his eyes.

I knew about the abuse, but...how did I miss this? Or did I ignore it? "Zephyr...I'm so sorry..."

"Why?" Golden hands shook as hard as his voice. "General is below everyone. Our whole purpose is to serve and protect, but I keep putting myself first. I kept failing everyone – placing myself above all..."

That's not what I saw...

"You should be disgusted by me." Turning on the Psych, rage lashed out. "Why are you here?! Why bother with a monster like me?! A monster who'd do this to his own people! His own family!"

Zephyr leapt forward, fists clenched. Flinching, Gongie bolted up – nearly falling out of bed as the older boys' dreams fought for dominance in his mind.

***

Elbie wasn't there anymore. Neither was Oya... Blue crystals scanned the room. Ferdinan didn't know where he was, he just knew he wanted to forget. He wanted to forget that horrible conversation – both of them. He wanted them to not exist.

It's not real. I want to forget that lie. Forget that lie. It's not real. It never happened...

Confusion set in and underworked muscles twitched, screaming to move. But he was so tired... *What was I...?* Softness touched his arm, startling him. *Sora...* Looking at her was too hard so he stared at the blank wall.

"What's wrong?" Her voice was as soft as her touch.

Ferdinan wanted to answer so she wouldn't worry. Wouldn't call anyone... But everything was numb and he was so tired.

"Are you cold? In pain?" A worried face blocked his view of the wall. "It's okay. I'm listening."

Nothing matters... Closing his eyes, he willed his mind to escape.

***

Onyx eyes gazed at the downpour beyond the window. Hours of non-stop school work. It was painful. The longer a Fighter and some Athletes forced themselves to be still, the louder their cells screamed to move. But there was no running or fighting in this weather.

A golden finger jabbed at his freshest wound.

Wind slammed rain against reinforced windows with such force they bowed inward. The rainy season... It was unnatural. But dependable. Violent rains came out of nowhere, lasted a month, and vanished. But lockdowns only happened when winds became dangerous. Like now. Bending those windows was a feat... *The Energists are going to be exhausted...* They always were during the rainy season.

The sharp pain of an open wound and constant ache of muscles needing to run kept him company. Tapping his screen, he pulled up the next series of assignments. *No stopping.*

And he didn't – shrugging off screaming muscles to keep working. Even when his fingers twitched. And his limbs.

His latissimus dorsi contracting, however... Zephyr choked back a scream. Rolling off the chair, he started the Fighter's "rainy day routine."

Windows bowed against wind and water, but Zephyr didn't stop until he noticed an unexpected sound. *What is that?* Straining his ears, Zephyr stood and followed it to his cousin's room. Golden fingers dug deep into the freshest wound. The wind reared and tapping became erratic. *This isn't good...*

Opening the door revealed a reinforced pane leaning against the wall – one tip rocking, tapping the armoire. Everything was drenched... Curtains. Rug. Furniture. The books were unsalvageable... Damp fabric and the early threat of mold struck his nose. *Cleaning this will be a good workout.* Possibly better than the routine that was interrupted.

First, an emergency maintenance request, then Zephyr surveyed his cousin's room. *What can I salvage?* There wasn't much. *He keeps everything in his lab...'cause I stole his home.*

Taking down the drenched curtains and stripping the bed, he put them in the tub and moved the furniture to the hall. The armoire was bulky, but he got it out – revealing something strange hidden in its shadows. *What's that?*

A stick of swirling fog sat against a six-inch metal cube. Next to it was a screen. Whatever it was, the armoire protected it from the water. Curious, he took it to the dining table. *Sheet music for a violin? But he learned the mandolin...*

And it looked nothing like a violin, save the bridge and bow. *Metal strings...?* Attached was a little green flower. *Who made this? It's too simplistic and rough for Ferdinan's work.*

The plexiglass body was light and a cord attached it to the box. *This can't be a violin...* But Zephyr turned it on.

He was nine last time he played, but it felt natural lifting the fog to his chin and pulling the bow across. Sound didn't come off the strings, but out of the cube. Alien, metallic, mechanical notes. There was nothing alive about it like the bizarre music floating around the island since Family Week.

Do I remember enough to play? The black dots lost their meanings years ago, but his muscles remembered – mostly. Shaky and halted, he produced a tune. *Why make such an odd instrument?*

Putting it down he cleared the rest of Ferdinan's room, but his mind kept returning to the stick of fog. *How hard would it be to learn again?*

***

Keeping a dying child comfortable was harder than Sora expected. She knew it'd be painful, had worked with sick children before – only, none as sick as the skeletal boy.

A cocktail of drugs and nutrients dripped down to pool where the IV met the tube protruding from the boy's shoulder. A dozen pillows kept him propped up enough to breathe. Blue tinged skin wrapped bones shivering for warmth.

If I could do something. Anything to help. This thought wasn't altruistic, there was greediness on her part. Even being one of the few capable of bearing children didn't mean she'd succeed. Or that the child wouldn't get sick or injured despite her best efforts.

What if her child became sick like this? Could she calmly watch? Could she bear seeing them? *Will he make it to North Oueshi?*

She swore something whispered "yes" directly to her heart, but it was probably wishful thinking. Returning to her screen she found her gaze wandering back to Ferdinan. Then it drifted to the screen laying precariously on his belly. And something insisted she look.

Ridiculous. Shaking her head, she went back to work. But that screen held her attention. *It's wrong to look through other's things.* But...

The screen was slipping – like it had a mind of its own and was testing her limits. Leaning forward she took it and put it on the bedside table. It turned on.

No code. No double tap. It just turned on. Neither would it turn off when she tried. Instead, an article in an ancient language appeared. A language she knew...

And that voice whispered to her heart again – begging her to read it. She shouldn't. But it begged harder.

The article was as old as the language it was written in. Something that should've been destroyed countless generations ago. *Where did he find this?* But the Artimuses said he was resourceful... Everything in the article described the boy sleeping fitfully beside her. Or what she'd been told about him. *Is he...?* *Would he go this far to get better?* But it was too late.

Still...

She sent the article to herself. This time the screen turned off and she placed it securely on the bedside table and went back to work.

Hematite eyes grew heavy.

A dimly glowing person walked up to her. They were broken and struggled to stand. Something about that flickering light made her think they used to glow brightly but this was now all they could manage.

Please. It can't be too late.

That voice spoke straight to her heart – filling her. Desperate and scared. Afraid if Ferdinan died so would they. "His heart's barely working. Unless that medicine repairs his heart, it won't matter."

She felt bad, but it was true. And when the glowing person knelt – placing their forehead on the ground, she felt worse.

Please. He's important to many.

"I know. But his heart's beyond repair. If I could fix it... Even then, everything the article said, Ferdinan's health is beyond what we can help."

V-Ech is gone, but Šari-a will heal his body when you get him to Oueshi. Just get him to Oueshi.

"Who in Oueshi can heal a dying heart?"

Please. Help him.

Crazed green eyes floated in front of her accompanied by a wild grin. "You should rest. I'll sit with my dear friend."

Jumping, Sora stifled a gasp. Studying the girl... *Am I still dreaming?* She was definitely in Ferdinan's cabin, but... Oya's appearance was so sudden. And those clothes...

Sora didn't think it was possible to wear clothing wrong... It looked like the slacks were pilfered from Jon. Two of her could've fit in the waist and the cuffs were rolled up 'til they were comically thick and still dragging the ground. A rope held the pants up and bare toes barely poked out the bottom. The top... Sora couldn't guess where Oya found it, but it was meant to tie on both sides and instead was wrapped around and tied in the back. Like the pants, it was too big.

And that grin. It felt like a dream, its intensity growing. Delicate hands lifted Ferdinan's screen and offered it.

The desire to show the article to Samuel tripled.

Inhuman green eyes glowed and Oya pressed the screen into her hands. "Not all dreams are nonsensical."

Who is she? The broken person's pleas filled her and Sora couldn't ignore them...

The crazed glow softened when Oya turned her gaze to Ferdinan's far too still body. And the surreal feeling of a dream faded to the harshness of reality. "It's my turn to sit with him. Go."

Chapter 11

"What do you think?" Sora asked when Samuel looked up.

Jon tensed in her arms and she squeezed him tighter – smoothing his hair and apologizing again. He should have Samuel's full attention, but this wasn't her place. Neither did she have the knowledge and skills needed to create the chemicals outlined in that article.

Samuel looked at her for a long time... Hope and distress and so many things battled across his face. "I can't live with myself if I don't try."

Though stifled they both heard Jon sob. Again, she squeezed him. "How long will it take?"

"The boat's well-stocked." Samuel put down the screen and stood. "Once I get full access to a research lab, it won't take long."

"Do it." That was all she needed to say. Not because this decision was her right, but because she didn't want Jon feeling like Samuel was choosing Ferdinan. So she decided. And neither of them would argue.

***

"You wanted to see me, sir?" Norger sat when Dæya motioned to the chair. Silence reined, save for the water hitting the window.

"I received unexpected news that affects the Scientists, Healers, and Artists." Dæya breathed out slowly. "Students we thought would come over the next couple years are starting after break."

"How many?"

"In addition to the Tinkerer and two Thinkers, you'll get another three Thinkers – ages three, four, and not quite five."

What do I do? Half the incoming thirteenth and fourteenth years were given permission to graduate early...

"A number of developments occurred in East Azuté – forcing a redistribution of manpower worldwide."

They're starting early 'cause the ones who should be caring for them are needed elsewhere... I'm not trained for this...

"What do you need to handle the extra Scientists? Nammie Ke said she'd need a co-Lead. A wonderful idea. Instructors are training with Master Lucé to deal with...the more delicate matters."

"I don't know..." How did he prepare for toddlers who shouldn't be here? "I need to think about it."

***

Morning came but her dear friend didn't move. He'd been awake for a while. But he laid still, propped up by a dozen pillows, tears leaking out of closed eyes. *What's taking Ozar so long?* Without Śarī-a's heir...

The door opened and Sora walked in. Dark circles stained her eyes and uncertainty strained her lips. The beautiful woman placed two vials on the night stand and grabbed a cocktail from the smaller trunk.

"My turn." Sora didn't look at her. "I'll do everything I can for him."

"Thank you." *Please don't be too late.* Of her three promises, this was the one she wanted to keep most. Before leaving, Oya grabbed some clothes from Ferdinan's trunk. It was disconcerting how well they fit, save being too long. Now to explore while she figured out what to do next.

Bare feet strolled the deck. Alien green eyes turned to the water. It didn't jump and splash and beg to play. Because it wasn't hers right now. But Û-ya'īn was safe with Yuyu unless she gave it away also. *So irritating.* To test Yuyu's capability, the girl needed to hold multiple charges. *I've searched two years for suitable guardians.* A task that easily took decades, sometimes generations. Umbacano showed no desire toward anyone. Until Yuyu introduced Elbie. *How did I not see it?*

But she was glad Umbacano found someone it connected to. Every charge deserved a guardian. *How suitable will Śarī-a's guardian be? They won't be ready to take it for some time though...* Unless Oya intervened, which wouldn't be pleasant. Delicate fingers tugged at her steel locket.

Bored of the deck, Oya climbed on the railing and enjoyed walking along the metal bar. Sometimes she swung down to a lower deck. Other times she climbed up the side of the boat, all while she thought, planned.

Why would Gongie sew the memories back in? Why force painful, unwanted things back in place? He wouldn't purposefully harm another, but those stitches ran deep. *I'll have to leave them. I hope Kámua's ri-*

"That's dangerous." A young boy, maybe Yuyu's age, stared at her.

76

A delicate brow rose high over an alien green eye. Everyone passed by blissfully unaware of her. Until now. *What happened to you....?*

For a soul so young to be so painfully warped... *I've never seen this.* It was like a machine grabbed him in twelve different places then pulled and twisted until the child was barely human. Large wounds were healed but still bleeding... And holes dotted his mind. *What could do that?* "I'm a balance expert. It's fun. And the water would never hurt me."

An incredulous look painted his face. "From this height the water'll be like solid ice."

"I'm not the one you need to worry about." Oya gave her most crazed grin and spun on the railing. It was tempting to figure out what did that to the boy's soul, but she had too much already... Giggling, Oya ran along the thin metal bar – orbs soring alongside in her peripheral.

***

"Volunteer healers need to pay attention to the symptoms I've mentioned. Please learn from our trials and errors." Samuel concluded his speech, eyes on his little brother. "All treatments are outlined and medicines' production methods are available worldwide to healers."

Sora was caring for Ferdinan and Oya was nowhere to be found, so Jon sat by himself, antsy and focused on keeping his breathing under control. *I'm almost done baby brother.* "If you have any questions find me later or send a message."

Jon's face brightened but the crowd murmured. Samuel didn't care; his family came first. Stepping down, he sat beside his baby brother. One arm wrapped around broad shoulders and the other took Jon's hand.

Resting his head against chocolate brown hair, Samuel whispered, "we don't have to stay."

The lights flicked off and Jon tensed. His breathing became shallow, rushed and he grabbed his shirt. "My chest hurts and my arm's numb..."

"Breathe with me. Just like last night. Just like this morning." Samuel readied to calm Jon's heart if he couldn't. Slowly, one exaggerated breath after another, they breathed. *Considering what he's been through, he's doing well...* "We don't have to stay. My presentation's over now."

"I don't want to be in the cabin."

"Would you like to sit on the top deck?"

Slipping out, they kept to the open paths - helping Jon relax as they made their way to the top deck. His baby brother didn't say much - just sat next to him on a bench near the railing. Together they watched the last of the sun disappear. And when darkness settled in, Jon kept his eyes on the bright moon - nervous and squeezing Samuel's hand tightly.

None of the dozen conversations Samuel attempted took root. But that was okay. If this was what his baby brother needed, then this was what he'd do. Seeing those he loved suffer was unbearable. If Jon broke, he'd never forgive himself.

If only helping Ferdinan was so easy. *At least he accepted Sora...* Kind of. That article gave him hope, but for the medicine and treatment outlined to work, they needed to get him to a healthy weight and the boy couldn't eat anymore...

***

Flexing muscles to stop them from cramping took everything he had. Running was too hard. Sitting up was too hard. None of it mattered anyway. A defeated sigh crawled out of Ferdinan. There was so much... But he couldn't fail. He couldn't...

Ferdinan waited for Emil's animosity, but all he felt was loneliness. Not the kind that comes from being by yourself, but the kind born when the last person rejects you utterly. *It's fair. I'd reject myself if I could...*

Boney fingers reached for his screen - bumping the tube hanging from his shoulder. He hated it. But without that cocktail he'd be useless. *I'll need to take it too... I'm so tired... I just want to die...*

"How're you feeling?" Sora offered the screen he had reached for.

"The trunk...a second medicine..." The screen appeared on his lap.

"What does it look like?"

"A small box...dosed vials..." He didn't want to, but it was his duty.

"What does this do?" She stared at the bottles and needles packed neatly inside.

What are the right words? Answering was too hard. If it were Jon or Mother or... But Sora...he was too tired to guess...

Colorless crystals fell on the screen in his lap. He should send a message to grandpa Huey...but...

But...?

Ferdinan wasn't sure how long he searched for the end of that thought, but it didn't matter. Energy flowed into him. A defeated smile twitched. *It really does feel like pure energy washing over you.*

"Thank you." Picking up the screen, Ferdinan stared at the dozen messages from grandpa Huey. He should call the man, but it was too hard. He needed to get the timeline and supply drops sent. And a contingency plan for if Ferdinan couldn't confirm the next drop.

"Wow. What is this?"

Startled, Ferdinan turned to Sora. The box was on the table and she had a different vial and needle ready. "It's..."

Though she waited patiently, smiling, Ferdinan couldn't think of how to tell her. It was a medicine he created for end-stage patients. It gave them energy and dulled their pain so they could enjoy their final days doing whatever they wanted instead of being trapped in bed. But he didn't have the right to tell that to a potential Oueshian mother...

Hesitantly, he pointed to the bottle she held. "What's that?"

It was her turn to hesitate, but she answered. "The medicine from your screen. I wasn't prying. It wouldn't turn off for some reason."

Ferdinan should be angry. But he was too tired. And it didn't matter anyway. A strange warmth filled him, but he didn't care. "Ok..."

Returning to his screen, he called in favors to have teachers come if he didn't confirm his presence two days before...

"Ferdinan?"

There were other concerns he had to address or be inundated with countless call requests from various contacts. *I hope it's good enough.*

"Ferdinan." Sora's beautiful hematite eyes leaned closer when she sat on the edge of his bed. "How're you feeling?"

"I'm sorry I've caused you trouble..."

"You haven't been any trouble." Slowly, she offered her hand.

The gesture made him want to cry. Her touch was soft. Not painful or disconcerting. It felt wonderful. But he didn't deserve any kind of comfort. But... A touch that didn't hurt... "I have. And I'm sorry."

Her hand didn't waver. "What do you need for your presentation tomorrow? I can have it rescheduled."

"No." Ferdinan looked away and drew the blankets up higher. "More of that medicine and I'll be fine."

"If that's what you want." Sora retrieved her screen and sat at his bedside. "Tell me everything you'll need for tomorrow."

***

While Samuel chatted with Kyo Jorani about the medical techniques described in his brother's presentation, Jon checked his messages.

He wanted them to go away, but he couldn't be rude to a Kyo. There were a few messages from each of is suitemates, but Jon didn't want to look at them. Didn't have the energy to respond. So he kept scrolling. Instructors were simple enough to answer. But the Superintendent... Skipping those, he continued – answering only the ones he had the energy to look at.

Norger? A message from the gent was unexpected...and the Kyo wasn't shutting up... Reading over it made him wish he'd skipped it. It wasn't long, but gave significant detail about a student he was expected to mentor. Jon felt himself growing sick. He couldn't. Even if he had to go back...he couldn't...

No. I won't be mentoring anyone this year.

Nearing the end, he found a follow up message to the security protocol request he'd gotten three lifetimes ago. *I started working on the program before... I could finish it.*

Securing a line, he pulled up his notes stored in his lab, and stared at them. The partially encoded system filled the screen. This wasn't difficult, Jon programed these for fun. But...he just stared. It was too hard to move his hands. Too hard to re-read the last line of code.

The screen blurred. Tossing it aside, he cradled his head. Cooking was a chore. Programing was too hard. He couldn't sleep. Everything was scary. Death surrounded him. He was useless. Helpless. Unwell. He finally had family, and he'd hurt them. *Will I infect them....?*

Chapter 12

Days of following faded tracks led Ozar to a complex series of caves. And on the other side was a hidden world. Every structure was either built into the land or covered with plant life.

How should I approach?

Ozar considered this until a pebble hit his arm. Turning, another grazed his chin – but he saw who threw it. Realizing she was caught, a little girl stood at yelled at him in a language he was forbidden to learn until his own camp and village were restored.

She's the heir.

Not what I'd expect from Śarī-a's guardian... Holding out his hand, he knelt. "I was sent by the Rā-yumôn."

Little fists rested against her hips and she pinched her lips to the side. Again, she spoke in that language he didn't know.

"I'm sorry. I wish I could respond."

Crossing her arms, she approached. It was hard guessing her age. She looked about as old as Evelyn, but had the air of one twice that. Thick, black curls swayed and hazel eyes glowed. Green tinged light shown off the gold rods in her right ear. Crossing her arms, she looked down at him. "You can't respond but know Rā-yumôn?"

Something silvery glinted from the forest. Ozar held perfectly still. Revealing who he was – depending on who held that arrow... "I'm North Oueshi's Hei-O. I wouldn't trespass on your village if I wasn't sent."

The glint of silver vanished.

Am I safe? "She sent Ajulagrá to find Śarī-a's guardian and me to establish a connection between her and the village."

Frowning, the girl scoffed. "Stay here."

He wasn't sure where she melted into, but she was gone. *She has three rods along her helix and two rods and a hoop in her lobe...* No matter how Ozar considered that, he was both impressed and pitied her. There weren't many reasons a child would have multiple lobe piercings. And three helix ones... *What sort of person is this child?*

***

The old man wouldn't let Samuel go. Apology plastered itself across his big brother's face but Jon knew it wasn't Samuel's fault the old man wouldn't shut up.

Each attempt to end the conversation failed – frustrating both brothers.

Annoyed, Jon rubbed his stomach and leaned forward a little. "I don't feel well."

"I'm sorry, baby brother." Samuel squeezed Jon's shoulder and guided him past the old man who was still trying to get a few last words in. "Gnux, please message me and I'll respond properly after taking care of my brother."

Once the man was out of sight, Jon straightened. "Sorry for lying."

"It's ok. He was being unforgivably pushy." Samuel squeezed his shoulders. "Sora asked for me. I promise, I'll be quick."

"Ok..." Jon wanted to leave, but he followed.

Samuel triggered the chime and Sora stepped out – giving them both a hug. "I'm sorry, Jon, but could you wait inside? There're a few things I need to tell Samuel and I don't want-"

Jon shook his head, waving his hands when she paled. He didn't want her apologizing, not when she was doing so much for his family. Not when she'd be family soon.

"Or on the bench down there." Samuel pointed.

"No. I can...once."

"I'm sorry, I wasn't thinking." Sora bowed, and gave him another hug. "I won't forget again."

"Thank you." Waiting for the two to walk away, Jon entered.

Ferdinan sat propped up on the bed with a handful of screens scattered around him. Despite the pleasantly warm temperature, the skeleton wore a coat and was wrapped in blankets. A disconcerting wheezing came from the gent between spasmatic coughs. Though awake and alert, the Tinkerer looked terrible.

He's still working on multiple projects? Jon frowned. Of course, Ferdinan would work until he died.

That thought made Jon's heart race. Closing his eyes, he forced himself to breathe like Samuel coached. But it was hard and terrifying. Weak coughs disrupted Jon's thoughts, but he didn't want to look at the gent, so he pulled a screen from his pocket. Maybe mom, his brothers, or his island brothers had sent a new message. He wasn't responding to them, but it was nice seeing they were there.

One additional message was waiting. *Norger?* Jon deleted it. He already said 'no.'

"I apologize... Someone came to see her... She should be back soon." Ferdinan's trembling voice had more life than expected.

"Working on your presentation?"

"Yeah..." Silence landed hard and settled oppressively until Sora returned.

***

"What're you doing? This programming's beyond you." Annoyance dripped in Norger's voice. "You'll end up hurt."

It's what I need for the gloves. Elbie suppressed a glare but turned off the screen. Master Ferdinan believed in him. Was excited when he tried new or difficult things. His mentor never doubted him. So why was Norger so negative? Umbacano nuzzled his cheek. If not for...whatever this bird was...

Mismatched eyes turned to Umbacano. He recalled wondering that before... And... *What was I...?*

"Well?" Frustration appeared two inches from his nose.

Elbie jumped back – head hitting the floor. The ringing of falling metal danced with the pounding of windblown rain.

"What're you doing?!"

Abrasive slime grabbed Elbie – pulling him to his feet. Dizziness and nausea hit hard. *No! Stop!* The more he pulled away, the harder Norger yanked him back. "Stop!"

Startled, the Thinker let go and Elbie flew back to the floor. Norger searched for what to do – freezing. "Clinic. Let's get you to a clinic..."

But Elbie was already closing the door. If only he could lock it from the outside. Norger wasn't wrong though. A head injury... And he was dizzy. But he'd get there by himself...once he found an Energist... *My screen...*

Something warm ran down Elbie's neck as he walked to the doors. *What is this?* Brushing the warmth away, little fingers came back dyed red.

"Session finished early?" Xhou's smile quickly faded as he shifted a box to look closer at Elbie's hand. Putting it down, he studied the Tinkerer's head before telling the Energist who escorted him to get a Healer.

"Why'd you leave like that?" Norger's voice materialized behind them.

"What happened?" Xhou knelt – looking at Elbie's eyes.

"I don't know. He managed to trip backward over a stool." The new Lead shifted in agitation. "Probably 'cause he wasn't doing what he was supposed to."

Heat and humiliation battled inside Elbie. He wanted to yell, to run. But he was certain his head wouldn't appreciate it.

"That doesn't sound like Elbie."

"Well, that's what happened."

"There's the Lead stuff I promised." Xhou gestured to the box, smiling at Elbie. "I'll care for Elbie."

There were no objections. The student Healer arrived and closed his split skin, but the mild concussion earned him a trip to Isolation for observation.

 Neither Umbacano nor Xhou left his side.

Once he was settled into a room, he was told "no work" and the screen he was designing Yuyu's gloves on was taken away.

Pale and shaky, Xhou smiled. "I don't know who'll be more upset I let you end up here, Yuyu or Haoyu."

Elbie giggled...and regretted it. "Haoyu'll have Cidi and Iilli to help him worry more."

"Mind if I say nothing 'til I'm safely off the islands?"

"I'd rather they focus on their fieldtrip." Elbie laid back. It was going to be a boring couple of days. *You'll keep helping me with Yuyu's gloves?*

The beautiful yellow bird shook its head and fluttered to sit on Elbie's toes.

"Please tell me what happened."

What happened... Elbie looked at his hands. "I was doing my own project instead of testing the teaching materials."

Blue-black eyes stared. "How did that lead to you getting hurt?"

Rain hit the building harder. "I was startled when he confronted me..."

"I don't believe that's what happened." Xhou leaned forward – giving Elbie an apologetic smile. "Even if it was – it's not your fault. Norger's responsible as both Lead and acting mentor. So, tell me again, what really happened?"

But... It needed to be Elbie's fault. If it was Norger's, he could start hating the older boy and he didn't want that. Silence reined until Elbie told Xhou everything. "Norger's not the mentor a new Tinkerer needs. He's impatient. And he doesn't listen. If he can't listen to me and Yuyu, he'll never be able to communicate with her."

"Ok." Blue-black eyes wide and overwhelmed, Xhou nodded. "I'll do everything I can."

A little beak pecked lovingly at his middle toe. "Thank you."

"Will you let me apologize on Norger's behalf?" Xhou smiled at Elbie's surprise. "He's dealing with more than Leads usually do 'cause of the blight. He also has his own unknown future to figure out. It's no excuse. But I promise, he's a nice, caring person. I should've realized how stressed he was."

It's not your fault. A realization hit as the rain quieted briefly. *It isn't anyone's fault.* But it was still unfair. Umbacano fluttered over to Elbie's shoulder and nuzzled his cheek.

***

Blue fingers offered Oya's histories to her. Everything was arranged for Azuté. Personal affairs were delt with. Ferdinan's presentation was soon. And Jon had Samuel. *What can I do for her?*

Spasmatic coughing forced the screen from his hands. His heart leapt and twisted – unhappy at the strain. He felt so weak. And numb. And tired...

"I apologize..." Ferdinan picked up the screen and offered it again, but she didn't take it. "Everything on here's amazing and interesting. It's been useful and comforting and wonderful. But it's time to return it to you."

Smirking, Oya leaned back. "It's an insult to return a gift."

"And if I don't need it anymore?" Ferdinan looked down. It was an amazing gift. There was nothing about it he didn't love, but he didn't deserve it and he couldn't use it much longer.

"It's yours for as long as you live." Crazed green eyes turned to the ceiling. "You can request who it goes to after you die, but it's yours 'til then."

It was odd how easily Oya spoke of death. Jon would pale and squirm. Most people would be uncomfortable at best and irate at worst. But Oya... "She's too young, but when she's older, Yuyu would love this."

"Not Elbie?"

"Elbie..." Elbie wasn't a bad choice, but... "He's more..."

The door open and Sora entered – holding more vials. She apologized and collected another from the medical trunk and injected both into his IV. He expected her to sit down and read, but she asked Oya about food preferences and left.

"Elbie's more?"

"He prefers dreaming ideas and making them reality. Yuyu's interests lie in bringing other people's ideas to life." Ferdinan laid back enjoying the energy rushing in. "She has wonderful ideas, but... It's... She knows she can create anything she can think of. But others can't. So she enjoys creating things that otherwise would only be ideas."

"What a sweet child. Like what?"

"The last one I know about..." Guilt hit hard. "Her friend was missing their menagerie and wishing they could have a pet on the islands without it disrupting the ecosystem. Yuyu came to me asking about making a pet robot."

Her grin grew soft as Ferdinan studied boney hands.

"I gave her one of my little robots to study, but I don't know how far she got..." *If I reached her fast enough there'd be robot animals all over the islands...*

"Ah." Oya grinned and leaned forward. "A hundred and thirty years from now, when old age has taken you, you can offer the histories to Yuyu."

Not knowing what to say, Ferdinan changed topics. "Are you ok here? I'm sorry there isn't much for you to do."

"There's plenty of boat to explore." Her mad grin grew. "All the talks are boring though."

I'm sorry. "Tomorrow there's three more speeches, then the formal dinner and dance. After'll be mini conferences..."

Those green eyes all but glowed when he said "dance." Her joy and excitement stole the rest of his words. *Ok. That's what I'll do for you.*

***

Pure excitement bounced on tiptoes, little hands clapped, and green-ringed black eyes watched eagerly as two young girls stepped off the boat with a Chūzite teacher.

Evelyn ran at them – making the two nervous – but Mother couldn't stop smiling. *Three granddaughters.* And Evelyn had siblings.

The new arrivals didn't move fast enough, so Evelyn started her greeting there on the pier. "I'm Evelyn! I'm also claimed! Except I'm from East Azuté... You'll love this family. They're giants! And they got so giant 'cause they're so loving!"

The girls clutched at the teacher's legs nervously, but the woman encouraged them to greet the overly excited Evelyn. The oldest of the two took the younger's hand – mumbling a thank you and their names.

"Tinny and Yin?! I love those names! They're really pretty!" Grabbing the girls' hands, Evelyn dragged them to their new family. "This is Grandma Artimus! Everyone calls her Mother...me too, even though she's my grandma... So you call her Mother too! And this is Pa-papa! He's Mother's husband and our Pa-papa! Though people call him Father. But I call him Pa-papa – so you can choose which one you want! Pa-papa's teaching me to cook. He's really good. Do you know how to

87

cook? If so, you can teach me too! If not, Pa-papa can teach all of us! It'll be lots of fun!"

Next, she introduced Xingho and Raonie, their new parents, then pointed to each of their new aunts and uncles – the ones who were in the country – and random servants she insisted be there. "Do you like bugs? I like them. They're cute and weird and creepy! There's lots of them in the woods! And also fuzzy little creatures! Lots of bunnies! Our school's really fun too!"

Tinny and Yin stood horrified at how quickly Evelyn spoke.

"Oooo! Which languages do you know? I speak common and Terric. Though I've gotten really good at Yemeri! Do you know Yemeri? If not, I'll help you learn!" Evelyn leaned in close – apparently wanting an answer this time. "Which languages do you speak?"

It looked like she was physically restraining herself while she waited for an answer.

When silence lasted too long, Tinny – the older of the two – squeezed the younger and mumbled, "Common and Panali. We're learning Chiih."

"Panali...?" Evelyn thought long and hard before her eyes tripled in size. "That's North Chūzo's national language, right? Will you teach me? Then I can talk to you in your language! Oh! That'd be my big brother's language too! Then I can talk to all three of my siblings! And we can learn Chiih together!"

Mentioning Ferdinan made Mother nervous. Father wrapped an arm around her waist. *How do we prepare Evelyn?*

"Oh! We get to share a room! You're going to love the bed, it's as big as a house! And I have a play cottage...but it's your play cottage now too!" Evelyn grabbed the two girls' hands and dragged them inside. "I'll show you!"

Chapter 13

"I'm sorry..." Samuel sighed. "I can't turn down the Master healer."

"I'm sorry..." It was Jon's fault...but it also wasn't, which gave him another thing to be conflicted about.

"I'll keep him company."

Both brothers jumped when Oya appeared wearing clothes which obviously weren't hers...or meant to go together... *Who did she steal those from?* And why? The Samutlz provided her with a full trunk. They might be terrible people - horrible family - but they were good hosts.

Samuel hesitated, but shook his head. "I'll ask him to meet with me during the opening dance."

Green eyes glowed and excitement laced her wicked grin, making Jon nervous. "When's the dance?"

"Ferdinan concludes the keynote speakers. After is a dinner for socialization and strengthening ties with others in various fields. Then there's a formal dance to further promote interpersonal connections."

Oya snorted. "What's the point of the next two weeks?"

Jon rolled his eyes while his brother blinked. "The first three days are introductions. The next week and a half are specialized presentations and creating plans to address the needs discussed. The last few days are interdisciplinary collaborations to finalize plans and timelines."

Oya snorted. "Sounds...long."

That was one word for it. And... Jon finally had family and there was a boat full of people he had to share with. *I hate all of them.* "Go. Putting it off will make it more annoying."

"Your health comes first."

No, it doesn't. It never does... "They'll keep hounding us when I need to be outside." Though true, it was an excuse.

Frowning, Samuel turned to Oya. "Don't leave him."

"Not 'til you return."

"Thank you." Hugging his baby brother, Samuel apologized and left.

Alone...again... Save for the crazed green eyes grinning at him. Bare feet skipped to a chair and floated up as blood red hair hung down below the edge of the seat. *She can't be my age...* "What're you doing?"

"Sometimes it helps to change perspective." Oya stretched, reaching delicate hands down to the floor. "Stop standing on the ceiling. It's strange enough with all the furniture up there."

Wrapping his arms around himself, Jon looked away. "Please, I'm not up for nonsense today."

"How much fun would it be to dance on the ceiling instead of the floor? Lights beneath our feet instead of above?"

Jon looked at the other chair. He barely fit in them properly, it wasn't possible to sit upside down. So he laid on the bed with his head hanging down and propped his feet against the wall. "Does this work?"

Golden-brown toes danced. "It works as well as anything else."

That was an unpleasant thought. "How? How are you ok? We were both trapped, but you were buried...covered in rock...leg crushed..."

"Only part of me was buried." Her grin intensified before turning serious. "Darkness. Being trapped. I faced them long ago and conquered. As have you. Once you realize it."

"How did you stop being afraid? Stop seeing death everywhere?" Jon's heart pounded. It wasn't bright enough. The walls...could he break free? And... *Why didn't she run? We would've been fine if she ran!*

"It's scary 'cause you're alone when your heart panics, and who'd understand when you can't? There's no reason, but it happens anyway. And it reminds you of the death you faced. How do you escape it again? It was luck you survived the first time." Gentleness and a strange kind of compassion filled Oya's countenance. "Luck...which consumes your power. How often will luck be on your side?"

His heart raced and his mind staggered. There was no solid ground. Just air. And he was falling. Falling into a darkness he couldn't escape...

Ice cold hands encompassed his cheeks and it all melted away...

"But you never were alone. Even when the last light failed, there was always one person next to you and one person fighting to reach you." Inhuman green eyes glowed. "And luck? It's simply circumstances and the people gifted to you. As long as those people are on your side, you'll always have luck."

That was...unexpectedly comforting... "Thank you."

"Don't thank me." Oya stood, sparking Jon to sit up. "Lean on your unique luck so you don't have any regrets."

"Regrets?"

Her grin vanished completely. Oya stared straight into his soul and Ferdinan filled his mind.

"He's not my responsibility anymore. I did my duty. I got him here alive. I don't have to worry about him." Jon lied, but he didn't want to think about the gent, didn't want to see anyone die. "There're plenty of people here who can care for him."

"Can you live with yourself if you ignore him 'til he's gone?"

"He's never gone. Never." Jon stood, but he couldn't look at her. All the comfort from before was gone and his heart raced again. None of this would've happened, he never would've...if Ferdinan wasn't haunting him! "He's always there making life difficult and stealing my family. Why should I put my needs behind his every time? I'm suffering too."

Oya stepped aside as he paced, panting, shaking.

"It took everything to get him here – I don't have any more to give. Even now with Samuel and Sora...he keeps stealing them from me. I need them. They're *my* family!" Jon wasn't sure why he was yelling, but it felt good. He'd been quiet and done what he was supposed to no matter what it did to him. So he got to yell. He got to be angry. He had every right to hate the gent! "Why am I not allowed what I need? Why should I give up more to one who's committed countless atrocities? Someone I've already given everything to and just keeps taking more?!"

"I'm not asking you to accept him or his beliefs. I want you to care about your own principles. I want you to care about your future self if you're trapped with a regret you can never rectify."

"I do care! Why do you think I'm here instead of home with my family? My entire family? Do you care how much I need them? I can't stand the lights being out. I can't sleep at night 'cause it's too dark. I need help to." *Regret...* That one word leached the fury from him. "But I did my duty anyway. I didn't abandon him when I had every right to. I pushed aside those atrocities and focused on the good they did so I

91

could look at him. Get him here. He's not my responsibility anymore. And even if he was, I can't. I'm barely keeping myself going. Dragging him along... I'm too weak...too tired."

"Then relinquish all claims to him. You'll not comment on or complain about how I help my friend." Oya stood tall. "He's my friend. My brother. And I'll stay by his side 'til the end."

Jon swallowed hard. Her words...but... *She's giving me an escape.* He simply had to take it.

***

Sora finished pinning her hair and adjusted her suit. *How will this go?* Samuel described Ferdinan's fear of healers and warned it was always worse after being at home. Bad enough the Dinta was actively avoiding the boy despite wanting to check on him personally.

How will Ferdinan manage in a room full of healers? There'd be military scientists, diplomats, and traders as well, but... *Will that be enough to get him through?*

Entering the adjacent room, she found Ferdinan out of bed. Barely. The sick child knelt half naked on the floor – forehead resting on the edge of the trunk. Weeping. A boney hand covered his face, but she wasn't sure if he was trying to stifle the sobs or hide from the world.

He can't present. That was ok. He was a child. This wasn't something he should be forced to do. Kneeling next to him, she offered a hug, but a broken voice begged her to leave. "You don't have to do this. Samuel can present your disks with the notes you've written."

Ferdinan flinched into a ball at Samuel's name. "I do..."

"Ok." She helped him to his feet when he struggled and laid out his outfit. "Ready for another dose?"

Pale, skeletal cheeks burned. "Please."

It didn't take long for the medicine to start working. Though miserable, the boy moved easier and finished getting ready quickly.

His tailored black suit emphasized how dangerously thin Ferdinan was, but radiated quiet simplicity. A neutral blue collarless button up. Matching blue socks and pocket square. It was all perfectly designed to check every box of professionalism without attracting attention away from his presentation. And Sora hated it. He was too sick to do this.

"Ready?"

Ferdinan gave a shaky nod.

The entire way he tugged at the suit. Skeletal hands rubbed nervously together and colorless crystals searched constantly for threats. The closer they got, the more people there were, the jumpier Ferdinan became.

A pained gasp rang out when someone brushed against the boy and that too thin body rammed into the railing. Crystals danced rapidly. *He looks like a trapped animal.*

Cautiously, Sora stepped close and whispered, "You really don't have to do this."

Pain twisted his face, but when he looked at her, his expression was hard, resolute. "Please stop saying that. If I didn't *have* to, I wouldn't be here."

"I'm sorry." Sora didn't like it, but the boy couldn't handle any more pressure, so she offered her hand and kept offering though he didn't take it. "I'll be next to you the entire time."

Ferdinan nodded - pale and shaky.

The preparation room was behind the stage. Ferdinan connected his screen for the presentation and read over his notes again. A lady entered briefly to inform them the opening remarks were starting and he'd be announced soon. The boy stood, pale and hugging his screen as though it were the only thing keeping him alive.

"Sit and relax."

Whether he didn't hear or was ignoring her, Ferdinan approached the wings and peaked out. His impossibly thin frame shook and boney fingers clutched at his chest - he struggled to breathe.

Sora rushed over and he recoiled into the shadows. *His heart can't take this.* "Sit down. Relax with me."

Eyes, wild and darting, struggled to focus on her. What little color he had vanished as he started hyperventilating.

This isn't his heart, is it? Keeping her voice soft and calm, she offered her hand again. "Can you tell me what you need?"

"I-I...I'm...f-f-f-ine..." Stick arms clutched the screen harder as he folded himself into a tighter ball.

What do I say? "I'm right here. You're safe. I'm not leaving."

His body spasmed - retching, drawing attention. And he couldn't stop.

"I know it's hard. But your heart can't take this stress. How can I help you calm down?"

Retching turned violent, but he accepted her help getting back to the couch.

"Is everything okay?" The lady from earlier ran over - horrified and ready to move as soon as she was given instruction.

"I'm caring for him." It wasn't easy keeping her voice steady, but Sora needed to calm Ferdinan down, not stress him more.

"I'll get hea-"

"No. I'm caring for him." Placing herself between Ferdinan and the lady eased Ferdinan's stress slightly. "Worry about your job, I'll fulfill mine."

Though uncertain, the lady obeyed.

What do I do? What'll help him? When Ferdinan clutched at his chest - eyes wide and terrified - she nearly panicked. "I know you don't like being touched, but would you like a hug?"

Eternity passed with only the painful sounds of retching and desperate gasps for air. Finally, scraggly loose curls waved side to side and he looked desperately at her hand. "...sorry..."

"You can hold my hand. You can hold it as long as you want." Breathing out slowly, she tried what Samuel did for Jon. Understanding, Ferdinan gasped in time with her. "I'm here. You're safe. I won't let anyone touch you. I won't let anyone hurt you."

Chapter 14

Oya walked along the railing, spinning, jumping, hand walking back, because the entire boat was a playground and there was no one else to play with. She could count on one hand how many children were aboard this conference. And she, Jon, and Ferdinan were three of them.

Paying attention would've been the polite thing. And she loved her dear friend, but she was bored and didn't understand what he was saying.

If he'd look up, she'd be silly for him. But he was struggling to speak without stuttering and shaking so hard she was surprised he could stand. Blue crystals focused on the giant screen behind him or Sora beside him, and his hands clutched the podium. *You're almost done, dear friend.*

"That's *really* unsafe. You'll get hurt." The boy from before looked around, confused at why no adults were saying anything.

How do you see me, young one? "What's your name?"

Disbelief coated him. "You don't know who I am?"

"Should I?"

Black eyes looked at her long and hard trying to figure out if he was in the wrong or her. "I'm Prince Kaz."

"Call me Oya." She offered her hand, but he just stared at her, so she gave him her most crazed smirk.

"Your title?"

"I have none," she grinned.

He scowled, puffing out his chest with an amusing level of authority. "A servant should show the Master's heir respect."

Mad giggles spilled out. "The Five Lauals are of no concern to me."

"Master–"

"Laual, Master, Kal, Nann, Tiili. It's all the same." Oya gave him a glimpse of her own authority, before turning Cheshire again.

Kaz blinked. Uncertain. Unnerved. "No one's above the Five…"

"Q-questions?" Ferdinan's trembling voice limped through the hall.

"This'll be interesting." Oya turned her full attention to her dear friend. She might not understand the disks, but Ferdinan was amazing at explaining things one on one. And...she was curious about some of these people. There was too much vitriol whispering around for her to not be.

"I can't believe they're putting a sick child through this stress." Kaz folded his arms, frowning. "This is for adults, why's a child presenting?"

"Jealous?"

"No." Kaz's gaze turned to a woman who stood. "Disappointed."

"Why's North Chūzo no longer honoring its trade agreements with Mid Oueshi?"

Kaz snorted – earning him a grin from Oya. As reward, she sat on the rail to put his mind at ease. Partly.

A dozen voices added to the complaint. Ferdinan turned translucent and his eyes stayed fixed on the podium. "My older s-sisters...are trained on foreign affairs. I'll ans-s-swer...any questions c-concerning...the disks."

An older gentleman stood.

Kaz's eyes widened and he chewed on his lip. "What does General Vvillic want with those?"

"Hm?"

"He's..." Kaz shook his head and listened when the man spoke.

"Lord Ferdinan, you claim these can replace a healer. Would you demonstrate how well?"

"Mostly. There's only s-so...much a device can do." Blue crystals focused on the man so hard Oya was certain Ferdinan blocked out the rest of the room. "If you'll approach, G-General, I'll demonstrate their diagnostic abil-lity...and treatment generation."

The man gave a lighthearted laugh and walked on stage.

"Hold it to your chest...p-pr...press the side button." Ferdinan demonstrated while giving verbal instructions before offering a disk.

"It can't be that easy," Kaz scoffed.

Alien green eyes pierced the ten-year-old. "But it is."

"May I use this one?" General Vvillic pulled one from his pocket. "It was requested I use healer Neel's."

"O-of c-c-course..."

The young Prince rose an eyebrow. "You know him?"

"He's my dearest friend."

The man did as Ferdinan instructed and the crowd waited while the disk scanned him. After a moment it flashed yellow, then green.

"Did he really make those? I've heard the healers. They say a scientist couldn't possibly make them, let alone a child."

"Adults are petty creatures. Even more so when children are involved." Oya giggled. "Be better than them."

"You have a health c-concern...though you m-m...might not notice any problems yet." A boney hand reached out, shaking and Sora approached the man.

Grinning, the General handed it over to her and waited for her to give it to Ferdinan. "Please, elaborate."

Looking over the results didn't take long. "Your p-pancreas isn't functioning as ef-f-f...effectively as it should, making it harder for your body to maintain blood s-sugar levels. Please see your healer b-before it becomes a chronic condition."

"And if I didn't have a highly trained healer?"

Ferdinan gave a shaky smile and read the treatment plan suggested.

Contemplating, the General stared at the disk. "What else can you get from it?"

Ferdinan's expression... *He hates that question...* Kaz didn't look thrilled about it either.

Shaking his head, the skeleton studied the disk carefully. "You have a c-concerning number of scars – both internal and ex-x-ternal. Th-there's excessive wear to your joints. You're a General in leadership as well as p-p-pr...practice...considering the p-placement of scars, you've enjoyed decades of training s-soldiers personally."

"Proper leadership requires assuring the competence of those under you." The General grinned and motioned for him to continue.

"You only have one working kidney."

"Excuse me?" The man interrupted.

"The one d-d-damaged by..." Ferdinan studied the disk again, trying to stop shaking. "...a pike...has st-stopped working. The healthy one's fine on its own, but s-something to be aware of."

"It can tell what weapon caused an old wound?" Awe coated Kaz.

"I doubt it."

That startled the young Prince. "But..."

"With how long he studied the disk, I guess he recognized the scarring pattern."

"How would a child know that by sight?" Kaz rolled his eyes.

"In late ch-childhood, you broke your arm at the growth p-plate... leaving your right arm slightly shorter than the left." Ferdinan looked like he could say more, but didn't.

"You can't begin to fathom his mind." Oya winked and pushed herself off the railing to stand beside the younger boy.

"I'll contact you later." Taking back the disk, the General grinned.

Another man stood – making Ferdinan cringe and returning his attention to the podium. "Impressive. Unbelievable a child could think of something like these. Tell truthfully, Lord, were these created by your father? Were you sent in his place due to his extended disappearance?"

This caught Oya's attention.

"You're his friend and didn't know his father hasn't been seen in years?" Kaz scoffed.

Shaking harder, boney fingers clutched his chest. "Th-that'd-d be easier."

How much longer will he last? "If he wanted to talk about his father, he would've."

Confusion coated Kaz and the rude man, but for different reasons.

While the man floundered, another stood – making the young Prince smile and Ferdinan struggle for breath. *Is he hyperventilating?* "You know her?"

Kaz nodded. "That's healer Paphula. She's the highest ranked healer here after the Master healer."

Ah...

"Why do you impinge on the healers' realm?"

All color left Ferdinan. The only thing keeping him upright was the podium. That skeletal body convulsed as he fought not to be sick.

Kaz's dark eyes doubled. "What's wrong with him?"

It was subtle, but Sora stepped closer, offering her hand to the dying child. Colorless eyes darted around. His body jerked and he gripped the podium harder. Desperation locked onto the woman's hand... Desire...

And he took it. Holding on tight. *He didn't flinch...* Alien green eyes turned to Kaz. "Is there anything you fear to the very core of your soul?"

"...no..."

"Then you couldn't understand."

The boss healer lady cleared her voice. "Well?"

Mimicking Sora, Ferdinan slowed his breath. When he spoke, it was to her. "N-no discipline ex-i-ists in isolation. This c-conference ex-x... exemplifies that. The efficacy of this c-conference depends on it. It's yearly oc-c-currence for generations without be-coming corrupted or losing p-purpose proves it."

Sora smiled encouragingly. Saying nothing. Simply holding his hand and breathing with him.

"Healers c-create wonderf-ful medicines that've saved countless lives. But every device they use was b-based on something created by an engineer or scientist. Or a c-curious person. They regularly s-send equipment to engineers to b-build or to improve them." Ferdinan paused, panting for a few breaths. "No discipline exists in isolation. And they sh-shouldn't. The sharing and interacting of d-different minds and knowledges allow us to grow instead of remaining stagnant. Why bother b-being here if you thought otherwise?"

That earned Ferdinan a scowl he never saw. "The folly of childhood's quite the sight to–"

"Well said." Another stood, interrupting the woman Oya didn't like.

Glancing over, Ferdinan paled further. He released Sora's hand and bowed – swaying unsteadily. "I apologize, K-Kyo Jorani."

"I see nothing to apologize for, Master Ferdinan. I do, however, have a question concerning these disks."

"Anything, K-Kyo." Ferdinan stayed bowed, the podium steadying him on one side and Sora the other.

Oya giggled. *Looks like I get to greet two.*

Curious eyes studied her. "Do you know them?"

Giving him a wink, Oya smirked. "Not yet."

"But you don't have a title..."

"I first saw these when visiting the Grasslands. Quite ingenious. Impressive. And the materials... I've been studying them for some time. Including their distribution."

Ferdinan leaned harder against the podium, but didn't straighten.

Oya snorted at Kaz. "Why does that matter?"

"The number you've sold is a fraction to what you've donated. Considering the rarity of the materials used, how've you managed this?"

Kaz couldn't find the words, so he turned back to the Kyo.

"I-I build them myself. And b-barter my skills for materials. I work with generous people who donate what they can to help."

"I see." Jorani's expression gave away nothing, but they smiled. "Thank you. Please continue your wonderful work."

***

Jon couldn't get Oya's words out of his head, so he came. But he wished he hadn't. Watching Ferdinan present was painful. On many levels. But when the gent took Sora's hand and held on both he and his big brother were surprised. Even in the cave the skeleton still flinched when hugging them, but the gent looked relieved with her.

More surprising was seeing Ferdinan at the mingle. He knew the skeleton didn't want to be there. *Why's he being stubborn?*

Jon moved closer to Samuel who chatted with another healer, but his attention drifted to his ally. He didn't want to see the gent. Didn't want to acknowledge the truths he knew. But he couldn't look away.

Ferdinan weaved cautiously through the crowd – always pausing to make sure Sora was there. That he hadn't lost her... *Where's Oya?* Not seeing that crazed grin by the skeleton's side felt wrong, but he couldn't find those inhuman green eyes or blood red hair anywhere.

Various people approached Ferdinan – few of them friendly. Most he nodded to and hurried on, but others he exchanged conversation.

An older gentleman approached, speaking Calbri – the language of the scientists. Though a generally dead language, scientists used it often due to its preciseness.

Ferdinan bowed to the man. "Lashi Imin. I apologize."

The man laughed and reached out to pat Ferdinan shoulder but he cringed away. Panicking, stick arms protected his head. Unpleasant memories filled Jon and the man's laughter died. Concern turned into endless rounds of apology between the two, before Sora stepped in – speaking Salwrigian. Both stopped and bowed to her, saying something.

Eleven? Chocolate brown eyes darted between his big brother and his ally. Samuel would leave if Jon asked. But so many were waiting to talk to his brother...

His gaze drifted back to Ferdinan as a woman bowed to the gent, speaking in a language Jon didn't know – but Ferdinan apparently did. *Twelve? How? He only started talking a couple years ago...*

Someone bumped into Jon, apologized, and continued past to greet his brother – drawing his attention to the crowd surrounding Samuel. Having so many people nearby was comforting. For Jon.

Ferdinan had his own little crowd. Nothing like Samuel's which kept growing. The one around Ferdinan gathered a few people, but as more approached, the ones that'd been there for a while left to find other scientists to mingle with. And with each new person, Ferdinan revealed another language he shouldn't know.

Why can't I stop watching him? He didn't want to see the gent. Didn't want to remember the last year. But his eyes kept going back...

An older scientist stepped up and greeted Ferdinan in Panali. Startled, Ferdinan blushed and responded in Calbri. And Jon thought about the mob.... *Does he not know his own country's language?*

He shook his head. He was done with the gent. He didn't have to do anymore. Finally. So why couldn't he look away? Closing his eyes, Jon pressed himself against Samuel and took his big brother's hand.

"Time to go?" Samuel whispered.

"No. I just..."

Reaching a hand across Jon's shoulders, Samuel squeezed his baby brother and return to the conversation he paused.

And every time Jon's gaze drifted to the skeleton, he forced it to the sunny sky over the open ocean. Or to the jovial people around him. Or anywhere the gent wasn't.

Until he couldn't find his ally. Or Sora... Where Ferdinan had been was a crowd of healers intently focused on something.

Jon's heart raced and he looked more intently for the two, but all he found was Oya's blood red hair approaching from the balcony. *Where's Sora?* Chocolate eyes searched frantically. Moving through the crowd...searching...

On the other side of the room, he finally spotted her trapped in a corner by a small group of healers. And on the floor, huddled in a ball – shaking, retching, clutching his chest – was the skeleton. Healers poked and shoved the gent, demanding answers for his rudeness. Others stood as a wall between them and the rest of the conference.

There should've been a thought in Jon's head. Emotions, feelings... But he was numb. There were so many things he should've felt when healer Paphula grabbed Ferdinan and pulled the skeleton to standing. He should've moved – reacted – when his ally screamed. Or felt relief when the gent broke away and fled. But he didn't...

It all felt surreal. That didn't really happen; healers wouldn't do that... Not to a child... Not to anyone.

Clapping filled the room. Not the deafening roar of many hands. But the piercing sharpness of two. The rhythm was slow and steady – mocking and chiding. And the crowd that had surrounded Ferdinan stepped back uncertainly.

Wild green eyes flamed with a fury no words could describe and her signature grin was frigid. Every healer withered under it. "Harassing a dying child to tears. How noble."

Oya vanished like she always did, leaving the room confused. And trembling.

Chapter 15

How's he so fast? Even adrenaline couldn't make someone as sick as Ferdinan run like that. It made Sora worry about his heart.

Sprinting, she didn't stop until she reached Ferdinan's cabin. Broken medicine vials splattered the walls and floor. Torn bags of IV cocktails laid strewn about. And lifeless eyes stared as boney fingers ruptured another bag.

Both the sick boy and floor were drenched. Careful not to slip, Sora rushed over and grabbed his hands only to be slammed into the wall. It hurt. But she tried again – this time pinning his arms to his side with an embrace.

Stick arms burst free. And her face was crushed into the floor. *How's he so strong!?* She couldn't move and the hand pressing against her head wasn't easing.

"I never did anything to you!" His skeletal body shook. "So why...?"

Who's he talking to?

"Why?! Why can't I help?!"

Shoes she didn't recognize appeared and rushed past her. Screams erupted and a struggle ensued. But she was free. Flipping to her back, Sora took in everything as quickly as she could. Kyo Jorani was doing what she attempted – but successfully. And Ferdinan was crying out, thrashing. "Release him!"

"He'll hurt you!"

"Let go! He'll die!"

Lips tight, Jorani did as they were told. Sora caught the falling boy. His eyes were still dull and lifeless. But he wasn't fighting anymore – just staring at his hands.

"Why...? Liars. Why's it wrong?"

He's not conscious...is he? Slowly, she wrapped an arm around him while one hand smoothed his hair. "I'm so sorry. You're safe now."

Crazed green eyes appeared. Crazed and full of fire.

***

What do I do about Norger? Xhou understood Tinkerers could be frustrating, but Elbie was the easiest child around.

Was naming him Lead too much? He has nothing left at home, so... Norger did best when working; what better position than Lead to stay busy? But if Xhou was wrong...

Blowing out a breath, he leaned back. *Elbie doesn't want to do anything. Feels he's at fault.* But Norger was clearly responsible. A head injury was serious, especially for a Scientist. It was like an Artist losing an arm or an Athlete with a crippled leg.

I already let Yuyu lose full use of her hands... Ferdinan would kill him if something happened to Elbie too. If the Tinkerer didn't kill himself first. *How was Ferdinan trained?*

Xhou didn't remember much. *He was cute...* But too timid and quiet to interact with. And Xhou didn't see him much that first year...

I need to talk to Master Dæya.

***

"I've traveled the world and seen many things. But that... I'll never forget." The Kyo held the door long enough for her to enter then started cleaning. "What just happened?"

"Don't tell anyone about this."

Kyo Jorani carefully gathered broken glass and IV bags. "What do you mean?"

"He couldn't handle it. And I don't think he'll remember anyway." Sora forced the pain she was feeling out in a long, controlled breath. It felt impossible for anyone to weigh so little, but there wasn't much left of the boy. She and Jorani got him into dry clothing and laid him down in her cabin to rest...to wake up... And Oya was watching over him while they cleaned.

The Kyo studied the pile of debris they'd collected. "What do you need?"

"A mop." Walking over, she looked at the pile and carefully picked up a piece of broken vial with the label still attached. "He'll need more of this."

Reading it, piteous eyes turned to the closed door.

***

She said wait. So Ozar did. For two days. Ajulagrá kept him entertained when bored, and calm when antsy. And eventually an older woman appeared.

She wasn't particularly old, just older than him. "A hei-o, here?"

Kneeling, he kept his head low. "The Rã-yumôn sent me as a link."

"Skuna told me."

"The little one who attacked me with pebbles?" *Or the archer ready to shoot me?*

"She's protective." The woman smiled – eyes grazing over the wall of jungle surrounding them.

"I understand." Ozar shifted to sitting. "Shall we?"

She sat comfortably and they closed their eyes. Taking her hand, Ozar called out to the Rã-yumôn. When they looked, they were on the twilight beach with the girl who was too young to be a Rã-yumôn.

"Welcome."

The new village elder bowed deeply.

"What happened?" Gold flecks shone in black eyes and long black hair glowed. "I'm sorry, you're name?"

"Iona." Straightening put the woman half a foot taller than the Rã-yumôn. "Destroyers came. Tanan led the group who held them back so we could escape."

"I see." The Rã-yumôn's lip twitched.

"We're planning a new village. Considering reestablishing the camp as well." Iona threw a frown at Ozar. "We don't have time or resources for a hei-o."

"He's not staying." An eerily familiar grin stretched across delicate lips as gold flecked eyes turned on Ozar.

***

Umbacano danced in the air. It was fun watching the beautiful bird, but Elbie wanted to work. There wasn't even sun to relax in. Other than messaging Li-Nouha's parents, all he could do was wander Isolation. But besides watching the blight medicine replicate itself, it was pretty boring.

Most of the gym equipment was off-limits due to his injury, so Elbie sat watching the beautiful bird. Alone. In the empty room. Isolation was rarely busy... *Why does this place exist?*

It was larger than the island population needed and inconvenient to get to, particularly for the main medical building...

A little beak nuzzled at his cheek – breaking his train of thought. *Sorry. I didn't mean to ignore you.* But it was quiet. Too quiet to do much but stare at nothing. *I should go back to my room. It's late and at least there I can hear the rain.*

Umbacano drew his attention to an older boy walking up behind him carrying a large bag. *He looks Tuel's age...* Red filled Elbie's cheeks. *Haoyu. He doesn't have to worry this much.*

Long braids swayed as the boy walked and dark skin stood out beautifully against white walls. But he seemed nervous, stopping an unusually long distance away. "Are you bored? Would you like company?"

Smiling, Elbie motioned to the bench. "I'm sorry, I don't remember your name."

"Marcus. I'm Tuel's suitemate." Long fingers placed the bag on the floor before sitting next to Elbie.

"How can I help you?" The young Tinkerer cringed at the first words his brain latched on to.

Marcus laughed – yellow fluttering around his head unnoticed. "You're the first person to ask and it not feel condescending."

"I'm sorry..."

"Don't be." The older boy relaxed. "Would you like to paint?"

"They only said I couldn't work." Elbie gave a sheepish grin and Umbacano pecked his cheek harder than normal. Rubbing at the spot, he gently headbutted the bird. *I'll be good. I promise.* "What do you usually paint?"

"Unless it's an assignment, I paint what I feel." Tying back his braids, Marcus laid out an assortment of art supplies. "Do you know what you'd like to paint? Or do you want to play with colors?"

Mismatched eyes looked at the magnificent bird. "I know exactly what I want to paint."

"Wonderful." Marcus set up two easels and offered a palette. "Guess *I* need to decide now."

Giggling, Elbie selected a brush and a few shades of yellow. *Sorry, Umbacano. I know I can't draw you as beautiful as you are, but I think Yuyu'll love it.*

Instead of dancing around, Umbacano sat on Elbie's knee not moving – like the perfect model. It was nice not having to think or worry about anything. Yellow and orange were all over his skin and clothes, the bench and floor by the time he finished. *Wow...this looks nothing like you.* Elbie giggled.

"Done? Can I see?"

Turning the easel, he blushed. "Can you tell what it is?"

"What a fun bird. Looks like it could be the sun's brother..." Something sad washed over Marcus's face and was gone as quickly as it came.

"Can I see yours?"

Picking up the board, Marcus showed him, but kept his eyes down.

Dark blues and grays filled the space. Swashes of purples and bioluminescent greens at the bottom lifted the dark colors. And a couple light swashes of tinted white dotted the top. "It feels like I'm at the bottom of the ocean..."

Sorrow tinged the older boy's smile. "Then I did it right."

***

What...?

Ferdinan woke up in a cabin that wasn't his, lying next to a sleeping Oya. And wearing pajamas... *What did I do....?*

He remembered healers separating him and Sora... His heart thrashed and blue crystals searched the room. But it was only him and the one generous enough to call him "friend."

The time? If he missed the dance...forced Oya to miss it... But he still had energy. Searching again, he found a screen and checked. His presentation ended a couple hours ago. *I didn't miss it.*

The door opened and Sora entered – relieved when she saw him. "Good! How're you feeling?"

His head hurt and humiliation drown him. *What did I do? How do I fix it?* He searched for a solution, but he didn't know where to start...

Tears welled as he slipped his feet off the bed and onto the floor. At least his muscles weren't screaming, but he didn't know if that was because of the cocktail or of whatever the healers did to him... Muffled pain followed the irregular thrashing of his heart.

"No. Stay in bed," Sora scolded gently.

"I'm sorry..." When she tried speaking, Ferdinan interrupted. "I've no right asking..."

"You can ask me anything."

Sitting up – Ferdinan looked at Oya. *Have I seen her sleep before? How tired is she? How much have I hurt her?* "The dance... I want to give Oya a day of fun... She loves music and dancing..."

"Your heart can't take the stress. You need to rest."

"We both know...I'm not walking off this boat...so I'm going to be selfish..." Ferdinan's gaze didn't waver from the one who called him friend. "The medicine...will get me through..."

Tears rolled down Sora's cheeks, but she listened.

"I want to dance with her... I want to make her smile..."

"And the healers?"

Silence fell. His heart thrashed. Black spots came and went. His face twisted in fear and pain. It was a fight, but he painted on a resolute expression. "I'll do my best..."

***

Zephyr didn't want to see anymore, but he searched anyway. Searched. For days on his own. And nothing. *No...I'm done...*

"Are you?"

Zephyr nearly fell off the silver ribbons when the elf appeared out of nowhere – Gongie behind her.

"Thank you." The Psych bowed to the elf.

"I'll attend to my other duties." Smirk fading to a grin, she wished them luck and disappeared.

I hate you. I hate both of you. Refusing to look at the Psych, Zephyr walked away.

"It's not that direction." Gongie's voice stopped him.

"Why are you here? After what you saw?"

"I want to help, that hasn't changed."

"What's wrong with you? Helping a monster."

"Zephyr..."

~

What could Gongie say? *The truth...* "I'm selfish."

The golden Prince stepped back – head and hands shaking.

"Like you, I also need this to be over." *What's the best way to approach him? Last time didn't work. But being forceful when he's suffering...* "Let's start."

The door appeared behind Gongie and on the other side was that horrible elf.

"How do you overcome pain and sorrow?" The elf stood regal and smug on her twilight beach. Before her knelt Zephyr, naked, stub nosed blade in hand.

"Whatever it takes." The golden Prince threw his fist down and silver embedded deep in his thigh. A long sigh eased out as blood welled.

And the elf asked again.

Watching this...will he want to hurt himself more?

Gongie did what he did the other two times. He searched. His heart constricted. The desperation of a child looking for someone who'll protect them but trapped at the mercy of their monsters – hope for salvation dying... *How terribly will he interpret this one?*

Dark eyes opened and he called for Zephyr to follow. They walked – looking for that desperate child until moonlight glinted off half buried bits of mirror in twilight sand.

"I don't want to see. I don't want anyone seeing..." Pushing golden fingers into purple sand, Zephyr lifted the broken pieces.

Shadows rushed forward.

109

Tiny Zephyr being scolded when searching for help. Being bowed to when he begged to be heard or asked to play. Requests outside the scope of his duties ignored or redirected countless times. Until he stopped. Until he crafted the image of a perfect Chūzite prince.

Then came the praise. The attention. The pride. And when he dared to step beyond that image, it all went away. So he encased himself inside...all while beatings played in the distance. ignored by those who should've stopped them.

"I already know I'm selfish, demanding. I already know what happens when a protector doesn't protect. What's the point of this?" Golden hands jerked and pounded at the air.

Remembering the previous night, Gongie kept his voice cold and steady. "Do you want an answer?"

"I...!" A golden finger tapped at his chest over and over until frustrated hands clutched black hair.

"Have you considered, maybe these events shaped you into who you are?"

"My family's wonderful, they'd never build me into this," golden hands scolded. "This was me. But she knows this already. So what's the purpose?"

Does the elf have one?

Another elf appeared – watching Zephyr slide down a smooth wall to land on a bed of needles.

When she carved off his skin, the Prince relaxed – cheeks red. "To punish me."

Chapter 16

"Have you decided what you need for...everything?" Xhou placed a cup of fruit tea in front of Norger.

"That's not what you came to talk about."

"It's one of many things." Xhou took a sip and sat back. There was too much on his plate he wasn't allowed to touch. It was nerve wracking. But he could fix this, hopefully. "I know she's young, but Banick's quick to adapt, efficient, and detail oriented."

"She already agreed to take on two apprentices." Norger interrupted. "I can't ask her to learn how to mentor and Lead at the same time. I've already forced too much-"

"Ok. Not Banick." *Don't be stubborn.*

"Just say it." Pounding rain drown out Norger's frustrated growl.

"Elbie? He said it was an accident. But..." Putting his cup down, Xhou stood. "Accident or not, as mentor, you're at fault."

"I didn't do anything. He was stubborn and refusing to talk. When I asked again..." A breathy growl left the new Lead.

"The accident isn't the concerning part."

"What?"

"Elbie's complained multiple times you don't listen. He feels invisible. Incapable. Like he isn't good enough." Xhou stared at Norger. "I understand you're stressed. We're facing similar... It's not fair. Nothing about the last year and a half is."

Norger's face hardened, becoming defensive.

"I know you're a good person and an amazing mentor. But this is obviously too much for you right now. And that's ok." Xhou offered an understanding smile. "Admit it and arrange help so six new Scientists don't hate it here. Or hate themselves, 'cause that's not fair to them. And they're too young to understand."

"There's no reason for him to feel that way. If he just listened..."

"Elbie suggested Jon or Master Dæya mentor her."

"Jon won't." Norger buried his face in his hands until he was composed enough to speak. "He won't take any mentee. Which is why Banick and Irri have two, Trea will have one for a year before graduating, and I have to take on one along with the Tinkerer."

"Choose a Co-Lead. Delegate." Xhou scratched his neck. "I'm arranging a meeting with Master Dæya. Before then, come up with a plan that'll make this next year smooth for you and all the Scientists."

***

The line of silent people was unexpected. Gongie recognized a few of them, there was even a copy of himself. "I don't understand..."

Zephyr's hands shook. "You don't see their scars?"

Gongie stepped closer, studying his doppelganger. It was faint. Like it wanted to be on the surface, but was buried too deep. His eyes were gouged out... *What's this...?*

Each had a scar. They varied from person to person and some had more than one. Ferdinan's was particularly horrific. Hands mangled beyond recognition, a deep slice over his heart and a gaping mouth with no tongue... "What is this?"

Life drained from the golden Prince. "The damage I've cause their souls..."

Impossible...

Lips trembled, but hands moved calmer than expected. And Zephyr smiled. "Like you said, just being here I've damaged Ferdinan and Jon...and you."

"You haven't hurt me. Neither did I say otherwise."

"I see it every time you look at me." Golden hands moved. "A monster hurts and destroys. Without thought. Without notice. I've damaged everyone's souls."

"That's wrong." *How do I help him stop believing that?*

"It's why you won't go away." Zephyr's voice shook along with his hands. "Who wouldn't want to save their loved ones from a monster?"

Dark eyes studied the line of people. *What does this actually mean?*

***

Sora took Samuel away from him again – leaving Oya in their wake... The site of her was something to behold.

"What're you wearing?" Jon stared at the crazed redhead who was hardly dressed appropriately for bed let alone a formal dinner with dancing. Nothing fit. Nothing matched. *Who did she steal these from?*

"Pants and a shirt?" Golden brown bare feet danced around the room – bored. "Is that a problem?"

Jon ran long fingers through his hair. He had the stylist cut it shorter than normal. It felt weird, but he wanted to remove as many reminders as he could... "Dinner isn't 'come at your convenience' tonight."

Oya paused and looked at him – delicate brow raised.

Jon returned the look. *Get back soon, Samuel.* "I know you already know. You always know about anything interesting and half the ship preparing for a major event would've sparked your interest."

She gave him a giant grin. "Fair enough."

"Ferdinan's going, isn't he?" Jon folded his arms not wanting to think about the gent but needing his worries from this morning assuaged.

"It's the last thing he should do." Oya sat on the trunk she'd been given and hadn't opened. "And the last thing he wants to do."

It took a moment for Jon to weigh both meanings of her last statement. What he'd give to have Samuel here. All of his family. Jon closed his eyes and imagined the warmth of their touch and the comfort of their embrace. The joy of smooshing them. And the safety of being crowded by them. Once he was off this boat...

But looking at her... His sensibilities overwhelmed his homesick heart. "It's a formal dinner. I'll help you get ready."

Giggles spilled out of her as Oya jumped off the trunk. Opening it, she selected one random thing after another. *Is she even looking?* As quickly as she pulled garments out, he vetoed them. If she wasn't getting annoyed, Jon would've sworn she was doing this on purpose.

Pushing her aside, he looked through the neatly packaged clothing. None of it suited Oya. Not the mischievous little trickster god he knew. But there were a couple things she wouldn't fully object to. Weighing the pros and cons of each, he selected a dress and held it out to her.

She scrunched her face at him and he rolled his eyes right back. "Ferdinan would love seeing you in this. The color will magnify the brightness of your eyes without clashing with your hair. And it's much easier to move around in than many of the others."

That didn't make her happy, but she conceded and took the dress.

"Before you put it on, let's do your hair."

Delicate fingers combed through the unnatural red. "All done."

"Sit." Jon motioned her to the chair and was surprised when she obeyed. *What's she up to?* Selecting a wide hairbrush, he worked it through thick, course strands. Much thicker and courser than most hair he'd played with, but at least it wasn't fine and wispy. "Why haven't you been by his side? Seems you spent more time with me than him."

"There isn't much I can do." Oya flinched when he hit a knot. "Sora's good for him. She's the first person he hasn't outright rejected."

"He never rejected you." Not sure what to do with her hair, he kept brushing. *Maybe flowers?*

"Many times." Oya grinned at Jon. "It's a mercy I'm giving him."

"What do you mean?"

"My dear friend would feel worse if I stayed beside him calm and quiet instead of running and playing. He'd feel responsible for stealing my fun...if he didn't die trying to join me. I'd have to watch my words 'cause he wouldn't tell me 'No.'" Oya turned her gaze forward so Jon could work. "But I watch over him at night and keep his dreams safe."

What does that mean? But she didn't elaborate, so Jon studied her unevenly cut hair. Mercifully, it was long enough to braid. Chocolate brown eyes searched the room – landing on the variety of bouquets Samuel was given. "Pick a couple flowers. Ferdinan loves flowers."

Red filled his cheeks. It was true, but Jon hadn't realized he'd been thinking it. Standing, Oya spun around the room until she picked three mismatched blooms. Their only commonality was each boasted different shades of yellow. Once she sat, Jon partitioned her hair. *This short... braid each side and join in back?* A braided halo... How ill-suited to her.

The blood red hair was surprisingly easy to work with. If only Oya was the same. Jon shook his head – he'd been rude to her this entire time and that thought was even worse. *Why's it so easy to disrespect her?*

"Odd that a boy can sculpt hair with such ease," Oya teased.

"Odd? All males should learn how to care for and style hair so their children can have whatever style they want."

That earned him a giggle. "I've never seen you do this before."

"Everything that happened at the hospital and since..." Jon weaved in the first flower. It was hard thinking about this - talking about it, but she was listening and... "Everything... Ferdinan stole what time, energy, and desire I had to do anything I enjoy."

He expected a rebuke, but it never came. "Your dad taught you?"

"Dad and Ozar. It was lots of fun. I loved playing with mom's and my brothers' hair." A band and hairpin held the first braid in place so Jon could work on the second. "Ilu and Marcus let me play with their hair too. But Xingho started losing his and shaved it off. And Jingjing, Rigel, and Ilu decided it was easier to cut theirs short. At least mom, Ozar, and Marcus kept theirs longer..."

"Gongie didn't keep his hair long for you?"

The second flower weaved in easier than the first. "He's... It's a cultural thing for him - almost religious."

"Religious, huh?"

Not sure how to respond, Jon finished weaving in the third flower before finishing the braid and pinning the two ends together - tucking them so they looked like one braid.

Picking two more larger flowers... It made him cringe, but considering the lack of cohesion of the first three, Jon made sure to pick two that also didn't match. Carefully he pinned them. Unless she tried, those flowers weren't coming out.

"There were two pairs of shoes that'd match the dress-"

"No." Oya jumped up and sat on the table - grinning broadly. "I'll wear the dress. I'll keep my hair nice. But I'm not wearing shoes."

***

Raonie eased herself onto the couch next to her mother-in-law. "I thought sisters would calm her down."

Mother laughed. Evelyn reminded her of another energetic child she loved more each day. "She feeds off people's energy. Her teachers still complaining?"

"Ooo! Ooo! I know!" Evelyn's shouts made Tinny and Yin flinch.

The Chūzite teacher looked exhausted. "No shouting. And please wait 'til I've finished the instructions."

Mother smiled encouragingly.

"They are." Raonie relaxed her shoulders. "If exercise wore her out... Any suggestions?"

What ended up working for him? "Talk to Leoniel."

"Kyo? He's energetic too..." Raonie frowned.

"He's calm compared to what he used to be." Mother smiled; those were tiring days. "She'll be impossible once she realizes what 'Oza' is."

"Mama! Mother! Listen to what I learned!" Evelyn dashed over. The young girl recited an old North Chūzite poem near perfectly. Getting those sound combinations right was impressive. "Did you know-"

"Lady Evelyn. I appreciate you're excited, but the lesson isn't over. If you're joining, you need to stay 'til the end."

"What?! No! I'm coming!" Evelyn ran - sliding the last few inches into place. "Sorry. I'm listening!"

Mother didn't mean to snort, but she couldn't hold back the laugh. "Always having people lined up to talk...she'd never stop going."

"I'll call Leoniel."

***

Am I capable of helping him? He wanted to fix this. Wanted life to be calm and safe for Jon. For the suffering to end.

At least checking on Elbie was easy. Opening the door to the middle student's gym, Gongie thanked the Energist and walked in. Something formless but undeniably yellow flitted past his mind. *What was that?*

Metallic fingers and circuitry he couldn't hope to understand danced around in various configurations - meshing with one kind of fabric after another only to be discarded and another paired. *The Tinkerer's creation process...* It wasn't often he experienced this, but it was amazing.

Shiny black hair swayed above an unusual sized screen. Excitement and thoughts of Yuyu flitted between creating. *Where's Tuel?*

Everything vanished. *How does he and Yuyu do this?* It taxed them, but they were the only non-Mind Talkers who could silence their minds.

"Am I troubling you?"

Mismatched eyes focused on him as the boy shook his head.

"May I visit while I wait for my friend?"

Elbie nodded.

Walking over, he sat facing the boy. "What're you working on?"

"What happened to Master Ferdinan?"

Gongie grimaced. *Where are you, Tuel?* "There was an accident. Jon and Oya were hurt, but Ferdinan saved them and got them medical care. They're with Jon's brother now."

"How badly?"

It was strange having a conversation with a perfectly controlled mind. Most people had random thoughts and feelings come and go. Oya...didn't exist. But Elbie was there without anything slipping past. "Jon needed minor care. Oya's leg was crushed, but is ok now."

"Good." Mismatched eyes turned to the screen as Elbie leaned his head against that formless yellow... "I'm glad. She's weird, but she cares about him."

"He cares about her too." Gongie searched for the late midday shadow. "She's the only person I've seen him care for."

Irritation flared. And indignation. "Master Ferdinan cares about everyone."

Regret hit when Gongie realized what he said. "I apologize. He cares deeply for his apprentices too."

"No. He cares about everyone. Helps everyone he can." Elbie didn't suppress his disappointment. "A Telepath should know that."

"I apologize. Guess I'm projecting my own struggles."

"Oh?"

Burdening a young child... But their conversation was interesting. And Gongie wondered how long Elbie could maintain this precise control. "I'm finding it difficult to help some people."

"If you don't help them for them, you won't get far."

This is a young child, right? "Thank you." A familiar mind finally arrived – apologizing.

"Here you are! I thought we were meeting at the younger student's gym. Sorry..."

Giggles filled the air and that yellow weaved through Gongie's mind again. *What* is *that?*

"Elbie? How are you?" Tuel patted the young boy's back.

Elbie flinched and Gongie gasped...nearly screamed. It felt like he was being torn in half. And Elbie... A million thoughts and possibilities filled the young boy's mind – making the Psych dizzy and nauseous.

"Are you ok?" Tuel leaned in, but his worry only made it worse. "Gongie?"

Everything vanished. Everything but Tuel's panicking.

"I'm sorry. I need to go." Elbie gathered his screen and bag and ran to the door – stopping at the wall of water. Sheepishly he turned back. "Um..."

Sorry, Gongie. Thank you for trying. Tuel flew over to the boy. "Where to?"

"Master Ferdinan's lab."

"Ok!" Opening the door, Tuel parted the water for them. *I'll be back to get you.*

"Thanks..." *What was that sensation?* Whatever it was, it took a while for Gongie to see straight again.

Chapter 17

What if the healers attacked? Nausea hit and his heart thrashed. He really wasn't walking off this boat. *I won't be a blight any more...*

Breathing deep, Ferdinan forced himself to calm down. It was fine if he didn't wake up tomorrow as long as Oya had fun tonight. Checking his message to Grandpa Huey, the skeleton made sure each contingency sounded innocuous. Next, he released the data, research, and details of his experiments into secure accounts for Yuyu and Elbie.

Composing the message though... If it was only Yuyu it'd be simple enough. But Elbie... Ferdinan rigged cradles and blankets so the tiny infant could be comforted without being hurt. Taught the toddler to walk and talk and basic life skills. Watched as Elbie went from unable to roll over to inventing things that shouldn't be possible...in only seven years...

How did he phrase this to sound like a reward and not a farewell?

Yuyu, Elbie

You've both far surpassed my expectations and myself. Watching your growth has been amazing. You've more than earned full access to my lab and all my resources. Blow are two of my most trusted contacts' information and their specialties. They've done more for me than I can list. I've also messaged them about you so they'll know to look for when you reach out to them in the future. I can't wait to see what you do next.

Ferdinan didn't know how to end the message, so he left it like that and scheduled it to be sent in a week.

A beep announced he had a half-hour to finish getting ready. Even with the medicine he doubted he'd last the entire night, so Samuel and Jon took her to the dinner and he'd arrive for the music. Besides, the less time he was there, the fewer opportunities for the healer to hurt him again. As long as they didn't hurt Oya...

Oya... A small smile twitched on his thin, blue lips and he grabbed a hair brush. Hopefully she wasn't pestering Jon too much.

Each sweep of the brush released a troubling amount of hair. It'd become so thin... But that didn't matter. Tying it back... Nearly colorless crystals stared at his reflection. At the pathetic monster staring back. *How does she stand being around me?*

But it didn't matter. Tonight wasn't about him. Grabbing the second vial, Ferdinan injected an extra dose into the IV port. Uncomfortable pressure proceeded irritating cold before the medicine dispersed inside him. Looking at the little tube was surreal, but it was inserted too deep to pull out, so he tucked it carefully under his shirt and finished dressing.

The door opened as Ferdinan buttoned the vest and Sora entered – beautiful as always. A pale orange dress fit her body perfectly and made her rich skin glow. Intricate braids wrapped around each other before cascading down her back. "Musicians are setting up."

Latching the last button on his jacket, Ferdinan slipped on dance shoes. *I look atrocious.* A horrifying monster in a suit. But Oya wouldn't care. "Thank you."

Dread and butterflies and hammers attacked in waves as they approached the ballroom, but Sora's smile helped him keep moving.

Notes sang, were adjusted, and sang again. And a tune he recognized started. It sounded different played live on appropriate instruments, but it was the song a younger Scientist selected for the show. And it was presented as a group dance...

In the center of the room Oya spun – watching the skirt of her dress flare out. It barely qualified as a formal dress but was fancier than anything he expected. A beautiful blend of purples and blues wrapped around her, flowing like a waterfall. A crown of yellow flowers floated in her beautifully braided hair. She looked like the Queen of fairies.

Exotic green eyes landed on him and her wild grin grew. Bare golden-brown feet ran up... *Is there any way to get her to wear shoes?*

Though he smiled at her, colorless crystal scanned the room for threats. But the closest was Samuel and he was half a room away. Enough space to escape...

"*I'm glad you're feeling better.*" Oya's grin didn't waver, but her eyes betrayed the truth she knew.

"*The dress suits you. Did Samuel do your hair or Jon?*" Ferdinan guided her to the dance floor when the opening song started. It was a traditional start to every conference. Once it ended, the dance would begin.

"*Jon.*" Oya skipped and spun – sometimes walking backwards and sometimes beside him until they claimed a less crowded spot of floor. "*How many other random skills does he have?*"

Moonlight glittered off the ocean's surface, making it look purple against the black diamond sky.

"*All North Oueshian males are trained early in domestic skills,*" Ferdinan smirked at her. "*Even being the baby didn't get him out of it.*"

She giggled.

"*But since he enjoys it…*" Ferdinan shook his head, not wanting to think about how much he disrupted those joys for his ally.

Wild green eyes fixed longingly on the ocean surrounding him then darted to the musicians. And it was nice. Standing near her. The comfort of her presence. Her unique beauty. He could look at her all night.

Moonlight made her golden-brown skin glow – clashing with her blood red hair. *She's beautiful…* But staring was rude, so he turned his gaze to the ocean. Energy was still building inside him; the full force of the medicine was coming to bear. "Would you like to dance?"

Inhuman green eyes tripled and excitement radiated at him. He recognized this tune too. It was the one Yuyu chose.

Dozens of instruments swelled together brilliantly.

Ferdinan smiled but flinched when her perfect void swallowed his hand. He took her waist and they floated. Just like the improvised dance they enjoyed during the Family Week show. Only, this time, he led. And she moved as if they'd practiced it a million times. Whenever room opened up, he spun her. And she laughed! The most beautiful laugh and as warm as the sun… And when he lifted her, she giggled.

Nothing existed but her perfect void and expert notes quickly winding down… But that was fine. There'd be another song. And another. He'd give her every dance he could.

Even when she stole a violin, he played without apology. All her favorites. Ones with energy she could jump and spin and kick to. No one knew what to do with them and he didn't care. This night was for her.

***

He won't stop. Her dear friend was panting and couldn't stand up straight anymore, but he kept offering songs and dances. If this wasn't what he wanted, she would've ended it a while ago. So she laughed and danced! But he couldn't take anymore. *Will I fail?*

Śarī-a's heir was with Ozar. If the girl found the host soon…

Taking the pilfered violin, she returned it to its owner then told Ferdinan she was done. His smile...it was sad and grateful and happy. And apologetic.

She took his offered hand and walked out with him. Boney fingers were cold – colder than hers – and she felt every knob of phalanges. Giving her best grin, she chattered about nothing and he returned in kind as they walked random halls, slowly descending through the ship.

Or not so random. Ferdinan stopped and opened a door to a much smaller ballroom than the one they left. It was empty save for a small table and chairs sitting on the balcony. An artistic array of fruits and drinks were laid out beautifully. *He planned this.*

She looked up at him – up at his apologetic smile. Grinning, she dragged him to the little table.

"*Your playing was wonderful!*" Oya grabbed something red she never seen before. It was small and didn't need to be peeled. "*You're impressive considering how long it's been since you played.*"

Pink flooded his cheeks. "*I apologize.*"

"*The violin is to use as you need.*" A strange combination of sweet and bitter and tart attacked her tongue and scrunched her face. This red fruit would take getting used to, but it was good. "*Which one's your favorite?*"

Ferdinan paled and looked away, but not for long. Bony blue fingers selected a purple fruit that look like a giant drop of water. Within moments it was peeled and offered to her. "*Careful, it's sour.*"

Though the skin was purple, the inside was yellow with red seeds. And it was impressively sour. Her face twisted as the fruit's meat paralyzed her briefly. "*That's quite the...*"

An unexpected sound caught their attention. Ferdinan was on his feet. The entirety of Oya's soul commanded Û-ya'ïn before her brain interpreted what she saw.

Strength seeped from her, but the water obeyed. She couldn't see it – but Ferdinan's expression said it all.

I'll hold him for you.

How many eyes are watching that Û-ya'ïn wouldn't lift him? The Rã-yumôn could demand it do so, if she had the energy to command it. Her body was already ten times heavier and her knees half as strong.

122

Ferdinan was across the room by the time she retrieved her shell dagger. Winking at the orbs, she sliced the strings lacing her dress. Energy filled her and both the dress and orbs fell to the floor.

Bare feet leapt to the top of the railing and pushed off. And she flew...fell... Until Û-ya'ïn embraced her, gradually slowing her dissent and lifting her to the surface next to the child. *How many layers is he wearing?* Û-ya'ïn was the only reason Kaz was floating.

Why's he unconscious?

You were slow to command me.

There was sound above, but it was too far away to understand. Grinning, she flicked her wrists...and nothing happened. *Oh yah...he deactivated them on the train...*

Ok... Alien eyes searched for a solution, but the ship was too big to see more than a portion. *A floating island with no beach...*

He's not breathing.

As if descended from heaven, a soft ladder fell into view. But not close enough to reach, especially while carrying an unconscious child in soaked clothing. *Thank you for answering, old friend. Can you lift us to the bottom rung? No one should see.*

Slowly the water swelled and they drifted toward the side of the boat. Delicate hands grabbed it, then maneuvered the boy onto her shoulder. The fight up the rungs quickly drained the energy the orbs gave her. A ten-year-old in wet clothing was *heavy.* But she kept going because it was the only thing she could do.

Thank you, old friend. Once we're safe, return to the Jinku.

Û-ya'ïn's warmth filled her – and its anxiety. Alien eyes searched... Whether it was the darkness or terrible luck, the flat surface of the hall was all she could see. The ladder shook far more than it should... *What?*

From the shadows Ferdinan's feet appeared. One stick arm wrapped around her while the other took Kaz from her shoulder. He didn't say anything, but his face was warped in pain and he struggled to breathe. But he didn't hesitate. He simply climbed – confident she'd follow.

More than once he stopped – desperately clinging to the ladder and Kaz before moving again. *He's so fast.* Anyone else in Ferdinan state would've died months ago. The things he did to himself, the medicines he created, couldn't keep him this long past his expiration. But he wasn't just a Tinkerer. *Could being a Fighter....?* Oya would have to study them more closely when she returned to the islands. If she returned.

Too many times Ferdinan stopped, gasping for air. But he forced himself to keep going. Once it looked like he was going to lose consciousness. And she knew...

Samuel avoided Ferdinan for Ferdinan's sake. But that wasn't an option anymore. Closing her eyes, she reached out to the man and told his heart he wanted nothing more than to come to the lower ballroom. Anchoring that desire in place, she returned to climbing.

By the time Oya reached the top, boney hands were pulling her up. She moved toward the unconscious boy, but Samuel and another were fighting to get Kaz breathing and Ferdinan...wasn't beside her. Spinning...

A skin wrapped jumble of bones laid slumped against the railing. The few lighted strings connected to his chest were fading. But she made three promises. Neither would she accept failing any of them without giving everything. Even if it meant twisting a charge's purpose.

Sitting beside her dear friend, she took his cold bony hand and closed her eyes. The orbs were exhausted and so was she. But they gave what was left of them. *Shēnó!* All the light drained out of her and more.

She sat on the twilight beach, Mr. Charlie and his charge facing her.

"Two children'll die." She addressed Shēnó directly. For a long time the lighted figure stared at her and she freely offered her mind because it was faster than talking. Faster than arguing.

He needs Śarī-a. But I can help the other.

"If Śarī-a was an option, I would've already called for it." Oya's statement made Mr. Charlie uncomfortable. Of all the charges to lose... "I don't expect you to heal him. Just do for him what you did for me so Samuel could heal my leg. Just give him life long enough to find Śarī-a."

That's a terrible thing to do to one who's suffered so much.

"I know."

Chapter 18

Samuel wanted to do this years ago. The first time Ferdinan almost starved to death. And again, the second. But his little brother refused and the Samultz denied their pleas to provide the care the boy needed.

The incision was small. Inserting and anchoring the tube was simple. This barely skirted propriety, but Samuel didn't care – saving lives mattered more than arbitrary rules. *Please don't be too late.*

If he could stay... These next few days would be extremely delicate for a regular human, but Ferdinan's mutations... How much to give and how often was guesswork. Making adjustments would be simple if he didn't leave, but if Ferdinan woke up while he was here...

Neither was it fair to Jon. The breathing exercises helped with the panic, but didn't stop it. Neither did they prevent the nightmares...

Don't die. Securing the cap, Samuel taped the tube to Ferdinan sunken abdomen. Last, he restrained those impossibly thin arms so his little brother couldn't tear the tube out.

Then there was Oya. No matter how he tried, he couldn't scan her. She was always a picture book. But since she was breathing and her vitals look fine, he convinced himself she was exhausted.

Double checking the neural blocker, Samuel inserted the first bit of formula. *A diode. I'll monitor him remotely and send instructions to Sora if there's a problem.* This way he wouldn't have to leave Jon alone...

Jon was right. Ferdinan stole me away again. Because that's how it always happened. Because the skeleton's needs were more severe. And because the child had no one else.

Dark eyes stayed fixed on the neural blocker and his ears perked for alarms.

***

Why is there another Tinkerer? Why're they so stubborn? So willful? And Jon! That spoiled child! Couldn't even do his part!

Stopping, the new Lead let out a slow breath before entering the reception area. Ms. Radery greeted him and he sat patiently until Master Dæya appeared, but the man didn't call him in. Instead, Dæya gestured to follow him outside. Down the beach. Way down. In pouring rain and gusting winds to a bunker tucked inside a hidden cave...

They were drenched and exhausted when they reached the natural shelter. A hidden path led past the bunker and branched multiple times. "Remember the confidentiality you agreed to before becoming Lead."

"Yes, sir."

"Good. Xhou didn't need to know since Lord Ferdinan took care of everything. Neither is he privy to this information now." Hematite eyes shone in the dim light. "Li-Nouha is the last Tinkerer born, so your successor won't be informed either."

That was...uncomfortable to hear. "I understand."

"No one knows how Lord Ferdinan trained Yuyu and Elbie. He was quite protective – wouldn't let anyone near them for their first year."

"Why?"

"I wish I understood him enough to guess." Dæya shrugged and continued past another branch. "Tinkerers before them were trained using a device developed specifically for their brains."

Disgust twisted Norger's face. "Excuse me?"

"Consider what you know about them."

"I won't desecrate a child." Norger turned but Dæya stopped him. "I don't know how I'll do everything, but I'm not defiling her brain."

"Imagine being trapped inside your mind. No matter how much you need to connect, no matter how hard you try. You're an ethereal being of immense intelligence trapped inside a broken machine." Polished hematites grew hard. "No escape. Imprisoned 'til death."

That...doesn't sound real. "There aren't many Tinkerers, but it's still cruel condemning them to a life like that." The man's gaze locked Norger in place – mind held tight. "Given the choice, which would you choose?"

Loneliness grew, twisting into desperation, and mutating into agony. Gentle cries for help became horse screams then mad ravings. And pain. Every kind imaginable. Blades and fire and tearing skin. Gouged eyes and dissolving bones. Norger held his own intestines, but there were no wounds. Universes crushed him. Multiverses of wonder and possibility trapped in this endless emptiness. Becoming heavier and heavier...

Stop. Stop! Let me out!

Cave surrounded him again and Norger was sick.

"Is saving someone from that a desecration?"

Catching his breath, he spit out the remnants of breakfast and acid. "Whose mind was that?"

"Someone who was never freed."

"I'm listening."

They continued down the hall to a locked door. Inside was a large room. A dozen bands with oval nodules hung on one wall and five boxes were lined up neatly. On the other side was a screen, a bio monitor, and a tiny bed. Aside from the screen, the tech was old and covered in dust.

"Bringing a child here would terrify them."

"It'll be moved to Isolation as needed. There's another storage with backups." The man turned serious. "Don't ever wear these, they're designed for Tinkerers. If a non-Tinkerer wore one... The damage..."

Norger flinched as the man shuttered.

"They'll react negatively for a few weeks, but calm down once they realize what it's doing for them. After, they stop complaining." At Norger's raised brow, Dæya explained, "Like any chore, a child'll fight 'til they get used to it. But Tinkerers are stubborn, so it can take a while."

True.

"Don't waver." Dæya waited for Norger's full attention. "It'll feel dramatic 'cause she can't speak. She'll scream. Like Ferdinan, she might become violent. But that's how they communicate 'this isn't something I'm used to' or to assert their dominance through obstinance."

"Why continue if it causes distress?"

"A total of three Tinkerers didn't complete the training." Picking up a screen, he handed it to Norger. "The first two died at their own hand before graduating. The last I've been fighting to keep alive for thirteen years."

***

Nanobots were fascinating. Their self-replicating property gave Elbie plenty to test too. *I wish Master Ferdinan was here, he could teach me faster.* Elbie couldn't imagine making these from scratch. *Will they work with the skeletal structure or do I need to redesign it?*

Mismatched eyes drifted to the carbon printer. Umbacano sat next to it watching as well. *Start simple.* A month wasn't much time to teach himself new information and skills, but he didn't have classes while the younger students were gone and the rains kept him trapped inside.

Yellow fluttered over to peck at the cylinder of nanobots and black eyes stared at him. *I should program them with something simple to see how much I understand.* Elbie rubbed Umbacano's head. *It feels so real.* Yuyu's skills were impressive. "How should I test them?"

The beautiful bird looked at Elbie and chirped – surprising him.

"You...make sound?"

This time the bird chittered and whistled. *She programed bird calls into it?* But something was off... "What are you?"

Soon, little one.

What was I...? The subtle movements of the carbon printer caught his eye. He was doing something... Happy chirps sang out – dancing joyously in the air. Elbie walked over to watch the printer. The first gem was printed. His project was officially done. This one was for his sister.

Watching the carbon printer was calming after frustrating sessions with Norger. If only it eased his worries about Li-Nouha. *What did Master Ferdinan do for us?* There were things they vaguely remembered... Planning for her arrival was difficult without knowing–

Stunning yellow fluttered around the room – dancing and weaving. Elbie laughed and petted the bird when it landed on his shoulder. "We want her to not be trapped. But I doubt she's free."

Jumping from his shoulder, the bird landed on the table – chirping...conversationally... *What a strange robot.*

"According to Xhou and the instructors, Ferdinan didn't talk 'til shortly before Yuyu arrived. None of the older Tinkerers talk..."

That wasn't quite true. Yuyu's mom spoke a little, but not until after Yuyu started school. "Why're we born trapped?"

Bright yellow hopped over to nuzzle his fingers.

A million possibilities filled his mind, but there was no shape or coherency. If he could make a device to help all Tinkerers past this... That required information he didn't have access too, but within those possibilities, that knowledge existed. He just had to find it.

***

How? Golden hands flew. "I don't understand. How do you find them so effortlessly?"

"I search for you." The Psych looked over the sea of Zephyrs surrounding them. Seemed there was one for every day he'd been alive.

"You're not telling me so I can't get rid of you." Hands clenched into fists and onyx eyes closed. *Why am I doing this?*

Reaching down, Zephyr grabbed the shards. Every copy of himself lined up as shadows appeared. Bowing. Paying homage. Praising their Prince and future ruler. Praise for his existence. His accomplishments. His words. Big and little things. Pointless and important....

There were so many... Citizens, strangers, peers... Even Denila...

Then came the march of his family. Mom. Dad. Rutoric. Aunt Tenalia. The Duchess. Cousins. North Chūzites and Grasslanders of various relations.

"The hope of our future."

"Continue improving and you'll be a fine General."

"Wonderful as always, my Prince."

"As expected from my heir."

"You'll make a great General."

"Already showing aptitude to rule, impressive."

Countless praises marched around, growing grander as he aged.

Gongie's face twisted with pity.

They deserve a real son, nephew, heir. A monster doesn't deserve family.

The shadows were still greeting his younger selves, but Zephyr understood. Spinning, he returned to the silver roads. "That's enough."

"Zephyr–"

Golden fingers thrashed at the air. "I don't need to see a continual repeat to understand."

Worry tainted the Psych's voice. "What do you understand?"

"I don't deserve family."

Gongie stopped him. "That's not-"

Flinging the younger boy away, the Prince's hands flew. "Monsters don't get to have a family! That's what this is. I've been poisoning them from the beginning."

"Zephyr..."

"Don't worry." Grabbing the Telepath's shoulder, Zephyr guided Gongie to the silver roads. "I never loved them; I wouldn't have become this if I had."

***

Trapped in the darkness. Boney fingers pressed against an invisible wall. *What's happening? Samuel would never keep me asleep this long...* But if he didn't break out this time, he could finally die. Finally...

"Giving up?"

He wanted to. Forced into unconsciousness while they did untoward things to his body...refusing to let him die. All so he could hurt more people...

Emil sneered in disgust. "Guess you finally get what you want. What you've always wanted."

"Why is that wrong?"

Emil bristled, scowling. "You'll never earn it."

"I know." Stick limbs drifted to sitting - too tired to care anymore. "But everyone else will be safe. Will be free."

Emile grabbed Ferdinan's shirt - fist held high, jaw twitching. Slowly, he let go. "It doesn't matter, you'll be forced to wake up soon."

Chapter 19

Ozar smiled at the girl sprawled out on the ground. "Comfortable?"

"I watch the birds now." Skuna waved him away.

"Perfect. I tell you the story of Śarī-a now."

"*Shush.* Birds."

Laying down, he joined her silent birdwatching. There weren't many, but the breeze was perfect. The Hei-O was starting to doze...

"Why would I take Śarī-a? Tanan was killed 'cause they were its guardian."

"A guardian's priority is keeping the charge safe. I don't know what changed that for Tanan."

"Why you?" Skuna stretched, returning to bird watching. "A hei-o."

"The Rã-yumôn sent me. I don't want any more charges lost. I was the closest." Ozar sighed. "I'm not sure. It was surprising being called with the other guardians to help Iinamī's new heir. I didn't know we'd met. But without Śarī-a there'll be countless unnecessary deaths."

Hazel eyes turned on him – delving deep inside his soul. Light glinted off the many rods in her ear. "Someone you love'll die."

Faces filled his mind and Ajulagrá sorrowed alongside him for those with limited futures. "At least three I love. Two *you* love."

"Ok." Sitting up, she got comfortable. "Tell me Śarī-a's story."

***

Straps held stick limbs and a band across his chest kept Ferdinan from hurting himself as he thrashed. Begging, screaming. Until he passed out from the strain.

Tears blurred his frail body – gasping desperately for air and too exhausted to shiver. Pulling the covers back in place, Sora gave a silent plea of her own. *Please stay asleep...* Chūzo's Master provided the best equipment and medicines – but Samuel and the Master healer...

"It's cruel doing this to a child." Kyo Jorani frowned, offering the neural blocker. "This is far more humane."

Sora didn't disagree. The royal family knew Ferdinan his whole life, but... Hematite eyes fell on the neural blocker. Tying down a dying child instead of keeping him comfortably sleeping...? A chime sounded.

Time for the next dose of formula. *I'm sorry, Samuel, but this is too harsh.* Taking the blocker, she placed it on the dying boy while the Kyo prepared the syringe. Taking it, Sora slipped it into the tube protruding from his lower abdomen. *They said they love him, so why do something so cruel? Why does Samuel insist we can't keep the blocker on him?* Every time he woke up... The screams. The pleading... It was too much.

Kyo Jorani sat and took her hand. "Rest. I'll watch over him."

If they weren't a Kyo, Sora would've declined. It felt like she and Samuel were being pushed away from Ferdinan more each day.

"I'll be in the adjoining room." Picking up her screen, she sent a call request and teared up at the immediate response. A sorely missed face appeared. Brown eyes with specks of green smiled excitedly until seeing her distress. They'd been together since childhood – there was no hiding anything. Which was one of many things she loved about Kinni.

"My love, what's wrong?" Long hair fell forward as Kinni leaned in.

Sora sat back and smiled at her beloved. "I wanted to hear your voice and see your beautiful face."

Kinni smiled softly. "I'll talk to the end of eternity for you."

***

"Thank you for your help." Herrard smiled and bowed to Mother Artimus, Xhou following suit beside him.

Mother's smile was strained. "You're addressing countries' needs to educate their people on edible vegetation in their regions?"

"That's a primary focus." Herrard glanced at Xhou. He didn't envy his island brother. "Please inform us if Ozar's able to reach Mundan."

"I will." Long fingers combed through thick, black curls. "However, Samuel might not be able to help with the Grasslands."

Xhou paled. "We need him..."

"Contact Am'ria. She's a native and has kept her ties strong."

"Won't that be viewed as a conflict?"

"By at least five countries." Mother gave an apologetic smile.

***

"Samuel!" Color and flare cheered. "It's been too long."

"It has." The Healer's face was grim. "Let me start by apologizing."

"Anything you need, speak." Samuel's tale was heartbreaking. *He was so sick at the hot springs...* Knowing Ferdinan had gotten worse...

"The Master healer isn't listening. He and Kyo Jorani are keeping me away from him too. If the Master claims him..." Samuel's face twisted. "He'll die alone and be buried by people who don't want him."

"He always has sanctuary in my home." A strand of lavender hair fell forward. "I'll talk with Jorani to see what they're doing."

Pain Samuel held in broke free. It took a bit to continue, and his words were terribly strained. "Thank you."

"Send me instructions for what he'll need when he gets here."

Samuel nodded but Leoniel didn't end the call. The exhausted Healer needed a reprieve, so he listened until something crashed in an adjacent room and a frustrated scream shattered the peace.

***

Norger? Jon stared at the call request. He didn't want to talk to the Lead, but he needed something other than the gent to think about. Or the darkness lingering in the distance.

"Jon Dinta. Thank you for responding."

Jon studied the incredibly handsome boy – certain what this call was about. "How can I help you?"

"I need to discuss your apprentice for next block so you have time–"

"No." Jon interrupted. "I already said no."

There was a moment of silence while Norger fought back whatever he was feeling. "It's your duty. You should've taken–"

"No." Jon interrupted again. "I can't."

"Banick and Irri are taking two. Trea's taking one for a year, even though it's unfair to a new student." Strain shook Norger's voice. "If you don't do your part, I'll have to take on two as well. I already have one, am Lead, and have a province I'm trying to put back together."

"I can't." Chocolate eyes looked nervously at the failing daylight. "I'm not well."

"You look fine. Stop being selfish and lazy. It's wrong to burden the rest of us 'cause you refuse to do your part."

Guilt and heat and the desire to scream welled up. "Giving a mentee a sick mentor isn't fair to them or whoever has to keep filling in."

"I'm not Xhou. I can't do it all. If you don't do your part..." Whatever vitriol was on Norger's tongue, the older boy swallowed it back. "I need you to do your duty."

"I can't. And it sounds like you need to say the same." Jon closed the box before Norger could argue more. Confusion and frustration and rage. Helplessness. Uselessness. So many things exploded inside him.

It wasn't fair! This wasn't his job! Or responsibility! He didn't ask for this! He didn't agree to it!

And it kept building, burning hotter, expanding beyond his body's capacity to contain it! Screaming, he threw the screen against the wall. He was so filled with white hot fire and limitation! It hurt! And he hated it all! He hated it all! He wanted it all to end!

And it just kept building. His throat was raw and his knees hurt. And he couldn't contain it. It was too much. Too big. Too painful.

Arms wrapped around him and it slowly faded. Leaving him with nothing but tears. Shifting, he grabbed hold of Samuel – burying his face in his big brother's chest.

***

Iona handed Ozar Skuna's bag. "We expect her back safely."

"I promise. The Rā-yumôn'll contact you once they've met."

Kneeling, Iona hugged the girl. "Don't cause too much trouble."

They had a short conversation in the language Ozar wasn't allowed to learn, then Skuna led them to the caves and out the other side.

"Now we're in your world."

Ozar smiled. "Then I'll lead."

Chapter 20

It was quiet. And boring. But Oya's vigilance didn't waver. Not when the man came to inject stuff into the belly tube and replace the neural blockers when they flashed red. Nor when Kyo Jorani had a contentious conversation with another Kyo. She simply watched. Because no matter how much she wanted to play or move or be nosy, she needed to be ready. The moment Śarī-a's host was found...

But it was mind-numbing... And Ferdinan's beeping screen was too tempting after days of nothing. She should leave it alone. But she was bored and her dear friend wouldn't be answering anytime soon.

Delicate fingers tapped on the screen – revealing a call request from Elbie. Propping it against the wall, she accepted the call.

Mismatched eyes widened in surprise, then concern, and a beautiful yellow bird landed on his shoulder. Rain pounded on the window behind him. "Hi Oya. Is Master Ferdinan there?"

Hello, Umbacano. Your impulsivity caught me off guard. "He is, but he's not well."

I've waited two generations. He's the one I want.

The young child chewed his lip before determination hardened his face. "I want to see him."

I don't object. Elbie's a good choice. "He's incapable of consenting..." Oya let the consequences linger unspoken – curious what the boy would choose.

"I understand, but I want to see him anyway." His eyes sharpened and his gaze held steady. "I deserve to know. I need to know...and for more than just me."

Good answer. Oya grinned and moved the screen so Elbie could see him. And she watched. Watched as those mismatched eyes took in the sight of someone near death. Someone the child considered a father. Or the closest thing Elbie knew to one.

A myriad of expressions flashed across the boy's face. Sometimes his lips twitched or his eyebrows knit together. At times his entire face twisted and his lips moved as if begging for another truth. Tears slowly clouded the boy's eyes until they fell. Over and over, he swallowed – searching for his voice. The entire time, Umbacano nuzzled Elbie's cheek or pressed against his neck. "How long?"

I'm sorry. "If everything goes right, decades. They might even get him over a hundred."

Elbie dried his face but a tear escaped. "Is everything going right?"

"It never does." Oya propped up the screen again. "I'll do all I can 'til the end. I wish I could give him comfort without hurting him."

"You..." Elbie hesitated. Even when he made up his mind, he delayed by drying his face again. "The top of his head. It won't hurt him if you touch him there."

"Ah..." Oya nodded and gave the boy a comforting grin. "He's never flinched when I touched his head."

Mismatched eyes grew distant and increasingly haunted.

"Why did you call? I'm not Ferdinan, but I'll help with what I can."

"I've been worried. No matter how many times I've tried... No one's heard anything from him. And..." Elbie looked down at his hands and the tears flowed again. "I received an automated message from him. He gave me access to all his research and inventions. All his contacts and passwords. He gave me everything."

This made Oya pause. *He executed his own will...*

"Don't tell him that's why I called."

"What would you like me to tell him?" Inhuman green eyes turned to her unconscious friend. *He's crying...* Tears slowly leaked from closed eyes and that pale bluish skin was growing ashen. She wasn't sure what was happening, but it looked like Ferdinan's body was tensed as well and a tiny red light on the blocker blinked angrily. *What's happening...?*

"I know what my next project's going to be... My next projects."

"Oh? What are they?" Oya grinned bigger. *They're already inventing together...? Good job, Yuyu.*

Though shaking, Elbie managed a smile before telling her all about his idea for gloves to give Yuyu back the fine motor control and dexterity she lost. When she asked about others, he gave a genuine, though sorrowful, smile. "I don't know if it's possible."

"Now you have to tell me." Her grin grew and she leaned in.

"I want to make touch normal for us." Mismatched eyes grew brighter and the yellow bird on Elbie's shoulder danced. "There's a new Tinkerer who'll be coming. I want to give Yuyu and her a normal life. I want us to know what comfort is."

If only the adults were so noble. "You'll do it. I know you will."

Silence fell and Elbie paled. Umbacano nuzzled his cheek, but it didn't make his smile any less sad. "I might not be able to."

"Why wouldn't you?"

"The information I need is improper." Little hands rubbed the bird's head. "Anything that'd allow me to collect it would be forbidden."

How opportune... If she failed, having Kámua already connecting to another... *Kámua. will you help him and Umbacano?*

There was a long pause. *If I can.*

Umbacano, watch over them both?

Anything for the Rã-yu and my guardian.

Oya grinned. Elbie wasn't ready to be a guardian, but he'd be easy to train. "Adherence to propriety is the source of all of society's ills."

"I see why Master Ferdinan likes you." A flickering light appeared next to the yellow bird and Elbie's hesitant smile became determined. "I think I'll study the materials he sent. There were tons of articles..."

"Happy creating." Her grin brightened. *Come back when I call, Kámua. Enjoy your time with him.*

***

"You don't understand his needs. He'll die." Samuel bit at the Master healer behind the door.

Jon slid to the floor – resting his head in his hands. He was so tired. This was the last place he wanted to be, but since he couldn't stand being alone, he waited in the hall between Ferdinan's sickroom and the office his big brother and the Master healer were arguing in.

"If *you* understood, he wouldn't be suffering like this."

They went back and forth, arguing needs, nationality, and neglect. And Jon wanted it all to stop. *If he'd finally die this would be over!*

Shock and self-loathing hit hard. *Do I really want Ferdinan to die...?* He searched, but every thought and truth led to that being the only solution to everything wrong in his life. And he hated it. But... *I need this to be over. I need everything to stop...*

Where's Oya? This was the perfect time for her to sow whatever chaos. To make him feel guilty for feeling these terrible things and point him to a solution he hadn't seen. To somehow stop what was happening. But...even she was powerless next to one of the Five. Even Oya had to recognize she was nothing next to the ruler of a continent. And Jon...

If he could go into that room and relinquish all claim he and his family had for the gent, he would. Because he needed this to be over.

"Are you ok?" That voice was young and held the trepidation Jon was fighting.

A boy around Yuyu's age stared down. Even the child's casual wear showed his rank. Shifting to knees, Jon bowed forward. "Thank you for your concern. I'm fine."

"I'm not."

That wasn't the response Jon expected. "What's wrong?"

"I died. But...this can't be the afterlife. Not an eternity of arguments separating my family."

Jon was certain he'd be sick. *Did Samuel do things he shouldn't to bring this boy back?* "You both died, but neither of you are dead. Your healer saved you."

"Then how come nothing feels real?"

Desperate chocolate eyes studied the boy. It was the same for him since the caves. Jon hadn't realized it, but...nothing felt real. None of this was real. It couldn't be. Because he'd never want someone to die.

***

Metallic notes drowned out the rain pummeling the building. If only it consumed the goo. It felt thicker and his stub nosed blade less effective...

Putting the strange violin down, he undressed and studied the wounds marring his leg. Pressing into the freshest... That goo muffled the pain – refusing to leave him. It wasn't enough.

Light glinted off silver shining in the dark gray world... Inviting... A shaky sigh left him. The promised relief...the lie... The goo in his chest expanded - taunting him.

Why am I doing this? A golden thumb pressed deeply in the newest wound, urging pain from the severed skin. But it felt numb.

Grabbing the stub nose knife... He shouldn't do this. Not so soon. But he needed it... The comforting weight and natural coolness-

A *beep* jarred Zephyr back to reality. Dressing... He should leave the blade. It'd wait for him to take care of whoever was calling... But just holding it...

Golden fingers clutched the gift his friend and rival gave him as he stared at his General's name on the screen. Water rammed his window with godly violence. It was so loud...and muffled... How could it be both? Sitting, Zephyr accepted the call request.

"Hello." Normally his hands danced, but now they gripped the stub nosed knife. It was his only relief.

Concern and worry marred her face. Golden fingers gripped the blade tighter. *I don't want to know.* It was just another terrible thing about himself. She spoke, but all his focus was on the metal in his hands and the goo in his chest.

Just a little? She won't see. His hands shook and Tenalia kept talking. He nodded when she paused and frowned when she did. *What's she saying?*

One hand let go, allowing the other to press the tip against his thigh. *Listen to her...* But the goo and the world - all of it crushing and overwhelming, filling him to bursting... He should listen to his General's words.

Ramming a blade into his body was easy. It was quick. But he missed so much compared to slowly pressing it through skin and meat.

Pulling out quickly to watch the red run down - to feel the goo leak out. It was wasteful next to this. Angling the handle forward. Slowly pressing. Slicing up...

He shuddered - soaking in these wonderful sensations. The goo didn't ooze out. It simply stopped existing. That shudder cut through all of it - banishing it. Every ounce... It'd been pressing against his skin and crushing his organs. But not now. Not as the blade moved...

Pressing it back in, he angled the handle the other direction, pushing so the tip tore upward. Pressing down as he slowly pulled it out so he felt every millimeter of dull edge drag...

"Nephew?"

Startled, Zephyr jumped. *What am I doing?* Opening his eyes, he shook his head - painting on an expression of surprise and confusion. "Did I hear you right?"

"Yes. Captain Multiz reported Ferdinan was near death, but Kannani said his condition was exaggerated. She treated his wounds and sent him to the conference. But..."

Zephyr froze - tightening his grip on the blade. "But?"

"When he returns to school make sure he gets the care he needs." Tenalia shook her head. "How can they overestimate his health like this?"

***

The skin wrapped skeleton lay lifeless on a medical bed - propped up, heated blankets giving him warmth. Various tubes and diodes attached to the frail body. Oya studied the red flashing neural blocker on Ferdinan's forehead... *Why do they keep flashing yellow and red?* Sora and the Kyo were confused by this too. It was a topic of many conversations the last few days - leaving Sora doubting her choice to agree with the Kyo.

Hovering above her dear friend was Shēnó's golden light. Oya wondered if it had something to do with it. *Thank you, Shēnó. Soon...one way or another...*

This is cruelty. If you care for him, show him mercy.

Inhuman green eyes turned to the screen with Kámua's histories. *I made a promise.*

It wasn't her favorite activity, but Oya sat on his bed - eyes fixed on her dear friend. Sora and Kyo Jorani slept in chairs beside Ferdinan. And Samuel was arguing with a man she didn't know.

The neural blocker's red light stopped flashing. Long frail limbs twitched, that too thin body convulsed. A scream as alien as primordial monster's slashed her ears...

What is this...?

***

"We agree this was a bad idea, but you don't have to worry. I talked to Dæya. We'll use the old training techniques." Norger held out a screen. "You're done with your apprenticeship. Sign this and it'll be over."

Not having to come back sounded great. But Li-Nouha... Signing the form, Elbie returned to the entrance. The Energist who brought him was gone. Rain poured down like always, so dark and gloomy it made him want to sleep... But Umbacano was bright and happy.

Students weren't supposed to walk alone in this weather, but he didn't want to be here anymore. Umbacano pecked his ear when he reached for the door.

Ouch! Reflex almost knocked the bird off his shoulder. *Yah...getting a robot wet isn't good...* But he didn't want to wait... Chittering chirps drew his attention to a hazy figure slowly getting closer.

The figure morphed into a smiling Tuel and entered – perfectly dry. "You're done?"

"You were going to wait this long?"

"I was getting tired and this was the nearest shelter." Dark eyes looked down the hall. "Who's getting you?"

"...no one..."

Frowning, Tuel opened the door. "Enjoy flying?"

"I don't need to go far, just to Master Ferdinan's lab."

"Oh?" Tuel smiled. "Then I'll rest there."

"There's a sleeping sac in the closet." That was meant to be a jovial offer, but the older boy's expression... "I have a project I'm working on. But you can relax there if you don't touch anything."

That sadness morphed into a grateful smile. "Thank you."

***

Jon never saw Samuel run that fast. But he'd never heard a sound like that either. It echoed straight to his bones – jarring and grating. A purely primal agony.

A deathly pale Kaz stood trembling, eyes tripled in size and the Master healer froze just past the door. Like Jon in the train station's courtyard, the man couldn't move. Held in place. Desperate to charge, to cry out.

And that sound rose up again – withering his insides. Kaz flinched. Samuel threw Sora and Kyo Jorani out of the way and tore off the neural blocker.

Memories Jon hated rushed in. That skeletal body twisted, face frozen in eternal torment. Nearly colorless crystals open wide. Tubes jutting from his body were pulled taut and every muscle contracted.

This wasn't what Jon needed. What any of them needed. *Just die! Please...I can't stand this...* Sinking to his knees, the growing giant watched his big brother grab stick arms. He didn't know what Samuel was doing, but it'd keep their ally alive. It'd draw this out longer... *Please...just let it end...*

Chapter 21

Working each muscle and keeping his little brother's heart going was exhausting, but Samuel slowly got Ferdinan's body to relax. *I'm surprised it took this long.*

Panting, retching, boney hands clutched at the Healer's arms. Pain warped Ferdinan's face but the boy knew not to let go before he finished.

Tears poured out and blue lips trembled. "O-ok...ok..."

"Lay back. Stay calm."

Colorless crystals flew open, but before Ferdinan could reach for his stomach, Samuel grabbed his wrists. *He remembers...* Every time he tried easing his little brother to sleep, the boy broke free. "Restraints!"

"Why?!" The skeletal body thrashed. Stick limbs fought to escape, to tear the feeding tube from his belly. And nearly succeeded. "Why did you do this to me!?"

"Now!" Samuel stopped Ferdinan from hurting himself, but couldn't keep hold long enough to calm him down.

"Why?!" Fury screamed – filled with betrayal and loss of everything precious. "Take it out!

The boy would kill himself if this didn't stop. Shifting to the bed, Samuel wrapped his body around the flailing skeleton – holding tight despite the screams – until he finally forced the boy to sleep.

This was exhausting – physically and emotionally. Laying his little brother back, he covered Ferdinan and secured those stick limbs when Sora offered the restraints.

Coffee eyes turned to the ceiling. There was so much inside him...and nothing. *I need to get him safe. I need to get back to Jon.*

Jorani frowned as the Master healer rushed in. "What was that?"

Turning, Samuel glared at them. And when he spoke, he yelled despite himself.

***

As always, grandpa Huey answered within minutes of Leoniel sending a call request.

Ocean blue eyes glistened above a giant smile. "Leoniel, son! What trouble're you into now? Or are you needing more supplies for Azuté? You've already horded most the world's fabric, mind you."

"Grandpa Huey!" Light glinted off the dozen rings he wore. "Your miracle man who makes medical devices..."

All the lighthearted energy from a moment before turned perfectly serious. "What's happening, son?"

"There's a child who'll die without a miracle. A child who's the world to my second family." When Huey's face dropped, Leoniel waved his hands. "I know it's unlikely he'll be able to do anything. But I have to ask."

"Haven't been able to contact him directly for a while. His last message was automated." Determination hardened the man's lines. "But I'll do what I can and hope. What's wrong with the child?"

"Massive damage to their heart. Their organs are shutting down and they can no longer eat." Leoniel's heart sank at how impossible his request was. "They might not reach me..."

"Why's this child important to you? Or is it all for your second family?"

"Planning some guilt to get the miracle man moving?" This was only partly a joke. The old man was genius at knowing how to motivate people when necessary. "They have a potential, a capacity for so much I'd love to see them recognize in themselves."

"Describes my feelings toward my miracle worker. You wouldn't believe how young they were when they earned the rank of Master."

"Considering some of the miracles you've described them making..."

***

Umbacano danced around the screen filled with ancient knowledge. Articles and research Elbie never dreamed of...

The brain was fascinating and these articles held so much knowledge... *Ancient humans figured out all this?* It was amazing.

Umbacano strutted - sometimes pecking at a file - and sometimes looking at nothing to his left. *How're they all so useful and in the one ancient language I read?* It was if an expert in these articles were helping him.

Where did Master Ferdinan get this?

Though fascinating, there was a problem. "Everything's on ancient human brains..."

Umbacano looked to his left then back at Elbie.

"How has the brain evolved over the millennia?" Sighing, Elbie picked up the screen again. "How different are Tinkerers' brains?" *Or the other mutations.*

The screen flashed and the options changed. Startled, Elbie dropped it. New articles...all about the evolution of the brain over millennia. *How....?*

***

Why won't this end? Jon sat alone outside their cabin. He tried waiting inside, but it was too small. Too dark. The cave kept flooding his mind. And on the deck, he could stare at the moon. Its light... It wasn't full, but it was bright.

Why did Samuel save him? Why did I? I should've let him die in his lab... Long fingers gripped the railing and Jon's face twisted. *I'm a horrible person. Terrible...*

He needed Samuel. Needed his family. And that wouldn't happen while Ferdinan was here - endlessly dying but never dead. *No.* Jon shook his head.

I'm terrible. I hate being like this. Pushing himself from the railing, Jon grabbed the door's handle but didn't open it. *Samuel should stay away from me.* He needed his brother - his family, but...

Why isn't this over? Done? No matter how exhausted he was, how close to death Ferdinan got, or how strongly another wanted the gent, he was still trapped.

Hours passed. Maybe eternities too. Sora checked on him a couple times but he told her to leave. No woman should be around someone as poisonous as him - as contaminated.

When his brother appeared Jon almost ran, but Samuel would follow despite being exhausted. Strong arms wrapped around him. An embrace he didn't deserve. "Stop. Go back to Ferdinan."

Samuel squeezed tighter. "You need me too. I'm sorry to leave you alone. I'm sorry I-"

"Don't. Stop focusing on me. He obviously needs you more." Jon hated Samuel apologizing to him. The guilt... He didn't deserve those words. Didn't deserve his family. Didn't deserve anything.

Concerned, Samuel opened the door and ushered his baby brother inside. "His needs don't negate yours."

"But they come before my ugliness." Jon hated saying it - hated feeling this even more.

"I'm listening. I love you. I want to help."

"But you shouldn't! You shouldn't! I don't deserve it." When his big brother tried hugging him, he pushed Samuel away. "He needs to die! I want him to die so this can finally be over. I'm terrible. There's no forgiving that. I'm terrible. But I can't take it anymore! I want him to finally die."

This time Jon didn't stop Samuel from hugging him. He didn't deserve it, not someone who wished death on a child...

"I love you. I want it to be over too."

Those words shattered Jon's insides - leaving only tears.

***

Rains raged against the buildings. Tuel was with the older Energists protecting the key areas of the islands. Ilu and the other Healers where healing Energists as they became injured or exhausted in the storm. Marcus and his fellow Artists helped instructors keep the younger students distracted. And everyone else was to stay in their suites for the time being.

Which gave Gongie time to worry. It felt like Zephyr's mind had broken off another part and hid it away.

How can I help him?

"How do I kill the monster? It needs to die."

What's he going to do to himself? Gongie ran.

~

How do I kill the monster? It needs to die. The stub nosed blade... It felt so good. Right. But he was lucky Gongie didn't catch him...

With each urge to grab his knife, the Prince played more violently until the unnatural violin screamed. Wrong notes made the sound harsher – more grating. And when the door chimed, he ignored it. Because nothing else could exist. It couldn't. So he kept playing. And playing. Onyx eyes longingly caressing the blade...

Metallic notes stopped though the bow kept moving. *I forgot.* Resident doors didn't lock during a shelter-in-place for safety and easy headcounts.

"Are you ok?"

Zephyr didn't look at the Psych. "I'm practicing."

"'How do I kill the monster?'" Gongie grabbed Zephyr's shoulder. "Talk."

Shrugging the Psych off, Zephyr stored the swirling fog and attached speaker. "About what? The truth's simple."

"You believe that so strongly..." Gongie looked helplessly at his hands. "Zephyr... A monster can't be killed. You can only teach it humanity."

***

Looks like they're done. Leoniel grabbed blankets for the two sleeping girls and their exhausted mother while Evelyn rambled in three different languages at his employees.

"I'll entertain her for a bit." Leoniel covered Tinny and Raonie then wrapped Yin. "There's a lounge with couches past the third door."

"Sounds wonderful." Raonie gave a grateful smile and shifted Yin. For two years younger, the girl wasn't much smaller than Evelyn. "Please message me your suggestions, I forgot half of them in the chaos."

"Of course." A wave of ringed fingers summoned two employees. One picked up Tinny and the other escorted them to the lounge.

"Leoniel..."

Her family aren't the only ones she's exhausted. Still, Teal and Pom distracted the girl as best they could. "Yes?"

Patting Evelyn's head, Teal mouthed, "Soon."

"Wonderful." Dark eyes watched excited energy tug Pom around. "Thank Illian and Rinie's partner for informing us. Everyone'll have a chance to visit when she's ready."

147

"Pom! I need you and Teal to care for a delivery. Evelyn. I was hoping you could help me."

Green-ringed black eyes tripled. "Ooo! With what?!"

His employees bowed and left - grateful for the escape.

"I'm taking clothes to give to people who need them." His smile outshone his rings. "But I have more than I can pack. Will you help me select which outfits to take?"

"Really? I can help with service this time?!"

"This time?"

"My big brother does service things too. Lots. But he's always done before he visits me. Though...he hasn't in a while..."

"Oh?" Leoniel led her to the boxes of clothes he and his employees spent the last year preparing. They'd be taking it all. But since Mother asked for an assessment... "He stopped?"

"Yah, after making everyone better..." Understanding warped her face into a comical O. "He keeps coming to see me... I'm stopping him from service! Oh no!"

'Making everyone better...?' "It's important to take breaks to care for your family and yourself." Leoniel opened a random box.

"Really?"

Mother's right, she's like me. The young girl was all over, running from person to person, talking up a storm. Until it was the two of them. *Adjust how we greet her and her family.* "Doing service constantly isn't good and he'd want to take time to ensure you're ok after being sick."

"For a whole year?"

A year? "Sometimes." Tipping the box allowed clothes to spill out and sent Evelyn into cheers. "Which ones do we choose?"

"Ooo! So many colors!" Little hands dived in - critiquing every piece and sorting them into three piles. Yes. No. Maybe.

Adding to his employees' work made him feel bad, but this was a perfect distraction to assess her...and gather unexpected information. The entire time she jumped between sorting clothes, telling Leoniel all about her big brother, and getting distracted by customers and employees who came too close – rambling at them about whatever random thing popped into her head. *So that's what I was like.*

***

"Why's it so cold?" Skuna shivered as little feet trudged through thick snow. "It's supposed to be summer."

"It's winter in the northern hemisphere."

"That's stupid."

Ozar nearly snorted. "That's how it works."

"It's still stupid," she glared. "Why couldn't you take me away from winter instead?"

"I'm sorry, we can't wait that long." The Hei-O frowned at the darkening sky. It'd be snowing soon. "You'd be in front of a warm fire if you hadn't insisted my home was wrong."

Huffing, she looked away. "It was the wrong place."

Ozar stopped her, but possible futures filled him – confirming she'd chosen correctly. *You could've told me sooner, Ajulagrá.*

She needed to choose to find Śarī-a.

The half-day walk in snow, ice, and freezing winds wasn't pleasant, but the girl didn't stop. Not until they reached a particular tree that looked like all the others...

Kneeling, she dug – and scolded Ozar when he tried helping. So he watched. And waited, blocking the bitter winter wind for her.

Little hands brushed dirt from a small piece of something once white but stained with age. Considering it was Śarī-a's host...

"I'm cold. And tired." She gestured for him to lift her, which he obliged. "We'll wait over there."

"Ok." He had no idea where they were, but followed where she pointed. An hour later, Ozar faced a home he knew well.

***

Dark... Everything... How long ago did the last light fail? Jon's heart moved faster searching for Oya. She couldn't move, so why wasn't she beside him?

Jon felt for her, for her tiny body that was always too cold – and found warmth. He needed to make sure she was safe. He needed to get her home. *Is she coming down with a fever? How do I treat a fever? There's no water. If she gets sick...if she dies... Where is he? Why isn't he here yet?!*

Chocolate eyes darted around desperately. Ferdinan should be there by now. Dim light...far away but real... *He's here! Ferdinan found us!* Leaping to his feet, Jon ran forward but instead of rock, he touched cold metal. *What?* Turning, he scanned the room. The large cabin room. There was the bed and Samuel asleep. *I'm not trapped.*

Something warm ran down his cheek. *We aren't trapped.* But his heart still pounded. *We aren't trapped anymore. I'm safe.* Sobs escaped – startling his big brother awake. "I'm sorry."

Samuel slipped out of bed, wrapped an arm around his shoulder, and guided him outside. A salty breeze swept away the scent of dirt and moss. There was no cave. It was dark, but stars and the moon filled the sky. There was no cave. Nothing confining him - trapping him. He was safe. But his heart pounded and the air was thin. He'd die. He'd watch his ally die. And Oya...

Tears came harder. Samuel hugged him tighter and sat them on a bench. "It's okay. I'm right here. You're safe."

"I'm safe... I'm-" Jon repeated but he didn't feel safe.

"You're safe. I'm right here."

"I'm sorry." Jon rested his head on his big brother's shoulder. Ferdinan was dying and Oya had vanished. But he was the one crying over a cave he escaped. He was the one with a racing heart and barely able to enter a bedroom. He was the one afraid of dying...of being trapped again...

Chapter 22

"You did well, young one." Black hair swayed, speckled with sunshine and shadows. Reaching out, Oya waited for Skuna to offer the host.

"If I give it to you, I won't be guardian, then why did I leave home?"

"You'll become Śarī-a's guardian once I meet you in person. There're lessons I need to teach you. And..." Gold specked eyes looked sorrowfully at the bone fragment the girl held. "It has needs you're not able to provide for yet."

"How long do I have to wait in this winter prison?"

"Not long. I'll be there before the month's out." Though Oya kept her hand out, she grinned and asked after the girl. "Are you having fun despite the cold?"

"It's ok." Skuna shrugged, but a tiny smirk said otherwise. "There's a strange man whose kind and really loves shiny things."

Oya giggled. "Enjoy the shinies 'til I arrive."

First the girl nodded, then started to bow, then shrugged. But she handed over the bone fragment. Thanking her, Oya released Skuna back to her dream.

Closing gold specked black eyes to the twilight beach; alien green opened to the sterile room her dear friend was sleeping in. Shēnó hovered dutifully above and Kámua was still with Elbie. Sora sat attentively, watching the sleeping skeleton.

And off-white stood proudly in her golden-brown hand. *Finally.* Now to make the transfer and claim the charge herself. This wouldn't be fun. Skuna was strong and determined, but the girl wasn't ready for this.

No one noticed Oya leave or skip down to the cargo hold. No one heard her *hum* Śarī-a's song or whisper the words to gather the charge to its chosen host. No one would know what she did – deep in the bowels of this island sized ship.

Making herself comfortable, Oya winked at the orbs. *Bear with me.* They weren't happy. And for good reason. But she'd do all within her power to keep her promises.

The bone fragment glowed in her hand. *Almost done.* "Who were you, once upon a time?"

There was no answer. Neither did Oya expect one. Wicked green eyes looked at the tired orbs beside her. "Lend me your strength if I'm too weak."

Hesitation froze the orbs in place, but bone glowed with what resolve it could. Śarī-a was ready.

"Lend me your strength." Delicate hands lifted the bone. "And after I'll give you mine."

Resolve and the world's life filled her – paralyzing her. *A little less...* But Oya couldn't blame Śarī-a. Losing a charge...

"Little one, would you accept Śarī-a? And through it enjoy the life you were denied?" Oya whispered to the small bit of bone resting in her palm – doing nothing until it agreed.

Grinning, she went to work molding it to an acceptable state of non-existence. Gathering the dispersed Śarī-a into it, Oya gave up a portion of herself – an offering needed for their union. Regardless of how brief.

***

Mismatched eyes fixed on the carbon tray as he pressed the button. Following the commands, it took form, becoming a crystal at a thousand times the speed. *My printer's useless next to these...* Surprisingly, the programing instructions for his printer worked well with the nanobots.

The first eighth of the diamond grew quickly. Then stopped. *What happened?* According to the command program... Elbie frowned.

Why did they self-destruct? Each individual bot fulfilled one command cycle then died and the next one moved in.

Elbie placed his head on the table. *How do I fix this?* And where to start on his second project? At least Li-Nouha's dad responded positively to spending the break here.

How do I delete the self-destruct, get them to connect the skeletal structure to her nerves, and find a non-restrictive material to cover her hands that didn't turn into goop?

Umbacano danced on the table – nuzzling his cheek. A universe of possibilities...solutions... *The second skin could work...* If he figured out the self-destruct... And programing... *Ugh...it's so hard!* Chirping directed his attention to the window and a blur disrupting the rain.

I haven't called for an escort... Elbie paled. Was this...? He saw how sick Master Ferdinan was. *I don't want to hear it...*

The chime sounded and Tuel peeked through the door's window. "Next wave's coming. Time to get back to the dorms."

Relief sighed out of him. There wasn't much more he could do here anyway. Grabbing his bag, he opened the door, but froze when he saw Gongie. Every thought and emotion drained from him. "Thank you."

Tuel took Elbie's bag and waited for the young Tinkerer to lock up. "What're you working on today?"

Mismatched eyes turned to the sheets of water falling on the other side of the door. His mind emptied automatically around a Telepath, but keeping it quiet was exhausting. "A surprise."

Umbacano fluttered around before landing on Elbie's head.

Gongie flinched, looking confused – dark eyes focused where Umbacano sat...

Waving a hand toward the exit, Tuel smiled. "For Yuyu or your suitemates?"

"Yuyu." One green and one gray eye focused on the rain. "I need to ask Ilu for something."

***

"I'll do whatever's needed." Sorrow dimmed Am'ria's delicate golden face.

That was easy... "Thank you for being so willing."

"I knew it was coming." Her tiny body straightened but she was too adorable to look regal.

Blue-black eyes stared intensely from across the room. "How should I approach the Duchess?"

"Don't worry about her."

"What?"

"The Duchess's role is nearly finished."

What does that mean? "Who'll stand when it's North Chūzo's turn to speak?"

"It could be Tenalia, Emelica, or Zephyr."

Zephyr...? He's a child. But this was North Chūzo and Zephyr was a noble. "Thank you. Please inform me as soon as you're able."

Once the Queen bowed, Herrard closed the screen and tore off his robe – bells freely offering their complaints. It wasn't uncomfortable, yet it was too confining, restrictive. It took three rounds of washing and special cleansers to get all the face paint off.

"Here." Xhou stood in the doorway holding a wide bristled brush.

Smiling, Herrard sat. His island brother had become quite proficient at undoing the elaborate hair and brushing the product out. "Thank you. What do you think?"

Deft fingers easily removed every pin before unweaving the strands. "Considering having a child speak for the Duchess? Something bad's happening."

***

"Thank you, dear friend." The chair shifted when Ozar plopped his exhausted body into it.

"I'm always happy to see you." Light from the fire glinted off a dozen rings when Leoniel offered the giant a mug of steaming tea. "This is the second surprise I've gotten this week."

Ozar didn't drink the tea, but he fully enjoyed the aroma and warmth. "What happened?"

"Samuel called." If a smile was appropriate, he'd offer one to his exhausted friend. "How do I make Ferdinan comfortable?"

Ozar leaned forward. "What's happening?"

I'm sorry, dear friend. "He's dying."

The two men sat in silence – firelight flickering and the winter night looming heavy beyond the window.

"Tell me everything."

Kyos often bore bad news, but this was the first time Leoniel had to impart terrible words and steal hope from one he loved.

Ozar didn't say anything. He simply gripped the cooling mug tight, building an internal defense at what Leoniel was about to say.

"They don't know what's keeping him alive and doubt he'll make it here."

"Two days 'til they make port in North Oueshi..." Dark eyes gazed at the cold tea – searching for something he wasn't finding. "He'll make it."

Leoniel gave a loving smile – preparing for when wishful thinking became pain. But Ozar always guessed right when things were unlikely. "What should I prepare? Beyond the medical – Samuel's already sent that information."

"Unfortunate it's winter. He loves flowers and gardens."

Flowers... Lips scrunched to the side, Leoniel ran long fingers through lavender hair. *Such a simple thing...* Grabbing a screen, he summoned his best employee and waited for her to arrive.

"I'm sorry, Kyo. Skuna woke up and it took a bit to get her back to sleep."

"Lashina, how hard would it be for your brother to move a green house to share a wall with Tuli Cottage tomorrow? The corner room with the full-length windows?"

The unusual question made her pause, but she gave an airy laugh. "With a little help, not difficult at all."

"Would you be willing to work at the cottage for a while? We're receiving a guest who needs extra care."

***

Wind hurtled rain into the window and drops rolled out of chocolate brown eyes. If Gongie could reach through the screen and hug his distraught friend, he would. *What does Jon need right now?* "I'm listening, unless you want me to talk."

"I don't know..."

Though Jon wouldn't look at him, Gongie held onto a gentle smile and quietly watched the growing giant cry. There was no one in the suite, but voices, anxiety, and boredom from everyone in the building echoed in his mind. Zephyr was particularly difficult to ignore. But he wouldn't waver from his island brother.

"I'm sorry..."

"It's ok. I'm listening. I'll listen for as long as you want."

Silence fell for some time before Jon spoke. "Oya disappeared and Samuel's fighting to keep Ferdinan alive...and I just want him to die so it'll all end. I hate wanting that. But I can't stop. I hate being a horrible person..."

That's...what do I say? "I'm listening."

"Why? I just told you I want a child to die!"

I see... "Jon. I love you. I've been inside your mind for eleven years. So, will you honestly consider my thoughts? If you're able?"

Jon glanced to the side then down, but nodded.

"You don't want him to die. You want him to stop suffering." When Jon broke down, Gongie continued, making his voice as soft and comforting as he could. "You can't stand witnessing it anymore. That's normal, understandable. Watching someone suffer is a pain all its own. It hurts and damages us. And it's easy to feel like we don't deserve to hurt 'cause we aren't experiencing what they are..."

Gongie wasn't sure how useful his words were for Jon – but they hit his own heart hard.

"You aren't the kind of person who wants a child to die. You're a person who's been forced to watch – helpless to ease the suffering and are unable to do so any longer." *I wish I could hug you.* "And that's ok. It's normal. Understandable. And I'm sorry I didn't do more to help."

It hurt watching his island brother suffer. If he did something sooner... *Those thoughts aren't helpful.* Neither could he change the past. But the guilt was heavy.

Gongie's full attention didn't waver from his dear friend. And once Jon was calm enough to talk, he listened – offering what comfort and insight he could.

***

Deep in the bowels of the island sized ship, dusty from neglect, Oya placed the little piece of bone on a small box she found and prepared. If only she could be carried to the center of the sea or camped on an isolated island... Not even Humawit would interfere with this.

It was worrying. She didn't know the ship's acoustics – where everything connected. There hadn't been enough time to explore it all, but this spot was the farthest away from people and required being small to reach. Having no control in an unknown environment...

Alien green eyes closed. *Breathe...focus.* Last time she was high on adrenaline and impulse. And it was the only option. Now...

I know it's not only Tanan you mourn for. Don't hold back your fears and pains. Give me everything. And in return, heal my dear friend. Protect Kámua.

I will.

Promise?

I promise.

There was no right choice. No best solution. Oya was either irresponsible for letting the girl suffer a pain she couldn't fathom or irresponsible for keeping her from being the only guardian to not experience their charge's mourning.

It was a terrible thing humans did, anthropomorphizing reality. Forcing mortal things they couldn't understand on them. But that wasn't a human trait alone...

Breathing out one last time, Oya opened her eyes. The soft sand of her twilight beach surrounded her. What was a tiny glow now stood tall – radiating orange instead of gold.

It's not fair to you.

"I'd never trade this duty. I've never regretted any of it." Oya held out her hand. "I'm sorry your guardian won't know you, understand you, as they should."

For a short while.

Bitter tinted her grin. "Very short."

Warmth wrapped around her hand and spread up her arm. Glorious warmth and concentrated agony. Of loss and being lost. Hurt and being hurt.

To an immortal being it was the first time every time. Because these were human things it was forced to bear. Things it never should've experienced. Things it couldn't be prepared for. Things – no matter how many times – it wasn't capable of understanding. It only knew it needed them to stop.

Pain and anger and fear. Loneliness. Abandonment. The end of existence. Everything a charge was never meant to know screamed out over the twilight beach.

Her world shook. Broke. Parts fell away. And Oya felt herself fade.

The grief of a timeless being trapped in a temporal world.

***

"Do you have all that?"

Xhou flopped back dramatically. "My head hurts."

So does mine. Herrard wacked his island brother's knee. "This should be easy for a Thinker."

"Being good at it doesn't make it any less boring. Or tedious."

"It's vital. Especially since you lack experience. Keep studying."

"*Ugh...* I hate this so much. Why can't they mind themselves and be happy there's food?"

"'Cause they're people." Herrard tossed a screen to his whiny suitemate. "Be glad you're not stuck with this schedule. Sixteen private meetings and four closed conferences. You better have decent progress to show by the last one."

"Supplies from groups helping with initial set up already arrived. More are coming in waves with each boat of volunteers..." Xhou trailed off when Herrard shook his head.

"Later groups won't matter when addressing critics of the treaty, only what you manage with the first set." Herrard stretched. He was getting hungry. "Manage a miracle with those, then everything else after will matter."

Chapter 23

"I'm working." The Prince tried closing the door, but Gongie wedged himself inside.

"We need to talk."

Golden hands thrashed. He needed to work so he could get everything done and leave!

"Not about you," Gongie waved to the couch. "Get comfortable."

Ice filled his gut – making the goo too solid for his lungs to move. *What's happening?*

The Psych hesitated multiple times during his tale.

This is all my fault... Every word the Telepath uttered. Golden fingers dug deep into the torn flesh of his thigh. Deep. And deeper. But the pain wasn't enough. It wasn't... *I need my blade.* The slow slice in. Rocking. Tearing...

Gongie stopped talking – looking horrified. Pushing those desires from his mind wasn't easy. He wanted it. So badly... *I hate Telepaths.*

"You need to stop."

I hate Telepaths! Leave! You have no right in here or my head!

Rich, dark skin turned ashen, but Gongie didn't move.

"Why are you still here? You are terrified! You shouldn't-!"

"Of course I'm scared, but I won't leave while you plan to hurt yourself."

"I'm not hurting myself." Zephyr knew the Psych said forcing innocuous thoughts was unpleasant, but he didn't know how else to stop thinking things he shouldn't.

"*Ugh...*" Gongie rubbed his head. "There's no point. I'm not leaving."

***

It'd been some time since Oya shook like this, but it was almost over. As much as it could be. Light rested in her arms – pulsing with horrendous things it'd never understand, but no longer orange.

No matter how many guardians it mourned for... *Sparing Skuna will cause Śarī-a worse later... What'll they do? Have other Rā-yumôns taken a guardian's duty? How will this affect them?* But this thought came far too late.

"Do you need more time?"

Yes. But I'll be ready soon. Thank you.

Hugging golden light was odd and wonderous. If she had the time, Oya would sit with it for eternity. "I need to prepare him. And myself. Rest as long as you wish – I'll return soon."

Giving Śarī-a one last hug, Oya opened the door to the silver roads. Wriggling tentacles reached out. *Who found me there?*

Alien green eyes opened to Kaz poking her arm.

"This is a strange place for a prince."

He nodded – coated in exhaustion. "I kept feeling I should come here. You wouldn't wake up, but that feeling wouldn't let me leave."

Sitting, she studied him. Somehow his soul was more warped than when she first saw him. Healed wounds bled harder and the holes over his mind were larger. Her curiosity surged. She needed to prepare. But... *How did it get worse here?* "May I ask what happened to you?"

"I died." He stared at her, eyes drooping. "I died. Like my older sisters. But they didn't come back. And...it feels weird. Why do I keep coming back? Or am I dead and don't realize it?"

Interesting. She was exhausted... But... Reaching out golden-brown arms, she swept him up when he leaned forward for a hug. Gently she eased him to sleep and delved deep into his mind.

I should've studied him earlier. The woman with silver-streaked hair was marked all over him. *How did a human manage this? How much time do I have? How do I fight this?*

Opening her hand, she took in her reflection off the broken piece of mirror. A normal one would've shown what she wanted to see. What she willed those around her to see. But this one was cruel – only showing the truth. It was terrible. But this was her truth and it wasn't going to change. At least she already held Dashū because she didn't have enough left in her to call and command a charge.

Dashū?

Yes?

You led him to me.

Yes. You need help.

You know I'm beyond your help. Oya smiled. She still loved it for its devotion and care. *But if the boy isn't, he deserves a reward for listening when he had no reason to.*

I don't know if I can fix this. I've never seen anything like it.

But you'll try.

I will.

I trust him to you while I prepare my friend.

Once Dashū wished her luck, she closed her eyes and opened them on the twilight beach...and nearly groaned. But he hadn't seen her yet.

Morphing into the elf, she approached the boy searching in all the wrong places for her. *How dependent are you on your abilities?* "You're the second to intrude upon this place."

Gongie spun, sighing out relief...until he saw her. Still, words slipped off his tongue. "I need your help."

Sitting, the elf breathed out her exhaustion. "Speak."

***

Jon didn't want to be here, but he couldn't handle being alone. Sitting in the corner, he watched Samuel... *What's he doing?* The gent's heart was beyond repair, but every day they came. Samuel injected a formula into Ferdinan's abdomen then held the skeleton's hand for an hour. It wasn't fair.

And he couldn't keep doing this. *If everything I feel is normal, why do I have so much guilt over it?*

A knock sounded behind them. "Everything's arranged."

Samuel withered at Kyo Jorani's announcement. "Thank you."

"Is there anything you and your brother need?" They stopped beside Jon and patted his shoulder. "Anything you want."

"My family." Jon's voice broke.

"No, Kyo, thank you."

161

"This is a rude question." The Kyo gave an apologetic smile. "Has he ever told you why he can't accept you?"

The air became impossibly heavy. "No. He always stops himself from telling us."

"Jon? You have more opportunities for him to open up since you school together."

Ferdinan never told him anything – it's what made the gent so infuriating. An oppressive silence smothered everyone. It felt like it wouldn't end if he didn't say something. And he just wanted this to end. "He says he's not one of us, wasn't chosen even though we claimed him. Constantly."

Coffee eyes widened then drifted to Ferdinan's unconscious body. An expression Jon couldn't interpret twisted Samuel's face. He wasn't the only one to notice, but the Kyo didn't ask further.

His big brother's reaction...there was significance. "*I don't get to be a part of you.*" *What did he mean when he said he wasn't chosen...?*

***

Zephyr escaped to the silver roads. Not to search. Just to escape.

Onyx eyes stared out at the eternity of black broken by strips of silver. It was chaotic and beautiful and perfectly peaceful. And he sat. *Would I fall forever? Would I die?* It'd be perfect...

Zephyr shook those thoughts from his mind every time they entered until a door opened beside him and two intruders appeared. *What happened to her?* Sapphire eyes were dull, proud shoulders drooped, and she didn't look solid...

"There're enough lives I'm..." The elf stopped herself. "You need to help each other."

"Help each other?" Gongie looked startled.

"Yes," the elf eyed them both. "Zephyr, have you found a single shard or door on your own?"

"No."

"Gongie, do you think your guilt will go away by not passing judgement on deep scars?"

Shaken, Gongie paled.

"Succeed and you'll help yourselves, each other, and countless people in your lives. But I can't hold your hands. There's too many I'm already holding." When they looked away, she shook her head. "Go. There's another who needs help."

Gongie looked desperate. "And we don't?"

"You won't die without it." Dull sapphires turned to Zephyr. "Not yet anyway."

Not letting them argue, she vanished.

She wouldn't leave me alone a few months ago...

They didn't speak. Didn't look at each other. What was the point?

"I don't want you to die."

"What?" A golden ring finger tapped at his temple.

"You keep looking at the emptiness like you're ready to jump off." Earnest concern radiated from the Psych.

"Death isn't an option for me."

Gongie scratched his neck. "I don't want you to die. Not 'cause of your duty or propriety. I want... You don't deserve death. And I want to not be responsible for it. And... Killing yourself doesn't kill the monster. It'll live on without you."

Golden hands jerked – frustrated. "I *am* the monster."

"No. It might be inside you, but if you die, it'll latch onto someone else." Gongie opened his mouth to say more, but stopped, staring past the Prince.

Zephyr looked. That door wasn't there a moment ago. *Go away... I don't want to. Not again.*

But it didn't disappear.

"No." Zephyr looked up. "No. I can't do it anymore."

***

If she could do this now... Alien green eyes stared at translucent golden-brown hands. If she didn't have two other promises, she'd force it.

Oya stood outside her dear friend's dream. If another distraction demanded her immediate attention, it better be before she stepped through. But everything felt empty.

Sapphire eyes replaced inhuman green and unnatural blood red hair became starlight. A silver leaf circlet wrapped around her forehead. *It's nice being tall.* She stepped through and into a black void.

Why won't he go to Evelyn? It's better than this...

"If he wanted your generosity, he wouldn't keep throwing it away."

"He's not throwing it away, he doesn't know how to accept it." The elf turned to Emil. Though ethereal, he was stable. Neither fading nor solidifying. "Shēnó couldn't keep him alive if no part of Ferdinan wanted to live."

"But he rejects your efforts. Your gifts. From the beginning."

"You know that's a lie."

"No more so than your costume."

The elf giggled before turning serious. "You know he's too sick to do what's needed to become healthy, but you won't help him."

Silence fell. A silence pregnant with trepidation and uncertainty. "You know that's a lie."

The elf sighed – not wanting to acknowledge the honesty of Emil's words. Instead, she made her way to the skeleton huddled in the dark waiting for death.

"It's cruel. What' you're doing."

"I know."

***

I guess she likes flowers too. Leoniel placed extra blankets on the bedside chair. "There're other green houses. If you'd like a view of one, I can have it-"

"I'm leaving soon." Skuna didn't remove her nose from the window. "I'm going back to summer."

"Understandable." Walking over, he stood beside her and enjoyed the wonderful colors. If only their perfume permeated the glass. "I prefer the freedom of warmer months as well."

Hazel eyes studied him, the intensity of her gaze wasn't right for a child. "They called you Kyo."

"Yes. I'm one of three."

"Even we know the Kyos. But I always wondered if you knew us."

Leoniel grinned. Meeting someone like her was a hope of his. "Gin Kyo told me there were people whose honors were metal instead of titles or tattoos. Ozar bringing you surprised me. But I'm honored. I can't imagine what you did to earn those."

Little fingers fiddled with the rods. "Many things."

The conversation lulled to a comfortable silence. Leoniel quickly realized she preferred it this way. Speak when there's something to say. Stop when it's been said. It was odd. But nice in its own way. "A sick child's arriving this evening."

"I know."

"Unless he wants company, don't bother him. He's..." How did Leoniel finish that diplomatically?

Skuna's gaze shifted from the flowers to the winter beyond – frown marring her face. Sitting, she closed her eyes and drifted off.

That's...unexpected...

***

Colorless crystals stared through the window. Ferdinan would move if his limbs weren't bound. Maybe... He had no interest in the motion around him. None of it mattered. But he couldn't tear his eyes from the scene beyond his reach.

The family of giants. A giant family of giants. They were all there – mauling Jon with hugs and love and affection... Even Evelyn was mixed into the chaos. Laughing. *Good. I'm glad.*

I'm glad.

I'm glad... Ferdinan's throat was tight. His heart constricted...but it didn't stop the family's happiness. The long-awaited reunion. Perfection. *I'll never ruin it again. Finally.*

Jon got the family he needed – the family he wanted and deserved. *Good. Stay with Jon. Fix the damage I've done to him.*

165

Once the traditional mauling subsided, Oya approached Jingjing. A living mountain. The man made his mom and brothers look small.

Whatever they said, were saying, he was glad he couldn't hear. He couldn't bear it. But Oya was making them laugh... *Good. Play. Be silly. They'll treat you well.*

Evelyn ran behind the group and emerged with two girls – one older and one younger. Though the two were shy and uncertain, the Oza didn't hesitate dragging them to Jon. She was so excited. Hands flailing, feet dancing. *Good. I'm glad you love your new family. Be happy. Become as great as your grandmother.*

"Ferdinan?"

It sounded like Sora had called him multiple times. But he couldn't look away from the world he nearly destroyed. It hurt to watch. But... *It's still broken. I broke it. But they'll repair it. It'll be perfect once I'm gone.*

"Ferdinan? Are you ready?"

Yeah... Closing his eyes, he waited for the dark abyss they kept imprisoning him in.

***

The scene was beautiful. A joyful family reunion straight from her dear friend's mind. And Oya felt the despair it caused. *Bear a little longer, I'll be done soon.*

Golden-brown bare feet stood starkly against fresh snow. Giants hugged and laughed – doting on Jon and the three little girls. Flakes glittered around them. Winking to the orbs in her peripheral she drew them to her. *Forgive me. I'll need a little more.*

They swayed and warmth filled her. Life made her whole then greater...until she pulled herself from their minds and walked away.

The docks were bustling. Unexpectedly alive for the dead of winter. Enjoying what chaos she could, the crazed redhead made her way to the trees. Finding a comfortable spot, she sat and called Skuna. If she was going to meet the girl, Oya had to reveal her new look.

Green eyes closed and opened onto the twilight beach. Smoothing delicate hands over hair and eyes, Oya became the girl she used to be.

"This is an odd time to call."

"I'm not far," Oya grinned. "Have you prepared yourself?"

"As well as I can. Ozar told me the story. You have the host. I'm not sure what else I can do but wait."

"We'll need another host." Oya almost giggled at the girl's annoyance. Holding two hands up, she stopped Skuna's complaint. "You're the guardian. There were some things I had to help Śarī-a with first. And in return, it made me a promise – one you'll have to keep."

"No choice? That's not fair."

"Nothing's fair." She sat on the soft sand and motioned for Skuna to do the same. "You know the soul is finite?"

Skuna blinked, giving Oya a strange look.

"Mine's at its limits or I would've already forced the promise."

"But mine hasn't been exercised."

"Close enough."

Shrugging, Skuna folded her arms. "What's the promise?"

"Śarī-a will heal my dear friend. We'll travel to him after I teach you how to make a transfer and perform the ceremony."

It looked like multiple questions were on her tongue, but Skuna only asked one. "Isn't using the charges for your own benefit corrupt?"

Hearty laughter rang out. "If only it were that simple. He's Kámua's keeper. And he's vital for fulfilling my duty."

"Ok."

That was easy. But straightforward was a prized trait in Skuna's camp. "Now, you should know, when you meet me, I won't look like this."

C R Saxon

Chapter 24

Gongie bolted for the stairs. Sharp pain hit. And lingered... Deep and twisted release expelled the goo. His leg never hurt this bad. *Ugh...*

Dark clouds grew thicker. Unrelenting. *I'm a monster. I hurt everyone.* The agony in his leg tripled. It felt like it was being torn apart!

Clutching his teeth, Gongie continued up. *Stop it, Zephyr!*

Activating the chime, the Telepath stifled one gasp and groan after another. *Ugh... His mind's so far away!*

He activated the chime again. And again. *Should I try a medical override?* But that'd bring eyes and questions... So he kept hitting the chime.

The tearing deepened... Gongie swallowed back a scream. *I'm sorry... But I have to stop you!*

The pain changed, becoming the jarring irritation of an injured limb forced to move.

"I told you, Denila. I have too much work."

"Open the door." Dizziness hit with panicked thoughts and emotions and pure frustration. But at least he didn't have to try *that*. "I already know, so open the door."

Resignation drained to despair...giving up. The door unlocked, but Gongie had to let himself in. Bloody footprints covered the kitchen floor and stained the common room carpets. Zephyr stood naked – silver glinting in one hand.

"I understand."

Failure radiated from the Prince. And... *Confidence?* "Understand What?"

A golden hand reached out. It bled from the handful of broken mirror bits he'd been clutching. "I can't fix it. I can never be forgiven."

What do I do....?

Wind rose up – battering rain and twigs against the window. The tip of the stub nosed blade poked and pushed loose meat and torn flesh. And those bits of mirror... Some fell to the floor; others were pushed deeper into that golden palm when Zephyr pressed it against the window.

"I can't fix anything..."

Gongie remembered the rages. A world completely red. But this... Wherever Zephyr's mind was, it was dark.

Heart pounding, Gongie stood perfectly still. If he did the wrong thing, said the wrong thing, would that red fill the world? Only this time with him beaten instead of Ferdinan? Could he survive?

Gongie was terrified to stay, but he couldn't leave. *What'll he do?* "I'm helping you through this."

"You can fix it? Everything?" Zephyr turned; knife held high. It wasn't aimed at Gongie but his golden belly. Dull, lifeless onyx eyes looked down. Down at his stomach. Down at his torn leg.

What do I do...?

***

The moment mom came into view Jon pushed himself away from his brothers. He tried smiling, but only managed not to cry. "Mom."

Her strong, warm arms wrapped around him. "Let's go home."

Mom walked him to the car – leaving the rest of the family behind. Slipping inside, he rested against her, feeling small in her embrace. Feeling safe. Protected. Just them.

"I don't know what's wrong with me. I'm always scared. I can't sleep. I'm so tired... I want terrible things just so it'll stop."

"You're safe now. We love you." She rested her cheek against the top of his head. "We love you. You're safe. We'll help you feel safe again."

"I can't go back." Jon's voice broke. "I'm sorry. I can't."

She squeezed him tight. "I want you to stay as long as you need."

Hearing that... Breathy laughter shook with tears. Not having to argue...or explain... "Thank you..."

***

Standing, Oya brushed the snow from her clothes. *It'll be interesting teaching her.* Transforming a host into a transfer wasn't difficult, but it wasn't easily taught. And the ceremony... Hopefully Skuna had a good memory. Śarī-a would help when it was time, but the more the girl remembered the less frustrating it'd be and the less likely there'd be mistakes.

I found a traveler.

You're excited to meet her.

You're exhausted.

A defeated laugh left Oya. *I can neither command you nor stop you, but I won't turn down the hospitality of a traveler.*

I'll return shortly.

Delicate fingers tugged at the chain she always wore. *To think I once commanded six...* Giving a wink to the orbs, Oya slipped a green band on her ear. And she walked – lost in the freedom of solitude and dancing with the countless snow sprites falling from the heavens.

It'd been too long. The islands were the longest she'd stayed in one place. Nearly three quarters of a year... Over a year with her dear friend and Jon. *I forgot how wonderful this was.* The purity of untouched nature...

If this were Ferdinan's country, how many buildings and people would I have passed unaware? But it wasn't the hidden world she found herself missing. It was the bright winter flowers. How much engineering went into making something look as delicate as its summer counterpart but hearty enough for the winter? It spoke volumes about his culture. The last month...

There was no one ahead of her – until there was. *You're impressively stealthy.* Raising a hand, Oya waved and they returned the gesture, moving forward.

"*I hardly believed... but I guess I wasn't going mad.*" Removing a hat and protective glasses, the old woman held out her hand.

Unlike Oya's green band, the old woman's was well worn. "*Call me Oya. And you?*"

"*Tac.*" Unwrapping the scarf she wore, Tac offered it to Oya. "*Even the most seasoned would freeze in these temps with no shoes and a light coat.*"

Though she didn't need it, Oya took it anyway – travelers didn't turn down each other's hospitality. "*I'm grateful for the company. It's been some time since I've gotten updated news. Unfortunately, the last travelers I met weren't in a place I could do so."*

"Trading's the best part." A thickly gloved hand waved nonchalantly in the distance. *"Got a pod if you'd like to travel in comfort."*

"Normally I'd prefer the walk, but there're some time sensitive tasks ahead of me."

"Pod it is."

The walk to Tac's pod wasn't far. Laughing, the old woman put it to manual control and guided the little bubble wherever the crazed redhead pointed. They chatted non-stop the entire time. Tac shared news from the various villages she'd visited that year and Oya informed her about the incident at Mr. Charlie's camp. The woman didn't believe Ferdinan's part for a bit – outsiders... But by the end...

"I must've missed that by weeks." Tac navigated the bubble playfully around the trees, slowing when Oya held her hand up. *"I'd like to meet an outsider who did that much."*

A wild grin turned to her. *"Depending on what happens, you might."*

"Sure this is where you need to be? Pretty empty out here."

"I'm sure." Alien green eyes turned to the darkening sky. *Will it be tonight or morning?* Regardless, she had a host to find. *"Going north or south?"*

"Haven't decided. Was simply enjoying the snow for a bit."

"There's a child who'll be going south in the next week or two. She's not a traveler and this is the first time she's been far from her village."

A sly old grin emphasized Tac's lifetime of wrinkles. *"I'm happy to wait."*

"Thanks." While Oya searched, Tac chatted, made a fire, cooked dinner, and called out when an unhappy, snow-covered girl appeared.

***

Why did saying "no" to a little girl make Jon feel like a terrible person? He was exhausted. All he wanted was to sit and cuddle with his family. That's all. To be surrounded by them – touching them so he knew they were really there.

But Evelyn was excited to show him so many things. A year ago, feigning interest would've been easy. But right now, he didn't care. He didn't have the energy to care. *I'm glad her new sisters are calm and quiet... I'm terrible thinking that...* Energetic children were a good thing. But he didn't have the energy for them.

"We'll play tomorrow, ok?"

Green-ringed black eyes glistened above a sad pout. "Ok..."

"Evelyn." Father Artimus waited for his granddaughter to face him. "Do you want to help me with dinner?"

"Oh! I can show uncle Jon how good I've gotten!" Turning back to Jon, she jumped on the pile of bodies to ring his neck in an enthusiastic embrace. "Tinny and Yin are really good too! Especially Tinny!"

The older of Evelyn's new sisters pulled the younger closer, but they nodded when Jon looked at them.

"Tinny! Do you want to make nu...o..nu... Those fancy cookies? Jon'll love them!" After the older nodded, a little finger pointed at the younger. "Yin! Do you want to decorate them? You did such a good job last time! They were so cute!"

Pink stained the younger girl's cheeks, but she nodded sheepishly. Evelyn climbed off the brothers and ran up to her new sisters. Taking their hands, she dragged them to the kitchen.

Thanks, dad...

Rigel chuckled and rested his chin on Jon's shoulder. "You can relax, we'll keep her occupied."

"Did she always have this much energy?"

"Hmmm." Bastian pulled Jon tighter against him – off setting the whole pile, but everyone readjusted automatically. "It grew as she got more comfortable. She's been steady at this level for a while."

"She reminds me of Leoniel." Jingjing's deep voice reverberated around the room.

It wasn't easy squeezing a hand as huge as Jingjing's, but Jon's being swallowed up in it was wonderful. "Leoniel's calmer."

"Leoniel was worse at her age." Xingho offered a cup of something warm and fruity smelling – mussing Jon's hair when he took it.

The warm tea reminded him of summer. Warm days under a bright sun. Playing in the water with his brothers. Open air. Good food...

It wasn't until Nazu took the cup from Jon's hand that he realized he was drifting. Finally. After a year...more than a year... Jon felt safe. Safe to breathe... To close his eyes... To sleep...

***

"Thank you." Samuel bowed – slightly out of breath. "I owe you more than I can express."

"Did Jon settle well?" Leoniel helped Samuel out of his coat and gestured down the hall.

"As well as expected."

"Ferdinan's comfortable and Sora's with him." The colorful man stopped until Samuel faced him. "He didn't wake up when we took the blocker off."

"That's..." Blockers were designed to gently wake the wearer upon deactivation. The only reason his little brother was still asleep was because he *couldn't* wake up.

"I'm sorry..."

Samuel's lip twitched. "Better be safe and put it on while I'm here."

They finished the short walk down the hall and Samuel waited for Leoniel to prepare the boy for his visit. When he walked in, Sora stood.

"I'm taking a break now. Get me when you're done."

"Take as long as you need." Samuel bowed. "Thank you. I can never repay all you've done for us."

"Make sure my children stay healthy and grow strong and I'll consider this debt paid." She gave a facetious smile before sad eyes turned to the boy. "How many honors has he earned? And how many more no one knows about?"

Samuel smiled. "More than I can imagine."

"Rest well, Ms. Sora." Leoniel gave his brightest smile and hugged her tightly. "The kitchens are open to you and a secure line's ready in your room. Sleep. I'll sit with him tonight."

Sora hugged the colorful man back, gave Samuel a squeeze, and left.

Sitting beside the skeleton, Samuel took that painfully frail hand and went to work stimulating atrophying muscles. *His body isn't reacting to my touch...* It didn't matter how futile it was, he tried healing the boy's heart again. But... Even if there were enough nutrients, even if his little brother's heart wasn't scarred, the rest of Ferdinan's body was dying too.

Leoniel stood and prepared the formula. "There're some things you and your family need to know."

"What things?"

"Finish with that, but leave the blocker on."

Doing as he was told, Samuel administered the formula and hung the next set of cocktails. And when Leoniel gestured for him to sit, he did. *I hate it when he's serious.* It always felt as if the world would break when Leoniel wasn't jovial and energetic.

"Kyo Jorani arrived earlier. They gave me some...serious information." Leoniel offered a screen – apology filling his face. "They're planning to draw up charges and was wanting the other Kyos' advice. I told them to do nothing 'til we've fully considered everything."

I don't want to see what'd make him talk so gingerly. "What things?"

"Various controversial treaties involving East Azuté, North Chūzo, and our own country. If this isn't handled properly, unrest could erupt around the world." Leoniel nodded for him to open the first box. "And...what the boy's autopsy shows."

He's not dead yet! But Samuel knew it was days away...if that long. "We won't allow an autopsy."

"You won't have a choice." Exhaustion sighed out of Leoniel. "Watch."

Two videos waited. Both left Samuel in tears.

"Did you know about either of these incidents?"

"No." Bitterness twisted Samuel's lips. Finally. Evidence. After it was too late. "We've suspected abuse for a decade but haven't been able to prove it. The other...shows how strongly he adheres to his cultural beliefs. It's made protecting him extremely difficult."

"What've you and your family done to protect him?"

Where to start? Answering that question took a while. Samuel was certain his family would be asked the same so he was as detailed as he could be.

***

It was a miracle. Like Zephyr was restrained by an unseen force allowing Gongie to bind his leg and hand and clean the blood.

The common room carpets were a pain. But Zephyr's room was a massacre.

After, he closed the door and held the Prince because he didn't know what else to do. The golden boy looked so fragile in his arms...

You've done well, little one.

Gongie searched. *Did I fall asleep too?* Golden light filled the room and settled on Zephyr. Though startling, it felt warm – safe.

Thank you for helping him. I'll guide him from here.

What are you?

An ally.

Chapter 25

Considering Skuna found the first host, Oya wasn't surprised the girl found the second despite all her searching. She was simply an interim guardian after all. "*Tac. You'll enjoy a rare experience if you choose to stay.*"

"*Wouldn't sit right leaving two children alone in the middle of nowhere. In winter.*" The old woman leaned forward. "*Can't say I'm not curious either.*"

Oya grinned, but the younger girl wasn't amused. "*Do you know what you hold, young one?*"

"*A host.*"

"*A sacrifice. A particularly precious one.*" Oya corrected.

"*How so?*"

"*It's the second given by the same source.*" Alien eyes looked longingly at the little bone chip. "*It knew the first wouldn't be enough and gladly offered a second.*"

"*That's unusual?*"

"*This whole situation's unusual.*"

Lips pursed to the side, Skuna studied her - shifting closer to the fire. "*How can something long dead choose its fate?*"

"*Ask them.*" A golden-brown hand gestured to the bone, but inhuman eyes stayed locked on Skuna. Watching. Tac watched too - curious by Oya's sudden intensity.

Looking uncertain, Skuna studied the fragment. Closing her eyes, her little fingers took in every jagged edge and rough spot, all the lines of imperfection along what was once a smooth surface. Then she froze and her eyes flew open.

Oya grinned. "*Was their answer satisfactory?*"

Both a little pale and more determined, the girl nodded. "*What do I do now?*"

"*Ask if they're willing to accept Sari-a again and enjoy a full life they were denied.*"

Clutching the bone tightly in both hands, Skuna pressed it against her heart and closed her eyes. Step by step, Oya walked the girl through the process of creating a host. Then came the ceremony.

It was a long, exhausting night, but Tac kept the fire hot and Skuna was enthralled. Watching two strangers become forever entwined... The joy guardians experienced when they truly met their charge... Pure exhaustion caused by the unfiltered emotions of something immortal. Things they'd never understand in a lifetime as short as a human's.

Golden-brown arms scooped up the exhausted Skuna and placed her in the pod.

It took a while for Tac's awe to fade. *"Leaving already?"*

"Unfortunately. Going with her poses a risk I can't take. There's nothing I can do anyway." Oya wrapped the girl in a couple blankets stored in the pod. *"I'm trusting you to get her home safely. Follow her instructions no matter how odd they may seem."*

"Gladly." Standing, the old woman approached and held out her hand. *"In all my years. This was a child's fairytale I've always dreamed of, but knew was impossible."*

"The impossible is often more possible than the possible."

Harty laughter filled the air. *"Thank you for fulfilling an old dream I never forgot, Rā-yu."*

"Am I someone so important?"

"I met your mother." The old woman winked. *"She was a wonderful Rā-yumôn. But there's no doubt, you aren't the same."*

"Ah! Travelers. We're the most frustrating bunch." Taking Tac's hand, Oya pulled her into a hug. *"Safe journeys. Do me one favor."*

"Anything."

Delicate fingers ran through her hair and smoothed over her eyes. *"Describe these the same as my mother's and no specifics about the ceremony. Other than that, enjoy embellishing your story to the moon and back."*

~

Both Ferdinan's and Jon's homes were winter wonderlands, but significantly different. Humanity chose invisibility in North Chūzo. But in North Oueshi – a short boat ride away – color and human influence won.

Nature was easily visible, but tamed and bent to human will. Instead of plants cultivated to survive the dead of winter, they sluffed off their brightness to hibernate, leaving humans to bring color to the muted world.

Buildings stood tall, proud, and beautiful. At least to a human eye. Oya doubted the rest of earth's inhabitants felt the same. But such was the egotism of humanity.

Following Jon's collection of strings, Oya made her way to what looked like a village of kings. Magnificent buildings obviously made for royalty spread out across rolling snowy hills. The ocean hugged one side and a forest another. The rest was walled off with building sized hedges and decorative gates guarding the few roads in and out. *No wonder he's so sheltered. In a grotto such as this...* Yes, there was sky above and the illusion of openness, but this was definitely a grotto.

Normally she'd want to drag people out of places like this. But until the dark clouds over Jon's mind were gone, this was the best place for him. And for her... She needed to rest or she'd be useless for some time.

Walking up the tallest hill, she entered the building sitting higher than the rest. Outside was awe inspiring, and inside... *This place is huge...* Intricate designs carved into the ceiling told a myriad of stories. Some of which shouldn't be in a place like this. In the home of a hei-o. Destroying them was tempting, but she'd leave that to the next... *Will there be another?*

Shaking her head, Oya followed the sounds of life and chaos. Inside an auditorium sized common room was an overwhelming site.

Aside from Evelyn and the two girls she was dragging around, everyone was significantly taller than her and filled with so much life to make them feel twice their size. In the center of it all was Jon, somehow touching every person in the crowd he was half buried under. It didn't look comfortable, but Oya had never seen him so relaxed.

Breathing out, she released their minds. It was a little thing to block them from thinking about her, but draining. So was reaching out to Kámua. There wasn't enough of her left to command it, only to say it was time to return to Ferdinan.

I'm coming.

If she could've caught her breath, she would've laughed. *No more 'til I properly rest...whenever that may be...* Bracing herself against the wall, Oya straightened, put on her biggest grin, and walked in. "This place is huge!"

"It's not much bigger than Ferdinan's estate...the main house..." Chocolate eyes blinked in confusion, but Jon pushed it aside to snuggle deeper inside the mishmash of bodies.

"Yah, but Ferdinan's estate didn't have twenty-foot carved ceilings and *cathedral* doors!"

"Huh? They aren't twenty feet...I don't think..." A dozen arms somehow hugged the Thinker at once, making him squeak. "What's *cathedral?*"

"Oh! Oh! Oh! You're my big brother's friend! I remember you from the screen!" Green-ringed black eyes appeared out of nowhere and tiny hands grabbed Oya's ice-cold ones. "Is he having fun at school? I haven't gotten to talk to him in a long time. I want to tell him about my new sisters! Will you tell him to message me so I can?"

"I'll scold him for not calling you regularly." Oya knelt and spun the girl so her arms were crossed before releasing one hand and pushing her to spin away. "You have new sisters? How exciting."

"Yes! Tinny! Yin!" Evelyn pointed at them.

They stood looking uncertain and troubled at the strange girl with inhuman eyes and blood red hair, but Oya grinned and let Evelyn burn through the excessive energy the girl enjoyed.

***

This is unexpected... Shivering, nose running, and wrapped in a blanket Leoniel didn't recognize, Skuna stood on his porch looking annoyed.

"I didn't lock the door."

Swooping up the half-frozen girl, he took her to the dining hall and placed her in a chair next to the fire. "How long have you been gone?"

"Long enough someone locked the door."

Motioning an employee over, Leoniel instructed them to bring warm tea and prepare breakfast for the girl. "It's dangerous roaming

182

outside when it's dark. And if you got lost in these temperatures! Please ask for an escort the next time you want to play outside."

"Who'd play in this?" Skuna leaned closer to the fire. "There's a promise that must be kept."

What...does that mean? Before Leoniel could ask, a warm mug was brought. Skuna gladly took it – drinking in the warmth.

"Sir." His oldest employee smiled and gestured to the hall. "Patrik is waiting in the common room. I'll watch over her 'til Lashina arrives."

"Thank you, Mr. Quilic." Leoniel turned to his young guest to find her shooing him toward the hall. "Enjoy your breakfast and please let us know before you go outside again."

"It was necessary."

He wanted to ask, but she'd turned her full attention to Mr. Quilic, and Jorani's messenger was waiting. *How do I convince them?* This situation was delicate and reached beyond Ferdinan. And, though terrible to think, the boy only had days left. They needed to focus on children worldwide that'd be hurt if they handled this wrong.

***

How long have I been waiting? It felt like eternities. Laying back in the dark abyss, Ferdinan ignored the golden light emanating from Evelyn's door. She was happy now. With siblings, grandparents, and more uncles and aunts than she'd know what to do with. Soon she'd have cousins. *She's happy.* And he was glad.

Emil's animosity radiated across the endless abyss – scoffing at his lame attempt to assuage his guilt at everything he stole from her.

Tired but somehow not yet dead, Ferdinan closed his eyes. If only he could sleep here. But...how did one sleep when they were already unconscious?

Warmth and life entered the abyss. Sitting up, Ferdinan found himself surrounded by a golden light as bright as the abyss was dark. *What is this?*

The fulfilment of a promise.

Slowly the intense light divided into three pillars. One radiated youthful energy. Another concern and duty. And the third, broken and flickering, was fatigued and filled with disappointment. It was the third that felt most personal. And it made sense. His very existence–

Thoughts like those keep ruining the gifts I've given you.

"I...I don't understand. Who are you?"

"It's the reason we're still alive." A frowning Emil stepped from the darkness. "They all are."

Why does he look faded?

"You are surprised? Haven't you noticed the medicine they've been giving you?" When Ferdinan looked away, Emil stepped closer. "Of course, you were hoping it'd kill us. Like always."

One of the golden pillars glowed brighter – separating them. **Which makes this cruel.**

Both Ferdinan and Emil turned their attention to the light. "What do you mean?"

"You're going to heal us again."

It's what I was sent to do. But you can't keep damaging this body. Either of you.

Ferdinan looked away while Emil scowled at the skeleton.

And this... There was a long pause before the pillar spoke again. *Your death will claim more than you. Neither is it fair for one to accept death while the other wishes to live.*

"The world would be better off without me."

"Our death'll claim more than ourselves? Why should I worry about nebulous others I don't know? How does my death hurt anyone?"

It'll hurt me and my siblings.

Emil scoffed. "Our death'll hurt gods?"

Kámua can't survive another loss. And unlike you, we can't birth more.

"Who's Kámua?"

The one who's comforted you for months. Who gave you medicine and stories. The broken pillar moved closer –

barely glowing. *The one who warmed you when despair took over.*

Ferdinan heard that voice begging him again. Pleading. Desperate. It stole strength from his legs and resolve from his heart.

Twice I've healed you 'cause I was asked. Will you reject me a third time? And by doing so kill my sibling and shatter the last hope of your dear friend?

Ferdinan's face twisted as he fought back tears and a stifled sob escaped Emil... *He's crying? Why?*

Emil walked away – keeping his back to both of them. "Do what you want. I'll be gone soon anyway."

Though silenced, you'll never be gone. This is as much your life as his.

That made them both pause and sent chills down Ferdinan's spine. That voice begged and filled him with more warmth. But it didn't stop those words from echoing around his mind. *Shatter the last hope of my dear friend? What does any of this have to do with Oya?* "It doesn't matter. You can't help this time."

Not completely. You've done terrible things to your body. But I can do enough. Will you accept my gift?

"Why can't it be over? Why can't everything finally end?"

Why can't it?

Ferdinan's lips twisted and he looked away. "I'm so tired. So broken. I... I should've never existed. So why can't I disappear?"

It's a cruel thing. Will you accept my gift?

***

That was an unpleasant exchange, but a peaceful transition between North Chūzo and East Azuté was imperative. Leoniel didn't know the boy well, but the success of these treaties would be top priority for one willing to be beaten to death for his people. Assuring them was the best Leoniel could do for his guest.

His bejeweled band chimed. Time to relieve Sora.

From the hall Leoniel heard Skuna's voice speaking a language he never heard. Inside Ferdinan's room, Sora slept peacefully in the chair and Skuna stood at the boy's side, hand hovering over his heart.

What's she doing? A strange light swirled around her arm – growing until it enveloped the boy. It vanished as quickly as it came. *Am I dreaming?*

Monitors cried out their various calls, but he was the only one startled by it. Smiling, the girl nodded as if at a job well done. Until she turned to find Leoniel.

Shrugging, she walked past him, "He doesn't get another. I'm resting now."

What just happened? Leoniel rushed to check on Ferdinan. *He's breathing easily...* And the blue was fading from the boy's skin. All vitals were improving before the man's eyes. "Samuel!"

Sora startled awake – poised to jump where needed – and an employee rushed in.

"Please bring Samuel here now."

"What's happening?" Sora's eyes locked on Ferdinan.

Not wanting the boy to wake up yet, Leoniel placed a neural blocker and motioned Sora over. "Am I seeing this wrong?"

Hematite eyes doubled. "How...?"

Chapter 26

Why can't I die? I'm not needed. Or wanted. So why? That dreaded warmth washed over him and Ferdinan found his gaze drifting to the screen with Oya's histories. Forcing blue crystals away, he stared at the wall... Tall windows gave a brilliant view of summer flowers in full bloom – safe inside the greenhouse sheltering them.

Sora shifted in the chair at his sudden movement. "Are you ok?"

"Yes."

"Is there anything you need or want?"

Please stop asking. There was only one answer. He lifted bound hands as far as the restraints would allow. *Which will break first, these or my bones?*

A tired sigh left her. Then the chair scooted closer and softness caressed his hand. It was unbearable, but he didn't want it to stop... He deserved pain. Punishment. Not this...

"Can you face me and honestly promise to leave the tube alone?" Gentle fingers brushed back his hair. "We don't want this either, but 'til you're healthy and eating on your own, it won't change."

"He had no right." Ferdinan growled.

"He had every right to help his brother."

"Then why's he here instead of with Jon?!" *He's not my brother! He never will be...* "Brothers. Parents. In-laws. Nieces... They're *his* family. His."

Fire crackled. Snowflakes danced on the other side of one wall and bright flowers filled the other. *Why can't I die?* Ferdinan hated himself for the weakness leaking out of his eyes.

***

Rain filled the world. Metallic notes danced fiendishly at his command. A monster's command. Wrong. Chaotic. Zephyr's heart raced and sweat dripped. Horrific attacks forced strings to bring notes to life.

Clenched teeth forbade internal screams from escaping.

All his soul commanded the monstrosity, those unnatural sounds. His heart pleaded. Agony poured out of him. And the goo eased, letting his lungs expand. Motion. Failing. Running away. All that existed was a monster, a monstrosity, and the demonic rain. All standing in a blood-filled room.

***

Father Artimus spoke after an eternity of contemplation. "And he was unconscious when he got better? He's been restrained the entire time?"

"Ya." Leoniel sighed and leaned back – dark eyes on the ceiling. Even if the girl's culture wasn't privileged information, who'd believe what he saw? *What was that light? And Skuna...* The girl was sleeping solidly. Just like a normal child who'd worn themselves out. "Him being awake would make a difference?"

"Confidentially?" Father waited for the colorful man to nod. "Medical devices and medicines. He's tested a number on himself. Made a few for himself."

I see... "What do you need me to do for him?"

"Make sure he doesn't tear out that feeding tube." Father sighed, exhausted. "We need to get him to a healthy weight, but it'll take some time even if he cooperates."

"I can't keep a child strapped down for 'some time.'" Leoniel sighed. "If not necessary to prevent him harming himself, I wouldn't allow it at all."

"Ferdinan always gets better in time to distance himself so he can get worse again." Father looked at the medical disk with Ferdinan's information. "I wish I knew how to stop the cycle."

"How should I approach Jorani concerning his improved condition? What'd be best for Ferdinan?"

"Tread lightly. Listen to him – both what he says and doesn't say." Father hesitated. "And...frankly, he won't trust either of you if Kyo Jorani presses on with their intentions."

"Thank you. I'll do what I can." Leoniel saw Father out and made his way to Ferdinan's room – surprised to find Skuna lurking outside the threshold – eyes trained on the boy. *Could she be....? But why's she here? And...how's Ferdinan connected to her people?*

Leaning down, Leoniel whispered, "Is there something I can help you with, Skuna?"

She jumped, but instead of looking guilty, she was annoyed. "Why's he bound? I have business with him."

"Let me see if he's up for a visit."

"He shouldn't be bound." Her hazel eyes cut through him. "It broke Kámua, it'll break him."

Who's Kámua? "We tried. It's unsafe to do so." Seeing anyone tied down, let alone a sick child, was gut wrenching, but the skeletal boy nearly tore the feeding tube from his belly when he woke up last night. It took all three of them to restrain him. If he hadn't passed out when Leoniel grabbed his ankles, the boy might've succeeded.

Skuna frowned at him. Stepping in the room, she called out in her native language. Her scolding voice made Ferdinan pale and look away. Turning back, she poked Leoniel's arm. "I'll return later."

Those three words held many expectations, ones the Kyo wasn't certain could be met. But he smiled and entered – first addressing the exhausted Sora. "Go eat and rest."

Giving the woman a hug, he took her seat beside Ferdinan's bed. The boy didn't want to be seen crying, so Leoniel pretended he saw nothing. "Let's try a trust exercise."

"...I don't feel like games."

"This isn't a game." Heavily ringed fingers reached for the nearest restraint. The closer he got, the harder Ferdinan trembled. *Why's he shaking...?* "I'm going to remove this band. What're you going to do?"

"Why are you doing this?" The boy's voice was strained.

"Many reasons. I love the Artimuses and they love you. I feel your genius and potential is amazing and will help countless people. I won't be able to live with myself if I don't. All children deserve to be healthy and happy. 'Cause you have a kind and loving heart – the world always needs more of these."

"They don't love me. They pity me. They feel obligation. I'm not a genius. Everyone's potential is greater than mine. I'm not...I'm not any of those! I'm just a burden. I couldn't even help–" The boy cut himself off and forced his face to the flowers, farther from Leoniel.

"It's ok if you can't see it." Praying this wasn't a mistake, Leoniel carefully undid the restraint. "The rest of us see it for you."

That boney hand jerked away, finally free. For a moment Leoniel worried. But Ferdinan rolled to his side and dried his face. "I'm sorry...for troubling you. I shouldn't be here..."

"I'm happy you are. You're welcome for as long as you need, as long as you want. My home's always open for you to return whenever you wish." It was hard sitting there while that frail body shook with stifled sobs. But what mattered was making this easier for the boy, not himself. "You're safe here. I won't let anyone near you unless you wish it. Neither will I allow anyone to take you from here without your consent. My home's now and forever yours."

Leoniel almost expected the boy to say he didn't want anyone near him or to send Samuel and Sora away. And as terrible as it was, the Kyo would do so to build trust. But the boy just wept.

***

It was all Oya could do to gasp out a laugh as the man returned her to her feet. *Which one is he again?* Such overwhelming height!

The other giants were smothering Jon somewhere, but this one was fun. He let her ride on his shoulders while giving her a tour of the "house." Nothing this big could be a house, even if it was for multiple generations of giants.

"Bastian, everything's arranged for tomorrow."

Oya turned to whoever spoke. The boy...young man...boy? It was hard to tell with his angular features. But he was nearly a head shorter than Jon. "You're not a giant, which makes you...Rigel?"

"Yes." A light blush colored is red-brown skin, but he cleared his throat and pointed at the appallingly mismatched and oversized clothes she'd pilfered from somewhere. "Somehow the trunk of clothing you were given disappeared, which makes you in need of a new wardrobe."

"There's plenty of clothing here."

Rigel chuckled. "I can only guess how many headaches you've given Jon."

"Many." Giving him a mad wink, Oya spun. "But few of them were over fashion."

190

Both brothers stifled a laugh and commiserated for their baby brother.

"We have Barago's booked tomorrow. If he can't make outfits you love, they don't exist."

Oya snorted at Rigel's confidence. "I don't know who Barago is, but I accept that challenge."

***

Skuna? Ferdinan didn't know who the girl was, but she had rods in her ear and spoke Oŭndo. She also told him to behave so she could go home. But why would anything he do affect her? They were strangers.

But that warmth. That broken light...it begged. *I need to move.* His muscles weren't screaming like they should be, but they were twitching. Soon... But the Kyo's household wasn't letting him do much.

Warmth surged and the screen with Oya's histories turned on. A new article appeared. And it was... It reminded him of the Washubae monk's meditative exercises. They weren't taught outside the Bae clan, but he watched some of them when he visited years ago. If this–

A chime signaled the colorful man to stop reading. Dark eyes fell on the neural blocker. "Samuel'll be arriving soon."

The unspoken question lingered – giving Ferdinan full power. Or, it felt that way. The man was a Kyo, but adults, healers especially, lied all the time. Why would Leoniel be any different? "He should go home."

"And Sora?"

That question was harder. If he could keep her touch...but he didn't deserve it. He was being greedy. "She should go home too. Her spouse misses her, keeping them separated is wrong."

"She's here 'cause she wants to be."

"She's here 'cause she feels obligated." *Just like you.*

"Ok." The colorful man pressed a button on his bejeweled bracelet then prepared the formula Ferdinan was forced to take. "Know that I do nothing out of obligation – only 'cause I want to."

Liar.

A servant arrived before Leoniel finished preparing the Formula.

"Please make arrangements for Ms. Sora and Healer Samuel to return home." Giving the woman a brilliant smile, he continued. "Thank them for everything they've given. I'll see them off properly this evening."

Ferdinan expected the servant to be surprised, but she nodded and left, giving the skeleton an encouraging smile on the way out.

Turning his attention to the man, Ferdinan waited, wondering how much of this was for show. A tray with three syringes were placed on the side table. The giant formula syringe he knew, but the other two...

"This one is a vitamin mixture and digestive aid. And this one... Samuel said you were familiar with it." Picking up the digestive aid, Leoniel moved to the IV cocktail, but stopped. "I know you want to administer the formula, but it'll be easier for me to do these. Is that ok or would you prefer to do it yourself?"

I prefer to be left alone. But the man could do those without risk of touching him - unlike the formula. "You can. Thank you."

Ferdinan expected to wake up groggy, but nothing happened after the man injected both. So he picked up the larger one. *I hate this.* Unwanted warmth coated him. As long as the Kyo didn't betray him... But he could tear it out! And be restrained again... Would Samuel *and* Father Artimus then be trapped here if he did? Ferdinan would never get rid of them...

This was demeaning. Humiliating. And...*ugh!* It felt so weird. So terrible! He just wanted it to stop...

Boney hands trembled. Fighting. He could tear it out. It was only Leoniel...but that man's touch...

"There's a child who wishes to visit with you." Leoniel removed the tray once Ferdinan put the empty syringe back on it. "She's one I can't guarantee won't come despite your wishes."

"The one who yelled at me?"

"Do you know her?"

"No." But considering the metal in her ear... *Three... Mr. Charlie had five, but most adults had two or three.* And she was young. "I should shower and dress."

"Give the medicine a bit longer. I'll prepare the bath."

I can do that. He wasn't an invalid... Nearly colorless crystals stared at boney hands. The blue was gone but they were the same. Weak. Useless. Destructive.

Dark eyes glowed under lavender hair. "I trust you."

Turning his back, Leoniel left the room.

Ferdinan grabbed the tube. Held it tight in his fist while his other hand pressed against the skin around it. And he shook. Even weak and useless he could do this. He could tear it out! But broken warmth pleaded for him not to. Guilt from the man's last three words... And that strange girl yelling at him to behave...

Nerves flared as he pulled the tube taut. One yank. He was never given a choice! This was done against his will! He had every right to tear it out! He wanted to. He wanted this all to be over...

It's a cruel thing. I don't expect you to see it otherwise. But will you throw away the gift she pleaded for you? The gift she gave part of herself to secure?

I hate you. Beyond words...

Good. Hate me so you can stop hating the one you should love.

***

Xhou was laying on the floor, feet propped on the couch when Herrard returned. "What're you doing this time?"

Blue-black eyes opened, but the Scientist didn't move. "Being lazy."

"Ah, enjoy it while you can." Waiting for Xhou to close his eyes again, Herrard grabbed a pillow and wacked his island brother's face.

"Ah! That's not how you be lazy!"

"But this is how you deal with floor slugs." It was dumb and Herrard had no reason to be obnoxious, but he felt like it, so he swung the pillow again. Though Xhou flailed, his brother didn't move. "No floor slugs!"

"Lazy!"

Taking the challenge, the Healer retreated to his room and gathered the bells he hadn't bothered putting away yet. All of them. Every set and returned to the common room. He sat next to his island brother's feet and selected one of the singular bells that tied to his entrance robe. *Flick. Jingle, jingle. Flick. Jingle, jingle. Flick. Jingle, jingle.*

Carefully slipping the closest band of bells on his wrists, Herrard shook them in the most obnoxious, offbeat rhythm he could manage as he slowly moved the single bell to hover an inch above Xhou's cheek.

Xhou growled comically. "Why can't you ever be lazy with me?"

"This feels lazy to me." He moved the bell close enough to brush the Scientist's cheek before swinging it back and forth.

"*Agh!*" Annoyed hands batted the bell away – again and again – but Xhou refused to move. "Give me that!"

Releasing the string let the bell *bop* Xhou's nose, but the Scientist grabbed it before it could hit the floor.

"One of the wrist bands too." A small toss and a cluster of bells landed on Xhou's chest in a cacophony of protests. He slipped them on his wrist and shook his fist in mock anger. "Come be a floor slug."

"Ok."

Rolling onto the floor, the Healer laid next to his brother and put his feet on the couch.

Side by side, they shook the bells as obnoxiously as they could – bumping each other to disrupt their focus and trying to outdo the other.

Both refused to be the first to give up.

Chapter 27

The elf's beach? Though considering what happened with Zephyr... *What was that light? And voice?*

Gongie looked up at the ever-full moon. *I wish I was back at the camp.* That thought startled him. He'd been so focused on Zephyr, he hadn't thought much about himself. But... *My efforts mattered there...* And... *I miss Ajani. And Larashi's teasing.*

The living conditions weren't preferable. But he was useful and didn't have to pretend horrible things weren't happening. He helped someone...

"So much for resting." A transparent elf stared down at him.

She's still like this? "What happened to you?"

"I did too much." The impressively tall elf sat, plopped back, and close sapphire eyes. "Tell me what's wrong."

Not sure what else to do, Gongie laid back and told her everything.

"You want to give up."

"That voice said it'd care for him..." The moon loomed heavily overhead. "Is that me wanting to give up?"

"Dashū's insistent Zephyr finishes the test." Transparent fingers dug absentmindedly in the twilight sand. "It didn't expect him to break like that."

"It...?"

"A story for another day." Standing, she offered a hand. "Dashū'll handle the rest. But if you don't want to give up, stay with him in the waking world."

Gongie was surprised how solid that transparent hand was. "I'm not trained for this."

"No one is anymore." A long breath slowly leaked out of her. "You've only to choose what you want to do."

The words that left Gongie's mouth weren't the ones he was expecting. "I want to go back to the camp. I want to truly help people again..."

A grin Gongie couldn't interpret spread across her face. "You don't think you've been helping him."

"I haven't..."

"That explains much." Turning, she waved open the path to the silver roads. "Give me time and I'll arrange a meeting with Mr. Charlie."

How many people does she know?
***

The shower was refreshing. So were clean clothes. Now Ferdinan waited. Sort of.

Breathing out, the skeleton followed each step of the first moving meditation the screen showned him. Moving slowly, as if through honey. Flexing and stabilizing each muscle. Forcing them to hold steady before slowly transitioning to the next step.

It looked smooth and gentle in his reflection off the glass. But his underused muscles trembled and he was sweating.

"*Good. Keep listening to Kámua.*"

Startled, Ferdinan spun. Skuna stood, arms crossed and smirking at him. Wiping sweat from his face, he bowed. "*You wanted to talk to me?*"

"*San-a healed all it could.*"

"*Who are you?*"

"*I'm Skuna, guardian of San-a, Ferdinan, keeper of Kámua.*"

What's she talking about? That warmth settled over him – insisting he knew. Proving how broken he was. That was all. He was broken.

"*You need to keep your promise.*" Skuna stepped forward.

"*What promise?*"

A little hand pointed to the screen of Oya's histories. "*Kámua's depending on you to live and heal so it can learn how to become whole.*"

"*I don't understand.*"

"*You don't? Do you truly not?*"

That broken warmth begged. Pleaded. It didn't want to die. It didn't want him to die. But this was all part of his broken mind. It wasn't real. He didn't want it to be...

"*There're others dependent on you too. Right?*" Stepping closer again, Skuna pointed to her ear, but not the three honors in her upper ear, the two rods and a hoop in her lobe. "*Each of these should bring joy. Not sorrow.*"

Ferdinan swallowed hard – not wanting to think about what she implied.

"*Even if yours are tainted with sorrow...you don't have to spread the taint.*" Again, she stepped closer. Numbness engulfed his hand and he fought to not flinch away. "*You can choose to cleanse it. Stop being a keeper and become a guardian.*"

She turned to the door, leaving him confused. And... As numbness faded, he realized he was holding something. A small box drowned in his boney hand. Inside was a tiny golden rod. "*Wait.*"

~

So many interesting guests. Leoniel didn't want to leave them, but Jon needed this and he trusted Lashina to watch over and provide for them in his absence.

This also gave Jorani an opportunity to talk to Ferdinan. But how much could go wrong? *He left the tube alone.* Kind of. Leoniel watched the boy grab it multiple times – ready to tear it from his body. But every time, trembling, face twisted by competing emotions, he let go and fought not to grab it again.

If Ferdinan kept overcoming the temptation... Or was it too much? A torture?

That strange language hit his ears. But it wasn't Skuna talking. Ferdinan's deepening baritone smoothly formed sounds Leoniel couldn't understand. The two sat on the floor facing each other – a little box placed between them. Every time the skeletal boy pushed it toward her, she pushed it back, scolding him.

Tapping the open door announced his presence, but only Ferdinan looked at him. Skuna sat there, arms crossed and lips pursed to the side, radiating irritation at the boy. It was difficult, but Leoniel held back a chuckle. "Kyo Jorani'll be here soon. I need to prepare my shop, but Lashina will care for you 'til I return."

197

Guilt forced blue crystals away, but Skuna only shrugged.

"Is there anything you need, Master Ferdinan?"

Red tinged pale cheeks. "No. I apologize for troubling you."

***

Berago's is huge and bright and open. And home. Jon's eyes teared up. He was certain he'd never see this place again. Never see his family. Or the sun. That he'd lost everything...

Oya dragged Jingjing through the opening that was barely tall enough for him. Bastian, Rigel, and Naizu laughed at the comical sight. Samuel and Xingho were taking care of various duties. And Ozar stood by him.

Giving his hand a squeeze, the Hei-O pulled Jon close. "We don't have to go inside."

No. That's not it. I just... Jon wished he could say why he was scared. It didn't make sense. "We should go before Oya causes too much chaos."

Laughing, Ozar wrapped an arm around Jon's shoulder. They entered in time to see Oya snatch Leoniel's aqua blue and pink sequined jacket only to dance around him.

"I want one like this but with teal and lime green!" She spun.

Leoniel laughed heartily. "Whatever your heart desires, my Lady."

Relief flooded into Jon at Leoniel's bright, energetic smile. And he realized... He knew Ferdinan was staying with the Kyo. If the gent had stolen Leoniel's joy then there was no hope for him to find his again.

Dead serious, Oya turned to the colorful man. "I'm not a lady."

"I apologize. A princess then?"

A full belly laugh burst from her. "Call me Oya."

"Ah, then you may call me 'Leoniel' or 'tailor,' whichever you prefer."

"But you *are* a Kyo." Perfect seriousness coated the normally crazed redhead before she giggled and slid over to Jon. "So, why're we here?"

"Seriously?" Jon grimaced at the mismatched pants and top she was drowning in. *Where did she steal those from?* "You need clothes."

Oya looked around. "They where are?"

198

Laughter followed as Ozar came up from the side. "He takes your measurements, you tell him what you want, and he makes it happen."

"Sounds more complicated than it should be." Wild green eyes looked Ozar and Leoniel over.

"Have you never been to a tailor?" Leoniel asked kindly.

"No, mom would sometimes make my clothes, though usually I got hand-me-downs. Even at school, they've just given me what I have."

Jon's initial surprise didn't last long. Considering her penchant to wear whatever she had access too, no matter how atrocious or ill fitted...

Leoniel grinned. "It'd be my pleasure to create clothing for you. Please, tell me what you like."

A delicate brow rose high over an inhuman green eye. "If I want an orange dress trimmed in purple and studded with peridot?"

"I have a number of cut peridots to choose from. You've only to choose the orange and purple fabrics you desire."

That trickster-god grin turned on Jon. "What do you think?"

"Sounds like an ugly dress, but Leoniel will make it work if you're serious." Jon looked about the room. It was so bright and spacious. Vaulted ceilings and brilliant amounts of natural light accentuated the plethora of colors. It was wonderful. "Where's Jingjing?"

"He was taken for some final fittings," Leoniel beamed.

There was someone else missing too. Someone Jon expected a big hug from. "Is he with Rinie?"

Dark eyes brightened under lavender hair. "She had her child."

"Really? Is he beautiful? Strong? Healthy?"

Leoniel smiled bright. "Definitely healthy. But I haven't visited yet."

***

Ferdinan bowed when Kyo Jorani entered. Trembling. Heart pounding... The skeleton spent the morning agonizing over what the Kyo wanted. His unacceptable displays at the conference... The trouble he caused them and Leoniel. Any number of things happening with food supplies... Or insults he hadn't realized he'd given. He didn't remember much of what he did the last couple weeks...

"You should be in bed."

"I'm feeling better. I apologize for troubling you."

"You aren't the one troubling me." The Kyo sat in the chair Ferdinan prepared for them. "Please sit."

Ferdinan did as he was told - keeping his head low. Boney fingers clutched at stick legs. "You wanted to see me, Kyo?"

Sighing, the Kyo shifted - moving closer until Ferdinan flinched away. If Kyo Jorani felt like Leoniel or Samuel he'd be helpless, unable to control his reaction. Making this worse...

"I apologize." Shifting back, the Kyo waved a hand to make Ferdinan look up. "I didn't mean to startle you."

"I'm sorry! I didn't-"

"It's ok." Jorani interrupted - voice smooth and steady. "I'm here to help."

Help...? Ferdinan's mind spun, searching for what they'd know he was connected to. But the disks were all he could think of. "I'm able to maintain stable production. Unless you have a large order, I can meet needs without difficulty..."

Silence lingered for a moment. The Kyo looked like they were about to say something, but changed their mind. "I'm sorry, which project are you referring to?"

"I..." *How many does he know about...?* Kyos were well connected and well informed, but only Grandpa Huey knew about most of his projects and the old man wouldn't say anything about him.

"Other than your disks, what do you do?"

Ferdinan offered the first innocuous creation to pop into his head. "Medical foodstuffs. Particularly for people who can't eat or have suffered starvation."

"Oh?" The Kyo smiled. "Did you find something that worked for you and decided to share?"

"No..." *What's their purpose? What do they want?*

When Ferdinan didn't elaborate, Jorani moved the conversation on. Seemingly random questions flowed organically. Ferdinan realized he made a mistake when the Kyo focused on the Artimuses for too long, but he was ready when the topics turned to his family and country. Though it confused him when Jorani didn't ask about food supplies. He was certain that was where this meeting was leading once his allies were mentioned. And when it ended... *What did they want?*

***

Humming danced happily around the room. It was a delightful tune, even if it was off key. Jumping and spinning on the air. Soring back and forth. Teasing all within earshot. And when it came to an end, the humming circled around to start again. And again.

It made everyone smile. But not Jon. Dark caves filled his mind. Trapped and thirsty. Oya should be dying. How long did it take for thirst to steal a life? How terrible...? Twitching muscles. Too hot...too cold...

"What a lovely song, Oya." Leoniel placed the last pin in the pants she randomly grabbed. "I've never heard it before."

"I was wondering the same," the mountain beside him spoke – deep voice reverberating through the room.

And falling rocks deafened him. Dirt choked him. Blistered hands pulled flying bodies over the crevasse. And the walls kept falling. Kept striving to bury him. To swallow them all!

"Are you ok?" A strong arm pulled Jon toward Ozar's whispered voice.

"It's a *folk* song of sorts from the people we helped on our fieldtrip." Oya spun in place before darting to a bolt of yellow fabric.

Leoniel chuckled – dark eyes looking over Jon before sending as much energy and color her direction. "*Folk?* That's a word I've never heard."

Jon buried his face in Ozar's arm as giggles filled the room. "I need to leave."

Taking Jon's hand, his big brother guided him out of Berago's while Oya made a mess of the fabric bolts. Outside was cloudy. He didn't know when the clouds came. It was bright and happy and–

A strong hand encased Jon's before Ozar's face drifted below his. It took a moment to realize his brother was kneeling. That anything other than the unforgiving rocks existed.

"You're safe. I'm right here. I love you." Ozar repeated this until Jon looked at him. "Tell me what you need."

"Safety..."

Tears filled his big brother's eyes. Standing, he pulled Jon into a hug and didn't let go.

Chapter 28

Blue crystals searched for an escape as his heart thrashed.

"Ferdinan, it's ok." Father Artimus didn't move. "I'm not coming–"

"Go away. It's my turn with him," Skuna *shooed* the King Father.

"There're things I need to discuss with Kyo Jorani. But..." Father sighed in defeat. "We'll talk later."

Adrenaline faded when the King left – allowing embarrassment to set in. *Why can't I control myself?*

Skuna sat in the middle of the room – expecting him to join her and ignoring his inexcusable behavior. Slipping out from behind the bed, he grabbed the box she gave. "*That was too rude. He's North Oueshi's King.*"

"*He's not my king. He's only a hei-o's child who wasted my time.*"

"*That doesn't make sense...*" He put the box by her foot.

An eyebrow rose high. "*You don't know what a hei-o is?*"

"*Hei-O is this country's heir to the throne.*"

"*It's the heir, but not to that.*" She snorted and pushed the box to him.

"*I don't deserve this.*"

A little hand pointed at his shoulder. "*You don't deserve that either, but it doesn't bother you.*"

Startled, Ferdinan looked to find scarred skin peeking through the top of his robe. Boney fingers pulled it fully closed. "*It's not the same.*"

"*You've earned them both.*" She tossed the box in his lap – eyes daring him to defy her. "*What's your decision? Once I leave; you can't change it.*"

Despair stole what strength he had. Pulling stick legs in, he buried his face in his knees. *I want everything to stop. I want it all to end...*

"*No. Look at me and tell me.*"

He felt Skuna move closer. Numbness touched his arm, and when he looked up, her face was an inch from his.

"Will you throw away Ṡarĩ-a's gift and abandon those who depend on you? Will you grab hold of your desires and make them reality? Will you stay by those who need you regardless of any duty you have to them?" Her face moved closer. *"I need to know 'cause that determines what I do when I leave."*

"I don't understand."

"If you choose your heart's desire, I'll prepare my people for what happens to Kámua. If you choose duty, I'll prepare my people for what happens to you."

A chime sounded, reminding Ferdinan of the messages he hadn't read. Grandpa Huey and Fulason. Yahmo. His apprentices... But it was too hard... Opening the little box, he stared at the golden rod. There was no winning. He caused pain, death, destruction. *I'm nothing but a blight.*

Golden light coated Skuna. She stood and retrieved the vial. She couldn't know what it was, but that glow... *How broken am I?*

***

Leoniel escorted them to an open balcony for lunch, but Oya had business with the colorful man. Once food was served, she grabbed a pale blue string jutting from the Kyo's chest and left. Leoniel following behind. *"You don't understand me, but neither are my words alien."*

"That..." The colorful man paled – looking closely at her ears.

"Kyo's are interesting people. The highest honor one can earn. Trying to earn it keeps you from achieving it, but unless your efforts are known and recognized, no one could award you the title." Oya giggled. "Despite this contradiction, it's recognized by two worlds."

"You're a Traveler." Leoniel bowed. "It's an honor."

Oya giggled. "I come from a long line of travelers."

The colorful man studied her. "That's not the same thing."

"Wise." Alien eyes drifted over the bright, colorful room. "Thank you for caring for Skuna. You're wrong about her, though."

"You're from a family of Travelers, but aren't one. Have no piercings, yet know of Skuna?"

"I also know the question haunting you." Crazed eyes flashed green at Leoniel's strained smile. "She's strange. And unique. But she's not the Rã-yumôn. Though you've met her. As have the other two."

Again, the man studied her – considering his words. "When did you enter their lives? Jon's? Ferdinan's?"

A giant grin split her face. "I have a story, a task, and a command."

"I'm listening."

"There once was a boy who couldn't bear the future. Though most would be envious for it, it made his heart sick. The disease spread 'til it nearly killed him." Oya grinned. He knew the story, but never heard it told. "A wanderer from the land of giants found him and took him home. Nursed him to health. And gave him every opportunity to thrive."

Watching closely, Oya took in every gesture, reaction. The paling of rich skin. Holding his breath. A trembling lip. He knew this story.

"Only, that future still awaited, so the illness thrived no matter how he smiled. And the giant understood. 'Til that future changed the boy would never truly be well." Stretching, Oya grinned. "The giant searched the boy's futures. Sifting through every reality 'til they found one."

She paused when Leoniel looked away at the painful story.

"It was a difficult future. Fraught with obstacles and resistance. The boy was resigned to keep to the future he knew despite how sick it made him, but the giant forged onward. For no child should be trapped in a future that'd kill them." A gentle smile took over her delicate lips. "The quest was long with too many battles, but eventually the giant won."

Leoniel's lip trembled. Dark eyes filled with an old pain. "They got the boy to the reality where the illness could be cured and he thrived."

"Yet he was crushed by guilt – allowing a new illness to take hold."

"The giants nursed him past it also. 'Til the boy was a healthy man."

"Healthy and happy and thriving." Oya circled him. "Now he takes in everyone he can – returning the kindness he was shown. I hope soon my two friends'll share that story."

Leoniel swallowed hard – nodding. "I understand."

"Tell no one save the Kyos about me. You're forbidden from letting the hei-o become aware of who I am. He has no right to this knowledge 'til his line has earned the removal of that title."

"You use that word as if it were a punishment or a curse."

"It is. An unfair one. But the only fair option." Oya softened her grin. "Don't worry. Every opinion you have of Ozar is correct. And his family. But that doesn't change the responsibility passed on to him."

"I understand."

***

Ferdinan placed the empty vial on the side table. *Why am I doing this? Why...?* Nursing a broken part of his mind was ludicrous... But he had a duty to fix East Azuté. Forcing that burden on strangers was wrong. And Elbie... He was a useless mentor, but the young Tinkerer didn't have a family. Ferdinan couldn't leave until he made sure the boy's future was secure...

Or maybe these were all cowardly excuses. A stupid, useless coward who never should've existed!

"Is everything ok?" A soothing voice interrupted his thoughts.

"I need these materials and equipment." Ferdinan grabbed a small screen and handed it to Lashina.

She took it, smiling. A real smile. Like this was what she'd been waiting for. "Anything else?"

He wanted to roll over and sleep forever. But he had a duty. "I don't want Father Artimus back here again. He has a country and a sick son to worry about. And I need to return to school to finish my mentee's apprenticeship. I've already requested the supply boat dock here. It'll arrive in a couple days."

"I can see to the first part..."

"I'm going back. I won't let anyone stop me." He felt terrible being forceful toward an employee who'd only been kind, but if he was going to stay... Blue crystals fell on the little box with the rod inside. *I'll do what I need.*

Lashina held the screen tight. "I know. But you can't eat. Is your school capable of caring for your needs?"

"It's not the school's responsibility. It's mine."

"Please tell me everything you need and I'll do what I can."

That surprised Ferdinan. *The Kyo's household is strange...* "Thank you."

***

206

A line of white and black keys sat untouched. No matter how Jon tried, his fingers wouldn't move. *When was the last time I played?* It felt like everything he loved disappeared from his life one by one over the last year. Even his trip to Berago's wasn't satisfying...

Excited squeals and cheers flew down the hall. Moments later Evelyn and Tinny crashed into Jon's knees.

"I won!" Tinny jumped, cheering.

"You're so fast!" Evelyn grabbed her hands, jumping with her and calling Yin over to join them.

"Racing inside isn't safe. That's what the trails and indoor gym are for," Jon half-heartedly scolded them. It was nice seeing them play. But it wasn't safe.

"We weren't racing! We were looking for you!" Evelyn took his hand and tugged, but Jon didn't stand.

Leaning forward, he smiled. "That looked like racing."

His newest nieces fidgeted, looking worried, but Evelyn wasn't fazed. "Remember the recipe Pa-papa taught me? Will you cook it with me? Please? You said you would!"

I said that? When...? Even if he remembered, the idea... Playing the piano felt easier and that was beyond him. Expectant eyes fell on him – crushing him with guilt. They were half-way to the kitchens before he realized he'd stood.

A million excuses filled his mind. But he was an uncle now, not the baby... Melancholy killed what little was inside him. He didn't want to cook. He just wanted to be held. He wanted to feel safe.

Anxiety welled when they entered the kitchen. What if cooking was painful here too? Like it'd become at school. Like at the camp? What if the joy was gone forever? He'd completely lose what he once loved most... The amazing gift his dad and older brothers gave him.

The room blurred. He batted away tears as quickly as they came, but it didn't help.

Bowls, spoons, scales, ingredients...they were all laid out and waiting. Evelyn climbed on her step stool. "Pa-papa says to make sure you have everything first!"

Jon thought Evelyn was talking to him, but she was facing her new sisters who watched intently.

Not sure what to do, he cleared his throat, hoping his voice didn't sound too strained. "Show me how much you know."

"Yay! Watch me!"

Evelyn went to work – chittering about what she was doing at each step or talking about school or describing the random bugs she found. It was exhausting keeping up with her mind, so when she stopped, it caught Jon's attention. Instead of asking, she was on tip-toes reaching for the knives.

"What do you need cut?" Jon grabbed the blade before she could.

"It's ok, Ma-mama, my big brother, and Pa-papa all taught me how to use a knife..." Evelyn stared into space for a moment. "But teaching me made them feel better, so teach me too so you can feel better!"

Her grandmother and Ferdinan? But she's only six... Jon laughed to not cry. Her offer was both ridiculous and adorable. "Thank you. Please let me teach you too."

He showed her everything his dad and brothers taught him and she mimicked him perfectly.

"Now I know four ways to cut!"

Together they prepped and mixed the ingredients. For assembly, Tinny and Yin joined. Jon was almost disappointed when it was time to put them in the oven. He couldn't remember the last time he had fun playing in the kitchen. The last time he cooked with people who wanted his food. *I'm glad...* It was a simple dish, but it was fun...

While he cried, Evelyn ran around like an expert – teaching her new sisters how to set the timers and properly clean and store everything.

It was fun... Making only what they wanted to make because they wanted to make it... And when the food was done, they took it, drinks, and a blanket to the indoor green house to enjoy a summer picnic in the middle of winter.

"Thank you, Evelyn." *I needed this.*

"Thank you too! It was fun!"

Chapter 29

The human body's fascinating. Elbie studied everything Ilu gave him about nerves between testing samples of the blight medicine – comparing it to Master Ferdinan's nanobots.

Whenever focusing became difficult, Umbacano fluttered to his shoulder and he was working again with better direction and renewed energy. *Will I finish before Yuyu gets back?*

Merging them with the second skin was unexpectedly easy. But the self-destruct... Umbacano's obnoxiousness helped him find where the bots and medicine differed, but not how to fix it. *How does such a small piece set these to repeat the command instead of dying?*

Jumping from his shoulder, Umbacano landed on the nanobot sample – toppling it over. Elbie jumped. "Careful. I need these."

Chittering, the magnificent bird moved to the medicine incubator – pecking at the buttons. "I need those too..."

How does a robot require attention? But Umbacano didn't stop tapping the buttons. Mismatched eyes doubled in size. *I can use the medicine bots instead.*

***

"Nut milk mint tea with a touch of honey." Lashina placed the warm mug on the little table before setting a small bowl next to it. "Lentils and fresh cucumber lightly salted."

The skeletal boy gagged despite the food being prepared exactly as requested. Apologizing, Ferdinan thanked her.

"Thank you, Lashina." Leoniel reached for the plate she offered, but paused when he noticed Ferdinan cringe. "I apologize. Would it be ok if I joined you?"

Thin lips trembled as nearly colorless crystals darted between the food and Leoniel. Whatever the boy was thinking, he paled and looked away.

"I'm sorry, Lashina. There's a project I should finish before eating. Please take it back to the kitchen."

"I...!" Ferdinan curled inside himself.

"It should only take an hour or so. I'll return then."

"Is there anything else you'd like or need, Master Ferdinan?" Lashina placed Leoniel's plate back on her tray.

"I'm sorry. No..."

"Enjoy." Leoniel stood and gestured his employee out.

When they reached the end of the hall, she stopped. "Will he be ok?"

"Our compromise." Leoniel pulled a medical disk from his pocket. Ferdinan was given more freedom, but Leoniel got to monitor the boy's vitals.

"I'm glad he's doing better. Though it's an odd name he's chosen."

Leoniel gave her his full attention. "Do you know him?"

"He was there...but..." Her eyes grew distant.

It was a look Leoniel knew well. Many of his guests and employees got that look when unshakable memories took over. Keeping his voice soft and soothing, he reminded her of where she was, who he was, and assured her she was safe. And he didn't stop until that look went away.

"A few weeks before Gin Kyo's team arrived, he wandered into the camp and stayed. He never spoke, but he listened when we called him Yeri. Three days before...he disappeared. We were scared they..." Lashina closed her eyes, taking a few deep breaths. "He gave his rations to whoever needed them most and he..."

Leoniel took the tray when she started crying and offered a hug she turned down. "You don't have to think about that place. And Master Ferdinan wouldn't have been ten yet, you don't have to remember for someone who-"

"His eyes. Blue's rare, but I've never seen any that pale, save Yeri. They'd be the same age if they're different people."

Leoniel wondered... Normally such a bizarre idea...but between Skuna and Oya... *What would a ten-year-old North Chūzite lord be doing in a slave encampment in West Mundan?*

Stepping closer, Lashina indicated she was ready for that hug, so he offered it freely. "I'm glad he was saved. That...*that* didn't happen."

***

210

"You're still missing one."

Golden hands danced, but words never came. Sitting on the twilight sand, Zephyr hung his head. "Only one?"

The elf sat beside him. Part of her felt bad for the distress this was causing him. Zephyr did terrible things, but... "Understanding will be the next step."

"Can't you torture me instead?" Golden fingers jerked aggressively – pounding and slicing his palm.

"If it were my task." Sapphire eyes glowed. "But it wouldn't be beneficial anymore."

"And this is?"

"Yes. So is this." A delicate hand pulled the stick of fog with a little green flower into existence.

"Where did you get that?"

"From your mind." Handing it over, she winked. "Play for me."

Frustrated, he blew out a breath. "It's not mine."

"But you practice every day. Even replaced part of your exercise routine with it." Grinning, she forced it into his hand.

"I don't like you being in my head."

"Neither does he." Leaning forward, she brought her nose down to touch his. "You need to stop."

Face on fire, the Prince scooted back.

Just as she had before, she poked the spot he'd first stabbed his leg. "Why do you feel you need to do this?"

He looked away.

Heaving a sigh, she studied his thigh. It wasn't infected yet, but it was bleeding along with his hands and his eyes. "If you keep doing this, you'll end up like Ferdinan. Your country will weaken, and when they discover how you keep yourself in control, they'll lose belief in you and the strength of your position."

Whether this was true or not, it sounded effective. "The only way to handle emotions is to experience them."

"I feel what I feel. I'm not ignoring anything."

"Then what's the sensation that keeps you from breathing?"

"Annoying, just like you." Releasing his grip on the odd instrument, Zephyr watched it vanish into thin air, only to end up in her hands again.

"Keep playing. You may realize yet." With a wink, the instrument materialized back in Zephyr's hands. "Good luck."

***

No more... Ferdinan pushed the bowl away... He didn't eat much, but he had to keep it down this time. Had to prove he was fine. Taking a capsule from his green mint tin, he slipped it on his tongue...but...if Emil refused to talk to him...? No. He needed these to give him an appetite and energy as well.

If only he could find the trunk his cuffs were in... His stomach twisted. Breathing through the nausea, Ferdinan double checked his final itinerary for his Azuté trip. *How did I miss so many errors? Make this many mistakes?* Blue crystals turned to the colorful flowers. *'Cause I'm useless. Pathetic.* So pathetic even his broken mind rejected him. Warmth flooded in – trying to force those thoughts out, but the unpleasantness made his stomach turn and twist. Gags took hold. He needed to stop himself before the retching started.

Footsteps rushed in and a chair moved beside him as color filled his peripheral. "It's ok. Can you relax? Would laying down help?"

Not vomiting in front of a Kyo again would help... Nauseating warmth set in, growing... *Breathe...* Placing his ice-cold hands on his neck eased the discomfort. "I'm fine."

"You don't have to rush." Leoniel smiled. "Only do what your body can handle while you're healing."

Ferdinan focused on the screen again, hoping the queasiness didn't get worse. But Elbie's last message mocked him. How did he respond? Scrolling past to ignore the guilt and the colorful man, Ferdinan didn't stop until he reached the oldest messages. Two from Grandpa Huey were marked "Urgent." Ice filled his gut. *What have I done...?*

"May I ask why it's so important to return now? I'd like to understand." Leoniel leaned forward, elbows resting on the little table.

Ferdinan's heart twisted as a boney finger hovered above the oldest message. "I've failed my mentee at every step. I need to at least finish his apprenticeship properly."

"Apprentice...?"

And it was unexpected... *A child with a dying heart...* "There's another student I need to check on. And my cousin...he's had so much to catch up with and was sick. And projects that've been delayed too long. And..." *The date...*

Leoniel waited a moment before responding. "That's a heavy workload. Especially when you're recovering."

"I have everything I need there." Blue crystals turned on the Kyo. *It couldn't...* Turning back to the screen, Ferdinan clicked on the second urgent message. *They were healed...around the time I was... He's a Kyo and Grandpa Huey–*

"What're you willing to compromise to keep the Artimuses from preventing you from returning to school?" Ringed fingers interlaced and rested on the table between them.

That...was unexpected and startled him from his contemplations. "I'm eating."

Leoniel smiled. "Besides eating. I'd rather you approach that at a rate your body can handle."

Compromise...? It was odd being asked this. And he couldn't give fake offerings. Not if Leoniel was going to do what he assumed. Not if the man already did what he suspected.

***

Apology filled the General's face. "You'll need to handle domestic issues while I'm navigating international ones."

Zephyr nodded. "Yes, sir."

"It won't be easy for you. Captain Rutoric'll stay by your side – use him, trust him."

Only Captain Rutoric? "And my parents?"

"Your mom's leaving to stand with the Grasslands." Tenalia looked down.

'Stand with the Grasslands?' Chūzite Royalty can't renounce their duty for another country... Did she use the wrong phrase on purpose?
"And my father?"

"Searching for Duke Samultz."

***

"Haha! You can't catch me!" Oya bolted for the trees.

There was a moment of shock before six little feet followed – crunching through thick snow. Continuing into the forest was tempting, but the three sisters were young and it was cold, so Oya looped back – allowing them to catch up by cutting part of the distance. Jogging around the main building, she led them to the kitchen entrance.

Bursting through the door startled Jon, but he rolled his eyes when the three caught up – nearly bulling into him. She kept going, but only two pursued. Evelyn stayed behind to ask Jon what he was making and if she could help. And if he didn't know, would he make some strange sounding thing with her.

Where should I lead you two? Out the kitchen. Down one hall after another, she brought them to an unused portion of the main building. Little feet stopped, so she turned back to find dark eyes glistening in awe as they peeked inside the room.

"What's wrong?"

The eldest held the younger's hand – both panting hard and gazes fixed beyond her. "We...we aren't...allowed...back here..."

"Ah." Stretching, she patted their heads and offered her hands. "Then where're we allowed?"

The two didn't answer – just kept staring into the forbidden room. *What's so interesting?* The lights weren't on, but sunshine poured in from the windows making precious metals shine provocatively. Light colored by perfectly polished gems painted the walls. *I see.* The "shiny effect" was powerful. But their eyes held more than simple awe. It was a perfectly human look, though disheartening to see it in ones so young.

Snapping, she offered her hands again. "What'd you like to play?"

They looked longingly a moment more before Tinny turned to Yin, waiting for the younger to choose. Hesitantly, Yin took Oya's hand and guided her to a shelf of books in their playroom. With encouragement from her older sister, Yin mustered the courage to give it to Oya.

214

"You like stories?" Both girls nodded. Opening it, Oya grinned. She couldn't read a word. "May I tell you a story from my home?"

They looked at each other a little disappointed, but curious. "Thank you, please."

Stretching long and tall, Oya melted to the floor. Both girls giggled and joined her. "A long, long time ago. Long before man went underground. There were dragons."

That caught their attention – big smiles took over their faces and they leaned closer...eerily quiet.

"Now dragons were terrible, fearsome creatures. Not like the fairytales we now tell. They were greedy and didn't care who they hurt as long as they could keep gathering wealth. For decades they stole and killed and cheated, gathering all the money and resources they could. But it wasn't enough. They always wanted more and more. Forcing billions!" Oya leaned in waving a finger back and forth. "And yes, humans numbered in the billions! Forcing billions to live with less and less 'til disease and starvation plagued the living and destruction consumed the world. The humans kept waiting for the dragons to die, but they just got stronger."

Yin scooted closer to her big sister and Tinny wrapped an arm around her.

"As the world was about to be consumed, gods arrived. They saw all the evil and the potential of the world if the dragons were dealt with. So they gathered the strongest of mind, body, heart, and soul and gave them the tools needed to slay the dragons." Oya jumped to her feet. Arms swinging like she held a sword and shield. "At first the fight felt impossible. The dragons too strong and the humans too beaten down. But they kept fighting. And they didn't stop. The dragons killed many. Destroying them utterly. But the selected kept fighting. 'Cause what was the point of living in a dying world full of evil? One where dragons had stolen all hope and destroyed what they couldn't horde?"

Tinny held Yin tighter, though the younger's eyes were wide with curiosity – waiting eagerly.

"And it worked. Not for the few selected, but for the gods who sent them. The select would never see the outcome. The gods knew this, but they also knew how important those select were." Puffing out her chest, Oya held out a fist as if planting a staff. "'Cause those select infected the population with hope and resistance and will. And when the last select fell, the dragons celebrated, secure in their total victory. But they didn't see the masses gathering. Building. Growing stronger as the things that were stolen from them – beaten out of them – were reclaimed, thanks to the select. Billions swarmed. Unrelenting. Tired of being at the dragons' cruel and twisted mercy."

Both sisters leaned in – giant smiles on their faces.

"A hundred million dragons fell to the billions they abused. And not a single dragon, old, young, egg, survived. Not one." Oya spun down to the floor. "And whenever the hint of a possible dragon evolving came, it was utterly destroyed without mercy. It took generations. And significant toil, but the world healed and the humans learned what living was."

Smiling, the two looked like they wanted more, but said nothing.

Oya grinned. Stories were what she knew best. "How about the lesson of Ticko the wise frog?"

Together they nodded, listening expectantly.

***

"Ferdinan was fairly reasonable." Leoniel sat across from Father and Samuel. "If he runs away, we know he won't come back. So what'll you compromise to not lose him? It won't take long for him to find a way out even if you try thwarting him. And I'm not going to imprison him."

Laying out what Ferdinan said, Leoniel gave them space to discuss their response. It took a bit and the two Healers often argued. But eventually, they settled on a counter offer.

Chapter 30

What happened to him? Ferdinan couldn't look at the King Father on the screen. Leoniel secured it so the boy's gaze could escape to the wall of flowers - but that skeletal body shook whenever Father spoke.

"It's not safe for you to return to school. They don't do what's best for you and despite our efforts you keep growing sicker there."

The boy didn't respond to Father's offer or pleas. Nearly colorless eyes focused on the color beyond the glass wall, planning something.

"What do you think?" Leoniel started, giving Ferdinan time to bring his attention back to the present. "Are you ok with that instead?"

The skeletal boy grew impressively red. "I'm sorry...please repeat that. I want to make sure I understand properly."

"We'll consent if you stay with Samuel in the guest apartments." Father leaned closer to the screen, but moved back when Ferdinan flinched. "And you'll need to return here over breaks 'til you're healthy."

Ferdinan grew incredibly pale. "I won't return over breaks."

"My home is yours." Leoniel smiled, reminding the boy of his earlier promise. "This room is yours whenever you want it."

Ferdinan shook his head, but he kept his gaze on the flowers.

"That's not the issue." The King folded his arms - deciding how far he could push. "One of us will go and help with your projects 'til you're healthy. A child should've never been traveling alone anyway."

He's been traveling alone?

"And who decides what that is?" Ferdinan flinched back. Pulling in his legs, he shifted his body to fully face the wall of flowers.

"Ferdinan, you're heart's permanently damaged. You nearly died." The word 'again' lingered unsaid.

What has this child been through? This information...would it affect his meeting with Jorani and Samuel later?
***

Everyone was at work or school. Except Ozar. Jon knew his big brother should be working, but he was glad Ozar chose to stay with him. Glad they could lay on the couch basking in the sun shining through the window. "I needed this. Being home. With everyone..."

"We love you and we're glad you're home."

A shaky breath left him. Curling up tight, Jon pressed deeper into Ozar's hug. "Don't make me go back. I can't..."

"You don't have to." Ozar rested his cheek against the top of Jon's head. "Focus on getting well. Don't worry about anything else."

Tears welled up. "If I'd tried sooner. Did more. Actually cared..."

"You did everything you could. More than you should've had to."

"This happened 'cause I didn't care about him. He was annoying and difficult and hates us, so I didn't think it mattered. But we'd all be dead if not for him. And I was still annoyed!"

Ozar squeezed tighter. "*None* of this is your fault. It's ours. You did everything you could. Everything you knew to do. This is our fault."

Long fingers grabbed his chest as if that'd stop the deep ache. "I barely tried... When Oya came, I was relieved 'cause she wanted to. She had the energy and desire. So I only did what duty required. 'Cause it was expected. I didn't want to. And I hated every second."

Strong arms held fast. "I remember how hard you tried including him. Your failed efforts. How it broke your heart. I remember. Even if you don't. You're a wonderful brother, I'll keep remembering for you."

***

"I'm sorry." Leoniel patted Samuel's shoulder. Jorani wasn't satisfied with any of their answers and it was exhausting. "A little more."

Sitting up straight, Samuel faced Kyo Jorani.

"How badly will Ferdinan be affected once these videos publicly escape North Chūzo's borders?"

"It'll kill him." Samuel clutched the screen tighter. "He'll blame himself for everything that happens to his people and family following..."

"How can I minimize this?" Jorani shot a glance at Leoniel.

"Contain it inside North Chūzo's boarders." Samuel slowly shook his head. "He doesn't check on his country except when he's tasked to do so. He trusts the Samultz to call on him when he's needed."

"He's a child." Jorani leaned forward, frowning.

"He's a Scientist. And noble." Samuel returned the frown. "To both himself and his people, it doesn't matter if we disagree or not."

"Let's take a breath." Leoniel stood. "We aren't here for our own ideals, we're here to help a child caught in a delicate situation."

Jorani and Samuel both sat back.

"Things have devolved this far." Leoniel held up the screen and pointed to the Duchess. "The videos circulating through the people are fueling aggression and rage. So how long do we choose to do nothing?"

"Indefinitely." Samuel's answer upset Jorani, but he didn't let them interrupt. "If we interfere, try to bend this to our ideals, we'll lose. We'll lose. Treaties will die – placing tens of millions into painful positions. And Ferdinan... Anything you hope to do for him...you'll never get to."

"So you'll let them beat him to death?"

Samuel rubbed his temples. "We have ways to keep him safe."

"How?"

"He rarely goes home and I'll be with him at school. I'll know when to have him summoned somewhere safe if needed." Samuel bowed his head to both Kyos. "Please don't betray his trust. He knows how to avoid Mom's summons, but he can't ignore a Kyo."

***

The North Chūzo-East Azuté treaties...Mother would've never guessed...but they explained much.

Naizu's still in school. Raonie can stay with her daughters if she cares for affairs. Rigel doesn't have much experience, but he can assist her. I need Samuel with Ferdinan. She'd prefer Samuel stand with the Grasslands, but since Queen Am'ria was willing...

Bastian's close with the West Azuté Tous. Xingho's best in South Oueshi and Jingjing's established in Mid Chūzo. Kidico was covered. And Mundan cut themselves off. *Three experienced negotiators and myself for six countries... No. Only two.*

She needed to find out what was happening in Mundan. *Ozar worked there before being placed for matching. I'll send him there.*

Her husband and her... *If Enri can handle both eastern Chūzite countries, I'll take the western.* That left Jon. And one Kyo.

It wasn't fair, but she didn't have many options. Grabbing a screen, she messaged the man she'd raised alongside her second born.

***

Joyful shouts filled the air. It worked! He made it work! Elbie and Umbacano danced around Master Ferdinan's lab. The nanobots automatically connected second skin, the skeletal structure, and his nerves for hours without any problems. When he removed the glove, it stayed a glove instead of turning to goop.

A chime interrupted their celebration. Mismatched eyes blinked at the call request and dread filled him. Elbie's heart ached. *I don't want to answer. I don't want to know...*

Bright yellow danced on the desk beside the screen. Tapping the accept button, Umbacano stared at him only to tap and stare again.

I don't want to hear... Elbie hadn't meant to cry, but it hit hard and fast. He saw Master Ferdinan wouldn't live long. But...he couldn't hear it...

Its ok. I promise.

Who? Elbie turned, but that voice seemed to originate from his soul and fill his entire being... *Has grief made me broken?* He didn't think his feelings were abnormal...but he was only seven...maybe this was what broken felt like?

Umbacano fluttered to his shoulder and nuzzled his cheek. Elbie's heart quickened and he realized he was holding his breath.

The universe of possibility opened in his mind. Only this time it wasn't focused on any one idea. Just pure possibility... And it was amazing. Wonderful. And... Elbie didn't know how to put his thoughts and feelings into words. He knew there was nothing wrong about this. Yet...how could this exist in a normal mind?

I chose you 'cause your mind isn't normal.

Who are you?

Umbacano. The one you see as a yellow bird.

220

I'm broken... Mismatched eyes flew open. Every time he wondered about the bird hit... *You've kept me from considering what you are.*

It wasn't time, but she's coming soon.

A bird no one can see...and I'm arguing with it...

You're mentor's fine, Śarī-a was found in time to heal him. He's returning soon.

That's not possible. Elbie saw how sick Master Ferdinan was. But... He wanted it to be true. He wanted to see his mentor.

Answer the call. And tonight, I'll greet you in your dreams.

***

It was exhausting, but they convinced Kyo Jorani to let North Chūzo's people decide their future. At least concerning the Duchess. *It would've been easier if Oya talked to them.*

With both guests gone, Leoniel turned toward Ferdinan's room.

Skuna stood outside – arms crossed and waiting. "I was going to leave 'cause you were taking so long, but I decided to wait."

"Leave?"

"I'm tired of winter." Stepping forward, she gave him a tiny smile. "Thank you for food and shelter. Make sure he doesn't die."

"You're welcome as long..." Leoniel started, but she turned to open the door. "It's dark and cold. If you'll wait 'til morning-"

"I have transportation." Calling out in that language he didn't know, she waved inside Ferdinan's room and an old woman he'd never seen walked out.

Who are you? Giving his best smile, he bowed to her. "Hello, welcome to my home. How may I help you?"

"A Kyo? So many people I didn't think I'd meet." The old woman smirked and held out her hand.

"You're taking custody of Skuna?" It was startling when she crushed his ringed fingers in her grip and wiggled them up and down. "May I ask your name?"

221

"Yup. Promised to get her home safe. Call me Tac." Letting him go, she turned to Skuna. "Ready, young one?"

Leoniel tried a couple times to convince them to stay to no avail. Standing barefoot in the snow, he watched the two disappear into the hedge... *A green band...that makes her a traveler....?* The stories Gin told... Shaking his head, Leoniel decided it was best to let them go.

Returning to Ferdinan's room, he was happy to find the boy sleeping. Since being healed, Ferdinan was either working or doing that strange dance. After warming his hands and feet by the fire, he checked on the sleeping boy.

Other than being dangerously thin and shivering, Ferdinan was looking good.

Straightening the blankets, Leoniel properly covered the boy. He hadn't seen the screen until it was falling. Catching it, Leoniel finished arranging the blankets and considered getting another out. *I'll see if he stops shivering.* The Kyo was about to turn off the screen and put it on the side table when he saw a name he knew well and a partially composed message.

Grandpa Huey? East Azuté? It was tempting to read the entire correspondence, but Leoniel stopped himself. Lashina's story came to him – making him think. Turning off the screen, he placed it under the antique green tin and grabbed one of his own.

A child who wandered into a slave encampment weeks before it was found and destroyed. A child who created a medical device that earned him a presentation at the World's Conference. A child discussing Azuté with grandpa Huey. *Father said he often travels alone. And he's already recognized as a Master. Who are you?* Opening a message box, Leoniel went to work calling in favors for information on the skeletal boy. Then turned to the secure search engines he had access too.

There wasn't much. Far less than he expected from a child noble, let alone one with the skill and knowledge needed to make those medical disks...as if Ferdinan's name was targeted for erasure. But there was one intriguing thing.

Opening a new message box, Leoniel sent a call request to a man name Fulason.

Chapter 31

"Wanting to finish Elbie's apprenticeship shows how wonderful and caring you are." Mother reached for Ferdinan's hand, stopping when he flinched away. "But please consider staying next block?"

Head down, Ferdinan studied the bright green string connecting to no one and the currently charcoal gray of Jon's. *I never want to see hers.* Never. He didn't want to know what false obligation looked like.

"Ferdinan?"

"No." Keeping his voice steady was a struggle. "You're Jon's home. Jon's family. He's hurt and sick and needs you. I'll make him sicker."

"That's—"

"Refusing to acknowledge this has only hurt him." Swallowing the bitterness wasn't easy. "Staying will steal his health and happiness. So no. I won't waste your time. Won't burden you. I refuse."

"You've never been a burden. Never wasted our time. You're our son. Our family. We want you. We love you."

Blue crystals squeezed shut. "I'm not the one who needs your love. Jon is. *He's* your son, your responsibility, put your son's needs first."

She shifted and endless falling consumed him. His gaze lifted and he wished it hadn't. Wished he hadn't seen her expression. It hurt.

A broken light that communicated through ancient articles. Healing dreams. Emil. Lighted strings only he saw. *I'm completely broken.* He poisoned them and he'd keep doing so if he didn't leave.

Selfishness kept him coming back, but he had to stop. "I promised the Kyos I'd cooperate. I'm promising you. Just...please. Jon's your baby. Your youngest son. Understand he'll never get better if I'm here."

"Ferdinan—"

"I need to finish Elbie's apprenticeship." *And prepare for break...* Ferdinan interrupted. This conversation needed to end. "I don't want to be here. I'm not needed and my presence will only make things worse. Do you know how much that hurts? Please stop."

***

Help.

Despair hit Gongie. The kind Zephyr felt before doing something he shouldn't. Kicking off his shoes, he crammed them in his bag and handed them to Ilu. "Please don't ask, just take them back for me?"

"You'll get hurt in this rain - if not lost."

"Trust me." Not giving his island brother a chance to argue, Gongie ran into the rippling gray. Mud swallowed his feet and water attacked his nose when he breathed. He reached the dorms gasping and panting...

Sopping wet, he trudged up three flights of stairs as invisible claws tore apart his leg. Activating the chime did nothing. *What do I do....?*

"Zephyr, open the door." Gongie gasped, but the Athlete's mind was so far away... Silver dug in deep. Muscle rose at the dull edge's force - not wanting to tear but unwilling to let go of its proper place. Choking back screams left him dizzy. *What do I do!?* The blade's nose pushed - relentless. Pain. Relief. Joy and guilt and so many things people weren't meant to feel at once made it impossible to think. "Zephyr! Stop!"

Rain and wind drown out Gongie's cry. Blunt steel forced its way to freedom, diving in slowly again. *Stop...I...I have to stop this...!* Ramming the door did nothing, but they were designed to withstand a Fighter...

I'm sorry... Forcing himself to breathe, Gongie searched. Pushing past the pain, he grabbed the handle and closed his eyes. Zephyr's mind wasn't easy to find. And when he did, it was shut behind a locked door. Two. Three. Four. *How far has he retreated?*

"He can retreat infinitely in the safety we provide. For short times."

Gongie froze. That was Zephyr's voice, but it wasn't the Prince.

"It used to be indefinite, but the elf took that away."

"Who are you?" *Was that two voices? He said 'we.'*

"Two. If you fail, there'll be a third." A masked Prince and a veiled, chained one appeared - both looking at a shadow without form.

"Stop. You aren't protecting him; you're letting him hurt himself."

The two looked at Gongie, filled with pity. "Can you protect him?"

Do I have a choice?

"There's always a choice."

"I'll do what I can."

The chained figure became a door - a terrible, gruesome door. Inside Zephyr stood in total emptiness - shifting between the tiny Prince and the one hurting himself beyond Gongie's reach.

"You need to stop."

"Stop what?" A voice both familiar and too young echoed.

This was wrong. Gongie knew it was wrong, but he grabbed the Prince and held on tight. "I'm sorry."

"What are you doing?"

"I truly am sorry. There's no forgiving this." Gongie's fingers dug into golden arms and he commanded the Prince to stop.

Nothingness expanded and Zephyr held his form.

"Open the door and let me in." *I'm sorry. As soon as the handle leaves my grip...I promise...* "I'm sorry."

The door opened and Gongie released the Prince - ramming his way in.

How did he walk like that...? Muscle hung, mostly detached. Blood cascaded down and wet, red footprints stained granite and carpet.

The injuries from last time. Scars from months of self-abuse. Zephyr stood naked, stubbed nosed prodding his torn thigh - detached from the pain. *He's still hiding in that room... Think! Will his muscle detach if he moves wrong? How much blood can an Athlete lose?*

"I'm sorry, Zephyr." Again, Gongie took hold of the Prince's mind, gingerly forcing the Athlete to sleep.

He needs a Healer... Holding onto that broken, tormented mind, Gongie found a screen. *I didn't think I'd collect this favor while still on the islands.*

It didn't take long for Herrard to arrive. Ushering the young man to the unconscious Prince, Gongie started cleaning.

"What-"

"This pays your debt." There was something else that needed to be done. "His leg and getting rid of that knife."

***

Ozar had to take a call from the Laual and Naizu wouldn't be home for a few hours, so Jon roamed - avoiding busy areas. He didn't want to be in the way and wasn't interested in the servants' attention.

Long legs took him down one hallway after another until he was staring at dusty rooms in a closed off portion of the estate. And Oya. Sleeping on the floor in a common room only used for large gatherings. Aside from the time she sat for a day with her eyes closed, Jon hadn't seen her sleep. He was starting to believe she didn't need to.

Waking her was a mistake. She leapt up, grabbed him, and threw him into the floor - pinning his arms and threatening to break his face.

Head spinning and lungs unable to inhale, he stared. Shocked. He should be worried about the golden-brown fist hovering above his head or the delicate hand pressing his throat into the floor. He was still figuring out what happened when Oya lowered her arm and got off him.

The delicate hand throttling him a moment ago offered to help him up. And he still wasn't sure what to do.

"It's dangerous waking me like that."

Jon sat up as Oya sat down. "I apologize."

Normally crazed green eyes were unusually dull. "Want to play?"

"No." *Have I ever seen her look tired? Or have I not noticed?* "Samuel told me about the agreement with Ferdinan."

"Really?" Delicate fingers played with the steel locket around her neck. "Thought they'd let you enjoy this break."

"Can you actually help Samuel care for him?"

"Does my answer matter since you don't trust I can?" A wicked grin grew. "You relinquished all claim to him. He isn't your responsibility or burden anymore. Enjoy being home. I'll care for my dear friend."

Jon shook his head. "I've seen him spiral too many times. This time nearly killed him."

"This time no one was with him. Samuel and I'll be there."

"You'll keep him stable on the islands while he's cooperating. But once he leaves or you grow secure that he's fine, he'll spiral again. And next time, he'll die."

"You're not the only one who can coax a heart to beat."

"I know!" Jon breathed out, calming himself. "But I know him. He's manipulative and sneaky. He'll do and say whatever he thinks will get him closer to his goal and he doesn't care about himself in all of that."

"Jon." Alien green eyes turned hard. "This isn't you're responsibility any more. It's mine. You gave him up. If he dies, it's my fault, not yours. All you need to worry about is whether you can live with yourself if you don't see him before we leave."

***

"Can we talk?" Mother smiled at the pile of her sons on the couch.

Jon didn't particularly feel like joking, but he joined his two awake brothers in pointing at each other – making her laugh. It was nice hearing that soft, safe, comforting sound. It was so nice...

"Jon," she clarified.

It took a bit to wiggle out, but he only woke up Jingjing, who went right back to sleep. Getting mom to himself was wonderful, but...would he poison her too? Would she realize how badly he broke and keep him from poisoning everyone else? He was her son, but she had three generations and a country to care for. Letting him compromise that...

Once in her office, she gave him a hug and placed a chair facing hers. "I want you to stay. I expect you to stay."

Jon's heart froze and his lungs wouldn't move. "What's happening?"

"A number of political issues are about to cause some interesting and unpleasant events." Mother offered her hand, smiling when he took it. "You and Rigel are still in school, but the rest of us are needed in other countries helping things proceed smoothly."

No...I'm finally home! "And you?"

"I've been summoned by Laual Runai."

Jon sighed as he leaned forward, not stopping until his forehead rested on her knees. *I hate everything.*

"Naizu and I'll return a couple times during your break, but the rest won't be back 'til everything's taken care of." Mother smoothed his hair and patted his shoulder. "I wish I knew how long... But I want you to stay. For the break. For next block. For as long as you need."

What's the point if I'm still alone....? But...it was better that way, wasn't it? So he couldn't infect anyone else... Jon didn't understand what

227

his mom said after that. All he heard was her voice, but it didn't form anything coherent. And it didn't matter. He shouldn't be risking his family anyway. But he finally had them...

***

"*If she doesn't give them a break, she's going to exhaust Tinny and Yin soon.*" Oya giggled.

"*I'm glad. She deserves a wonderful family.*" Ferdinan gave the best smile he could manage. "*Thank you for playing with them.*"

"*You should visit her or let her visit you. She's excited to tell you everything she's learned and done and all about her sisters.*" Stretching, Oya leaned against the window with the greenhouse on the other side.

She's so beautiful framed by flowers... Like the scene was built for her. "*No. She needs to bond with them before I intrude.*"

"*Liar.*"

Tears welled, but he blinked them away. It hurt. Hearing how happy Evelyn was – how much she loved her new sisters, new life. Knowing she only had to do this because he failed... *I don't want to destroy the life she's built back...* He closed his eyes and forced himself to calm down. "*I hate that house. But it's perfect for her. For the Oza...*"

Oya didn't speak. Not until the sun slipped below the horizon and stars appeared. Standing, she looked out at the winter window – pointing to the sky. "*Langer, the constellation with two hearts. Do you know the story?*"

"*Astronomy isn't an interest of mine beyond navigation.*" Boney arms wrapped around Ferdinan's middle for warmth, to keep his stomach from complaining, and to protect himself from whatever she'd say next.

"*Legend goes, Langer was a wise man who spent his life traveling from village to village, serving those he met along the way. He grew to love the people he served so much; his body grew a second heart to hold all his love.*"

"*That's a weird story.*"

"*True. But how comforting to think one person could love that much? The world could use him again.*"

Chapter 32

"I'm surprised you're telling me this." Samuel scratched the back of his neck. It was too soon for another fight.

"It's only a suspicion. I'm meeting with a few people over the next week to confirm, but I'm telling you now so you can prepare yourself." Ringed fingers combed through lavender hair. "How'll you respond when you 'find out' he's going to East Azuté?"

"He'll die there. No medical care and no access to the supplies he needs just to eat." Samuel wished it was as easy as saying no. "And that's only the physical. The emotional suffering when he sees abandoned farmlands... Even his short time in the main capital nearly killed him. We can't let him go."

"Emotional? What connection does he have there?"

"Confidentially?" Ferdinan didn't know they knew. "Evelyn's first family. He was close to her grandmother. I think that woman was the first person whose love he accepted. She had a farm and orchard, Ferdinan visited there almost every break."

"Do you think you can keep him away?"

"No..."

"Consider what's going to happen in North Chūzo."

Samuel cringed. That was another thing he didn't know how to protect his little brother from.

"Wouldn't it be easier to keep him safe and away from the news engines if he's busy serving in a devastated country?" Leoniel gently squeezed Samuel's shoulder. "You'll miss an important opportunity as well."

"Opportunity?" When it came to Ferdinan, those were rare and usually false.

"Instead of fighting him, praise him for his actions, ask to help. How much better will this be if you assist his efforts? You can be there supporting and helping him while he stumbles through the pain of mourning someone he loved. Probably multiple people."

"I doubt it'll work. He'd insist on going alone even if we were completely supportive."

"Then compromise. Tell him your limits and give him the space to prove he'll respect them."

"You haven't known him as long as we have."

"Does it matter?"

Samuel didn't want to admit it. Being supportive was always better for building trust...but he'd pulled Ferdinan from death too many times, he didn't want to do it again. And letting his little brother go to the ruins of a world forever lost - no matter how hard Ferdinan worked to rebuild it... It'd break the boy. "I'll consider it. Please confirm your suspicions as soon as possible."

***

"If you'd come sooner, we wouldn't have let him in," the veiled Zephyr frowned.

The elf stood with the veiled and masked figures. Watching Gongie bend the helpless Prince to his will - taking control of a mind that wasn't his.

Telepaths are scary.

Gongie vanished.

My turn... But Zephyr's mind stopped and faded to nothing. Annoyed, she opened the silver roads. *Dreams are easier anyway.*

Stepping onto her twilight beach, she called Zephyr. He appeared but didn't look at her. Didn't talk. And when she offered the plexiglass violin, he ignored it.

"I'm continuously surprised at how similar you two are."

Onyx eyes glared before burying themselves in golden arms. "We are nothing alike."

"He'd agree. But you're both wrong."

"You're wrong."

Again, she offered the violin her dear friend made that somehow became important to this boy. "Prove it. Play for me."

Zephyr shifted to his knees, hands flying. "Why!? You won't believe me!"

"Play for me." Sapphire eyes grew wild. "Play me all your sins."

Teeth clenched, he growled – pounding twilight sand with golden fists. "Fine!"

Grabbing it, Zephyr gave all his anger to the instrument, punishing its very existence. But he played. *How would such playing damage the real instrument?*

"What truths have you learned?"

"I'm a monster!" He screamed with the notes – a song belonging to his soul. "I told you that already!"

"What else?"

"I'm a failure! I shouldn't have family! I'm the lowest, but put myself above everyone. I damage souls! And destroy instead of protect!" Golden hands danced on the strings faster, harsher and the bow tried slicing the stick of fog in half. And he shook – crumbling at the edges. "I need to be punished. But I'm not! No one will punish me! When I confess my sins! When they see me hurt others! Even when they know how monstrous I am! Why won't they punish me?!

"Everything'll fall apart! I'll hurt more!" Zephyr bashed his anger and regret and frustration against the instrument. The last semblance of music devolved into chaotic notes. Tears filled onyx eyes. Rage made way for despair. "I hurt everyone. I'm supposed to be a protector. I'm supposed to protect. But I'm hurting everyone... I'm a failure..."

"What've you failed at?" Her question was cruel, but she didn't have the time to be gentle.

"Everything..." Chaos became melancholy clawing its way back into a tune. "I failed so miserably I became a destroyer. An abuser. Instead of a protector."

"It's impressive how thoroughly wrong you are." The music turned harsh. "Understanding'll start after you've found the last truth."

Zephyr let his hands fall. "What more could there be?"

The elf grinned and took back the violin. "The one that'll put the rest in context and fix the mirrors."

Zephyr withered – terrified, pleading for it to be over.

"Growth, repentance, maturing, understanding, change are all painful things." Long, delicate fingers combed back his hair. "Experiencing them all at once... Survive and you'll become the General you want to be."

***

That dream was amazing. But... Was Elbie broken or was this real?

Umbacano still sat on his shoulder and flew around. Still nuzzled his cheek and provided comfort. Still helped him when he couldn't figure something out.

Master Ferdinan was healthy like he promised... Mismatched eyes turned to the shiny purple cloth wrapping Yuyu's gift. And...it explained how he made those so easily, with little effort...

"Ready?" Tuel smiled from the open door.

"Thank you." Together, they walked to the pier where other Energists were there waiting for the younger students to disembark. "There's something personal I need to give Yuyu, in Master Ferdinan's lab."

Though concerned, the older boy smiled. "I'll take Haoyu to his suite and come back for you after."

"Thank you." Excitement rose in his chest and Umbacano danced on his shoulder. *I can't wait to see her face...*

Yuyu and Haoyu ran down the plank – protected from rain by an invisible barrier. Two sets of hands mussed his hair. "I've missed you!"

Pink eyes grew serious. "Answer your messages! Do you know how worried we've been?"

Haoyu's stern look added to the lecture.

"I'm sorry." Looking down, Elbie bowed. "I was... Master Ferdinan's lab..."

A smile blossomed on her lips and Haoyu looked curious. Tuel escorted them there – Elbie dodging questions to not ruin Yuyu's surprise.

"There're treats waiting for you, Cidi, and Iili in the suite." Elbie smiled, not inviting the Energists in. "When I'm done here, I want to hear everything. Ok?"

Haoyu gave a worried smile. "We'll see you soon."

"How can I help?" Yuyu waved the two off.

Inputting his access code, Elbie held the door for her - pointing at the purple bundle sitting on the table. *Please work.*

Her beautiful smile brightened the room - growing intrigued when she unwrapped it. "What're these?"

"Gloves. To return your lost fine motor control and minimize the strain on your hands so you can work without hurting them." Elbie expected her to laugh or shout excitedly. He wasn't ready for her to cry. But he'd be crying too in her place. "There's one last calibration."

"Can I help?" Yuyu dried her face.

"I need your hands." Offering her a set of goggles, he picked up the laser designed to remove the second skin.

Pink eyes turned away as goop fell off her hands. Scarred and withered. This was the first time he saw them... Umbacano nuzzled his cheek and hopped to Yuyu's shoulder to offer her the same comfort.

It's ok. This is going to work no matter what her hands look like. He clipped on the skeletal supports. Once he triggered it, the nanobots would connect these directly to her nerves for perfect control.

Next came the monitoring diodes. "I'm sorry, this is going to hurt."

"It's ok."

Disinfecting and numbing her palm, Elbie checked the diode was working and properly linked to both pieces. *Don't be scared...*

But no matter how detailed the instructions and diagrams; he was cutting into his sister while burning ice scorched his fingers. It was terrifying. The diode slipped in easily, attaching itself to the bone. After dusting the incision with Master Ferdinan's healing powder, he was finally able to breathe.

"How often will I have to remove them?"

"You won't. They're self-cleaning and self-repairing." Placing a small ball of nanobot infused second skin into each of her disfigured palms, he watched them spread out and consume her hands, stopping at the wrists where the base of the skeletal structure connected. Tapping the screen, the black rippled until it matched Yuyu's natural skin. "I'll monitor and adjust them 'til they're exactly what you want."

Her hands looked normal. Flexing, wiggling her fingers, examining every inch of them... They were normal. Just like before the fire. Pink eyes filled with tears again. "I'm sorry... I'm just...so happy..."

Elbie's heart never hurt as much as it did with the pain of her joy.

***

"If I wanted to see him, I would. If he wanted to see me, I'd go." When was Samuel getting back? Jon understood the skeleton was important to Oya, but he wished she'd stop pestering him.

Disappointment filled those wild green eyes – giving her the air of a real god instead of a trickster. But she was neither. She was just a girl... Jon shook his head. When had she trained him out of basic respect and politeness? Before her, he'd never feel so angry and bitter toward a girl. Snapping at one. Being rude...

"Can you live with yourself if you ignore him 'til he's gone?"

Instead of anger and frustration, something strangely twisted filled him... "He's never gone. His heart was damaged beyond repair and now it works. His body's no longer dying despite organs shutting down and being starved beyond what any human could survive. I don't know how he does it. But every time... And now they won't let him starve himself anymore. He's never going to be gone."

"But his soul's still dying. As is yours." A delicate golden-brown hand patted his arm. "You can't fix his soul, but you can mend your own."

He hated her for saying that. For pointing out the toxins inside him, the poisons he was infecting everyone with. And...and! His soul was too corrupt to be fixed. Someone who could hate a girl. Who could want a child to die. Jaw clenched, Jon swallowed back the heat and rising bile.

"Can you live with yourself if you ignore him 'til he's gone?"

Everything from a moment ago leaked out of him – deflating his shoulders and lowering his head. *That's what led me here.* Ignoring the suffering. Being angry at Ferdinan for simply surviving a situation the gent had no power in. And whether his ally died or simply went away, could he live with himself if he did nothing? If he did worse than nothing. If he kept ignoring the gent. Why did she always make him think like this? "No."

"What you choose to do now, choose for you." Those wicked green eyes glowed – intense and unyielding. "Not for him. Not for your family. Or country. Or the world. Choose for you."

How? Where did he begin to figure that out? After everything he'd seen and now knew?

Shifting to tiptoes, Oya patted his shoulder then left the room. She didn't disappear or stop existing. She actually walked out.

Leaving Jon alone with countless thoughts and emotions he didn't know how to process.

***

Frustration grew, but not his own. "You won't find it. I don't know where it is, but I should've taken that knife the first time."

Golden hands flew. "It was a gift–!"

"I know the sentimental value, but you aren't getting it back 'til that," Gongie pointed at Zephyr's leg, "isn't an issue anymore."

You've no right you stupid Psych! Zephyr glared – hands thrashing. "At least tell me who you called. 'Someone who owed me a favor isn't a good enough answer."

"That's all I can offer." Gongie understood Zephyr needed some element of control – the broken Prince was powerless and drowning. *What can he have total power of without hurting himself?* Dark eyes scanned the room looking for an idea. "How did you get that?"

"What?" A golden finger tapped his cheek.

"Ferdinan's violin."

Zephyr looked away, biting back irritation, the humiliation of helplessness, and a desire to get his hands on a blade.

"When he stood on stage with it... I wasn't expecting an instrument."

"The storms broke the window in Ferdinan's room. I'm storing it."

"Ah." Memories of Zephyr playing until exhausted filled Gongie's mind. "I'd love to hear your music."

Palm face down, Zephyr sliced it away from his body. *No.*

Not the control I was hoping for. But it was still control. "Then school work?"

Zephyr repeated the gesture. A sadistic expression twisted his smile. "If you won't go away, you're joining me."

Gongie grimaced at the exercise routines floating around Zephyr's mind. This wasn't going to be fun. "I can't do near what you can."

"I don't care."

***

Presenting to the school was always terrifying. But watching Elbie listen to all their adventures...this school was cruel sometimes. Yet he smiled – excited for everyone who spoke. *He's too sweet.*

There were times Yuyu wished she could be that truly amazing. If she had such a pure heart, what kind of person would she be? Looking down at her hands... These gloves were wonderful. Her hands didn't hurt all the time, didn't get tired – and she could do detailed work again! *I'm only a child, but I can do this much for my little brother.*

Yuyu's name was called. Despite a pounding heart, she walked to the edge of the stage. Mismatched eyes locked on her – wide with anticipation. *No one else is here. Only Elbie.* Smiling, she displayed the blueprints she and Haoyu worked on together and told him everything she knew he'd find fascinating. It didn't matter if only a few others would understand, because this presentation wasn't for them. It was for him.

All the little details of her daily tasks interested him. Describing the wild field and how it inspired her and Haoyu to design it into different kinds of parks for the three connecting schools made his eyes light up. And he laughed at all the different ways she and his suitemate got into trouble for always being late. When she talked about the different ideas they tried, she could see his mind spin, creating his own ideas. She told him about their fun and how Haoyu helped without thought when her hands were tired. *I won't have to worry about that anymore...*

She'd still have Elbie help. Because it was fun. Because he wanted to be there. And because she loved having him beside her.

Not once did Elbie's smile waver. *I know it's not the same, but I hope you felt like you were with us.*

Chapter 33

Boney fingers forced the capsule past his lips before resting on the disgusting thing protruding from his belly. *How do I live with a Healer? A liar who did this to me?* This was demeaning... But if he stopped, he'd be stuck here. If he stopped, more Healers would come...

He wasn't strapped to the bed anymore, but his hands were still bound. He was still trapped. Before thoughts of death could enter his mind, that unwelcomed warmth washed over him – infuriating him. He hated it as much as he hated this tube. How weird it felt. How uncomfortable it made him. He wanted to tear it from his stomach!

But...then he'd never escape this place... Skuna's scolding hit. Why was this his responsibility? He never chose it. He never wanted this!

Stillness and the penetrating gaze of hate and worry and conflicted emotions bore into him. Turning... *Jon? Why's he here? Go home! Be with your family! Leave me...* Something sharp stabbed his heart. Jon's expression – the emotions behind it – they were the same his ally bore since his first visit to the Artimus estate.

"Why do you keep coming back?" *If he left... I never could've hurt him.* And Jon's string...it was flickering. Fading. *Good... He's finally going to throw me away. Good. I'm glad. I'm glad... I'm glad...!*

"I don't know. It's not good for either of us." Jon's lip trembled. "We can't keep doing this. *I* can't keep doing this."

"I know. But *you* keep coming back. Why? Why did you come in the first place? I told you not to. I told you so many times..." Ferdinan didn't want to see the pain he kept causing his ally, but he wouldn't look away; he needed to make sure that string vanished for good... "All I do is hurt you. I hurt you...! And you keep coming back... Why?"

"I don't know!" Silence fell. Jon stood looking from side to side, clenching and unclenching his fists. "'Cause my family loves you. 'Cause I respect your genius. 'Cause I can't stand knowing you're suffering. No matter how much you irritate or hurt me. No matter how much we clash and how we can't stand it. I can't do nothing while you suffer alone."

A bony hand covered his face. *I'm not suffering!*

"Why won't you accept us? If you did, you wouldn't be alone! We've done everything... Please." Jon's voice broke and the rest of his words shook. "My family loves you. Why can't you accept them? You'd be happy...healthy if you did. We all would be."

How many times do I have to say this before he understands? "They aren't mine. The Artimuses aren't mine. They're yours. *You* were picked. Not me. They're your family...not mine... I don't get to be a part of you."

"You always have been." There was no describing Jon's expression.

"Why can't you stop this? It hurts." Neither could Ferdinan take anymore. He broke so much. How did he put it back together?

"You know you shouldn't go back to school."

"I'll keep stealing your family." Ferdinan dried his face. "I don't want to, but I will, 'cause that's what I do. Even though they aren't mine."

"It doesn't matter. I'm going back with you."

Nausea hit hard – paling the skeleton. "Why?!"

"I want to...I need to...it's the right thing to do."

"You don't want this! It's the worst thing for you!" Ferdinan closed his eyes to force himself to stop yelling. Kneeling, he bowed his forehead to the floor. "Dinta, please stop before I destroy you."

"Don't ever call me that!"

Ferdinan wanted to cry. To scream. And the string flickered harder. *I'll break it. I'll break it and he'll never come back!*

"Why are we like this? Why can we never be better?" Jon begged.

Why? Where did Ferdinan begin? How loud would he have to yell before he was heard? Was there any way to speak the truth and have Jon hear him? Could this have ended differently? Could he repair what he broke? Ferdinan shook on the cold floor – fire crackling behind him. Were there words Jon would hear? If so, where did he find them?

Something between a growl and a sigh escaped the Dinta. The growing giant fidgeted, waiting. Growing more agitated. Until he turned away. "Fine! I tried. But this is all I can do if you refuse to say anything."

By the time Ferdinan looked up, Jon was reaching for the door handle and that flickering string was fading away. If it disappeared... *Good. Disappear. Disappear!*

Ferdinan's family didn't want him. He couldn't have the people he loved. He failed everyone. Even now, he was the source of grief and pain for all those dealing with him. And once this battle over him ended, he'd be forgotten by those who lost, and thrown away by the victor. Because he was useless. Worse than useless. A curse. A defect.

He'd be alone again. Like his whole life. Finally. Alone. It was safer. Easier... Until he met Oya and became unforgivably intertwined in Jon's life. Those weeks fighting the earth to reach them. His heart dying every day – knowing he killed them... And then they were alive...

It's fine. Even if I lose them, they're still here. Living. Happy.

Bony fingers wrapped around that fading string. There was a dying warmth. Tangible. It wasn't possible. So many things the last year... What was one more? This figment of his broken mind... Holding it to his chest, he mourned the loss of something he never had any right to.

Jon's footsteps stopped but the door never opened. Looking up, Ferdinan found chocolate brown eyes staring at him – uncertain why they were still there but unwilling to leave.

Holding tightly to the string...words flowed off his tongue. "I don't know how many times I pushed you away, insulted you. I'm terrible and mean. There's nothing I won't do...'cause it's all I know to protect you."

Jon stood stunned.

"I don't know how I became like this. Why this is the only way I know how to be, to protect. And you fight me – like a contest between us. Who can bend the other first? Who can deal the most damage? I'll say what I don't mean and do what I don't believe 'cause it's my duty." *I don't want to be alone. But that's the life I was born to. You can't change that...* "You are kind and naïve. Stubborn and beautiful. No matter how many times I hurt you, poison your soul, we keep coming back to this."

Tears ran down Jon's face, but Ferdinan couldn't figure out why. He was a terrible person. His ally had known that for years.

"I'm tired of hurting you. But that's what I am. A defect. A blight infecting all I encounter. And you've been poisoned for the longest." *I don't want to be alone. But I can't stand hurting anyone anymore...* "I'm sorry. I was selfish. I should've pushed you so hard you'd never look at me again. But I didn't 'cause of that selfishness. I'm vile. I'm sorry for not doing what I should've the first time. So I'm doing it now. Go away. Take your family and go. 'Cause I'll destroy you if you don't."

Ferdinan didn't know where those words came from, but they reminded him of his place. Hopefully they'd give Jon what the boy needed to finally find happiness and peace. Safety far away from him.

Enjoying the fading warmth of the flickering string a moment longer, he released it. But it didn't go away. It didn't fade to nothing or jump a foot from his chest. It stayed. Connected beside the green string. *Why...?*

***

A few hours... Abrasive chemicals tickled Zephyr's nose, but it was the only way to fully get the blood out. And it kept him from thinking about that last truth.

Gongie sat up and rubbed the sleep from his eyes. "Are you ok?"

"I'm fine. Move."

"Sit." Dark eyes asserted their dominance.

What's the point? He'll never leave...

"Your 'truths.' You have them wrong."

"You've been here. Know everything..." Zephyr shook his head. It was crushing...seeing them over and over...

The Telepath steeled himself. "How can a protector protect when they never learned how? How can you protect another when you need protection?"

Heat flared up at the idiocy!

"No! You'll listen 'til I finish." Though shaking, Gongie's jaw was set. "What you did to your cousin destroyed him. And he in turn hurt someone I love many times. But that's all you were shown. It's not that you don't deserve family, you deserve a family who cares about Zephyr more than 'the heir.'"

I am heir and they do love me!

"Those thoughts. That self-hatred, his is greater. Your feelings can't compare to how gruesome of a creature he sees himself." Gongie

240

swallowed hard. "And like him, you need help but don't believe you deserve it. And so you keep rejecting it."

That goo swelled. How could someone who'd been in his head for years be so utterly wrong?

"You aren't a monster, Zephyr." Gongie stood. "Monsters don't care if they're monsters. Monsters don't feel remorse. Regret at the pain they've caused. And monsters have no desire to change."

"Is it my turn?" Zephyr snarled, golden hands flying – becoming more animated when Gongie sat back down. "Protecting others was my first lesson. It's the first part of being a General. I've been loved and coddled and given every opportunity. Every resource and support... And I failed. I put myself above everyone. I chose to destroy instead of protect, build, uplift. *I* chose to destroy."

"Then how come you had to tear your mind to create someone who'd protect you? Twice?"

"That was me being too cowardly to face how terrible I am."

"You don't learn to protect from a book or verbal lessons. You learn from being protected. Having to break yourself to find shelter means no one was protecting you when you needed it. There was no one for you to emulate."

Flying to his feet, barely contained violence and frustration filled every gesture golden hands threw. "You don't know anything! All you've seen is here! You've never...!"

Shaking, recoiling, Gongie forced himself to stay. To not run. He sat there in a battle of wills between the two of them and his own instincts.

What am I doing, scaring him? I'm the worst. Zephyr forced himself to calm down. "Giving me outlandish lies to hide behind so I can feel better, doesn't change the truth."

"You might've been coddled and spoiled with more than you could know to want. But if you were protected, you'd be like Jon instead of Ferdinan."

"We're nothing alike–"

Gongie still shook, but his voice grew stronger. "It's Ferdinan's twisted view of his own truths that've nearly killed him multiple times and left him in the state he's in. He refuses to see reality so he can keep hurting himself with false truths. 'Cause he believes he deserves it. He believes he needs to be punished. And he does everything he can to do so, including triggering you."

***

That was quite the confession. If Leoniel had arrived any sooner to get Jon, it wouldn't have happened. Now the man wasn't sure what to do. Eavesdropping was wrong, but that told him so much about those two. So much the Artimuses didn't seem to realize. If either of them was to heal, this was important for the adults to understand. So Leoniel did a terrible thing and kept listening – watching the edge of the mirror through the cracked door.

Despair twisted Ferdinan's face.

The muscles in Jon's jaw twitched but he was pale and having trouble swallowing. "What've you been protecting me from?"

Ferdinan shook harder and he bowed his head to the floor. "Everything at the hospital. The plague. Nei Hannai. Linar's Grove. Fifth year's ball."

Ferdinan continued listing names and events that were obviously significant to Jon.

"And I keep failing no matter how hard I try..." Ferdinan trailed off, straightening enough to stare at his chest – dismayed by what he saw. "That's a lie. I've only told myself I tried my best... I should've been protecting you from me."

Chocolate eyes studied the trembling skeleton. "Why?"

Ferdinan clenched his jaw shut – shaking his head. And when Jon insisted, he answered harsher than expected. "If you wanted to see it, you would. So I'll keep protecting you. 'Cause it's my duty."

Silence lingered. Slipping away down the hall, Leoniel made his footsteps a little heavier as he approached the room again. It was still quiet when he tapped on the cracked door.

Jon answered. Giving the boy a hug, the colorful man smoothed his hair and wiped loose tears from his cheek. "Samuel's ready now, unless you'd like more time to talk."

Jon shook his head. "We're done."

Chapter 34

"You wanted to talk?"

Gongie stood in a colorful meadow facing the giant. Sunlight warmed him on all sides. This place... "This is a strange dream."

"Only if you believe it is."

"Mr. Charlie." *It feels like the elf's twilight beach...but...* But alive. Changing. Growing. Gongie held out his hand. "I want to spend my school break there. I want to work and help. I'll do whatever you need."

The man laughed and took his hand - pulling the boy in for a hug. "Ajani and Larashi are waiting for you. When'll you arrive?"

***

"Coming with us?" Oya smirked at the growing giant lazily watching snow fall past the window and plopped the overly large bag on the floor. It was possible her family never had so many clothes in all their lives.

Even when Jon finally turned to her, he didn't look confident.

"It's your last chance to see him before we're gone."

It looked like he was gathering all the courage inside him. "No."

Giving her best Cheshire grin, Oya lifted the bag. *Good job, Jon.*

"Not asking if I can live with that? Manipulate me into going?"

Hefting the bag over her head, Oya secured it across her body - grin as wild and wicked as ever. "Why? We both know the answer."

"W-What?"

Walking up to the growing giant, she gave him a hug. Amazing how his head was in-line with hers when he was sitting. "I'm proud of you."

Jon looked as if she'd placed an impossible weight on him. "Why?"

"You might not realize what you accomplished, but I do. I see it." Inhuman green eyes looked at the solid string that was flickering not long ago. Now for it to become vibrant - once Jon cared for the clouds over his mind. "Get well. And don't worry, I'll be nice to your suitemates."

"That...makes me nervous...and worry more..."

"Next time you take responsibility for something, make sure one you choose. 'Cause they'll know." Giving him one more hug, she vanished from his sight. His startled look was always amusing, but resignation settled in faster each time she did this, so it didn't last long. Adjusting the bag, she walked out. "Good luck, Jon."

***

Tea steeped milk and a vegetable-lentil medley. It wasn't much, but it's what Ferdinan wanted, so Leoniel happily had it made. *He's leaving today but still can't look at Samuel...so....?* The Kyo made his way to his guest's room, carrying both their meals.

"...mentor. You deserved much better." Ferdinan's voice shook.

"Master Ferdinan, please stop apologizing..."

"We're relieved you're ok. And look! They work great!"

The second voice was definitely a girl's, but the first was young enough it was hard to tell.

"What happened wasn't your fault. It was beyond your control." The first voice spoke again.

"I failed you."

A tired sigh came from that young voice. "You taught me how to learn and work. Gave me tools and knowledge to complete my projects and Yuyu's gloves even with you being gone. That's not failure."

"You taught us. Helped us. Even while you were saving lives." There was silence before the girl continued. "Of course, we knew."

"No. It was my responsibility to mentor you, to put you first. And I didn't. I'm sorry. I shouldn't-"

"Master Ferdinan." The youngest voice interrupted. "I don't want you to apologize to me anymore. I want you to take care of yourself so you don't feel you need to."

Eavesdropping on one deeply personal conversation was bad, but two put Leoniel at his limit. Slowly, quietly, the Kyo backed away. *I'll come back later.* But the information he learned in those few words... *Two apprentices?* And young. The first sounded barely old enough to start school and the other couldn't have been much older.

"While you were saving lives." Is she talking about different events? And the youngest doesn't want him to apologize anymore... How...?

244

Leoniel wasn't sure how to end that last thought. There wasn't much information on the boy and he'd called in some debts searching. *How many favors will Grandpa Huey let me owe him before he says "no"?*

***

No matter how cold the shower, it couldn't wash away Zephyr's fury. He needed his blade, but the stupid Psych hid it somewhere.

"Jon!" Gongie's voice dripped with worry. "Are you ok?"

"No...I'm sorry. I just wanted to not be alone. And everyone's working or at school...and..." Jon's voice shook, but continued when he found the determination. "I'm not coming back for a while."

Closing his eyes, Zephyr drowned in his regret. *I poisoned him too...*

"Call whenever you want."

"I will." Jon's voice broke. "I think I'll need to talk often. Can I?"

"Of course...!" Gongie started enthusiastic, but trailed off.

"What's wrong?"

"I'm going back to Azuté over break. But I might stay here instead."

He's going back...? Zephyr focused on rinsing off the soap. This was annoying. If the Psych would go to his own room the Prince wouldn't be forced to eavesdrop.

"You should go." Jon's voice shook with fake cheer. "I won't need a secure line to contact you there."

A long pause followed before the Telepath spoke. "You aren't losing me. I'll happily come to you."

"No. You need to go. Whatever you want to do there, do it."

This conversation could end quickly or become more intimate and Zephyr didn't want to listen to anything more personal. Shutting off the water, he dried and dressed as quickly as he could.

"Um... They're on their way back with Samuel..."

"They're letting him come back? When he's that sick?"

"He did what he always does! Somehow got better..." Frustration shook Jon's voice. "I can't do it anymore. I can't stand the idea of talking to him... But... Would you...?"

245

Pulling on his shirt, Zephyr tried focusing on anything other than Jon's voice. *A running outfit and a dinner one. What's in my closet?*

"I can't get close to Ferdinan, but I'll check on Oya regularly."

Shoes...

"Um...are you sure it's ok? To call...I won't... I can't...over a screen...right?" There was a long pause. "A screen makes it safe...right?"

Zephyr stopped. *How much damage have I done?* Golden hands opened the door as quietly as he could. The Prince didn't know what he grabbed from his armoire, but he'd deal with Denila teasing him later.

"Even in person it's fine."

"I know it isn't."

So did Zephyr. Ignoring his intruder, he stayed out of sight of the screen as he grabbed shoes and a bag and bolted for the door.

"Sorry, Jon, can you give me one minute?"

Moving faster would've caught his ally's attention, but at this pace Gongie caught him before leaving the suite.

"Jon's struggle is from being buried alive. Not you."

"A decade stuck with Ferdinan pushed him to that." Zephyr slipped on his shoes. "I broke Ferdinan and he infected Jon."

"That's not how it works!" Gongie grabbed the golden Prince. "If you can't fight the temptation, don't go."

I deserve to be punished. I need to be destroyed.

"Zephyr. It's terrible that Jon's trauma is proper, but yours isn't. I never thought much about proper and imp-"

"I cause trauma. I haven't experienced it." Zephyr broke free and threw open the door.

"Don't give in." Gongie called out. "I'm focused on you."

I hate you.

***

I hate mud. It never comes off and carrying around extra shoes was a pain. *Only one more rainy season.* Leaving mud-coated shoes by the entrance, Norger slipped on clean ones and made his way to Master

Dæya's office. The man was ready when he arrived, but there was something he needed to change about the arrangement. "We need to talk first."

"What's wrong?" Dæya gestured Norger into his office.

"It can't be in Isolation. Not if I'm doing it."

"This training is why Isolation was built where it was."

"I'm tired. I have too many responsibilities to also shuttle a non-verbal toddler across the ocean every day." Norger didn't waver. "It needs to be closer to the dorms or the Scientists' island. I don't care which. I'm happy to set it up in my lab."

"She can't be near Psychs 'til her training's done."

"Psychs?" Norger nearly scowled. "My lab's on a different island."

"But Psychs go near there."

"Then restrict them." Psychs had no right inconveniencing Scientists on their own island. "It's *our* island."

The tattooed man frowned nervously. Grabbing a screen, he studied it before handing it over. "How about here?"

Quarantine? This isn't better.

"She'll be housed there so you won't have to escort her."

"It's cruel separating a child from everyone and who's staying with her? 'Cause I'm not." Norger made his line clear.

"It's near the spouse's homes, they'll take turns watching her."

"A normal person?" *Marrying someone with abilities doesn't prepare them for raising a child with them. No. I don't have the time or energy.* "I'll trust your judgement."

***

Closing out the screen, Herrard stood and removed his robe. It was all arranged. Entering his bathroom, he stared at the stranger in the mirror. Bright colors highlighted his features, making him look inhuman. Perfectly placed light and dark powders emphasized this.

Their rooms were emptied and deep cleaned – ready for the incoming eighth-years. Belongings were ready to load onto the supply boat arriving in the morning. He should have another two weeks... But with everything they needed to do...

As soon as I step on that boat in the morning... This stranger in the mirror was all he'd be allowed...

Xhou entered, walking past him to stare out the window – brush in hand, but his island brother didn't say anything.

Blowing out a silent breath, Herrard started the obnoxious process of removing the painted-on mask. Time to give up his life here. His family. The people he loved. And taught. And grew up with. *A few hours and it all ends.* Every falling tear was used to removed pigment. Because that's all they were good for. *I don't want this to end...*

"I just wanted..." Xhou's words trailed off when he turned to face Herrard. When he saw the tears fall as fast as the Healer could wipe them away. "I'm sorry for all the trouble..."

"It's not that." It was hard forcing words past his painfully tight throat. "Tomorrow, I lose my freedom and my humanity..."

Blue-black eyes looked out the window, and past the door, taking in every inch of the home they loved for fourteen years. It was over. And the future... "We're still brothers 'til we step off the boat."

I don't want any of this to end... Herrard kept attacking the tears and face paint, but couldn't say anything. A warm arm wrapped around his shoulder. And everything broke. The harder he wept, the tighter Xhou squeezed. Neither said anything. They simply stood mourning. Mourning until Herrard was calm enough to finish cleaning his face.

But Xhou kept his hand on his island brother's shoulder. "Let's make the best of the last few hours."

Chapter 35

Sweat coated Ferdinan despite the cold air. The moving meditation was intense while appearing peaceful. And it was perfect for thinking. *The gloves Elbie made Yuyu are genius. I knew his mind was amazing...*

Using the nanobots and second skin to directly connect her nerves for complete control... *It's perfect for Maelel and the others at the camp who need prosthesis. How many pieces can I print before break? How many are needed?* There wasn't time to build any, but he could work on them while traveling and during downtime between teaching.

If I go to the camp near the end, there should be time to finish. But I should go first to see how many are wanted. Would that take too long? How much has Tansu learned? If I show her how to assemble them...

"Been a while since I've seen this." Oya slipped into the luggage room he was using for the moving meditation. "Mind if I join?"

"Please." It was an eternity since his muscles screamed for him to stop. And it felt wonderful! Slowly transitioning from one position to another, they moved as if trapped in time. Until his legs couldn't hold him any longer and evening dark encased the storage room.

Laying back, Ferdinan panted. Oya's comforting presence appeared and he found himself relaxing as her unnatural red hair rested in the space between his shoulder and head. *I forgot how comfortable this is...* Blissful. Soothing. She was perfect. *I wish I was good enough for her.*

At least she put up with him. That green string caught his eye. *Why doesn't hers connect? Why did Jon's suddenly?* It couldn't be as easy as pressing it against his chest... And it changed colors again. It should've broken. Vanished. Faded away. Something. Not become a dull blue...

"It seems they shine the brightest when it's dark."

"What?"

A delicate finger ran the length of Jon's string until it pointed at the diamonds beyond the window.

"That's generally how stars work." He gave her an obnoxious grin and her giggles filled him with a joy he didn't deserve.

"A broken universe created near infinite worlds and life. Can it really be so bad?"

"I don't understand." *What kind of question is that?* Reaching for his bag, Ferdinan slipped a capsule from this tin and swallowed it.

"Langer, the man with two hearts."

"Hm?" Nearly colorless crystals turned to her. "The constellation? I'm not seeing it tonight."

"He was the first to see them."

"The stars?" Uncertain, Ferdinan sat up and listened.

"The strings."

His breath caught in his throat. *She...sees them?*

Wild green eyes gazed at him. "Langer truly lived and cared deeply for those around him. He could've easily had two hearts for all the love he possessed. Like everyone else of the time, he was born and grew without seeing the sun. At the age of ten, the long-awaited sirens called. The air was finally clean, the ground healthy again.

"So man removed the protective plates and found beauty beyond their imaginations. Wild forests and beasts new and forgotten. Nothing looked as the stories of old. And most beautiful of all was the perfect blue overhead and living green all around them. These were things out of legend – stories so long told they were believed to be fantasy.

"It wasn't easy. Taming land after generations underground... But Langer was young and eager and did the work of two men. Every day they tamed a little further, and every day they learned the wonderful and harsh realities humans left behind. And slowly, men thrived. This little part of the world held and coddled them as they grew stronger.

"More land was needed with each wave of humans, so Langer scouted." Wild green eyes glowed. "He founded many towns, and each thrived. Eventually he met a woman. Sweet. Kind. Compassionate. He loved that about her, and wanted to be an acceptable match. It was a long, hard battle, but she noticed, and in her own gentle, subtle ways, nurtured him as he worked to become the man he wanted to be.

"The final call came. The last of the humans were returning to the sun. There were more of them than any group previous, so they needed an area of land larger than before. Without hesitation he volunteered.

Setting out, he searched high and low and eventually became lost. Every attempt to find his way back ended with him farther from home.

"Falling to his knees, he wept for all those who needed a home. Closing his eyes, he prayed long and hard. All through the night and the next day. And when the stars appeared, he opened them again to find lights of all colors surrounding him. Some connected to him, some to other strands, but all came from the same direction.

"He sang out in praise for the help he'd been given and followed the strings. Along his way was a great hill hugging a huge lake which formed into a river, and he knew this was where they needed to be. Marking the path, he made it home and finally helped the last of mankind to settle."

"...I've never heard that story of the emergence." Taking a moment, Ferdinan tried piecing truth from fantasy. "What about the woman?"

"Her strand was as deep a blue as his – and he knew she loved him." Oya sat up. "The story varies. Some say they had one child who became the first Guardian. Others say they had five children who became the five Lauals. Others say the claimed eighteen became kings and queens."

"And what do you say?"

"Me? The five ruled each continent and the eighteen ruled each country. By the third generation, they were forgotten by all save a few."

***

"I have to ask, did you find a second miracle worker?"

Leoniel smiled at Grandpa Huey, but those ocean blue eyes were serious. "One appeared on my doorstep and left just as suddenly."

"If you're going to tell a tale, make it a tall one." The old man laughed and leaned in. "I'm glad. Only recently heard from my own."

"Strange how your miracle worker resurfaced as soon as the child needing them recovered." A lavender brow rose high, communicating Leoniel's suspicions.

Ocean blue eyes returned the look. "Indeed. I'm glad they got the help they needed regardless."

"I hope my request doesn't cause them undue stress or guilt." The Kyo waited long enough to soak in Huey's reaction. It'd be much easier to say it directly, but the Kyo couldn't risk losing what trust Ferdinan gave him – something he suspected was the same for Grandpa Huey.

"As for your request..." Huey changed subjects, but it didn't make the path they were treading any easier or less dangerous. "Mind, I can only offer this *suggestion* 'cause you're a Kyo."

"Based on the various itineraries I'm organizing, I'd suggest visiting the Helch settlement third, after helping with the Twelve-A crew and the cluster of mini-settlements to the south." The mostly bald man looked at the screen he held – finger hovering.

There was something unnerving about seeing this man consumed with hesitation, but Leoniel waited silently, smiling gently until he finally tapped the screen. A message appeared on the Kyo's end.

"Take your time in Helch. Considering how much the Oza had to leave behind, there'll be plenty for you to record, document, and pack."

"Thank you. Evelyn Oza's young, but I want to make sure she has access to her history when she becomes interested in it." There were so many questions Leoniel had for the man, but he doubted Grandpa Huey would answer any of them. Already, this was skirting limits he wasn't entirely sure of. "Anything I should know before entering Master Mingjing's home?"

Tension faded as Huey laughed. "There's this monster statue in the yard her son carved when he was young. And she was an avid journaler."

That's what I need to find. Huey's sudden seriousness confirmed his thought. Weeks of searching hadn't uncovered how Ferdinan knew Evelyn. The girl said he'd always been part of her family and Master Fulason confirmed the boy knew Evelyn's grandmother before the Oza was born – so how did he come to know an old woman on the other side of the world? She wasn't a noble, scientist, or part of his generation.

If not for knowing the boy personally and firsthand accounts from the Artimuses, Master Fulason, Evelyn, and the little information healer Yahmo willingly shared, it'd be hard to believe Ferdinan existed. "Thank you for your suggestions. Would you make those changes to my itinerary? There's a member of my second family I need to help today."

"It's already done and shipping schedules are being adjusted as we speak."

"Thank you." Ending the conversation, Leoniel left for the car.

Ferdinan needed help, but the boy was beyond his reach for a short while. And Jon... *He'll be in Helch...* Huey's "suggestion" would put him and Jon there ahead of Ferdinan so he'd have time to sort through Master Mingjing's home...*if* Jon decided to join him.

The ride to the Artimus estate wasn't short, but gave him plenty of time to consider ways of approaching the sick boy. Offering trust took him far, but how did he use this opportunity to build on that foundation? *This'll help Jon too, he wants his family so badly. Crossing paths in Helch will give Samuel a break he'll be needing by then...*

The biggest unknown was what he'd learn from those journals. *How much will reading those impact Ferdinan's trust?* The car stopped and a servant was there to greet him and escort him to the youngest Artimus son. Of all places, he didn't expect to find Jon laying in bed staring at the ceiling – gaze in another world.

~

"Mind if I visit?"

"Leoniel!" Jon jumped up off the bed and hugged the colorful man.

"How're you dear?"

"I'm..." Jon shrugged. What could he say?

"Facing death isn't easy for anyone. Let alone a child." Wrapping an arm around the tall boy, Leoniel guided him to the sitting area.

Jon focused on the full moon – beautiful and bright. "Umm...?" *What do I say?* Jon didn't want to worry this wonderful man who'd always been in his life. But...

"I'll listen for as long as you want. Or just sit with you."

He already knows... But saying it. Will saying it make it go away, make it leave him finally? "It wasn't just me... Oya's leg was crushed, I kept waiting for her to get sick...to die...then the lights went out..."

"That's terrifying. I can't imagine." Ringed fingers gently squeezed Jon's shoulder. "How did you get out? How did you save her?"

"I didn't...there was nothing I could do. We were trapped...I was alone." Breaths became erratic and tears filled Jon's eyes. *Just like now. Everyone's leaving me when I need them...* He would've been better off at school with his island brothers than alone at home...

Pulling Jon against him, Leoniel held the growing Giant. "I'm leaving for East Azuté and will be gone about six weeks."

He's leaving me too...? Good. I can't infect him that way...

Leoniel took Jon's hand when he squeezed his eyes shut – tears falling. "I'm distributing farming supplies, clothing, and food to revitalized farming towns and was wondering if you would join me."

Join...? This isn't a goodbye? "I don't think it's safe for you."

"Traveling can be quite therapeutic." Leoniel smiled. "I'd love your company and it'd give me a chance to cook for you. We can talk as much or as little as you want and meet interesting people."

Jon wanted to. Wanted to not be alone all break...or however long his family would be scattered. But he didn't want to infect anyone. He didn't want to break them – make them suffer like this.

Leoniel smiled, squeezing Jon's hand. "You don't have to worry about anything. Just choose what you want 'cause you want it."

Gongie's going there... Will he be close? A Telepath would be safe from his poison; their minds were built to withstand the broken. "If we end up near where my friend will be, can we make a small detour?"

"Of course. I've scheduled extra time. Contact your friend." Pulling out a small screen, Leoniel offered it. "The itinerary."

"Thank you..." *But...is this ok?*

"How're your shoes? And your travel clothes?" Leoniel winked. "There's a little time..."

Jon couldn't help but smile. He loved the clothes the Kyo made. Drying his face, he stared at his hands to avoid the dark window. Could he talk about it? Over a month with someone who loved him... *I don't want to be broken forever.* Maybe...if he started with answering the questions he was asked... "Ferdinan saved us. Saved me. Oya. And a dozen others... Then took us to a hospital in Chuzo..."

Surprise lined Leoniel's face. "Ferdinan saved you?"

Jon wrapped his arms around himself and nodded.

***

Zephyr wandered the silver roads. *Why do I break everyone?*

Aren't you tired of being fragmented?

His heart froze. *Did that come from my mind?* Strangled laughter shook out of him. *A broken monster... What could be worse?*

What if you could be whole?

"What are you?" A golden pillar appeared. And...it was familiar.

If you could be whole, would you?

Golden fingers tapped his shoulder and both hands swiped away – crossing each other. "You should fix my victims."

To make them whole, I must heal you.

Golden fingers flew. "That's a lie."

There's still one piece. The one you keep rejecting.

"I already know I'm an unforgivable monster." Zephyr turned from the pillar. Again. And again. But it appeared in front of him no matter which way he went. "What do you want!?"

I want one with the will to look at themselves and desire improvement. Don't lose that will.

"I try changing and still hurt everyone! A monster can't stop being a monster!" Fingers and hands and arms flew – his entire body screamed. "I broke my family. Damaged souls! Hurt everyone! Nothing forgives that! Nothing fixes the damage. Nothing makes it right... Or stops me..."

If you could fix the souls around you? Would you?

Ridiculous... But...he yearned for it to be possible. No one should suffer a life shattered by a monster. "Yes. If it were possible..."

The broken mirrors appeared between him and the pillar.

Find the last piece and fix them.

"Why are these mirrors so important?"

You can't heal others 'til you've healed yourself. Will you heal?

I need punishment, not healing.

What better punishment than facing the truth?

I hate you. The mirrors faded and the pillar vanished. Behind him the elf appeared. *I hate all of you.*

Slowly she turned, grin wicked and amused. "The guilt, shame, and regret o' past years will fill us 'til we drown. We hope and swim 'til we reach the shore, and there we come to groun'."

I'm so tired. Onyx eyes looked down and saw a glint of moonlight on glass. The first one he found alone. "Why can't I finish drowning?"

***

After a *long* and unproductive meeting with the tattooed boss man, Ferdinan escaped to find Elbie, so Oya left to fulfill her own duties. Making her way to Ferdinan's island, she laid back and closed her eyes. Opening them, she found herself in a small boat, rod in hand, and surrounded by an infinite blue-green ocean. "It's been a while."

"We were worried." The Fisherman gave her a strained look.

Oya was about to comment when something caught her eye. She couldn't quite see its form, only that there was more than one. *What are those?* But first... "Ready for a tale?"

"I love a good story." Grinning, the Fisherman added, "You can skip what you told the boss man."

"But that's the most epic part."

"And most 'never happened.'"

"Fair." She lounged back, fingers tickling the water's surface. "But after, I need to rest. I've tried a few times, but can't seem to manage."

"That's why I called them." The Fisherman gestured to the things she couldn't quite see.

That's what they are. Her story took as long as the tale she weaved for Dæya, only this one was completely true. And it was easily the most exhausting story she'd told in her life.

"The chaos you attract..." Sharp eyes and pursed lips shook at her. "...when you don't manufacture it. Kumi sends a warning."

"I don't like being bored." Every inch of her lean body stretched. "Already a year. I've flitted half my time away..."

"Almost. Have you learned what you need to?"

"Some." Oya stood. "The one most fit to help me with the next part is healing. What information does Kumi send?"

"Their first two bases failed." The Fisherman stood. "The facilities in Mundan are permanent. They're securing land in two other places."

"Get me Mundan's information." The formless creatures advanced. "Do you know why someone could see me when I don't want them to?"

"You've done terrible things to that boy's mind."

"There was another. One I hadn't met before. It didn't even occur to him he couldn't not see me."

"Then terrible things were done to him." The Fisherman looked up.

"He said he died like his older sisters but came back."

The Fisherman froze. "I'll ask Kumi to investigate him."

Time to stop wasting time. "I'm ready for them. Would you stop my dear friend from wondering about me?"

"He doesn't need any more stress."

Consequences

Epilogue

Sunshine warmed Oya's shoulders. *Impressive in such thick mud.* Though he stumbled, Elbie didn't stop running toward her dear friend's lab – only Ferdinan wasn't there yet. Which was what she wanted.

The last two weeks she did nothing but rest while Ferdinan taught, prepared countless random materials, and avoided Samuel. But she was energized now. As much as she could be. Besides, they left this evening and there was an impatient yellow bird guiding mismatched eyes to her.

Little feet stopped at the open door, but Umbacano continued – landing on her outstretched hand. The bird chittered excitedly, nuzzling her nose. *Thank you.* Inhuman green eyes and a mischievous grin grew.

"Can...can you see him?"

"Of course." Oya turned to the bird. "Glad you're having fun, impatient one."

I've waited generations for one like him.

"There's a reason we left the islanders alone." Oya moved the bird to her shoulder. "But it seems that time has passed."

"Um...can I help you?"

"No." Oya roamed the lab, grabbing a skeletal piece from the extra set of gloves Elbie was making Yuyu. "Such magnificent things you do. Wonderful things you want. Umbacano wasn't wrong to choose you."

"I can't compare to Master Ferdinan."

"Comparing yourself to one with eight years more experience isn't fair or accurate." Oya sat on a table. "Be smart and kind! Accept your amazingness, use it to help others and you'll always deserve Umbacano. 'Cause, unlike the others, it can choose to leave if you lose your heart."

Mismatched eyes blinked, confused.

Holding up a glove, she grinned. "How do they work? Wouldn't gloves make using her hands harder?"

"Skeletal pieces strap to her fingers and nanobots connect to her nerves so they receive the signals instead of her hands." Elbie blushed.

"Impressive."

"Umbacano's help made it easy. Not like studying the brain will be."

"Oh?"

"I can't see what it does. Or how. I can't learn about something I can't see or touch."

Oya looked at the metal fingers. "You can't see or touch nanobots or nerves, but were able to build secondary hands for a Tinkerer. How's the brain different? Isn't it nerves and chemicals?"

Umbacano jumped from Oya's to Elbie's shoulder. The boy froze and a look she loved seeing consumed him. But he forced it away, shaking his head.

Alien green eyes studied him – holding him captive, unable to move. *He rejected it?* "There once was a girl who knew life could be more. Be better. Be everything humans couldn't imagine. But she could. And she did. The more her ideas improved life, the more the gods blessed her with strength and energy to continue. And when she grew old, she did the most remarkable thing of all. Grand and terrible and wonderful."

Elbie held his breath. "What did she do?"

"She gave life to thirteen immortal things that never were supposed to live. Her successors gave life to five more." Oya gently headbutted the bird when it returned to her. "Keep doing what you love."

"But..." Elbie blinked. "What was I...? The brain..."

Oya winked at Umbacano. *Watch over him. No matter how brilliant he is, he's still a child.* Light steps approached – sparking Oya to slip into the shadows. If there were people who could see her without her knowing, she needed to focus on stealth again.

Chirps and whistles filled the lab. And... Elbie turned to the bird. "How do we do that?"

Impressive...

"Elbie." Ferdinan was visibly holding back an apology, but still bowing. "Is everything ok?"

"I wanted to help you load the boat and see you off."

About the Author

Psychologist, writer, crafter, and colored hair enthusiast... When CR Saxon isn't coming up with new and terrible things to subject various characters to, she can be found attempting projects with more ambition than skill, getting lost in random research, or catching up on chores. Her life is generally one of chaos and glowy screens – all while mentally living many lives in the name of fun, adventure, and storytelling.

Consequences

ISBN: 978-1-955644-06-8